The First Assassin

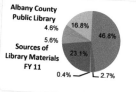

The
First Assassin

A NOVEL

John J. Miller

Mariner Books
Houghton Mifflin Harcourt
Boston   New York

The characters and events portrayed in this book are fictitious.
Any similarity to real persons, living or dead, is coincidental
and not intended by the author.

First Mariner Books edition 2011
Text copyright © 2010 by John J. Miller

www.hmhbooks.com

First published, in a slightly different form, by Woodbridge Press in 2009
Published in 2010 by AmazonEncore

Library of Congress Cataloging-in-Publication Data
Miller, John J.
The first assassin : a novel / John J. Miller. — 1st Mariner ed.
p. cm.
ISBN 978-0-547-74499-5
1. United States Army — Officers — Fiction. 2. Assassins — Fiction.
3. Women slaves — Fiction. 4. Washington (D.C.) — History
— Civil War, 1861–1865 — Fiction. I. Title.
PS3613.I53857F57 2011
813'.6 — dc22
011028597

Printed in the United States of America
DOC 10 9 8 7 6 5 4 3 2 1

For Amy, who told me to write it

The real war will never get in the books.

—WALT WHITMAN

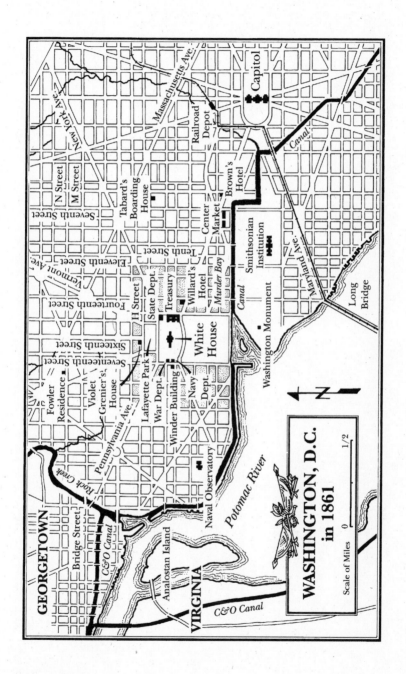

WASHINGTON, D.C.
in 1861

Scale of Miles
0   1/2

I

Saturday, February 23, 1861

When Lorenzo Smith heard the chugging of the train, he felt for the revolver at his side. His fingers met its smooth handle hidden beneath his black coat. Then he found the short barrel and the trigger below. Smith had reached for it a dozen times in the last hour, but he wanted to be certain that the gun was still there. It will make me a hero, he thought. It will change history.

Listening for the rumble of the train had been difficult. A loud mass of people waited for its arrival at Calvert Street Station. Smith did not know how many were there, but they must have numbered in the thousands. The noisy throng spilled from the open-ended depot onto Calvert and Franklin streets. Inside the station, where Smith stood, shouts bounced off the walls and ceiling. This place of tearful departures and happy reunions had become a hotbed of agitation.

The train's steam whistle pierced the din of the crowd. The engine would pull into Baltimore on schedule at half past noon. Heads bobbed for a view. Smith struggled to keep his position near the track. He had picked it two hours earlier, when the flood of people was just a trickle. He was not sure precisely where the train would stop, but he thought he had made a good guess about where the last car might come to a halt. He wanted to be within striking distance.

As the locomotive's big chimney came into view, a man standing next to Smith bellowed, "Here he comes! Here comes the Black Republican!" A roar of jeers and insults filled the station. Smith craned his neck. He saw the engine's massive oil lamp mounted on top of the smoke box. It gazed forward like the unblinking eye of a mechanical cyclops. Behind it were the cab, the coal tender, and a line of cars. Flags and streamers covered them all. The whole train glistened from a recent cleaning. At the rear, Smith spotted a car painted in orange and black. He reached into his coat another time and tapped the gun. Just making sure.

For the last ten days, the train carrying Abraham Lincoln on his inaugural journey from Springfield, Illinois, to Washington, D.C., had taken the president-elect through six Northern states—all populated by the abolitionists who had voted him into office. Applause greeted him at almost every stop. But on this morning, as Lincoln's train turned south into Maryland, it had entered slaveholding territory for the first time. Baltimore was the only city on the trip that had not extended a formal welcome to the incoming president—an obvious snub that pleased Smith when he thought of it.

Smith scanned the crowd and saw several men wearing hats with blue-ribbon cockades. This was the fashion among Baltimore's secessionist set. Each cockade had a button in its center displaying the palmetto tree, the symbol of South Carolina. That state had quit the Union in December, before any of the others. Many Marylanders now wanted to join the growing Confederacy. The moment Lincoln pulled into the depot, the members of the mob would let him know that he did not have their support. They did not even respect him. In fact, they hated him.

Rumors had circulated for weeks that Lincoln would not be safe when he reached Baltimore. But the president-elect had no choice about the visit. The only rail route into Washington from the north required going through Baltimore. Lincoln had to stop and switch to the Baltimore & Ohio Rail Road line at another station more than a mile away. That meant the presidential party would have to make a slow transit from one depot to the other, surrounded the whole way by an angry swarm. Lincoln was supposed to catch a three o'clock departure for Washington, where he would arrive about an hour and a half later.

Smith could not keep from grinning. He could hardly have asked for a better opportunity than the one handed to him here and now. He was about to become a hero— the hero of a new nation. He had planned for this moment from the day he heard Lincoln would pass through his city. He had visited the depot to see where the trains stopped along the platform. He had walked the route Lincoln would take to the other rail line, checking alleys and side streets for the best escape routes. He had studied a picture of Lincoln that had appeared in a magazine. When he learned that the president-elect had grown a beard, he drew whiskers on the picture and studied it more. Smith had cleaned his revolver over and over, trying to keep it in perfect condition. He had tried on his entire wardrobe, testing the gun in trouser pockets, through belts, and in his coat. He bought himself a new pair of shoes and broke them in.

They felt good on his feet as Lincoln's train crawled into the station. The shouting grew louder and louder. The engine rolled past Smith slowly, from right to left. His eyes met the conductor's for a moment. The man was shaking his head from side to side. Smith wondered what it meant, but not for long—there was too much going on. The cars kept moving by him. The presidential car in back crept closer. He could see the silhouettes of a few heads through its windows. A fellow up the platform from Smith began to smack the car's exterior with his cane, but it rolled out of his reach a moment later.

Then the train hissed to a halt with the presidential car directly in front of Smith. His meticulous planning had paid off. He jumped onto the car's metal steps. His feet clanged against them as he thrust himself forward and up. He heard men rushing behind him. At the door into Lincoln's car, Smith hesitated. He quickly surveyed the depot from this elevated position. It was so full of people that he was not sure how he or anybody else could make a hasty exit. He would have to slip into the crowd and count on its anonymity to envelop him.

First things first, he reminded himself. Several other men stood beside him on the back of the car. Smith thought he recognized one of them from a secessionist meeting he had attended. His hand was hidden inside his coat. Smith saw a slight bulge. So at least two of us are ready to perform the job today, he thought. Then Smith reached into his own coat and clutched his revolver. He was about to pull it out when the door flew open.

"Stop right there!"

The shout came from within the car. Before Smith could comprehend it, he saw the end of a pistol pointing at his face, just inches away. Behind the weapon he met the gaze of a man who looked ready to pull the trigger.

"Raise your hands!"

Smith knew that before he could even lift his gun, he would be shot between the eyes. But he did not loosen his grip. He was too close to his goal.

"Where's Lincoln?" he yelled.

"Raise your hands, sir, or I will shoot!" came the reply. The man leaned forward. His pistol almost touched Smith's forehead.

Suddenly Smith felt a commotion in the depot. He sensed that the men backing him up were pulling away. The tone of the mob's shouting had changed too. He could not hear exactly what they were saying.

"One last time, sir: raise your hands!"

Smith released the revolver. It slid back into his pocket. He showed his hands.

"Lincoln is not on this train," said the man. "You won't find him in Baltimore today."

Smith peered over the man's shoulders into the rest of the car. It looked like a room in the mansion of a wealthy family. The red walls and heavy furniture bore all the dainty trappings of Victorian elegance. Blue silk covered the space between the windows. Little tassels dangled from the chairs and shone in the light of the open door. As Smith peered inside, he realized the man with the gun was actually letting him study the car's interior. He wanted Smith to see who was aboard—and who was not.

Toward the rear, Smith noticed a plump, round-faced woman with her arms wrapped around a couple of frightened girls. A hulking man stood beside her, his arm on the back of her seat. A couple of boys sat nearby. Smith was certain he had seen the woman before. She glared back at him, her eyes glowing with anger. Then Smith realized who she was. He had seen her photograph. It was Mary Todd Lincoln, wife of the president-elect. He spent another few seconds looking at the other faces. Mrs. Lincoln's husband was definitely not aboard.

The man with the gun spoke again: "There's your proof. He's not here. Now leave this train immediately!"

Smith studied the man. He was in his early twenties. Except for a thin mustache, his face was clean-shaven. His features were soft. He did not look like the sort of fellow who would pack a gun and protect a dignitary, but there was a steady determination in his gaze. Smith had no doubt the young man was willing to pull the trigger.

Smith still did not move. "Who are you?" he asked meekly.

"I am John Hay, secretary to Abraham Lincoln, who at this very moment is relaxing in Washington. He passed through Baltimore early this morning, in darkness. Now, back off or I will shoot!"

Smith retreated a step. The door slammed shut. Smith realized that he now stood on the back of the car with a single companion, the man he had recognized. The others who had followed him up the steps were gone. He looked at the mass of people surrounding the train. He heard voices up the track: "Lincoln is not on the train! He's not on board!" Someone at the front of the car must have delivered the message, which spread quickly through the crowd.

Dozens of faces now turned to Smith, hoping he would contradict this report. But they saw a demoralized man. "It's true," he said. "Lincoln is not here."

The catcalls started again. "Lincoln is a coward!" "He's a sneak!" "He's lucky he's not here!"

Smith slumped his shoulders and looked at the man beside him.

"We have failed," he said.

Then he stepped off the train and vanished into the mob. On the way out, he did not touch his gun.

II

Monday, February 25, 1861

Langston Bennett threw down his copy of the *Charleston Mercury*. The pages fluttered to the floor as Bennett balled his hands into fists. "Damn him!" he said, sharply but to himself. His anger crested and began to subside. Bennett could almost feel it flow from his body. That was how it always happened—a moment of lost control followed by a quick return to his senses. He let out a sigh, leaned back in his chair, and closed his eyes. He ran his fingers through the long gray hair that touched the collar of his shirt. "Something must be done," he said in a low voice.

He opened a drawer in his desk and pulled out a blank sheet of paper. Instead of writing, he arched his back and gazed out the window in front of him, through the trees in Battery Park and across the harbor. He could see a couple of ships on the water. Farther to his left, at the harbor's mouth more than two miles away, he spied a tiny flag flapping above the waves. His eyes narrowed and returned to the page on his desk. He dipped his pen in a small bottle and rattled it around. When he brought it to the top of the page, the pen made a short black mark and ran dry. Now Bennett frowned. He could not even write the first letter of the date. He put the pen down, reached for a bell on his desk, and rang it loudly.

Footsteps sounded on the staircase. The door opened and a tall black man walked in. His wrinkled face told of many years. Bennett remained seated.

"Lucius," he said. "I've run out of ink. Please fetch me some."

"Yessir."

"Is there money in the till?"

"I think so."

"Very well."

Lucius bent down on one knee and began to pick up the newspaper pages scattered around Bennett's feet.

"Thank you, Lucius. I became aggravated. That menace Lincoln slipped through Baltimore in the middle of the night on his way to Washington. So he has proven himself to be not only a villain but also a coward. I still have trouble believing this man will actually become president in a few days."

Lucius could not read the *Mercury*, but he reassembled the pages and placed them on Bennett's desk before leaving the room. Bennett thought about standing up, but it felt too good to stay seated. This was a sensation that he had started to feel more often, and it might have bothered him if he had actually let it. He was already an old man, having been born seventy-one years earlier—in 1789, the year George Washington was elected president for the first time. Bennett liked to joke that he was as old as the republic itself. That remark was once tinged with pride. When he made it nowadays, though, it sounded more like a complaint—partly because he really was getting old, but mostly because he had lost faith in the republic.

Looking again at the dot of a flag by the harbor's mouth, he wished he had enough ink in his pen to blot it out: this was Fort Sumter, and inside it a company of men flew their banner in defiance of South Carolina. For two months, Bennett had glared at the flag every day. It was just a dash of color in the distance, but Bennett knew it displayed stars for South Carolina and six other states that had formally withdrawn from the Union. That flag must come down, he thought to himself. It will come down.

He could do nothing about it from the second story of his home and with no ink in his pen. He pushed back from the desk but did not rise to his feet. His leg ached—the left one. He reached down and rubbed it. Sometimes he still bristled when his hand touched the hard wood below his knee. His leg had become a stump fourteen years earlier, during the Mexican War. The surgeons told him it was a choice between his leg and his life, and before Bennett even had a chance to think about what they had said, they had sawed it off. He was glad they did, and he wore the peg like a badge. Many of the wounded men who returned from Mexico tried to hide their disfigurements, but not Bennett. He rolled up his trousers and exposed the peg for all to see.

The leg was a heavy price to pay for service in Mexico, but Bennett bore no regrets. He had bought himself a commission in the army, ready for an adventure. His wife had died many years earlier in childbirth, and his two sons were finally grown. Yet the war was not just a simple diversion for Bennett. The term "Manifest Destiny" had entered the public's vocabulary, and Bennett believed in it. California and New Mexico belonged in the United States, not in a corrupt Mexico. But more important than any of this, the war would allow the expansion of slavery into new territories. To stay strong, the institution needed to grow. Many Northern politicians, especially those abolitionists in New England, opposed the war for exactly this reason. But the war came and went, with the United States acquiring vast new holdings and the slavery question put off for another day.

About this time, Bennett first encountered the name that now haunted him. The South Carolinian had returned to his plantation home to nurse his wounded limb. In newspapers, he read of a first-term member of Congress who charged the administration of President James Polk with illegal acts in starting the war. This upstart continued the assault for a month with speeches and amendments, and he backed off only when Polk's treaty with Mexico ending the war arrived in the Senate for ratification. Bennett did not make much of the incident or of the congressman, who did not run for a second term. But he remembered the name. He knew for years that he did not like Abraham Lincoln.

He liked him even less after Lincoln became the Republican nominee for president—and then went on to win the election. Now Bennett was delighted to see the man humiliated. The *Mercury* carried a story about Lincoln's craven arrival in Washington. Instead of taking the train through Baltimore at noon, as he had been scheduled to do, Lincoln passed through that city in the early morning, while it was still dark, and arrived in Washington at dawn. By the time a huge crowd had assembled at the depot in Baltimore, Lincoln was comfortably checked into a second-story suite at Willard's, a hotel near the White House.

The incident already was proving to be a huge embarrassment for Lincoln. Supporters said the president-elect had had a warning about a plot against his life in Balti-more, and this news required him to take drastic action. How typical, sneered Bennett. The man had condemned the Mexican War from afar, while others fought and died for their country. Now he was showing himself to be fearful even of the American public. Bennett took some consola-tion from the fact that Lincoln's flight through Baltimore had no shortage of critics, even among his allies in the Northern press. Almost nobody thought it was necessary. Bennett smiled at the thought of Lincoln making problems for himself even before his inauguration, when he would suddenly have to confront many other problems not of his own making.

That sense of satisfaction soon faded. The truth was that the president-elect had outfoxed his enemies. He was still alive and unscratched.

A knock on the door interrupted these thoughts.

"Come in," called Bennett.

Lucius entered the room with a new inkwell.

"That was quick," said Bennett.

"We had this downstairs, sir."

Lucius stood still for a moment. Bennett shifted his chair back behind the desk and dipped his pen in the new inkwell. It came out shimmering black. Bennett grinned as a drip of ink came off the end.

"You know, Lucius, my hair was once this color."

"Yes, I do know," said Lucius, who allowed himself a smile.

Bennett's hair had started to turn gray when he shipped out to Mexico. Upon his return, it had gone almost com-pletely white. Now he wore it in the shoulder-length style of many Southerners, and it framed his broad face. His head rested on top of a big-boned body. He was once a muscular man, and traces of his former strength were unmistakable. Even at his advanced age, sitting in a chair, Bennett exuded a sense of brute power.

"Thank you, Lucius. That will be all."

"Yessir," said the slave, who exited the room.

For most of his life, Bennett had looked younger than he really was. He owned a large, upcountry plantation that grew cotton and rice. He spent about half his time there. Many plantation owners were content to let their slaves and hirelings do all the work, but not Bennett. He enjoyed the physical life of the farm and participated in it whenever he could, even after the wooden leg took away much of his usefulness. He had always hired overseers, and now he relied on them more than ever before. Yet he continued to go into the fields regularly, giving orders and sweating in the sun alongside the slaves whose own toil helped make him one of the wealthiest men in South Carolina.

This habit puzzled Bennett's peers, who did not understand why he would choose to spend so much of his time so close to slaves engaged in manual labor. They preferred a soft life of leisure. But Bennett believed the work was good for both the body and the mind. When he went off to Mexico in his late fifties, he looked and felt a good fifteen years younger. His presence in the fields also had a positive effect on the whole plantation. Bennett knew there was no such thing as the "happy slave" of legend, but he also knew there was more contentment among his slaves than there was among other slaves on neighboring farms. Just as soldiers appreciated seeing their general near the front lines, slaves appreciated seeing their master in a crop field.

Bennett himself believed strongly in the institution of slavery. He despised the Northern abolitionists who wanted to destroy it. They were radicals who had no appreciation of history, he thought. Aristotle regarded men as innately unequal and considered slavery the most natural thing in the world. It made plain sense that some would rule and others would serve.

There were some in the South who had doubts about slavery. George Washington, the Virginian, was one: he had freed his slaves upon his death. Bennett, however, considered slavery a positive good. Northerners who wanted to meddle with the South's way of life were supreme hypocrites, he thought. The industrial labor all around them was just another kind of forced servitude. Workers were wage slaves living in urban squalor. Northern industrialists cared only for making money. Bennett provided for his slaves in ways that went far beyond compensating them for their time on the job. Some of them, such as Lucius, even felt like family.

He knew the name of almost every slave on his plantation—and there were more than two hundred of them. When one died, he often delivered a short eulogy and was able to cite a few personal characteristics. He made a special effort to keep families together too. This was not always possible, but Bennett regarded himself as generous when it came to these matters. When he did sell a few slaves, he tried to sell them as families. When he had to split up a family, he tried to sell them to a neighbor and allow visitation. When he bought slaves, he often inquired about whether close family members were also available. He could recall several times purchasing slaves he did not really need, just to keep a family in one piece. It was something no Northern industrialist would have understood.

Gazing out the window again, his eyes settled once more on Sumter. "Here is a family that won't remain together," he muttered. The Battery below him had been fortified some years ago, and before that it was a place for hanging pirates. He imagined Sumter's commander, Major Robert Anderson, swinging from a tree. Then he reflected on the likely consequences. That seawall would need to be lined with cannons again.

There was no way to avoid strife between North and South now. Passions ran too high. Bennett felt betrayed by what had happened to make it so. Even after Mexico, he had done his part to hold off the sectional conflict. During the 1850s, he helped finance the filibustering expeditions of Narciso Lopez and John Quitman to Cuba as well as William Walker's forays into Nicaragua—again with the purpose of national expansion foremost in his mind. They were total failures, but Bennett nevertheless remained committed to doing what he could to keep North and South bound together by a single constitution that permitted the South to keep its way of life.

Bennett might have maintained this optimism even now if it had not been for what had happened in Kansas—or "Bleeding Kansas," as the press had taken to calling it. His two sons also had served in Mexico. Soon after returning, they moved to Kansas, with their father's encouragement. The idea was to found a new Bennett plantation as soon as Kansas could be admitted to the Union as a slave state—but both young men became entangled in the violent disputes over the territory's future. In 1856, within a few weeks of

John Brown's Pottawatomie massacre, antislavery factions gunned down both Bennett boys. Neither had married, so their deaths left Bennett without an heir. He was totally alone, except for his slaves.

That was the moment when his mind turned on the question of union. Like virtually every other member of Charleston's elite society, Bennett now believed the time had come for his state to part ways with the rest of the country. First he gave his leg, then he gave his money, and finally he gave his sons—all for the sake of preserving a country that seemed to show no appreciation for these sacrifices. Children should expect one day to lose their parents, but parents should not have to lose their children after they have weathered the vulnerabilities of youth and grown into healthy adults.

And still this was not enough for the Northern radicals, who had just elected this foul man to the presidency. Lincoln's name had not even appeared on Southern ballots. The unionists say they are for Union, thought Bennett, and yet they elevate a man whom thousands of citizens did not even have the privilege of voting *against*. How could any democracy worth its name permit that to happen? It was an insult to half the country. More than half of it, really—a few weeks earlier, Bennett had added up the popular vote totals cast for Lincoln and his three opponents. The president-elect had won less than forty percent of all the votes cast. Now he would rule over more than thirty million Americans. He was a false president. Life in the South would change in fundamental ways. Bennett imagined that even the local postmasters, named to their patronage jobs by this thieving politician in Washington, would stop censoring the abolitionist screeds from the mail.

Bennett finally rose from his chair and walked to a globe resting on a pedestal nearby. The curving coastline of West Africa pointed up at him. He gently rotated the globe to his right, his eye following a line across the Atlantic Ocean until it reached the shore of South Carolina. The map marked the borders of each state. Presented this way, he thought, they looked like separate nations. As well they might be. South Carolina had formally seceded from the United States at the end of December. Mississippi, Florida, Alabama, Georgia, and Louisiana had followed in January, and Texas had quit the Union on the first day of February. Just a week ago, Jefferson Davis was sworn in as president of the Confederacy in Montgomery, Alabama. Several other slaveholding states remained in the Union, but Bennett suspected that they would leave as well. If they did, the Confederacy would span from Maryland to Texas. It would be geographically larger than what remained of the so-called United States.

Now Bennett's eye wandered farther south on the globe, to a long and narrow island in the Caribbean. Florida seemed to point like a finger at Cuba. Had things gone differently these past few years, perhaps it too would have been in the Confederacy. Or perhaps Cuba would be an actual state, with its admission to the Union delaying the conflict that was now erupting. President Buchanan had wanted to buy the island from Spain, but abolitionists in Congress stopped the purchase.

The island remained outside the American sphere of influence, and yet it was strangely close. Bennett, in fact, once had spent an entire winter there. He had even considered buying a sugar plantation but decided it was impractical to run from South Carolina. Even after that, he continued to correspond with some of the leading figures in Havana. He was able to do this in Spanish, having picked up the language during his time in Mexico. Bennett once had rated the Cuban episode of his life a grand waste of time, or at most a missed opportunity. Yet his letters to and from Cuba had increased tenfold since last fall. Now the time had come to send one more, which he believed would change the course of everything.

Bennett dipped his pen in the inkwell again and scrawled the date on the paper. He paused for a minute, trying to decide which words to use. Then he began: "*Estamado Señor, le solicito su ayada en un tema urgente.*" As Bennett formed these words on the page, he mumbled a translation to himself: "Dear Sir, I seek your service in an urgent matter…"

III

Monday, March 4, 1861

The two men looked like hostages as they bumped down the street in an open carriage. Armed soldiers surrounded them on horseback. Troops marched in front and behind. Hundreds of spectators lined their path. Many of their faces were sullen, as if they were watching a foreign army seize control of the city. Shutters up and down Pennsylvania Avenue—or "the Avenue," as the locals called it—were closed tight. Most of the onlookers were at least polite. A few even cheered. Yet this was not what Washington, D.C., had seen in years past. The procession seemed more like a military exercise than an inaugural parade.

The carriage riders exchanged few words along the way. Their silence would have felt awkward were it not invaded by shouts from the crowd and the clattering hooves of horses. The men had met only once before, and they had had little to say to each other then. Now there was practically nothing at all. Both welcomed the steady stream of noise that filled the space between them. It provided a convenient excuse for avoiding conversation.

The pudgy, older man was James Buchanan, the outgoing president. A shock of his white hair bounced whenever the carriage hit a hole in the street, which it did every few feet. The jolts also made him grimace, but he looked more pitiful than menacing. He could barely see out of one of his eyes, a debility that forced him to squint constantly. In fact, he appeared a bit disoriented, as if he did not understand why he and the fellow seated beside him were the center of so much attention. Some of his critics would have considered this a fitting summary of his whole dithering presidency. Buchanan himself mostly felt relief. In recent weeks he had wanted nothing as badly as this day to come, and with it the lifting of a burden he believed he could no longer bear. He wanted to be done with the responsibility of the presidency. His thoughts now were focused on Wheatland, his home in Lancaster, Pennsylvania. He would plant flowers soon.

His companion kept a somber look, occasionally broken by a quick smirk or a slight wave. His crumpled face was not handsome, but it was distinctive. One glimpse and it was hard to forget, with deep-set eyes, a high forehead, and a big nose. The beard was new. He had only recently grown it. People accustomed to his face from pictures were not used to the new look. It made him appear older and more serious. Perhaps that was the point. All of this was set atop a tall and spindly frame. Many of his features seemed out of proportion, and a black stovepipe hat exaggerated his considerable height even further. It might be said that a good caricature resembles its subject. Abraham Lincoln, on the other hand, was a subject who resembled a caricature.

Colonel Charles P. Rook rode on a horse alongside the carriage, dressed in his blue uniform. His thoughts kept returning to a single question, which he could not chase from his head: would he take a bullet for Lincoln? Rook was riding with the president-elect for the specific purpose of protecting him. The other horsemen surrounding Lincoln were under his command, and he had planned all the security arrangements along the inaugural route, as well as at the Capitol, where Lincoln would give a speech and be sworn in. At Eleventh Street, Rook looked up and saw sharpshooters peering down from the rooftops of buildings facing the Avenue. They held Sharps rifles and had orders to use them if necessary. When he passed Tenth Street, he checked for the mounted soldiers who were there, just up from the intersection and ready to charge should the need arise. And in the crowd, mixed among the parade watchers, he sometimes spotted a familiar face—an undercover agent, keeping tabs on the people around him. Rook had planned it all.

The only thing he had not planned was the weather. It had rained lightly at sunrise, but unfortunately not enough to dampen the dust on the Avenue. At least the air was crisp and cool, a welcome change from the unusual warmth of the last several days. Rook figured this would keep his men more alert, rather than tempt them into sluggishness. He worried that a loss of concentration for even a moment, somewhere along this path, would give an assassin the small opening he needed. If a gunman were to pop his head from a second-story window on the south side of the Avenue, it was possible that only Rook's flesh would prevent Lincoln's death.

Rumors of conspiracy had run around the capital ever since Lincoln's election sparked the secession crisis. Opinion in Washington was split between those who supported Lincoln and thought the South was in the midst of a grand bluff, and those who truly hated the president-elect. There was no middle ground.

Rook was from Kentucky, and soldiering came naturally to him. His ancestors had fought in the American Revolution and the War of 1812. He had graduated from West Point in 1845, and within two years found himself fighting for his country in Mexico. He landed with the invasion force at Veracruz in 1847. On the march to Mexico City, Rook won brevets at the battles of Molino del Rey and Chapultepec. His military career was off to a brilliant start.

Then he quit. He discovered that when there was no war to fight, life in the military was unrewarding and the pay too low. He tried banking, but that failed when his treasurer ran off with most of their money. Then he went into surveying. The never-ending travel had prevented Rook from finding a wife. Most men of his age had a family. Rook, some said, was married to whatever job he held at the time.

He happened to be in Washington a few days after South Carolina seceded, when Lieutenant General Winfield Scott learned of his presence. The two men knew each other from Mexico. They discussed the national crisis and the particular threat to the District of Columbia, nestled between two slave states. They also considered the safety of the incoming president. After a time, the old general announced that he had a meeting with President Buchanan. Rook walked him down to his carriage. At the door, Scott paused.

"Our most immediate problem is that many of the citizens of the District of Columbia would like to defend the government and their next president—but they have no rallying point. There is nothing to bring them together."

"What may be done?" asked Rook.

"Make yourself that rallying point," Scott replied, stepping outside the door and into his carriage. From the vehicle, Rook heard him repeat his words: "Make yourself that rallying point!"

Three days later, Rook was mustered back into military service with the job of organizing the District's security and protecting the president-elect. It felt good to be back in uniform. Unlike some military men, Rook was far from vain about his appearance. He took a small measure of pride in a neatly trimmed beard that came to a sharp point below his chin, as if it had been chiseled into shape. Overall, however, he displayed the slightly rumpled appearance of a man who felt most at home in a field camp.

For the past two months, Rook had worked tirelessly to ensure that Abraham Lincoln would survive until this day. Yet Rook did not care much for Lincoln. His candidate in the election had been Stephen Douglas, the Democratic senator from Illinois. Douglas actually had defeated Lincoln in a Senate race just two years earlier, in a contest that the whole nation had watched. Rook did not believe Lincoln was the best choice to lead the country—and he was not sure that Lincoln was even a good choice. He worried that the abolitionists behind his rapid ascent did not have the interests of the Union in mind. They were blind advocates of a radical cause, no better than the fire-eaters of the South who now committed treason. Had their positions been reversed and the South pressed its views on the North, Rook believed it was the abolitionists who would be seceding. He wished both sides would keep the nation's interests in mind rather than flirt with a deadly conflict.

Rook had suggested holding the inauguration indoors. Lincoln, however, rejected the proposal. The open-air inauguration had become a habit ever since the British had burned the Capitol in the War of 1812 and forced the ceremony outside. The president-elect also turned down Rook's recommendation that he stay in a private house rather than a public hotel like Willard's. His experience in Baltimore probably explained it. Lincoln wanted to avoid another embarrassment.

From his first days in Washington, Lincoln had made clear his distaste for security. He told Scott that he did not want to be accompanied by thugs everywhere he went, like a dictator whose own people despised him. Rook had been forced to post plainclothes agents at Willard's because Lincoln would not permit an overabundance of men in uniform. The president-elect, in fact, probably did not realize how many men Rook had sent there to guard him—there were about half a dozen at any one time, and occasionally there were more. The hotel was constantly packed with job seekers and other creatures of patronage, so Rook's men were barely noticed. But a careful observer would have detected them there, day after day. Scott and Rook had not bothered to ask about the inaugural escort. They simply informed Lincoln of their plans and let him assume that they had been made under Buchanan's direction, even though this was not true.

As Rook crossed Seventh Street, he looked over his shoulder. The entourage had journeyed half a mile since starting at the president's mansion, where it had picked up Buchanan at noon, and then made a short stop at Willard's to get Lincoln. Rook couldn't see the White House—the

Treasury Department stood in the way—but he marked his progress. Seventh Street was the midpoint, roughly. The Center Market was there, a big building full of grocers and fish-sellers. Behind it lay the seamiest part of the city, south of the Avenue. Some people called it Murder Bay. Rook thought that this might very well have been the most treacherous part of the trip, and he was glad to have it behind him.

Getting this far had taken long enough. Rook wished he could have hurried the carriage from one place to the next with more speed. Somebody once called Washington "a city of magnificent distances." Rook did not consider the distances so magnificent. The city seemed empty and incomplete even when it was full of people, as it was today. He could only imagine what it was like during the summer, when the politicians and all the hangers-on were absent. It must seem like an abandoned village or a ghost town, he thought. In the meantime, he was concerned that the man he was supposed to protect was exposed, an easy target for someone taking advantage of Washington's wide-open spaces.

Now he looked up the Avenue, over the heads of the marching men in front of him, and on to his destination: the Capitol. The building's original dome was gone. A new one was rising in its place, slowly. Iron girders bent upward, looking like the ribs of a carcass. They hinted at the dome's eventual shape, but a large crane right in the middle towered over everything and made plain that this was a work in progress. Rook wondered if it would ever really be done. West of the Capitol, the Washington Monument also lay incomplete. The main difference was that nobody had worked on it in six years. The subscription meant to fund this memorial had run out of money with the obelisk only one-third its intended height. Now it just sat there, dwarf-like and ignored. So much of the nation's business was unfinished, thought Rook, and yet the country now tottered closer to collapse than completion.

The presidential carriage banged over a big rut, rattling Buchanan and Lincoln and causing Rook to tense at the sound. It would be nice if they finished the Capitol dome and the Washington Monument, thought Rook, but right now he'd settle for fixing the Avenue. No European capital would allow its streets to deteriorate so badly. Lincoln caught Rook's eye and smiled as he reached up and adjusted his tall black hat.

As he looked away from the next president, Rook's mind returned to the question he had asked himself all along the inaugural route: would he really put himself between Lincoln and a killer? So many others had decided they would not even serve under the man. Over the last two months, he had seen many of his fellow soldiers leave the army. Every day seemed to bring a new name. Most had departed for the South. Was it possible that one of them had stayed behind, plotting the ultimate treachery?

Scott and Rook had set in motion a security plan for the inauguration that would be difficult to betray: all of their subordinates knew only their own orders, not those of others. Rook felt he had guarded against some of the more outlandish rumors that had been circulating around the city, such as the suggestion that Lincoln and his cabinet would be kidnapped and smuggled to the Confederacy. He took every precaution he could imagine. Just twelve hours earlier, he had found himself racing down the Avenue in darkness to investigate a report that someone had planted explosives beneath the east portico of the Capitol, where Lincoln soon would appear. His search turned up nothing, but he posted a soldier on the spot. At daybreak, another dozen soldiers reinforced him. The colonel wanted no surprises.

As the entourage crossed Sixth Street, Rook looked at Brown's Hotel, on his left. This was a headquarters of secessionist sympathy. Southern politicians lived here when Congress was in session. Now they were gone, having abandoned the city in droves over the last several weeks. Still, the hotel was full, just like every place of lodging in the city. When Rook looked into the crowd along the Avenue, he could not fail to notice the large number of carpetbags. Hundreds of people visiting the city simply had nowhere to stay.

Fourth Street came and went, then Third Street, the site of the Washington Hotel and the St. Charles Hotel. After these landmarks, the crowds dwindled. At First Street, the parade found itself at the foot of Capitol Hill, which was really more of a slight rise on a flat landscape than something deserving the honorific of "Hill." It was as if the politicians who worked atop its low summit could not resist exaggerating even this simple fact of geography. Rook felt safer near the grounds of the Capitol, where there were fewer buildings to hide conspirators. In the distance, he saw a few pieces of light artillery—an extravagant gesture, he thought, but one that Scott himself had insisted upon in case there was actually an organized attack on the new president.

The procession now turned off the Avenue and circled to the left. Minutes later, the presidential carriage halted on the north side of the Capitol, where a temporary covered passage protruded about one hundred feet from a doorway leading into the building. Lincoln had barely stepped off the vehicle before Buchanan offered him his arm, and then they were hustled down this corridor. Rook waited for them to disappear. Then he dismounted and entered the Capitol himself.

The entrance was on the Senate side of the building. Inside, several attendants brushed off Lincoln and Buchanan to remove the dust that had collected on their clothes during the ride. There was a mad scramble all around them to get in position for the formal movement onto the platform where Lincoln would give his speech and take the oath. Senators, congressmen, Supreme Court justices, the diplomatic corps, and guests all had to take their assigned places.

Rook had assigned soldiers to guard the windows above the platform. He decided to make sure they were in position. He left the Senate chamber, turned left, and climbed a staircase. As he was going up, a man was dashing down—a late arrival frantic to take his place in the procession. The rest of the building was empty except for the soldiers at the posts. Everything was as he had expected it.

Peering from a window, Rook saw thousands of people gathering to hear Lincoln's speech. They stood shoulder to shoulder, covering acres of ground. Some had scrambled up the leafless trees for a better view. There were plenty of troops among them too. All looked well.

At the last window he intended to check, Rook came upon a bright-eyed soldier. "Any trouble here, Private?" he asked.

"No, sir."

Rook looked outside again. Dignitaries were filing out of the rotunda and onto the platform. Suddenly Lincoln appeared. His back was to Rook, but there was no doubt about his identity. He stood several inches taller than the people around him. There was also that hat. And then there was the applause—wild cheers the likes of which Rook had not heard all day. If the crowd on the Avenue had treated Lincoln coolly, here it adored him. These were his people. Rook realized he probably did not need troops in this throng. If any person tried to harm Lincoln, he would be swarmed by a mob of avengers. This was the climax of the inauguration, the moment when Scott had speculated Lincoln would be most vulnerable to an assassin. Rook suddenly understood that Lincoln had never been so safe. He felt a tremendous sense of relief. It had been impossible to rehearse for this day, and now for the first time he was confident the inauguration would be peaceful.

He stepped away from the window and leaned against the wall. He took off his hat and rubbed his forehead. The soldier across from him was still standing at attention. The whole point of his being here was to make sure another man with a gun would not be. His job was done too.

"Shall we listen to the inaugural?" asked Rook.

"Yes, sir!" The young man was excited at the invitation.

They watched Edward D. Baker introduce Lincoln. He was a senator from Oregon and also one of the incoming president's closest friends. Rook and the private strained to detect his voice above occasional gusts of wind blowing by the Capitol. It was just possible to hear him, but listening demanded total concentration.

When Baker finished, Lincoln rose to loud applause. From the corner of his eye, Rook noticed the private wore a huge grin—he was obviously a supporter. Lincoln removed his hat, but then realized that he did not have enough hands to hold his hat and protect the pages of his speech from the wind at the same time. He appeared uncertain about what to do. Then a stocky little figure on the stage got up. This was Stephen Douglas, the man Rook had supported for the presidency. The senator took the president's hat and returned to his seat.

The exchange took place a few feet behind the edge of the platform, and Rook was not sure how many people in the crowd saw what had just happened. That small gesture astonished him. Lincoln's greatest political rival had come to the rescue. Lincoln was a few lines into his speech before Rook even noticed he had started speaking, he was so struck by what Douglas had done.

Yes, thought Rook to himself, I would take a bullet for Lincoln.

IV

Thursday, March 14, 1861

"This man is gonna help us, Lucius! It can feel it! All the slaves been talkin' about it!"

Lucius looked at the short woman standing before him in the foyer. She was trying to speak in a soft voice but could not keep from raising it. This was Nelly, the neighborhood busybody. She had come from next door to borrow a cup of sugar. She was always doing that. Lucius doubted that she really needed the sugar. She just wanted to talk.

"I tell you again, Lucius: he's gonna to help us!"

"How's he gonna to do that?"

"He's gonna to come down here and free us! Why else would all the white folks be so upset? I've lived through a bunch of these presidents, Lucius, and sometimes the white folks get upset about them. But they ain't never been upset like they upset now. This is a whole new kind of upset!"

"Lower your voice!" said Lucius in a sharp whisper. He turned to look at the staircase leading upstairs, as if he expected Bennett to come down and scold him for listening to Nelly's nonsense. He knew his master was waiting for a guest who would arrive soon.

Lucius was used to Nelly's nattering. She seemed to know everybody on the Battery—and everything, too. Nelly had opinions on most subjects and enjoyed sharing them with anyone who at least would pretend to listen. It always amazed Lucius how she talked with such certainty about things she could not possibly know. Today it seemed as if she had sat in on a dining-room conversation with the Lincolns the night before.

"He's gonna to help us, Lucius," said Nelly again. "Hear me now. That man Lincoln is gonna to come down here and let our people go, like Moses did to Pharaoh."

"What makes you think a white will ever care enough about a black to do that?"

"Lucius, I know of whites right here in Charleston who would free the slaves."

"You're crazy, Nelly."

"I ain't fibbin'."

"Maybe Lincoln is a good man. But there ain't a single white person in Charleston who cares about the slaves, except to make sure they do what they're told."

"Have you heard of the Underground Railroad?"

"Of course, Nelly. Don't say it so loudly."

"There's a station right here in Charleston."

"That ain't true."

"Lemme tell you something, Lucius—"

A hard knock came from the front door.

"Nelly, you gotta go now."

"I'll slip down the hall. You get the door and I'll come back."

The knocker pounded again, this time more urgently. Lucius sensed impatience on the other side. He raised his eyebrows. "Go, Nelly," he said. "You know where the sugar's at. Get some and get outta here."

The knocker banged against the door again, even harder than before. Lucius started for it. He placed his hand on the knob and looked over his shoulder to where Nelly had been standing. At last she was gone. Sometimes the only way to make her leave was to send her on her way. Lucius turned the knob and opened the door.

A man stood on the porch, his hand raised as if he were about to knock again. It was getting dark outside, but Lucius recognized the caller immediately. This was Tucker Hughes, a familiar face in recent weeks. He stepped inside without an invitation, brushing against the slave's shoulder. Lucius wondered why he had even bothered to knock. Before he could ask for Hughes's hat, it was shoved at him. "Is he upstairs?" inquired Hughes.

After a lifetime in servitude, Lucius had become accustomed, even numb, to the dozens of little indignities he suffered each day. But for some reason the behavior of Hughes gnawed at him. Over the last year or two, Bennett had taken a fatherly interest in Hughes and treated him almost as a surrogate son. Hughes was a frequent caller when Bennett stayed in Charleston. He had come by every few days since the middle of January.

Hughes raised his eyebrows. "Is he upstairs?" he asked again, this time enunciating the words as if he were speaking to a half-wit.

The nasty tone snapped Lucius out of his thoughts. "Yessir, Mr. Hughes, and I can take you—"

Before Lucius could get the words out of his mouth, Hughes turned toward the steps and started up. Lucius tossed the hat on a chair and sprang after him.

This treatment perturbed the slave. It was not merely the rudeness. He was used to rudeness from white folks. It was the total disregard for the role Bennett had assigned Lucius to play in this house. Lucius should lead Hughes upstairs and announce his presence. If Hughes just barged in, Bennett would think Lucius was not doing his job. The slave would look bad and Hughes would have gained nothing. It was supremely inconsiderate.

Lucius wanted Bennett to think well of him. He had lived with Bennett almost his entire life. They were born the same summer at the Bennett plantation. Lucius's mother had looked after both of them during their early years, and they played together in the rough egalitarianism of childhood. But it could not last forever—not when one of them was white and the other black. Bennett's father, Richard, separated the boys around Langston's seventh birthday. Lucius became a full-time slave hand. Bennett's father introduced his son to the life of a plantation owner. In the mornings, a tutor taught him grammar, history, and arithmetic. In the afternoons, the overseers showed him how to manage a team of slaves in the field. In the evenings, Lucius would lose sleep when he heard the groans of fellow slaves who had been whipped that day by Langston. The boys rarely spoke to each other then, and they certainly never traded words about the past. Sometimes their eyes would meet and exchange a knowing look, but in a moment it vanished. They had their separate roles.

One day, when Lucius was about fifteen, he walked by an open window at the Bennett manor and heard the familiar voice of Langston arguing with his father. Eavesdropping was a skill that slaves honed to perfection, and Lucius decided to listen.

"I won't do it, Father! I cannot!"

"Langston, he is a slave and you are his master. There can be no favorites on a plantation. You must set aside whatever childish feelings you once had for him from what your responsibilities are today."

"You are asking me to punish Lucius for no reason—for a reason I am to invent! This test you have devised for me is not fair to him!"

The boy was shouting, but his father replied with cool insistence.

"Langston, you are becoming a man, and you must bury those sentiments. They do not befit a member of our class."

"No, Father, I cannot do it—and I will not do it!"

Lucius heard footsteps stomping across the floor followed by the slam of a door. He decided he had better get on his way when he heard the elder Bennett mutter something to himself. The words were hard to make out, but Lucius thought he could hear them well enough: "If that's how you're going to be, Langston, then there's only one way to deal with the problem."

A week later, Lucius was sold to another plantation ten miles away. The night he arrived, an overseer led him into the fields, where two other overseers waited in the darkness. They beat him senseless. "Just breakin' you in, boy," said one of them. Lucius crawled back to the slave shanties when it was done. The overseers knocked him around the next night too, and the one after that. The beatings grew more sporadic over time, but they never stopped—and they rarely occurred for a reason.

The abuse went on for years. Lucius grew into manhood, but he wondered how long he could hold up. During the day, he was forced to work harder than ever before. He had managed to escape whippings at the Bennett farm. At his new home, with its owner in Charleston most of the time, the overseers had the run of the place. They were cruel men. Lucius felt the lash constantly. He believed the overseers had it in for him. He believed he was a marked man. There were other slaves who were more resistant to authority, and some who did not work very hard. Lucius thought he was the only one to be singled out for torture.

Not once was he given a pass to visit his mother, who still lived on the Bennett farm. Slaves who had close kin nearby routinely earned this privilege. Lucius thought about running away, but he was kept in such a state of exhaustion and pain that he did not consider himself capable. He figured he would be caught and beaten worse than ever before. Was it really worth going on this way?

Lucius decided it was not. He resolved to end it all. One day, he positioned himself alone in the fields, away from where the other slaves were working. It was sure to attract the attention of an overseer. By the middle of the morning, it had. One of them started walking in his direction. Lucius thrust his hand into an overgrown patch of weeds, and his fingers grasped the handle of a butcher knife he had stashed there. As the man approached, Lucius thought to himself, This is going to be easy.

The overseer stopped about twenty feet away from where Lucius crouched. Instead of hurling insults at the slave and demanding that he move into the other field, he just stood there for a moment. He was not even holding his whip. This confused Lucius.

"If you think I wanna beat the life out of you, boy," sneered the overseer, "you'd be right."

Lucius tightened his grip on the knife. Just take a few steps this way, he thought. The overseer needed to come a little closer before Lucius could pounce.

"But I'm not gonna," said the overseer. "It's your lucky day, boy. Follow me."

He turned around and started walking to the manor. His back was to Lucius. He seemed completely unaware that the slave presented any kind of threat. Perhaps this was the time to strike. But now Lucius was curious. He looked down at the knife. It will cut just as well tomorrow, he thought. He hid it and followed the man whose life he had spared.

A few minutes later, he stood in front of the manor. The overseer told him that he had been sold.

"You're going back to Bennett's," said the overseer. "I think you're worthless, but they must want you bad. I hear you fetched a high price. They must wanna rough you up too—when you came over here a few years back, old Mr. Bennett insisted that we beat you as much as we pleased and then some."

The overseer said all this with a smile on his face. Lucius hated him for that. For a fleeting moment, he wished he still had the knife in his hand. "Here's a pass to their place. You have to be there by sundown. You know the way," said the overseer. "Now get out of my sight!"

Lucius collected a few belongings. Then he walked back to the home he had not seen for years. That evening, as he reacquainted himself with familiar faces that had grown several years older, he learned the news: Richard Bennett had died two weeks earlier. His son Langston was running the plantation.

These memories flashed through Lucius's mind as he followed Tucker Hughes up the stairs. He was determined to catch the younger man.

Bennett had treated Lucius very well as the years passed into decades. He had let Lucius start a family, gave him a prestigious job inside the plantation house, and now rarely traveled anywhere without his favorite servant. Lucius once heard it said that the art of being a slave is to rule one's master. He knew that nobody ruled Bennett, but he also believed that he had achieved a position of reasonable comfort. He doubted that someone who was not white could have a better life in the South. At the same time, he privately shared Nelly's hope that his whole race might be free one day. He wanted that for his grandchildren more than himself. He never said such a thing, of course. Not even to Nelly.

The urgency of the moment again intruded on these thoughts. Hughes was about to enter the study.

"Please, Mr. Hughes! Let me!" said Lucius.

Hughes looked up irritably but took a step back. Lucius nodded to him—a thank-you that was not heartfelt—and opened the door. Inside, Bennett looked up. Piles of books and newspapers cluttered the room. Both Lucius and Hughes knew that Bennett was a voracious reader. He read almost every word in every issue of the *Charleston Mercury* and *De Bow's Review* plus several other periodicals. He even used to get *Harper's Weekly*, which was published in New York. Yet the local bookshops stopped carrying it when it printed pictures of Lincoln.

"Mr. Hughes is here, sir."

Hughes entered the room, arms outstretched. "Langston," he said, with a big grin on his face.

The men exchanged greetings. Hughes eventually took a seat and picked up a book on a table beside him. He flipped to the title page: *The War in Nicaragua*, written by William Walker and published by S. H. Goetzel & Co. in Mobile. On the facing page, a picture of Walker made him look harmless, even effeminate. It was hard to believe this man had led a small army of American adventurers into Nicaragua and had briefly become the little country's president.

"It's surprising how photographs are appearing everywhere," said Hughes.

"It may be a passing fancy," grunted Bennett. "I've never had mine taken."

"Really? We have to do something about that." Hughes continued to flip through the pages of the Walker book. "Are we mentioned in here?"

"Fortunately not."

The light in the room brightened. Hughes looked up to see Lucius adjusting an oil lamp.

"It arrived last fall, around the time of Walker's death," said Bennett. "He wrote it to raise money for that final expedition—the one that killed him."

"I was sorry to hear what had happened," said Hughes. "There was a time when you and I believed he held promise. His success might have changed recent events for the better. If some part of Spanish America had been integrated into the Union, we might have averted this whole secession crisis."

"We did what we could. Yet we were foolish to think the Northern states would ever permit a filibuster like Walker to succeed in one of his conquests—and let Nicaragua, Cuba, or any part of Mexico into the Union as a slaveholding state. I am coming to believe the North actually wants this calamity."

Hughes set the book back on the table where he had found it. "How exactly did he die? All I heard was that he was executed."

"The Brits caught him in Honduras plotting a new incursion. They handed him over to the locals, who put him in front of a firing squad." Bennett lowered his voice. "After they had riddled his body with bullets, the captain walked over to his slumped form, placed the barrel of his musket in Walker's face, and pulled the trigger. The shot obliterated his features."

The image made Hughes cringe. "You might have spared me that detail," he said, shifting around in his chair. He noticed the pleasure Bennett seemed to take from his discomfort.

"Today, of course, I'm much less interested in the events occurring outside our borders than those occurring within them," said Bennett.

So now it was down to business, thought Hughes. Bennett seemed uncommonly serious this evening.

"Lucius, would you please excuse us? I'll call if we need anything."

The slave left and closed the door. Alone in the room with Bennett now, Hughes stood up. He found that pacing made it easier to think.

"Tucker, do you seriously think we can win a war against the North?"

Bennett knew the answer to that question, thought Hughes. They had debated it plenty of times before. It was a rather famous disagreement between the two of them. Why raise it now?

"My opinion on that has not changed, Langston. The South may prevail. We have better leaders, and we will fight a defensive war in protection of our homes and our ways. That gives us a significant advantage."

"Your ideas on that are thoughtful," said Bennett, "even though they are wrong." He paused to let that comment sink in. "Open warfare is exactly the wrong approach. The men now aiming cannons across the water at Fort Sumter are hotheads. They are ready to fire, and they have not given any consideration to whether Virginia will secede, whether they can secure agreements with the border states, or whether they can make treaties with foreign nations. They will act, then think—rather than think, then act."

Hughes had heard this before too. Their discussion this evening was like attending a play he had already seen several times. He knew how it would end. Yet Bennett seemed to want to go over the same ground another time. When would the old man ever broach the subject of inheritance? He had no heir—not even a relative. Everybody in Charleston thought he would name Hughes as the main beneficiary of his estate. But so far, he had not. Hughes had hoped tonight might be the night. Then again, this hope seized him every time Bennett summoned him for a visit. Time to return to the script, he thought. I have a part to play.

"Perhaps this business with Sumter is a welcome development," said Hughes. As he strolled around the room, he spotted some correspondence sitting on a table near Bennett. He immediately wanted to read it: "We've known for years that preserving our institutions may require war. Better to strike a blow for our freedom and our culture now than to curl up and let Lincoln destroy them over time and on his terms."

Bennett shook his head. "That fight cannot be won against the Northerners, at least not in the way you imagine. They have men, money, and material on their side. They are manufacturers. They have a navy. We are an agricultural people. We have rice, sugar, and cotton. It is not enough to win a war. We must consider other options. I want to do something for South Carolina, Tucker—one last thing before my days are done. I want to strike one final blow for the whole South."

This is new, thought Hughes. Bennett had not hinted at a specific plan of action before. "You puzzle me," said Hughes, stepping leisurely to the table. Bennett's back was to him. "One moment you sound like a conciliator who wants to avoid war. The next you say you want to do something for the South. I hope that what you intend to do is something besides giving up."

"I will never surrender," sputtered Bennett. "There can be no compromise on the slavery question. We cannot live under politicians whose idea of democracy is that when three people get together, the two shall rule the one. Our institutions must survive. It is our right that they do. And therefore, we must aim directly at the heart of Black Republican rule."

Hughes was struck by the old man's passion, but his mind was on the table. "War must be considered," he said, angling for a view of the papers. "If we show the North we are willing to fight, it may acquiesce."

Making sure Bennett could not see him, Hughes leaned over the table. A letter on top read, "*Su español es bueno, pero mi inglés es mejor.* Your offer is generous. I would like to meet in person to discuss it. Expect me in Charleston by the middle part of April." The letter was not signed.

Hughes could not read the first part, but he knew it was written in Spanish. Did Bennett have some unmentioned relation in Cuba? The thought worried him.

"But it may come to bloodshed," said Bennett.

"Yes, it may," said Hughes, returning to his seat. "And if it does, we will have to fight. Even if we lose, we may preserve our honor. But I think we may very well win a war."

Bennett said nothing for a moment. He appeared to be collecting his thoughts. Then he stared directly at Hughes and narrowed his eyes. "Let's talk of your inheritance, and how it may help us achieve our goals."

Hughes slanted forward. "What do you mean?"

"I don't want a war."

"I know that."

"I want a death. I want a murder."

Hughes sat up sharply. "What are you talking about, Langston?"

"I'm talking about Abraham Lincoln."

In the darkened hallway outside, Lucius pulled his ear back from the door. The sound coming from within was muffled, but Lucius was certain of what he had heard. Without making a sound, he walked to the steps and crept downstairs. He was glad Nelly was not waiting for him.

V

Friday, March 15, 1861

Rook's head jerked up as his horse came to a halt outside the Winder Building on Seventeenth Street. The animal seemed to know instinctively where to stop. It had become used to the routine since the inauguration: a daily walk around Washington's rutted roads and cratered streets so that Rook could inspect the bridges leading into the city and the pickets that guarded the roads to the north. Rook had become used to it as well, so much, in fact, that he had nodded off a couple of times between his last stop, at the Chain Bridge out past Georgetown, and his destination here.

He hopped down from his mount and yawned. It was dusk when he had set out, and since then the sun had gone down completely. Lights glowed from inside the building in front of him. An attendant materialized to take the horse.

"I expect to be here a little while," said Rook. He gazed across the street at the War Department and the Navy Department buildings. They were small—perfectly adequate for peacetime, thought Rook. Beyond them, he saw the president's mansion. There were lights on over there too.

"Colonel!"

The call came from across the street. A figure waved to him and approached. When he got closer, Rook recognized John Hay, a personal secretary to the president.

"Good evening," said Hay, holding out his hand. Rook grasped it. "How are things with you?"

Rook had met Hay only a couple of times previously and never at any length. They certainly were not intimates. He was struck by the young man's familiarity—he behaved as if he and Rook were old friends.

"I'm well, but a bit tired," said Rook.

"Aren't we all?" laughed Hay, who certainly did not look the way Rook felt.

Rook didn't know much about Hay. He had come with Lincoln from Illinois, and he actually lived in the White House so he could be near the president at all times. He was perhaps twenty-two years old.

"Maybe I'll get some sleep after my meeting with General Scott," said Rook. "He wants updates every day on Washington's military preparedness."

"Isn't it past his bedtime?"

Rook smiled. Everybody knew Scott's reputation.

"The general may not be in the springtime of his career," said Rook, "but he's a hard worker who demands a lot from the officers beneath him."

"Let's hope your meetings are more productive than mine. I spent half of my day dealing with government accountants. In the White House budget, there's only one slot for a secretary to the president. But there are two of us."

"Sounds like a headache."

"It's a battle between the president's will and an administrative won't," said Hay. The line seemed well rehearsed.

Rook got the feeling that he was not the first person to hear it.

"Are they trying to make you quit?" asked the colonel.

"Not at all. They're giving me a clerk's position in the pension office and assigning me to the president's staff."

"Isn't that the same thing as putting you in the White House?"

"Absolutely. But on paper there will still be just one secretary. It seems that in Washington, the purpose of paperwork is to obscure reality. At least that's my lesson for today." Hay rolled his eyes for effect.

Rook chuckled. He found himself liking the young man.

"I've detained you long enough, Colonel," said Hay, starting to go back across Seventeenth Street. "If you ever need something, you know where to find me—not in the place where my paperwork says I should be!"

Rook watched him go. Then he turned and walked into the Winder Building. The gas lighting and marbled wallpaper were rarities in Washington. It was one of the most attractive interiors in the city. Rook immediately smelled dinner. Scott often ate at this hour. From the room outside Scott's door, Rook inhaled the aroma of roasted chicken. He was one of the few people allowed to walk in on the general unannounced, though it was hardly a surprise for him to show up right now, when he was expected.

"Hello, Locke," he said to Scott's personal secretary, Colonel Samuel Locke, who was sitting at a desk by the entrance to Scott's room.

"Good evening, Colonel," said Locke, who did not look up from the newspaper he was reading.

"Anything in the news?"

"The general is waiting for you."

Rook did not like Locke. The man was a dandy—the kind of officer who was always looking at a mirror to make sure his buttons were shiny and his hair was just so. Rook could not imagine Locke in the field, doing the rugged work soldiers were meant to do. Yet the modern army needed all kinds, including paper pushers whose place was at a desk rather than in a saddle.

What really bothered him about Locke was the rudeness. Why was it so difficult for him to engage in small talk for a minute or two? Rook knew the answer: he had the job that Locke had wanted for himself, the responsibility for Washington's defenses and the president's security. Rook could not actually imagine Locke in that role. Apparently Scott could not imagine it either, because he was the one who had passed over Locke in favor of Rook. For his part, Locke seemed able to forgive the general and chose instead to channel his anger toward Rook and create a rivalry where none, at least in Rook's opinion, needed to exist. Rook found the behavior both baffling and irritating. At least Locke made no attempt to hide his resentment. The worst enemies were the ones who pretended to be friends.

On the other side of the door, Rook found Lieutenant General Winfield Scott removing a napkin from his collar. The old man was still chewing but wiped his mouth and took a sip of wine from a glass that was almost empty. A plate piled high with bones sat before him. It appeared as though he had just devoured an entire chicken all by himself, which didn't surprise Rook at all. The man's meals were always feasts.

The general's face was bloated and his body, enormous. It was hard to believe this fat giant was the same commander who had cut such an impressive figure in Mexico. Scott always had been a big man—he was six foot four and one-quarter inches tall, as he often reminded people. Yet the years were not kind to him. He was now so large that he could not mount a horse, and his carriage had to be specially designed to ride low to the ground because the general was not able to lift himself into anything higher. That little mountain of chicken bones on his plate, thought Rook, was not going to make it any easier.

"It is good to see you, Colonel," said Scott, swallowing his last bite. "Let me get this cleared."

He picked up a small bell on his table and rang it. A black valet shuttled into the room and began to remove the dishes and tablecloth. He was about to take the wine glass when Scott reached for it and gave him a hard look before pouring the last contents down his throat. Scott wiped his mouth again and placed the glass and napkin back on the table. The valet snatched them up and was gone in a flash.

"Please, sir, have a seat," said Scott, gesturing to where Rook always sat.

The general pushed his own chair away from the table. Grunting as he struggled against his own bulk, he succeeded in moving it less than a foot. Rook had seen this before too, and once he had offered to help Scott position himself in his seat. The old man would have none of it. Attendants had surrounded him for years, and accommodations a more vigorous man would not have needed now filled up much of his life. Even the president occasionally would come down from his office in the White House and meet the general in the driveway so that Scott would not have to strain himself getting in and out of his carriage. Even so, there were a few things Scott insisted on doing without assistance. Making himself comfortable in a chair was one of them.

When Scott finally settled in, he took a deep breath. The effort had exhausted him. At last he looked at the colonel.

"What is the latest?" asked Scott.

Rook delivered his standard report. "There continues to be civilian movement out of the city," he said. That morning, two families had departed the city by the Long Bridge, both bound across the Potomac River for Richmond. Their carts were stuffed with their belongings, indicating that they did not intend to return for quite some time, if at all. As was the custom, the soldiers guarding the bridge questioned them. "One fellow didn't want to talk," said Rook. "The other one admitted that he wanted to get out of the city because he did not support the new administration and the types of people it has brought here."

"This is typical."

"Yes, an ordinary day at the bridges."

"Is there more, Colonel?"

"I lost another lieutenant today," Rook said.

Civilians were not the only ones turning their backs on Washington during the secession crisis. Officers were leaving as well, resigning their commissions and heading home. Everybody in the chain of command knew about this problem, including Scott. The army was full of Southerners, especially in the officer corps. The drain was beginning to take its toll.

"Where is this former lieutenant going?" asked Scott.

"North Carolina."

"That state has not dissolved its ties to us." For a moment, Scott was silent. Then he waved his hand dismissively. "He was only a lieutenant," he said. "You will not miss him."

That was true enough, though the problem was far bigger than any single individual. Collectively, these losses were starting to affect manpower and morale. Every day seemed to bring a new desertion. By doing nothing in response, the army appeared content to let its men slip away at their leisure and join the ranks of a rebel movement.

Rook worried that these resignations were not even the biggest problem. What if some of the officers who remained in uniform were actually disloyal? And what if they stayed behind because they wanted to become subversives? He recalled how he had ordered a captain to patrol a wing of the Capitol the night before Lincoln delivered his inaugural address. With all the rumors about the president's safety, Rook wanted to be sure that the building was free of people who did not actually belong there. The captain seemed to do his duty well enough, and there was, of course, no trouble on the big day. Yet the man was gone within a week, after deciding that he owed more allegiance to Alabama than to the federal government. It made Rook realize that the army was perhaps vulnerable in ways that nobody had anticipated.

"I'm beginning to wonder whom we can trust," said the colonel. It was a risky thing to say. Scott was from Virginia, and there was talk among some Northerners that even he could not be trusted. Rook certainly did not want to make any such implication.

"If we acted against these men, the consequences could be terrible," said Scott. "It might strain relations between North and South even further—"

Rook could not stop himself from raising his eyebrows in disbelief. He immediately regretted it. The expression had caused Scott to stop talking, as if he had been interrupted. The general did not like being interrupted.

"Colonel?"

"Seven states are already gone, sir," said Rook. "They have seceded. How much more strained could relations become?"

"There is no fighting."

"Not yet. But if you weren't worried about the possibility, you never would have brought me into your service."

Before the general could reply, Locke burst into the room. He made straight for Scott with a piece of paper in his hand.

"This just arrived from the telegraph office," he said. "It requires immediate attention."

He handed the paper to Scott, who held it at an angle to catch the light of a lamp. He grimaced. "It's from Crittenden," he said. The contents clearly irritated him. "Bring me pen, ink, and paper!"

John Crittenden was one of the country's best-known politicians. He had served as attorney general for three different presidents. Most recently he had been a senator from Kentucky, a state that permitted slavery but which had not seceded. It would not secede if Crittenden had anything to do with it: he was a strong unionist.

Locke scampered out of the room and came back with pen, ink, and paper. He handed them to the general, who did not move his chair to the table. That would have required an enormous effort. Instead, he leaned way over to his left and scribbled a message.

He waved the paper in the air to help the ink dry and looked at Rook. "Colonel, we have fallen upon evil days. To think that a man who has known me so long and so well as my old friend Crittenden should find it necessary to send me a telegraphic dispatch to which I have to make such an answer as this." He thrust the paper in Rook's direction. Rook rose for it. He knew the script well, as he had taken written orders from the general many times previously. Its message was typical of Scott, concise and blunt: "To the Hon. John Jordan Crittenden. I have not changed. I have not thought of changing. I am for the Union. Winfield Scott."

Rook handed the note back to the general, who gave it to Locke. "It seems these days as though no man has entire confidence in any other man. Crittenden is my old friend!" said Scott, shaking his head. "Locke, get this message off promptly."

Locke closed the door behind him. A hush descended on the room. What had just transpired obviously disturbed the general. All loyalties were in doubt, even those belonging to a national hero like Scott.

"Was there anything else, Colonel?" Apparently the general did not want to discuss the loyalty or disloyalty of his subordinates. That was all right with Rook. Something else weighed more heavily on his mind than the departures.

He leaned forward. "You've heard the rumors about the president. They haven't let up. It is the talk of the city. Mr. Lincoln's life remains in danger, no less than it did on his inauguration day."

Scott frowned. "Of course, I've heard some rumors. Who hasn't? The air is hot with them."

"Do you know what today is, General?"

Scott did not like being questioned. He scowled but answered anyway. "Friday."

"That's not what I mean. It's March fifteenth."

"Yes?"

"The Ides of March."

"Are you giving me a history lesson, Colonel? I know my history. Today is the date of the death of Julius Caesar."

"And the anniversary of the most famous political assassination in world history."

Scott rolled his eyes. "Your dramatics do not transform fable into fact. Rumors are not the same thing as evidence."

"If we cannot act on well-founded suspicion, we won't ever collect evidence—and we may fail our duties," said Rook. "We have no hard proof that Virginia is about to march an army into the federal capital, and yet we've ordered a guard at all the bridges leading into the city. My men at these posts are under specific instruction to watch for organized movement across the river and to warn us the moment they spy anything suspicious. We've set up pickets along the roads into Maryland for similar reasons. We don't know whether there will be any trouble from Virginia or Maryland. We merely suspect that trouble may come—and so we take precautions."

"These precautions are simple and they cost us nothing," said Scott. "But the rumors of threats against the president's life are little more than idle chatter in an anxious city. I discount all of it. The time to strike against the president directly would have been before or during the inauguration. It would have created panic and confusion here in Washington and throughout the Northern states." This was the conventional wisdom among those who thought seriously about the security of the president: an assassination now, or even an attempt to assassinate, would create many problems—but most likely would strengthen the resolve of the Northern states and make them less inclined to compromise.

"Any student of history knows that assassinations rarely achieve their political ends," continued Scott. "They almost always backfire. Caesar is a perfect example of this. His killers wanted to preserve republican government, but they wound up with an emperor. I do believe we crossed an important threshold when Lincoln took the oath. You might even say we crossed the Rubicon." Scott smirked at his own cleverness.

"The president is hated in too many quarters. All it would take is someone willing to—"

"Colonel," interrupted Scott, "the other thing you must realize is that no American president has ever been assassinated. I know of only one attempt that's ever been made. You are perhaps a bit too young to remember it yourself. It was about twenty-five years ago, during the second term of Andrew Jackson." Scott spit out the name with distaste, as Jackson was an old nemesis. He described how Jackson was walking through the rotunda of the Capitol when a madman—a house painter called Richard Lawrence—leaped out from behind a pillar and pointed his pistol at the president. He pulled the trigger, but the gun failed to fire. So Lawrence reached for a second one, aimed it at Jackson, and pulled its trigger. Again, the gun did not go off. By this point onlookers were able to grapple with Lawrence and disarm him. Investigators later determined that his powder and bullets had fallen out of his guns when they were still in his pockets.

As he told the story, Scott was animated, but then he sighed. "Jackson accused his political enemies of plotting against him. That was typical. He tried to turn this astonishing event to his political advantage. In fact, there were those who thought the whole episode was a stunt, manufactured by Jackson for the specific purpose of letting him rail at his opponents." Scott obviously believed Jackson was perfectly capable of such behavior. "But it turned out that Lawrence was simply deranged. Francis Scott Key prosecuted the case, and the jury decided Lawrence was a lunatic not responsible for his own actions. He was confined to an asylum."

Rook had heard of the incident, but not in such detail.

"If Lawrence had not been crazy," the general went on, "he would not have tried to kill the president. This is the great problem with assassinations. The killing is not the hard part. A half-wit like Lawrence might have pulled it off, but then only a half-wit would have made Lawrence's mistake. The tricky part isn't pulling the trigger. It's getting away. No man except a fanatic or an idiot would try to murder the president without an escape plan, and the president is almost never alone. Evading capture would be close to impossible. The man who might succeed probably would be smart enough not to try."

Scott folded his arms at the conclusion of this little speech. Rook sensed that the old man did not want to be challenged.

"I have a modest proposal," Rook said at last.

"And what is it?" The general sounded skeptical.

"There are men like Lawrence out there. There are also men who have Lawrence's murderous intentions, and most of them aren't crazy. Therefore, we must increase the number of men assigned to protect the life of the president—"

"Absolutely not!" Scott was almost shouting.

"Just a handful of men, sir—surely we can spare a few from their posts at the Armory and Treasury—"

"That's not the issue," said Scott, lowering his voice but remaining stern. "I am sure we could spare them. The problem is that they aren't wanted where you would like to put them. The president is completely opposed to a plan along these lines. He won't tolerate more security than he already has."

"Sir, the current security arrangement is not adequate. The president's house is open to the public at all hours. It would not take much for a lone gunman to slip inside without arousing suspicion. Assigning a few additional men would harm nothing and help much. I'm also concerned about the president's protection when he leaves the grounds of his mansion. He is sometimes with only one or two men. At these moments, he is especially vulnerable. We really should demand more security."

"Are you done?" asked Scott with impatience.

"Yes."

"Good. Now you've gotten it off your chest, Colonel. And the answer is still no."

"Might he at least consider keeping himself out of view? Perhaps he could limit his public appearances."

"The answer is no, Colonel."

"Doesn't he understand the danger?"

Scott raised his palm, signaling Rook to silence.

"Colonel, your misgivings are noted. They are also rejected. You know how much criticism the president received for his passage through Baltimore, even from some of his closest friends. It was an awful start to his time in Washington. And then the inaugural security was very tight. Some believed it was too tight. Nobody failed to notice it. You did a superb job that day. I commend you for it. Yet our actions have their critics. They thought the security was overwhelming, even anti-democratic. I know the president himself shares this view. He has told me as much. We are fortunate that he has accepted the guards who surround him now. It is my concern that one day he will order them away. We should be grateful that he doesn't walk though the city in the dark by himself. I'm learning that he can be a stubborn man—he is probably capable of going for a midnight stroll in Murder Bay just to prove a point. I appreciate your concerns, Colonel, but you must put these notions out of your head."

There was no getting through, Rook realized. It sounded as though Scott possibly agreed with him at some level. That was not the same thing as the president's agreeing with them, of course. Rook understood that he was supposed to abide by the orders of his superior officer, and now he realized that Scott was simply following orders given by the one man in the whole country who could tell the general what to do.

"Is there anything else, Colonel?"

"No, sir."

"Then I will see you tomorrow. Good night."

VI

Thursday, April 11, 1861

Bennett and Hughes sat unsmiling in chairs just a few feet apart. They were dressed almost exactly alike, both in dark frock coats and black gloves. Each rested a cane against one knee and propped a hat on the other. They looked ready to go somewhere, but they sat perfectly still.

"Steady…steady…"

The men fixed their eyes on the same point across the room. Hughes appeared at ease, relaxing in his chair as if he could sit there all day.

"Steady…steady…"

Bennett, however, was clearly perturbed. For him, sitting motionless required total concentration. His face slowly twisted into a frown. His wide-open eyes blazed with intensity. He seemed ready to burst.

"Steady…steady…done!"

A man on the other side of the room gently placed a cap on a small tube projecting out of a wooden box. The contraption stood on three legs about five feet off the ground.

Bennett bolted up. He let out a loud hack and collapsed back into the chair, exhausted from the effort.

"We're almost done, Langston. Only one more picture, I promise," said Hughes.

"Let's see how this one came out," said the photographer, a wiry man with curly blond hair. His sleeves were rolled up, and silver stains covered an apron he wore over his shirt. He turned to his subjects and rubbed his hands together. "Would you like to see how the process works, Mr. Bennett?"

The old man grunted. "No thank you, Mr. Leery. I would not even begin to understand it."

"Very well."

The photographer removed a slide from the camera. It was housed in a protective case, out of the light. "Hold this, Marcus," he said to his assistant, a light-skinned black boy who looked about twelve years old. Then Leery disappeared into a large box covered by a red curtain.

"Where did you find this man?" asked Bennett.

"He opened a shop on King Street last fall. He came down here from New York City."

"I could tell that just by listening to him talk. I don't trust people with a Yankee accent."

"Many of the New Yorkers are on our side in this, Langston. You know that. They depend on us for trade. The whole merchant class there needs us. Besides, photography has nothing to do with the crisis. It's just a diversion. You don't need to be so grumpy about it."

"I am restless. Our days are filled with waiting."

Hughes could not disagree. He was coming to Bennett's house every afternoon now. They spent long hours together, sharing meals, talking, and reading in each other's presence. Mostly they just waited. Hughes thought the novelty of a photo session would help them pass the time, especially after Bennett had remarked a month back about never having had his picture taken. Leery performed most of his work in his studio, but Hughes had convinced him to visit Bennett's home—it was the only way he could get the old man to consent to having his photograph taken. Yet Hughes also understood that the exercise was more than a diversion. Sitting for a portrait with Bennett made him feel like an heir.

Hughes stood up and looked out the window. There were a few ships in the harbor. Perhaps one of these will end the waiting, he thought.

"They'll demand surrender soon," said Bennett.

Hughes moved his gaze toward the little fort just barely visible in the distance. "Yes. I suppose they will."

"If Sumter falls, war will come."

"I agree."

"But it won't change our goal."

Hughes took his eyes off the fort and looked at Bennett, still seated in the chair. He knew the old man was determined in just about everything he did, but he had not known him to be as determined as he was now. On the day Bennett told him about the plan, he had also said he expected it to be the final important act of his life.

Suddenly Leery called out from his portable darkroom. "We're done," he announced. The photographer stepped out, squinted briefly, and studied the picture. He held up a glass plate and looked at Bennett. "This is called the negative," said Leery. "It's a reversed image. Black is white and white is black."

"That's what we're trying to stop," muttered Bennett.

Hughes smiled at the crack as he went to see the picture. It was well focused. The lines were sharp. It was an excellent photograph from a technical perspective. The only problem was Bennett. He was scowling. In negative, he looked like a fiend from the pits of hell.

"Langston," said Hughes with a sigh, "let's try it once more."

"We have done this twice already," complained Bennett, still sitting in his chair across the room. "I am really quite fatigued."

"Looking pleasant really takes no effort, Langston. This will be the last one. I promise."

Bennett sneered. "No more after this."

"Prepare the next picture, Mr. Leery," said Hughes triumphantly. "This time, I would like to observe."

"Certainly, Mr. Hughes."

They squeezed into the portable darkroom, a small space when only one person occupied it. For a moment they just stood there. Then Leery's arm reached out of the curtains. "Marcus!" The boy put a clean glass plate in his hand. Leery pulled it into the darkroom. He seized a vial and uncorked it. "This is the collodion syrup." He tipped the vial and poured its contents onto the glass, then twirled the plate in his hand until a thin coating covered the whole surface. "Now we let this dry," Leery said, setting the plate down on a small shelf. "It will take a few minutes."

When the two men emerged from the darkroom, Bennett was still sitting in his chair. Leery gestured to his assistant. "Drop the plate into the silver nitrate when it's ready." Marcus disappeared behind the curtains.

"This can be a dirty line of work," said Leery, pointing to the smears and streaks on his apron. "I let Marcus handle some of the grubbier chores. He's a smart boy. If he were a little older, he could probably run this whole business for me."

"And if he weren't a slave boy," sniped Bennett.

"Actually, he's not a slave boy," said Leery. "He's free and lives on Nassau Street, in the free black neighborhood. I employ him."

"Really," said Bennett. His disapproval was obvious.

Leery either did not catch the reproach or he ignored it. "After Marcus pulls the glass from the silver nitrate, we'll have to take our picture while the plate is wet," he said. "The air is moist today, so we probably have about ten minutes to get the job done—plenty of time. Now let me show you—"

The sound of a short knock interrupted him. The door to the room opened, and Lucius walked in. He stepped gingerly around the photographic equipment spread across the floor and approached Bennett.

"There is a visitor, sir," announced Lucius. "He won't give his name, but he says he's from Cuba. He insists that you know him."

Bennett looked at Hughes. "Perhaps our wait is over," he said. Then he turned his attention to Lucius. "Give us a moment to arrange ourselves."

The old slave exited the room. Bennett rose to his feet and looked at the photographic equipment. "Mr. Leery, you will have to excuse us. Mr. Hughes and I have a pressing appointment. You must leave immediately."

"I understand." The photographer turned to his assistant, but Marcus was already cleaning up. He spoke again to Bennett. "Shall I make prints of these photos for you right away? I can drop them off here, and you can review them later today at your convenience."

"That would be fine, Mr. Leery. See that Lucius gets them."

As Leery and Marcus scrambled to pack and go, Bennett put his arm around Hughes. "I will do the negotiating with our guest," he said in a hushed voice. "You are here primarily as a witness."

"I know. We've gone over this," said Hughes.

The photographers did not need long. Marcus stuffed the darkroom full of pans and solutions, collapsed it, and carried it away. Leery took the camera. At the door, he paused for a moment. "Thank you very much for this opportunity, Mr. Bennett and Mr. Hughes. I am sure you will be pleased with the result."

"Yes, Mr. Leery. Good-bye," said Bennett.

Hughes frowned at Bennett's curtness. "Thank you, Mr. Leery. Please do deliver those prints. I will be anxious to see them."

With that, Leery left. The two men could hear him and Marcus stomping down the stairs with their load. The front door opened and closed. There was silence for a moment. Next came the faint sound of footsteps moving up the stairs, getting louder.

In walked Lucius. "Sir, your guest."

A figure stood in the doorway. He was clean-shaven, lean, and about average height. The man's hair was the color of sand. Long exposure to the sun had reddened his skin. His expressionless face was long and narrow. Two bright blue eyes took in the whole room before settling on Bennett.

"Welcome," said Bennett. Lucius thought he had never seen his master's grin look so guarded. There was even a touch of dread in it. Bennett shook the stranger's hand, and then Hughes did the same.

Bennett hobbled across the room and motioned to a chair for his guest. The visitor followed and sat down, and Bennett and Hughes took seats facing him. The visitor turned his head deliberately, looking over his left shoulder in the direction of Lucius, who remained standing near the door. His silent request was perfectly clear—he wanted Lucius to leave—but what immediately caught Bennett's attention was the ear on the right side of his head. Or what remained of it. Half was missing, and most of the rest was mangled. The only unaffected part was a drooping lobe that would have looked large on a fully attached and healthy ear. On this one, it seemed like a bizarre, dangling growth.

The sight distracted Bennett for a moment. Then he spoke. "Lucius, please leave us," he said. "Why don't you go see if Mr. Leery needs help?"

The three men listened to Lucius go down the steps. There was a pause, and then the front door opened and closed.

"I have not been in the United States for many years," said the visitor.

"This is not the United States anymore, you know," said Bennett earnestly. "This is South Carolina. We have seceded."

"Ah, yes," chuckled the visitor. Bennett was not sure whether he was being laughed with or laughed at. He decided he did not want to know the answer.

Bennett shifted in his seat. "How was your journey?" he asked.

"Agreeable, thank you," came the reply. "The weather was fine too, and I have found the people of Charleston to be simply delightful." He smirked. "Shall we set aside these meaningless pleasantries? They are distractions. I know who you are, and I think I know what you want."

The man spoke excellent English. Bennett had not been sure that he would. There was perhaps the slightest trace of a Spanish accent, but Bennett wondered whether he noticed it only because he was expecting it. Maybe it was not there at all. This man, at any rate, sounded like an American. From the North, he thought.

"What do you know of me?" asked the old plantation owner.

"Quite a lot, I suppose. You are Langston Bennett. You are one of the wealthiest men in the whole Southern part of the United—I mean, in South Carolina," said the guest. "Forgive me." He smirked again. "You own an enormous amount of land in the countryside and also keep this house in the city. You've spent time on my little island. *Usted aprendió a hablar español.* You were a supporter of Walker and Quitman and probably other filibusters as well. You have sent letters asking after me, and you have received responses recommending me for whatever job you have in mind."

"Your knowledge is comprehensive," said Bennett.

"A man in my line of work survives by staying well informed, Mr. Bennett."

"Then you must know what I want."

"I think I do, although it is not through any direct knowledge," said the guest. "It is a matter of deduction."

"So what have you deduced?"

"When a man like you meets with a man like me, there is generally only one thing he has on his mind. There is a certain kind of job he wants executed, and he wants it done by a professional. In your particular case, given your interests and recent events, I would guess that the job is a bit north of here." He paused for a moment. "I would guess it's in what you call the United States. Or at least what remains of it." This time, he did not smirk.

"You are an intelligent man."

"I am paid to be intelligent."

"My offer is an attractive one."

"You said it would be, and I believe you. That's why I'm here."

"Why should I hire you rather than someone else?"

"Because you need me."

"And why is that?"

The visitor did not move. He did not even cast his eyes downward, Bennett observed. A less confident man would shift in his seat or look away, he thought. This fellow did neither. Bennett found himself liking his guest—or at least approving of him. It was true that the reports he had received from abroad gave his visitor high marks.

"You need me because nobody else can do the job," said the guest. "I am aware of the reports that others have considered doing what you are about to ask of me. Yet they were ruled by passion and therefore doomed to fail. You must understand that I do not care about your ultimate ends. I do not care what you hope to accomplish by employing me. I care only about the job I am given. That's why I'm effective. I'm never desperate. I'm simply lethal."

Bennett absorbed this comment. He began to believe that he had found the man he had set out to find.

"We want you to rid us of this meddlesome president."

"Right," said the visitor. "Now give me a good reason to do this."

"You may know that I have no natural heir," said Bennett. "Ever since I lost my two sons, I have searched for a worthy man to assume control of my properties after I am gone. In Tucker Hughes, I have found that man."

Bennett gestured to Hughes, who nodded his head at the visitor. Then Bennett rose and wobbled over to his desk. He opened a drawer and removed several documents. "This is a copy of my will," he said when he returned. "Please, take a look at it."

The guest took the pages and scanned them. "As you can see," said Bennett, "it lists all of my property and deeds virtually the entire estate to Mr. Hughes."

"That is indeed what it says here."

"I am an old man," said Bennett. "It is doubtful that I will survive more than a few years." He handed his guest another document. "This is an unsigned codicil. It was drafted the day I received the letter saying you would come for a meeting. It amends the will you have just read to provide half of my property to a person who completes a certain unnamed task to my satisfaction. if I am still living, or of Mr. Hughes, if I am not."

The visitor looked it over. "This does leave matters a bit open-ended," he said. "But I think we can work with it."

"I figure a man in your line of work has the ability to enforce legitimate contracts if others do not," said Bennett. "You need not worry about it coming to that, however. We are men of honor. Mr. Hughes has every incentive to make good on our promise. He wants the result it will obtain as much as I do."

"Then perhaps this is settled," said the guest.

"You find our terms acceptable?"

"I do."

"Excellent," said Bennett. "Now, in terms of the planning—"

The visitor interrupted. "I will plan everything myself. In fact, you will not hear from me again until I have completed the assignment. I will not tell you where I am going or how I will accomplish it. But it will be done, and it will be done in a timely manner."

"How will we keep track of you?" asked Hughes, speaking for the first time.

"You won't."

"We won't?"

"No. There is nothing you can provide me."

"That may not be true," said Bennett. "I have a friend in Washington who may be of some assistance. She is an ally to our cause, and she has resources you may find helpful. I won't insist on it, but I believe it would be a mistake not to make use of her."

"Who is she?"

"Her name is Violet Grenier. She is near the center of the city's social life. She knows many things about many people. Some call her the most persuasive woman ever to live in Washington. She will almost certainly have intelligence you will want to know."

The visitor said nothing. Bennett took this as a sign to continue.

"I have taken the liberty of writing her a letter of introduction," he said, handing an envelope to his guest. "I suggest you give it to her and see what she can do for you."

The visitor studied the envelope. It was sealed. He turned it over in his hands several times before looking up.

"Very well," he said at last. "I will consider making contact with this woman. In the meantime, I believe this concludes our business. You will know when I have succeeded. Sometime after that, you will see me again."

He stood up to leave, but Hughes stepped into his view. "This may sound strange, but who are you?"

The visitor shot a look at Bennett.

"It may be best that you not know more than you already do," said Bennett.

"What is your name?" Hughes persisted. "What if we need to contact you through Mrs. Grenier? How are we to do that? There must be some name that we can use."

The visitor glared at Hughes, and it made the young man feel small. Hughes could see a vein in the guest's forehead throbbing. He was suddenly afraid of this man.

"You need not answer him," said Bennett.

The guest did not move. Hughes felt himself withering. Then the guest smiled, though not in a kindly way. His eyes seemed to threaten.

"You may call me," he said, pausing briefly, and then speaking with a full Spanish trill, "Mazorca."

The sky was overcast as Mazorca stepped off the porch of the Bennett house. He was satisfied with the arrangements made inside. It was quite a bit of land. When he completed the job, he would gain a small fortune. Mazorca had every intention of collecting.

He walked toward the water, where a few people strolled around the Battery. Off in the distance was Sumter. The day before, on the ship sailing into Charleston Harbor, Mazorca had seen it up close. He could tell immediately that it would not survive a coordinated attack. It was meant to serve as one part of a harbor defense rather than stand on its own. Its enemies were expected to come from the sea, not from the land. If the guns of Fort Moultrie started pounding away, Sumter's fall would be only a matter of time.

Mazorca halted at the Battery's edge. Green water lapped against the seawall. He stood motionless for a while, watching the waves roll up and down. He thought about the job that lay ahead. The objective was a familiar one. Yet it also felt like the most ambitious assignment he had ever accepted. There was much to learn, much to plan. He would enjoy the test and savor the success.

The papers in his pocket—the will, the codicil, and the letter to Grenier—pressed against his chest. He pulled them out, reviewed them, and put them back. Then he looked down at the water again. Its constant flow fascinated him. He stared at it for a few minutes, engrossed in the way that some people are when they stare at a fire.

About thirty feet to his right, Marcus placed a cap on the lens that had been pointing at Mazorca for half a minute. As Mazorca turned around and walked toward King Street and the heart of the city, he did not see Marcus. Nor did he see Lucius pat the boy on the back.

VII

The wagon creaked forward, inch by inch. Somebody had taken everything he could manage to remove from his home and piled it onto the cart. The heap of trunks and furniture soared twelve feet off the ground. Two horses strained to pull this load toward the base of the Long Bridge, where Fourteenth Street and Maryland Avenue converged. It was incredible to think they had gotten the wagon to move at all.

For Colonel Rook, the sight was no novelty. The slow evacuation of Washington by Southerners had been going on for weeks. Some packed lightly because they did not think they would be gone for more than a few months. Others, like this man, seemed to take everything they owned.

Rook was convinced that even more people would leave now: the fall of Fort Sumter was inevitable. On Friday, the rebels in South Carolina had started firing. There were rumors the next day that Major Anderson had surrendered, but nothing was confirmed. Rook knew it was just a matter of time. Without provisions, Anderson could not withstand a siege. Sumter was finished.

The wagon crawled closer to the aptly named Long Bridge. The Potomac River was nearly a mile wide here, and the Long Bridge was the only direct route out of the city and into Virginia that did not involve getting into a boat. Rook had his men keep a tally of how many people left each day. It was usually just a handful. Across the weeks, however, the numbers added up. He thought this information was helpful, but even more useful was talking to people before they set foot on the bridge. When he could, Rook liked to conduct the interviews himself. It was a good way to gather intelligence.

"Good morning, sir," hailed Rook as the wagon came to a stop right before the bridge. A man sat in front of his big load, and a slave beside him held the reins. The man looked annoyed at having to stop.

"Where are you bound?" asked Rook.

"Richmond."

"Looks like you expect to be there some time."

"Quite a long time." The Southern accent was unmistakable.

"And why is that?"

The man glared at Rook as if the colonel were an imbecile. He hopped off the wagon and swept an arm toward the half-assembled city of Washington. "This will be gone in a few weeks—all of it," he said. "The city will look like an earthquake had wrecked it. I don't intend to be here when that happens."

The man paused, but Rook said nothing. He knew from experience that interviews often produced their most valuable information when subjects were allowed to speak without interruption.

"Friends have written to me for months with a single message: 'Robert Fowler, get yourself out of that city.' When

I heard that Fort Sumter had come under fire, I knew they were right. I regret leaving behind my house, and I couldn't possibly take all of its contents. But Virginia will secede very soon, as will the rest of the South. This is a time for choosing sides. Surely, Colonel, you must know that Washington is not adequately defended. When Virginia and Maryland withdraw from the Union, it will be surrounded and it will suffocate."

Fowler was about to get back on his wagon when Rook spoke.

"What makes you so certain Virginia and Maryland will secede? They haven't yet."

"No, but they will. I don't intend to be here when trouble comes."

"Do you have a family?"

"My wife and children boarded a train for Richmond yesterday. I plan to join them. Now, sir, I'd like to be on my way."

"Of course," said Rook. "You may go."

Fowler climbed back onto his wagon. The slave tugged at the reins. The horses strained for a moment, and the wagon's wheels began to turn.

Rook watched them go. He took a piece of paper from his pocket and made a mark on it. Then he thought of the man's words: "This is a time for choosing sides." The colonel's eye wandered upriver, to the right, and settled on a big house that overlooked the Potomac from the Virginia side. This was the home of Colonel Robert E. Lee, and almost everybody in the army wondered what this talented young officer would do when his own time for choosing came.

The sound of a racing horse pulled him from these thoughts. "Colonel! Fort Sumter has given up!" shouted a sergeant as he dismounted. "We just received the official word by telegraph. Anderson gave up yesterday and the firing has stopped. The formal surrender is today."

"This will stir things up."

"Yes it will, sir."

Sergeant Frank Springfield was young, though mature beyond his years. He looked ordinary—brown hair, medium build—except for one thing. He had the bushiest mustache Rook had ever seen. It was so thick above his lip that Rook wondered if the man could breathe through his nose.

Originally, Rook had been skeptical of him: Springfield was an abolitionist, and Rook regarded all abolitionists with suspicion. In his mind, too many of them were radicals who placed the interest of their cause above national unity. Yet Springfield had impressed Rook as an unusually competent aide. It was just like him to hear about Sumter and track down his superior officer. Many men of his rank would not have bothered unless they had been ordered. This ability to take the initiative was why Rook had posted Springfield at Willard's prior to the inauguration, and why he had come to rely on him even more in the weeks since then.

"Thank you, Sergeant. Will you accompany me to the Winder Building?"

The two men got on their horses and headed north on Fourteenth Street. They soon reached an open field, where a few cows and sheep grazed. The truncated Washington Monument was on the left. To their right was the Smithsonian Institution, a dark red castle that looked like it belonged in medieval Europe. About a mile beyond was the unfinished Capitol. Neither man paid it much heed. They were distracted by the stench of what lay ahead: the canal. It was really an open sewer pit that cut through the city. People emptied all kinds of raw waste into its filthy waters. They occasionally dumped dead animals. The smell would have been bad even if water had flowed through it rapidly, but sometimes the water appeared not to move at all. Attempts to dredge it had failed—the abominable thing kept silting up. Rook and Springfield spurred their horses to pick up the pace and were glad to get beyond the canal's foul reek.

They turned left and passed just south of the White House. Then the Winder came into view. At five stories, it was one of the taller buildings in the city. It was more functional than magnificent, and that was to Rook's liking. In a city cluttered with potted streets and stinking sewers, functionality was nothing to take for granted.

It occurred to Rook that unscheduled meetings might take up a good part of his afternoon, now that Sumter had fallen. There would be talk of war. "Sergeant, would you mind riding out past Georgetown and inspecting the Chain Bridge for me? I'm afraid I may not be able to get there today."

"Yes, sir," said Springfield. Rook watched him trot another two blocks to Pennsylvania Avenue, turn left, and disappear behind a building. The colonel passed his horse to an attendant and went inside.

"I just heard about Sumter," he said when he saw Locke. Rook figured that the news might allow the two men to hold an actual conversation.

"General Scott is not here," said Locke. "He's meeting with the president."

Then Locke raised his eyebrows. "That coward Anderson. I think he's a traitor for giving up so easily. He didn't put up any kind of fight."

So there would be a conversation—a disagreeable one. Rook bristled at hearing the word *traitor* applied to Anderson. He knew many Northerners would criticize the fort's commander for his decision. Some of the press commentary on Sumter noted that Anderson, like Rook, was from Kentucky—a slave state. Until recently, the major had even owned slaves himself. At West Point, he had been a close friend of Jefferson Davis. His loyalty was under severe scrutiny, and many would doubt it after this new turn of events. But Rook was not convinced. If Anderson were disloyal, what did that make the men who had fired upon him?

"I don't think he's a traitor," said Rook. He recounted Sumter's plight: low on ammunition, running out of food, no chance of resupply. "Besides, the fort was not built to repel an attack mounted from the guns on shore. Major Anderson was in a terrible position. Under the circumstances, I think he probably did as well as anybody could."

"As well as he could for whom?" asked Locke, scornfully. "Men are picking sides right now, and it looks to me as though Anderson has chosen his. He's from Kentucky, you know."

Locke is trying to provoke me, thought Rook. Anderson had been ordered to Sumter several months earlier specifically because of his commitment to the Union. Some Northern newspapers had questioned the choice, especially as the crisis in Charleston escalated, but Rook knew that they talked without really knowing what they were saying.

That was typical of newspapers. Locke himself should have known better.

"Anderson is a good man. If the federal government cannot rely upon men who feel the tug of divided loyalties but nonetheless stand for the Union, then the United States truly is doomed," said Rook.

"Feeling a tug, Colonel?"

Rook felt the urge to punch him, but he settled for words rather than fists. "Watch what you say, Locke."

The general's aide rolled his eyes and sighed loudly. He returned to the newspaper spread across his desk. An awkward silence fell over the room.

A few minutes later, Scott ambled in. "Both of you," he said sharply, "come into my office."

The general collapsed into his usual chair. He looked worn out and distressed. "Tomorrow, the president plans to ask the states for seventy-five thousand soldiers to help put down the insurrection," he said. "I hardly need to tell you that this will be controversial. I suspect that we will lose several states over it, including Virginia. What a blow that will be."

Scott frowned. "Virginia has symbolic importance. She is the mother of statesmen: Washington, Jefferson, Madison, and so many others. The prestige of her entering this so-called Southern Confederacy is immeasurable. I'm afraid that losing her may take a military toll as well. It will be difficult to field an army of raw recruits without some of Virginia's sons at the helm. Worse yet, our capital will become instantly vulnerable. Can you imagine if Maryland leaves too? This city will be like an island surrounded by an ocean of enemies. Colonel Rook, I would like you to put all of your resources behind defending the city from military attack.

Do this exclusively. It is clearly the most important threat we now face."

Rook wanted to reply, but Locke blurted out a question. "Who will lead Lincoln's army?" he asked.

"As you know, I'm too old for another campaign," said Scott. He patted his belly. "I'm not fit for one either. I think the best candidate for the job is Colonel Robert E. Lee. He proved himself to me firsthand in Mexico. I marked him back then as a man with a bright future. He displayed his skills again when he captured John Brown at Harper's Ferry a year and a half ago. I'm going to sleep on it, but I believe that tomorrow I will recommend him to the president."

"I think that is a very fine idea," said Locke.

"He's from Virginia," said Rook. "Do you think he will remain loyal?"

"It is possible for Virginians to remain loyal," snapped Locke. "The general is for the Union."

"Of course," said Rook, irritated that Locke would try to twist his words. "The general has made his loyalty quite plain. Lee has not announced his intentions. He has put off his own time of choosing."

"If Lincoln takes my advice and makes the offer to Lee, that will force the question," said Scott. "It may even inspire him to do the right thing. He is the best man for the job."

The general looked at both men. "I would like some time alone now. Is there anything else to discuss?"

"I do have a small suggestion," said Rook. "Let's not forget about the personal security of the president."

"Oh please, Colonel," said Locke, full of contempt. "Now is not the time for this."

Scott shook his head. "I can assure you that the president feels entirely secure. This morning he walked to the Presbyterian Church on New York Avenue, attended a service, and walked back—without any kind of escort."

"I've had a couple of men keeping an eye on secessionists. I believe their activity should continue."

"I just gave you an order to concentrate on the city's defenses," said Scott. "I expect you to obey."

"We need to orient our defenses in two directions—toward an outside threat as well as an inside threat," persisted Rook. "I know that we can't place more men around the president. I'm talking about something else: investigating people who may pose a threat to the president, following the same rationale that allowed me to place undercover agents in the lobby of Willard's two months ago." Rook reached into his pocket and produced a slip of paper. He rose from his seat and handed it to the general. "I'm not talking about a long list of names. With your approval, I would like to begin surveillance of these people and others like them."

Scott looked skeptical. He studied the list for a moment. "Why is Robert Fowler crossed off?"

"He left the city this morning. I saw him depart by the Long Bridge myself, just before coming here."

Scott continued to examine the list. "How did you come up with these names?"

"I just wrote down a few prominent secessionists, or people who are known to hold secessionist sympathies. I only mean to use a handful of men who are already under my command."

Scott looked up from the list. "Just the other day, the president mentioned to me the problem of what he called the 'secesh dames.' It's a peculiar term, but that is how our president talks. Anyway, I notice that your list is composed entirely of men."

"Is there a woman you would add to it?"

"Violet Grenier is certainly a 'secesh dame.' She is also one of the few Southern sympathizers who maintain friendships on both sides of this controversy."

"So let me check on her. It might be helpful to know who is within Mrs. Grenier's circle of influence."

"Snooping on ladies?" said Locke, sounding exasperated. He looked at the general. "This is absurd."

Scott nodded, ever so slightly. "You see, here is the dilemma," he said. "You seem to be suggesting that people who know Mrs. Grenier can't be trusted."

"No, I simply think if anybody is conspiring against our city or our president, keeping an eye on someone like Mrs. Grenier may help us avoid a calamity."

"Mrs. Grenier is an acquaintance of mine," said Scott. "William Seward, the secretary of state, is a frequent caller as well. I will ignore the implications of what you have just said. Do not think on this matter any longer. I will not allow it." Scott then made a show of taking the list of names and ripping it in half. "Moreover," he continued, "I just gave you an order to devote your attention to the military security of the city, and away from the rumors that have occupied so much of your time. Our main concern can no longer be spies and collaborators. It must be soldiers who intend to march on Washington."

"I think that is the correct decision, General," said Locke.

Rook hardly could believe the man's posturing. He struggled to hold his tongue.

"Good day, Colonel Rook," said Scott.

Rook said nothing as he got up and left. He stormed out the door of the Winder Building, fists clenched in anger. Across the street he noticed the dingy, boxlike buildings of the Navy and War departments. He peered around them for a view of the White House in their rear, as he usually did when he emerged from one of these meetings with Scott. He imagined Lincoln inside it right now, still talking with his advisors about what to do.

Rook, for his part, had no doubts about his next move: he would disobey Scott for the sake of the president.

The fort was defeated, not destroyed. Round divots pock-marked its brick walls where cannonballs had crashed into them. But the walls still stood high and appeared service-able, especially with some patching. The parapet was de-molished. A few chimneys peeked over the walls, though a couple of these had been smashed. One looked charred.

A small group of gentlemen and ladies in fine dress stood at one of the fort's angles. A man was addressing them, waving his arms around in excitement. He was obvi-ously telling a story to a tour group. High over their heads, flapping in an ocean breeze, flew a blue-and-white palmetto flag alongside a flag representing the new Confederate na-tion. The flag of the United States was gone.

Mazorca studied the scene for a few minutes. He had lingered in Charleston for several days after his meeting with Bennett, reading everything he could find on the cur-rent crisis. He wanted a complete understanding of the scene before him, and this excursion was the final part of his research.

The ride out to Cummings Point on Morris Island had been long and roundabout. He could not get any closer to Fort Sumter on dry land than this. Perhaps three-quarters of a mile separated the fort from the Battery on the point, where a slanted wall of railroad iron protected the cannon that had fired on the fort just three days earlier.

When Mazorca was satisfied, he turned his horse around and galloped off. He had a train to catch.

VIII

Wednesday, April 17, 1861

Little Maggie was the first to see them. She dropped her basket and sprinted down the tree-lined lane, yelping with the unbridled excitement of childhood. A few others heard her and joined the chase. Soon a dozen dark-skinned kids were running toward the three approaching carriages, whooping all the way.

Bennett always enjoyed the approach to his plantation manor. The innocent glee of these children gave him a deep satisfaction. He felt like a hero returning from a long absence, or a general from a great victory. This first encounter with the children never failed to stir the sensation of fatherhood in him. He loved this moment and looked forward to it every time he departed Charleston and headed for his ancestral home—his true home—in the South Carolina countryside. He leaned forward and waved from the window. The kids kept on running. They seemed oblivious to him, but that was okay. It was dusk, and hard for them to see inside the carriage.

Up ahead, at the foot of the porch, a small group of grown-up slaves gathered. Sundown was quitting time, which meant that most of them had come in from the fields for the day and were near the manor. Bennett could see a bustle of activity behind them as several of the house servants performed last-second tidying. He knew they would have a hot meal ready for him by the time he walked through the front door.

The thought of food reminded him that Hughes had not yet made up his mind about staying for dinner. The young man's own plantation was only a few miles away, and the pair had decided to travel from the city together. Bennett usually made the journey with Lucius, but this time he sat with Hughes, whose small cab was a bit cramped for three. Lucius rode behind in the Bennett carriage. It had been a long day for everybody. Yet neither Bennett nor Hughes was tired. In fact, they were both in an exceptionally good mood.

"So will you join us at the table this evening?" asked Bennett.

Hughes was peering out the window at the assembly of slaves. "I am anxious to get home," he said, almost to himself. Then he snapped to attention and looked at Bennett. "But yes, I think I will join you, Langston."

"That is good. You can send your carriage on and take one of my horses when we're done."

They rolled to a stop in front of the big house, which gave the children a chance to catch up and scramble around one of the carriages. They must think I'm in that one, Bennett thought.

Hughes hopped from the cab and then turned to help Bennett down. The aging plantation master stepped onto the gravel, treating his peg leg with special care. He expected the slave children to swarm him, but their attention was fixed firmly elsewhere. "Lucius! Lucius!" they cried, first in chaotic shouts and then a chant. Bennett felt abandoned.

"Lucius! Lucius!"

The old slave now emerged from his carriage. He wore an enormous grin on his face and greeted several members of his welcoming committee with quick pats to the head and some words Bennett could not hear. Lucius looked up and saw his master about twenty feet away, just standing there and staring. The slave's smile disappeared.

"Lucius! Lucius!"

Lucius shushed the little throng and reached into his carriage. He pulled out a broad-rimmed hat and a big cane and walked at a brisk pace to where Bennett stood. The slave's miniature entourage followed right behind, not yelling any longer but giggling the whole way.

"Here you are, sir," said Lucius as he handed Bennett the hat and cane.

"Thank you, Lucius."

The two men looked at each other in silence. Bennett could see that Lucius was anxious at the apparent snub his crowd of young admirers had just delivered.

"It must be good to see your family again," said the master.

"Yessir," replied the slave. "Sorry, sir."

"Don't worry about it, Lucius. I can see a couple of your grandchildren here. Hello, Maggie," he said, bending over to look at a small girl clutching Lucius's leg. She took a step back. Bennett smiled and straightened up. "They ought to be happy at the sight of their grandfather!" he laughed, turning to the adult slaves who had just watched all of this. "And look, Lucius: over there is Portia. How this fine granddaughter of yours has become a lovely woman!"

Portia blushed. "Good evening, Mr. Bennett," she said.

"Good evening, everybody!"

A buzz of activity erupted around the plantation master. A handful of slaves started to tend to the carriage and its horses, a couple more unloaded boxes and trunks, and a few others inquired about the ride. Lucius dashed into the house. As this was going on, a white man came into view from the far side of the manor. He barked orders from a hundred feet away in a booming voice, making it impossible to hear anything but his bellowing:

"Get those bags off and inside right away! Unhitch those horses! I want them cleaned tonight! Make sure there's a table setting for Mr. Hughes!" The slaves were already attentive, but they seemed to move even more quickly at the sound of this loud man.

"Where did you ever find such an overseer, Langston?" asked Hughes. "I think they can hear him all the way to Charleston."

"This place would not function without him," laughed Bennett. "Hello, Mr. Tate."

"Hello, sir. Welcome back. We missed you a few days ago."

"Thank you, Mr. Tate. I longed to return too. But I could not ignore the recent events in Charleston."

"Did you see the bombardment?"

"The whole city did. The entire population must have descended upon the Battery, even before dawn. Hughes and I managed to avoid the crowd by rising above it—we watched for two days through a spyglass on my rooftop. Nobody could actually hear the barrage because a strong wind was blowing out to sea. But we saw the wisps of smoke rise from Fort Moultrie and Morris Island and knew that Sumter was getting pounded. Every puff from our cannons won a cheer from the Battery. Around eight o'clock on Saturday morning, we could see a huge fire at Sumter, with enormous clouds of smoke billowing upward. This gave everybody a thrill. We thought Sumter would surrender at any moment. But the men inside continued to hang on for a few hours more. They must have been covered with soot, and I still wonder how they breathed."

Bennett leaned on his cane and waved his arm about as he told the story, and Tate listened intently. Several of the slaves paused to hear the tale as well. The only person nearby not to give Bennett his full attention was Hughes, who could not take his eyes off Portia. She was short and fit, with bright eyes and caramel-colored skin that suggested race mixing somewhere in her background. Hughes guessed Portia was about eighteen years old. She was quite pretty—actually, she was beautiful—and he found himself desiring her. He quit looking, though, when he noticed the burly slave beside her. The big man's arms were as thick as Hughes's own neck. He stared directly at Hughes. It felt like a challenge. Hughes resented that. He refused to let a slave get in the way of anything he wanted.

As Bennett described Charleston's jubilation when Sumter finally did surrender—ringing church bells, hot-blooded speeches, and bonfires lighting the sky through the night—Hughes gradually maneuvered himself beside Portia. Her concentration was fixed on the story, and she did not notice him approach. He leaned over and placed his lips next to her ear. "Mr. Bennett was correct," he whispered. "You are a lovely girl."

Portia trembled at the words. She looked at Hughes, who gave her a rakish smile. She frowned and took a step toward that big slave. "Joe," she whispered, though she hardly needed to get his attention. She tried to focus on Bennett again but kept casting nervous glances in the direction of Hughes, who would not stop staring at her.

By now Bennett had returned to the subject of the federal troops trapped for weeks in Sumter and how they must have suffered, especially on the second day of the attack. "It is hard not to admire an enemy like that," said Bennett. "But it is easy to feel contempt for the man who would force them through it. This Abraham Lincoln is a beast, Tate. He was not within his rights to keep the fort. I didn't think he could sink further in my estimation, but he did when he made those poor men defend a cause as hopeless as Sumter's. There was nothing they could do. Their effort went to waste, except that it must have satisfied Lincoln to let them endure pain and privation so that he could frustrate South Carolina, however briefly."

Bennett's face reddened as his excitement turned to anger. "Curse that man! He will stop at nothing to confound us. Look around you, Tate," he said, gesturing to his house, his fields, and finally a few of his slaves. "All of what we have here will be gone if this man has his way. He is a danger to our lives and everything we hold dear. There is no other word for it: Lincoln is evil!"

Suddenly Bennett quit his harangue. The sermon had exhausted him. He breathed heavily. His forehead glistened with sweat. He removed his hat and rubbed his face with a handkerchief. Tate and the slaves wondered whether he was done and did not move. The old man replaced his hat and looked at the porch of his manor, where Lucius now stood. He had come back outside just as Bennett was concluding his outburst.

"Mr. Bennett," called Lucius. "Dinner is ready for you and Mr. Hughes."

"Well, Mr. Hughes, shall we venture in?" asked Bennett.

"Let's do that," said Hughes. He made eye contact one more time with Portia and winked at her. She looked away. Then Hughes locked arms with Bennett and helped the old man climb the steps of his home. At the top, he turned and spoke. "Mr. Tate, please be good enough to see that my carriage gets off." He went inside without waiting for a response.

Tate began shouting orders again. His first one went to the huge slave near Portia. "Get a move on, Big Joe. Start unloading that carriage." The slaves who had halted their work to listen to Bennett returned to their labors. Portia was the only one not to budge. It was almost as if she did not hear Tate. She just stared at the ground.

Lucius saw her. After Bennett and Hughes entered the house, he moved down the steps and touched her chin. She looked up at her grandfather.

"What's the matter, Portia?"

"It's nothin'. I just been a little tired."

"I hope it ain't more than that." Lucius slipped into an informal dialect that he tried to avoid around Bennett.

"Don't worry about me. I'll be fine."

She took a step toward the house, where she knew she was needed. But Lucius clasped her elbow. She stopped and gave him a questioning look.

"Portia, we need to talk about something very important."

Lucius glanced quickly in all directions to make sure they could not be overheard. Then he leaned forward. "Meet me by the stables later tonight, after Mr. Bennett has gone to bed."

A woman seated beside a window was the first to see it. "There's a secession flag flying over the Virginia capitol!" she said. This prompted a general commotion on the train. Passengers scrambled for a view. Atop a hill sat a white building that was designed by Thomas Jefferson and looked like a Roman temple. Above it flew a red, white, and blue flag, but not the federal one. In the fading daylight, they could see that it had three stripes, with a handful of stars displayed on a blue field.

"The stars and bars!" shouted a voice from somewhere within the train. The formerly subdued car burst into cheers. Had Virginia really seceded? What else could it mean? Just about everybody on board was thrilled at the prospect. This would give the Confederacy a fighting chance. The silence of nervous anticipation soon took over as the train slowed down on a bridge over the James River and then stopped at a depot on the other side of the water.

Within seconds it was confirmed: that very day, Virginia had voted to leave the Union. Strangers who had not spoken to each other on the ride now embraced. Men made martial boasts, and a group of women near the front cried with joy. "We shall have war now," one of them announced amid her own laughter and tears, "if Lincoln is not a coward." Her equally ecstatic friend replied, "But he is a coward! He is a coward!"

In the very last row of the car, a man with a hat pulled down to cover his face did not move. Mazorca pretended to sleep.

Corporal William Clark tried to suppress a yawn and failed. It had been a long day, sitting in the foyer of Brown's Hotel and reading the same newspaper over and over again. It was not even a newspaper he wanted to read. The *National Intelligencer* was Washington's leading daily for Southern sympathizers. Clark, a native of Maine, certainly felt no sympathy. He would have preferred not to hide this fact, but his current assignment called on him to wear something other than the blue dress of a federal solider. Ordinary street clothes were his uniform now. The *Intelligencer* was a part of his disguise as well. It helped him blend in and perform his job, which was to loiter around the lobby of Brown's, observe the comings and goings of its patrons, and listen to their conversations. If any of them acted strangely or said something interesting, he was under orders to report the information to Colonel Rook.

Like the other hotels along Pennsylvania Avenue, Brown's was big and ugly. Southerners from around the city congregated in its lobby, and many of those from out of town slept under its roof. Located at Sixth Street, it was convenient to the Capitol and therefore a favorite of Southern politicians. When Congress was in session, dozens of them stayed there. Even when it was not, the hotel's lobby remained a favorite meeting place and watering hole.

It had become even more popular following a scandal at its main competitor, the National, which sat on the other side of Sixth Street. Four years earlier, around the time of President Buchanan's inauguration, scores of people fell sick with what became known as "National Hotel disease." One of them was Buchanan himself, who was bedridden for the first several weeks of his presidency. Many wild-eyed partisans were convinced that National Hotel disease was not a disease at all, but rather a poisoning—a sinister plot, hatched by abolitionists, to contaminate the food at a place frequented by Southerners and their political allies. The real source of the problem was most likely a sewage backup that had flooded the kitchen, but flamboyant conspiracy theories rarely lacked for believers, especially in a Washington divided by regional loyalties and mutual suspicion. Although the National was forced to shut down briefly, it had recently begun to regain its former popularity. For now, however, Brown's Hotel was on top.

Clark had been coming to Brown's every day for a week, usually arriving in the early afternoon and staying well into the evening. He suspected that a handful of regulars began to notice him, but they probably regarded him as merely another transient who would vanish just as quickly as he had appeared. None of the hotel's employees seemed to mind him—each day, he ordered a couple of mint juleps and tipped well enough to keep them happy. The mint juleps, Clark had decided, were the only thing he liked about Brown's.

Business at the hotel had slowed down recently, as many Southerners had packed their bags and left the city. Yet the lobby remained fairly busy, and Clark had eavesdropped on scores of discussions. Much of the talk was about politics. How would the Lincoln administration respond to the surrender of Sumter? Would more states secede? Conversation often turned toward the fate of Washington itself and the predicament the president would face if Maryland decided to follow Virginia in quitting the Union. And then there was the military question: could the city actually defend itself against an enemy force? The consensus was that Washington would fall, at least without additional troops from the North.

Clark listened to all this chatter, recognizing that most of it was a combination of uninformed speculation and wishful thinking, often fueled by alcohol. Hardly an hour went by without hearing someone condemn Lincoln, but these were expressions of frustration and loathing rather than actual threats. There was talk from time to time about plots against the president. One day it was a plan to kidnap Lincoln. The next it was a proposal to put him on trial in Alabama. Clark understood that in both cases he was hearing rumor and bluster rather than gaining actual information, but he dutifully passed on what he heard to Rook.

After flipping through the *National Intelligencer* for what seemed like the hundredth time, Clark considered calling it a night. Then he noticed a group of men come into the lobby from their rooms. They had caught his attention a few hours earlier, when they showed up at the hotel covered in dust. Clark had watched them negotiate for several rooms. They aroused his interest because these days the hotel's clients were much more likely to be checking out than checking in. They were also remarkable for their filth. They looked as if they had gone for weeks without bathing or changing clothes.

Clark had not thought much more about them until they reappeared in the lobby. At first he did not recognize them because they had cleaned up. As they took a table and began ordering bourbons, however, Clark decided to find out what he could about them and their business in Washington. He let the men settle in and finish a first round. Then he rose and moved in the direction of their table.

Before Rook had assigned him to Brown's, Clark had had no experience at professional eavesdropping. Everything he knew he had learned on his own. The most important rule, he realized almost from the start, was that positioning was everything. It was best to arrive at your location before the talkers arrived at theirs. In this case, Clark had to maneuver into a seat about ten feet away from these newcomers, and with his back turned to them. It was hardly ideal, but it would have to do. He held open his newspaper, though by now he felt as if he could recite it as easily as he could read it.

Clark had trouble hearing the men at first because they did not speak as loudly as he had hoped. As they drained their drinks and ordered more, however, Clark began to pick up bits and pieces of their conversation. From their accents, he could tell they were Southerners. Much of what they said was unexceptional—talk of a long ride behind them, a good night's sleep in front of them, and a lot of drinking in the meantime. Clark also understood them to be Lincoln haters.

There was nothing remarkable about this fact, though one exchange did interest him. After a period of hushed talk that Clark could not make out, he was convinced that he heard one of the men say, "I can't wait to see that building crumble." Clark might not have regarded the comment as meaningful except for what another man, whom he had taken to be the group's leader, said next: "Shut up! We agreed not to talk about that tonight."

Silence followed for a few minutes. The men eventually returned to their previous topics of conversation. They sipped their bourbons for another hour or so and then left for their rooms. Clark wasn't entirely sure what to make of these men, but for the first time in a week he thought he might have something worthwhile to tell Rook at their next meeting.

Lucius listened to Bennett climb the stairs to his bedroom on the second floor. It was a familiar sound, made distinctive by the man's wooden leg: thud, clack, thud, clack. Lucius had heard it hundreds of times before. He could almost count the number of steps Bennett needed to reach his door down the hall. He waited for the creak of its hinges and then the bang of it shutting.

Bennett had been animated throughout dinner. He denounced the new president in some of the most colorful terms Lucius had ever heard him speak. After about an hour, Bennett was plainly tired. The journey from Charleston was one that had fatigued him even when he was much younger. Lucius ordered the plates cleared quickly. Hughes grasped the hint and announced that he would be going. The pair bid farewell in the foyer, and then Bennett excused Lucius for the night and made his way upstairs.

Lucius was tired too, but he would not let himself rest. Not yet. There was one more thing he needed to do. He poked his head into the dining room to make sure the other house servants were cleaning the table and setting it for breakfast. Satisfied by what he saw, Lucius walked back into the foyer. He stopped at the foot of the steps and listened intently for any sound of Bennett. He waited for several minutes but heard nothing. Then he walked onto the porch and looked down the long lane that led to the road he had ridden from Charleston. To the left he could see the manor's white clapboard outbuildings: the kitchen, a smithy, chicken coops, and much else besides. It was like a little town, all of it run by slaves—and now closed for the evening.

The silence of the plantation at night was always something Lucius missed when he was in the city. Charleston had its quiet moments too, but it had been full of noise at all hours for more than a week. He was glad to be back here and looked forward to visiting with family and friends he had not seen since the first part of December, when he and Bennett left for the social season. They had wound up staying much longer than expected, thanks to Sumter.

Lucius knew that he had a good life with Bennett—about as good a life as any slave could expect. Not every slave on the plantation actually liked Bennett. Their master was capable of employing all the cruel mechanisms at his disposal to maintain order on the farm. But most of the slaves regarded Bennett as fair, and that was high praise coming from the inside of an institution filled with unfairness. Lucius knew that he and his kind could take nothing for granted, and there was plenty to appreciate about residing on the Bennett homestead. There was a certain prestige attached to working at such a large plantation. Most slaves didn't actually work on large plantations. They toiled for small farmers who could afford to own only ten or twelve slaves at most. That meant they faced the constant threat of having their families split up when a harvest went poorly or their owner needed a little extra money. It happened all the time.

Lucius enjoyed special advantages on the plantation. Not only did he have all the normal privileges a house servant held over field hands, but he also shared an old relationship with Bennett. He was possibly the second-most-important person on the plantation, and he might have wielded more influence over Bennett than Tate or any of the other overseers. Lucius was the one slave who never had to endure one of Tate's tongue-lashings, let alone a real lashing. Tate knew better than to lay a hand on him. His big family was treated well too. His wife had died years ago, but he had two sons and a daughter who still lived here, plus ten grandchildren. His relatives all benefited from a small degree of favoritism.

It was a good life, he thought, perhaps the best he could have and better than he might hope for. That was why it had taken him so long to decide that he was willing to betray his master.

He stepped off the porch and made his way to the lane of buildings on his left. The stables were not in sight of the house—that was one of the reasons he had picked them for his meeting with Portia. He was certain she was already waiting for him and hoped she had not been there for long. More important, he hoped that she had not been noticed.

When he rounded the smithy, he saw that she was not alone. Her back was to the wall as she faced a man towering over her. In the darkness, Lucius could not tell who the man was, except to see that he was white. Neither of them saw Lucius approach.

The man grabbed Portia's arm, but she yanked herself free. "Stop it!" she said. The man started to pursue her but halted when he saw Portia's grandfather. Lucius recognized him now: Hughes.

Portia scurried behind her grandfather. Lucius raised his fists. He knew he was no match for the younger man, but perhaps he could hold him off long enough for Portia to get away. He was relieved when Hughes took a step back.

"Good evening, Lucius."

It was the first time Lucius remembered Hughes ever using his name.

"I was just trying to find a horse to ride, and your granddaughter was here."

He smiled awkwardly and took another several steps backward. Lucius stood his ground and said nothing.

"It's getting late, so I think I'll be going."

Hughes disappeared into the stable and a moment later emerged on top of a brown stallion. He kept his distance from Lucius and Portia and headed toward the lane in front of the manor. When he reached it, he spurred his horse into a full gallop and rode away.

"Did he hurt you, child?" asked Lucius.

"No, but he was comin' for me," said Portia. "I was waitin' in the stables, just like you told me. I heard somethin' and thought it was you. But it was him. He grabbed me, and then you showed up just in time."

"He's gone now, but we'll see more of him. He came to Mr. Bennett's home in the city most every day. It's like he's Mr. Bennett's son."

"I'm frightened, Grandpa. What if he comes after me again?"

"I don't wanna scare you, Portia, but you know white folks. They like to have their way with us."

"Why do we let 'em? There are more of us. We could take over this place and—"

"Stop talkin' that way right now," said Lucius. "It wouldn't work. It would get us killed."

Lucius put his arms around Portia. If Hughes insisted on having his way with her, there was no guarantee he could stop it. He was not sure talking to Bennett would solve the problem either. That might even make it worse. Bennett's new affection for Hughes had grown so strong that Lucius thought he might even give Portia away if he knew of the young man's interest.

These circumstances only added to his resolve. He led Portia into the stables. They sat down on overturned buckets.

"I'm sorry Mr. Hughes found you. If I had known about him lurkin' around, I wouldn't have asked you to meet me here. But what I got to say is very important."

Lucius stood up and wandered around the stables for a minute, sticking his head in the stalls to make sure they were truly alone. Then he returned to Portia.

"You heard of President Lincoln?" he asked.

"Everyone says he's gonna set us free."

"That's what I've been hearin' too."

"So what about him?"

"I want you to deliver something to him."

"What?"

"I'm serious. I want you to deliver something to him."

Portia was confused. "What do you mean?"

Lucius reached inside his pocket and pulled out a picture. He handed it to her. It showed a white man standing in profile. The image was a little blurry, but Portia could make out the man's features. She noticed the half-missing ear.

"Who's this?"

"Mr. Bennett and Mr. Hughes call him 'Mazorca.' They've hired him to kill Abe Lincoln."

"How do you know?"

"I overheard them talkin' about it in Charleston, and then this man came by. He's gonna try to murder the president."

"And you want me to take this picture all the way to Washington?"

"I would do it myself, Portia, but I'm too old. It's gotta be someone young."

"Why me? Why not one of my brothers?"

"I thought of that. But they ain't as clever as you, and you're gonna need wits for this. They'd also be missed around here sooner than you. The dogs would be runnin' on their trail by the middle of the morning. Also, you're the only one of my grandchildren who's been to Charleston."

"Charleston? I thought you wanted me to go to Washington."

"I know someone in Charleston who can help you get there."

"Why didn't you take care of it while you were still there?"

Lucius grimaced. "Maybe that would have been best. At first, I had the picture and wasn't sure what to do with it. Then I was thinkin' that maybe I'd just forget about it. Why risk gettin' caught? Comin' up to the house today, though, seeing you and all the little ones—it convinced me that something had to be done." He paused and looked straight at his granddaughter. "You're the one to do it, Portia."

"Can I think about it?"

"No. There ain't no time. That man could be in Washington already. I need to know right now if you're gonna do it or if I gotta find someone else."

Portia sat in silence. She stared at the picture, and then her grandfather. She knew he would not ask her to do something so extraordinary unless it really mattered.

"I don't know," she said. "I don't wanna leave this place. There are so many people I'd miss. I might never see any of you again."

"I know that, Portia. But this is more important than any single person."

She was not sure what to say. Then she thought about Hughes, and so she said the one thing that came into her head: "Okay."

"You'll do it then?"

"Yes."

"Thank you, Portia. You're a brave young woman. I knew you wouldn't let me down. Meet me here tomorrow night, when there's no more light in the sky. Be ready to go."

IX

Thursday, April 18, 1861

The big, black ball rested on top of its pole above the Naval Observatory's dome. That meant nobody was late. At least not yet, thought Rook, as he walked the final block toward his daily meeting with Springfield and Clark. For several weeks, they had gathered at the foot of the observatory, right by the river at the corner of New York Avenue and Twenty-third Street. They were supposed to begin promptly at noon, a time marked by the ball of black canvas, which was as wide as a doorway. It dropped at twelve, every day and without error. Across the city, people set their clocks by its fall.

Rook watched Springfield approach. As the sergeant came near, Rook nodded a greeting. "Where's Corporal Clark?" he asked.

"He'll be here," replied Springfield.

The black ball twitched and began its slow descent. Just then, Clark turned a corner and came into view on New York Avenue. He was walking at a swift pace. Springfield chuckled as Rook made a show of gazing up at the ball and then at Clark, who got the message immediately and broke into a trot. By the time he joined his companions, the ball was resting on the top of the observatory's dome. "Sorry, sir," he said, looking up at the ball.

"Instead of being sorry, be on time," scolded Rook, who then turned to Springfield. "If you let a subordinate break little rules, it won't be long before he breaks big ones."

This was more than Rook could say for himself. Here he was, meeting with Springfield and Clark—both good men— to discuss activities that his own superior officer had told him to stop.

"Sergeant, what's the latest from Lafayette Park?" he asked.

Like Clark, Springfield was dressed in plain clothes rather than his blue uniform. He had been posted to Lafayette Park, across Pennsylvania Avenue from the White House. Instead of keeping an eye on the president, however, Rook had ordered him to watch over the houses that lined the park. These were some of the most prominent addresses in the city—James and Dolley Madison once had lived there, and now the neighborhood was home to everyone from Secretary of State William Seward to Massachusetts senator Charles Sumner. Rook had told Springfield to pay close attention to Sumner's residence. Among Southern radicals, perhaps only Lincoln was more scorned. Just five years earlier the senator had been assaulted on the floor of the Senate by a South Carolina congressman who objected to one of Sumner's abolitionist speeches. Southerners hailed the attacker as a hero. It took Sumner more than three years to recover from his injuries.

Yet protecting Sumner was not Springfield's only objective, or even the main one. Rook actually had told Springfield to spend most of his time watching over the neighborhood's Southerners—his primary duty was not protection, but surveillance. Rook wanted the sergeant

to determine if any of the secessionists in the neighborhood were more than mere agitators. So far, he had not
experienced a great deal of success. A single man covering several city blocks can accomplish only so much, and
Springfield's most interesting observations up to now involved a couple of households packing up and departing
across the Potomac. That was the content of his report on
this day as well: yet another family with Southern loyalties
was making plans to move away. Alarmed by Lincoln's plan
to call up troops from the North, they decided to leave before it was too late.

Rook listened to this patiently and then asked the question that had been on his mind since his last conversation
with Scott.

"What can you tell me about Violet Grenier?"

"An interesting woman. Definitely a secessionist. She
lives in a big house across Lafayette Park from the president's mansion. She receives many visitors, including plenty
of important ones—senators, congressmen, and so on. Not
all of them are Southerners. Most in the secesh crowd stick
with those who agree with them. Grenier is the exception."

"Anything suspicious?"

"No, I don't think so. It's a busy household for just one
woman, but I don't see anything suspicious in that. Just bear
in mind that I haven't kept an eye on her around the clock.
I may have missed things."

"Please watch her closely. I'd like more information on
her. She seems to pull many wires in Washington."

"Yes, sir."

Now Rook turned toward Clark. "And what have you
seen at Brown's Hotel?"

Clark described the events of the previous night—the sudden appearance of ragged-looking strangers, their re-appearance in the lobby, and the snatches of overheard conversation. Rook listened without expression until Clark got to the part about them apparently planning to watch a building crumble.

Springfield perked up. "Do they plan to sabotage a building?"

"I don't know," said Clark. "But that seems like a pos-sibility."

"Unless we're letting our imaginations get the better of us," said Rook. He was not trying to rebuke Clark for mak-ing the report or Springfield for taking an interest in it, but he did want to encourage clear thinking.

"There's more," said Clark. "I went back to Brown's this morning and got their names from the hotel registry. That's why I was late getting here a few minutes ago. It was a dumb oversight on my part, not doing it last night. But I didn't think of it until I had walked out the door, and I hardly felt like I could go back and check and remain inconspicuous."

"So, what are their names?"

Clark reached into a pocket and pulled out a slip of pa-per. He handed it to Rook. As the colonel looked at it, he raised his eyebrows.

"Jeff Davis? Alex Stephens? You can't be serious."

"That's what I thought too," said Clark. "But those are the names they used when they checked in."

"You mean Jeff Davis, as in Jefferson Davis? And Alex Stephens, as in Alexander Stephens, the vice president of this so-called Confederacy?" asked Springfield.

"Yes."

Springfield craned his neck to see the paper Rook was holding. In addition to Davis and Stephens, there were two other names on the list: S. R. Mallory and Bobby Toombs.

"The other names are taken from the Confederate cabinet," said Rook. "Mallory heads their war department, and Toombs is their secretary of state. Your friends must have something to hide. Even so, going by these particular assumed names strikes me as reckless."

"It's like they're trying to taunt us," agreed Clark.

"I want to observe these men myself, Corporal. Keep them under close watch. Tomorrow's meeting here is canceled. Instead, Clark and I will go to Brown's."

* * *

With the sun almost straight overhead, Portia stood beside the trunk of an oak tree to catch its shade. She had spent the night awake, worrying about the promise she had made to her grandfather. Several times she had decided to back out. But she kept returning to the sight of him staring at her in the stables, his bright eyes shining in the darkness with an urgent plea. She imagined that this was probably how she had looked at him whenever she had wanted some small favor growing up. He had been so good to her over the years. Just last night, he had turned away that awful man Hughes. Her grandfather might not be around to protect her the next time. By morning, she had resolved to escape. But there was something she wanted to do first.

Portia leaned against the tree and watched a few dozen slaves stoop in the fields. She saw her two older brothers trying to fix a broken plow. She recalled how they had run off before. Anthony and Theo were always talking about getting away. Anthony was a dreamer. He boasted of making it to the North and earning enough money to buy his whole family from Mr. Bennett. Portia could remember him getting away three times, but the longest he was gone was about two days. He had only traveled a few miles when the slave catchers found him.

Theo's plans were not nearly as grand. He just talked about freedom and cared less about where he found it. He also had escaped three times, but he had not headed anywhere in particular. He just went lying out in the woods nearby, fishing for food and sleeping under the stars. Once he was gone for almost a month. But each time he came back, usually because he had gotten hungry—it was a lot easier to eat food from a plate than it was to catch rabbits. Her brothers were punished for what they did, but not so severely that they never thought of taking the risk again.

What if she ran off and was caught? She would suffer the lash, the bite of which she had never known. It would be unpleasant, but she would get over it. A worse feeling would come from the knowledge that her grandfather had made an earnest request and she had turned him down. That kind of pain might never heal.

Anthony and Theo continued to fuss over the plow. They argued until a third slave approached. He seemed to know exactly what was wrong. The brothers stood silently as he explained what to do. The sight gladdened Portia—not because she cared about the plow, but because this was Big Joe. He was exactly the person she wanted to see.

"Hello, boys," she said as she walked up to the group.

"Hey, sis," said Anthony and Theo together. It was how they always greeted her. Big Joe was silent.

"Did Joe show you how to fix this thing?" she asked.

"He showed Theo how to fix it," said Anthony. "I knew what to do all along. Your dumb brother wouldn't listen to me."

"Shut up, Anthony. You don't even know which end of this thing goes in the ground."

"Who's tellin' the truth, Joe?" asked Portia.

"They would've figured it out eventually," he said.

Portia smiled. She really liked Big Joe. His modesty attracted her. He did not speak much, but when he did, he generally knew what he was talking about. She had seen him end plenty of arguments just by offering a piece of advice. Everybody called him Big Joe because he had grown so much larger than his father, who earned the name Little Joe as soon as his son began to dwarf him. Little Joe was not small, but his only boy was the size of an ox. He was probably the strongest man on the whole plantation, and one of the gentlest, too.

Portia had noticed Joe staring at her every now and then over the last several months. A lot of the male slaves eyed her—she was probably more eligible than any other young woman on the plantation. Her mother kept telling her she was definitely the prettiest and that she ought to find a man before one found her. Her brothers just teased her about it.

"Come with me, Joe. I gotta talk to you about something," said Portia. She glanced at her brothers. "And I wanna do it alone."

Anthony and Theo whooped when they heard this. Their racket made Joe blush.

"Boys!" shouted Portia. "Shut up and fix the plow!"

This only encouraged them. "She knows what she wants!" "Portia and Big Joe, steppin' out!" They were getting louder and starting to attract attention from the other slaves. Portia did not know what to do, so she turned and stomped off a few steps when suddenly they quit their taunts. She looked back and saw Joe holding both of them by their collars.

"The lady told you to fix the plow," he said in a low voice. "I showed you how. Now do it." He released his grip and walked toward Portia. The brothers did not utter another word.

"Sorry about them," said Portia as she walked with Joe toward the slave cabins.

"No harm done."

They walked for a few minutes in silence through the fields. Portia was about to say something when she spotted Tate. The overseer jogged toward them. His whip, coiled through a belt, bounced at his side.

"Where are you going?" he demanded.

The two slaves stopped. Portia could tell Big Joe was nervous.

"Joe's mama asked me to fetch him. She wants him to move something."

"It can wait. Joe, get back to work."

Joe started to turn away, but Portia grabbed his elbow.

"Hold on," she said. "Mr. Tate, Joe's mama is cookin' something big for tonight's dinner in the mansion. She's got a huge pot of stew goin' and needs it moved. I'm not even sure what she's tryin' to do with it. I just know it's big and she needs a quick hand. She asked for Joe. He can move it and come straight back."

Tate glared at her. He said nothing for a moment, and then he looked at Joe. He caressed the lash on his hip with the tips of his fingers. What an intimidator, thought Portia.

"Joe," he said at last, sticking his finger in the big slave's chest, "I'll give you ten minutes. Don't make me come looking for you."

"Yessir, Mr. Tate."

The two slaves walked off as Tate watched them. Big Joe had an extra spring in his step now. "You didn't say nothin' about my mama," he said as soon as they were out of Tate's range of hearing.

"No, I didn't."

"Why not?"

"Because I haven't seen your mama all mornin'."

Big Joe paused in his tracks. "What's going on?"

"Just come with me."

"I don't know," he said, looking in Tate's direction. The overseer had his back to them now and was starting to holler at some poor slave for not working fast enough.

"He's tryin' to bully you," she said. "He's probably already forgotten you're over here."

He looked down at her, then back at Tate.

"Joe," she said, touching his arm lightly, "please come with me."

"All right. But we can't be long."

They walked briskly now. When they arrived at a row of slave cabins, Portia stopped and looked around. Nobody in the fields could see them. A pair of old ladies sat stitching shirts and trousers about fifty feet away. Portia knew Mary's hearing was not very good, and Bessie had gone deaf. Other than these two, they were out of sight and alone. As it happened, they stood right outside the cabin Joe shared with his mother and a few others.

She gestured in the direction of the kitchen, which they could see up the path near the mansion. It was separate from the plantation home because fires so often started in kitchens. It was much easier to rebuild a kitchen than a mansion. "He'll think we've gone there."

"What's this about, Portia?"

"I'm leavin' the plantation tonight."

"What? You been sold?"

"No. I'm runnin' off."

Joe became wide-eyed. "Don't do it, Portia. They'll catch you and beat you. A lot of the folks talk about gettin' away, but they ain't never made it. Not once. You know that."

"I'm goin', Joe, and you can't change my mind."

Joe did not reply immediately. Portia could tell he was wondering about something.

"Why are you tellin' me this?" he asked. "It would be better if I didn't know."

"I want you to come with me."

"What?"

"You heard me."

"Portia, I like you. I like you a lot—"

"I know you do, Joe. And I like you a lot too." She touched him on the arm again. "That's why you gotta come with me."

"I don't know—"

She sprang onto the tips of her toes, threw her arms around his neck, and planted a kiss on his lips. Joe was so startled he hardly kissed her back. Then she was standing in front of him again.

"Joe," she said, "I'm leavin' tonight. We're goin' together and I don't want to hear excuses. The worst thing that happens is they catch us and bring us back here. Tate won't like it, Bennett won't like it—but we'll have tried it together." She was speaking louder now, unable to contain her excitement. Joe did not say anything, and Portia took this as a good sign. He wasn't objecting. His resistance was weakening.

"There's a photograph," she continued. "It's a picture of a man who is gonna to try to kill Abe Lincoln."

"What?"

"We have to help him."

"Can I see the picture?"

"I don't have it with me. My grandfather's got it."

"Everybody says Lincoln is gonna free us."

"He won't if he's dead. Please, Joe, let's take the photograph to people who can keep him alive. We've gotta escape, and we gotta start tonight."

Just then the door behind them flew open. It was Joe's mother.

"Mama! What're you doing?"

"Did I just hear what I think I heard?" she said, in a voice that was worried and outraged at the same time. Her name was Sally, and Portia believed she was jealous of her son's affection. She had not gotten along with Sally ever since Joe's interest became apparent.

"Mama, we're just talkin'."

"You can't do it, Joe! You can't leave here! You're my baby!" Sally came down the steps and glared at Portia. "Does your granddaddy know about this?" It was not a question but a scold. "Get away from my baby boy!" Then she hugged her son and started sobbing.

"We're just talkin'," said Joe, hugging his mother back and patting her on the shoulder. "We're just talkin'."

Portia circled around to where she could see Joe's face. He continued to pat his mother, but he stared right at her. His eyes were a little moist. He looked torn. She did not know what he was thinking or what he would do. She figured she had done her best to persuade him. The choice was now his. He kept on staring at her, as if he were waiting for something. She raised her eyebrows and without speaking mouthed the words, "The stables. Tonight. After dark."

* * *

Rook was talking to a private in front of the War Department when he saw Colonel Robert E. Lee exit the Winder Building across the street. The gray hair and beard were unmistakable, and they gave Lee a natural appearance of dignity and maturity. His uniform was crisp and clean, as if he had put it on only a few minutes earlier. His white riding gloves looked as though they had never been used before.

The man carries himself like a king, thought Rook. Lee was, after all, a member of Virginia's aristocracy. His wife was even related to Martha Washington. There was only one reason for Lee to be at headquarters this afternoon: a meeting with Scott about taking command.

Rook tried to guess at the outcome as Lee mounted his horse, but he had no idea. For a moment, Lee sat in his saddle and stared at the Winder Building. Was he sizing it up or giving it a last look? Then Lee's head turned to the War Department. He caught Rook's eye, but his face was expressionless. He nodded to Rook and then headed down Seventeenth Street. He was moving south, toward the river.

Rook hurried across the street. He raced to Scott's office and immediately saw the disappointment on the old general's face. Locke sat with his hands folded on his lap. Rook knew instantly what had happened.

"I have just received some very unwelcome news," said Scott. "Colonel Lee has declined the offer to lead our soldiers."

"I don't understand how a man could turn down such an opportunity," said Locke. "What did he say?"

"He said he opposed secession and civil war, but that he could not stand against Virginia. 'If the Union is dissolved and the government disrupted, I shall return to my native state and share the miseries of my people and draw my sword on no one except in defense,' he said. It was a neat little speech, and he seemed genuinely moved by the offer that was made to him."

"Did he resign his commission?" asked Rook.

"I fully expect him to resign now. I suppose Secretary of War Cameron will receive a note from Arlington in a day or two stating as much."

By now a few other officers in the building had gathered around the doorway to Scott's room. They all wanted to hear the account too.

"Did you tell him he was crazy?" asked Locke.

"I told him he was making the greatest mistake of his life. He is a strong-minded man. It is one of the qualities in him that I like best, and one of the reasons why I thought he was ready for this duty."

Scott noticed the small crowd. "Let us talk of this no more. No good can come of it," he said, waving his wrist at the men. They took it as an order to disperse. Locke stood up and shut the door. Rook was annoyed that Locke did not put himself on the other side of it.

"Amid this bad news, today we have received some good news," said the general. "I was heartened by the five companies of troops that arrived from Pennsylvania this morning."

"It certainly makes the defense of Washington an easier task," said Rook. "I suppose we could repel an organized attack now."

"That depends on the size of the attacking force," said Scott. "I think we need between four and five thousand men in order to defend against any troops raised by Maryland or Virginia in the near future. We are far short of that goal. We simply require more men, and I hope they come soon. I know some are on the way. They cannot get here quickly enough."

"I have not received any reports of hostile armies assembling nearby," said Rook.

"Nor have I, but we shouldn't wait for that to start. If the Virginians raise an army before we prepare to defend ourselves, it will be too late. Just the other day, I heard the president remark that if he were General Beauregard, fresh from firing on Fort Sumter, he would try to take Washington immediately. It probably wouldn't take much to defeat us here. I just hope they don't think of it."

"I believe we'll be ready for them," said Rook. "We'll need more men, but they're on the way. Virginia will need time too."

"Colonel, do you know where you are?" asked Scott.

"Excuse me?"

"Do you know where you are?"

"I'm in your office, sir."

"And where is that?"

Rook had no idea what the general was getting at. He selected his words slowly and carefully, like a man facing a prosecutor during a deposition. "I'm in the city of Washington."

Scott smiled to ease the nerves of his colonel. "You are in the Winder Building, of course. Do you understand the significance of that?"

"I suspect that I do not."

"You will recall what happened in 1814. During our war with Britain, the enemy landed an army in Maryland and marched toward Washington. Our troops met them at Bladensburg, just a few miles from here. The soldiers of our country were routed, and Washington was laid bare before the redcoats. They burned the Capitol and torched the White House. If you look closely at those buildings, you can still see the burn marks in a few places. It was a terrible humiliation."

Rook knew this. He said nothing and let the general continue.

"The American general in command that day at Bladensburg was William Winder. This building, which now houses the headquarters of the United States Army, is named for him—the man who is more responsible than anyone else for our country's most notorious military defeat."

Scott let the story settle in Rook's mind. Then he rammed home his point: "I may sit in a building named for Winder, but I will not follow in his footsteps. On my watch, Washington won't fall."

Rook said nothing when Scott was done. He thought that perhaps he should have paid more attention to his history professor at West Point.

"I knew about Winder and the Battle of Bladensburg," offered Locke.

Rook balled his fists. He wished he could slug Locke.

"Let's just make sure history doesn't repeat itself," said Scott. "That reminds me, how goes the conversion of the Old Capitol?"

The general was referring to the three-story brick structure just to the east of the actual Capitol. It had been built quickly as a place for Congress to meet after the fire in 1814. For a decade, lawmakers met within its walls on the corner of Maryland Avenue and First Street. Since their departure, the building had served as a school and a boardinghouse. The federal government had just repurchased it for use as a prison.

"It will be able to accept prisoners any day now."

"Excellent. Now, tell me about the arrangements for the new soldiers from Pennsylvania."

There was a shortage of places to put the troops—the government had mustered several federal buildings into service. The Pennsylvania soldiers would stay in the Capitol. The Patent Office and the Treasury were also available.

"I presume that putting soldiers at the Treasury won't interfere with our other plans for that building," said Scott.

"That's correct," said Rook. "The Treasury remains the place where we'll send the president and his cabinet in the event of an attack on Washington. It's quite a large structure. The basement has enormous storage capacity."

"I wish we didn't have to use the Capitol."

"I agree, General. But you know we don't have many locations to put soldiers on such short notice. I'm intending to put Jim Lane's men at the White House when they arrive."

"Very well. That ought to ease some of your concerns about security."

"I certainly don't think we will go the way of General Winder, sir. Our vulnerabilities are elsewhere."

"Not this subject again," sputtered Locke.

Scott held up his hand to silence Locke. "Colonel Rook, let me make myself perfectly clear: I do not want to discuss your conspiracy theories anymore. Do not raise them with me again."

* * *

The man who called himself Jeff Davis looked groggy when he finally arrived in the lobby at Brown's. It appeared as though he had just gotten up, run a comb through his hair, and stumbled downstairs. Although it was the middle of the afternoon, none of his companions was around. He took a table away from the hotel's front door, in a corner.

Clark sat about a dozen feet away, sipping a cup of tea and pretending to study a newspaper whose entire contents he had already read twice. He avoided looking directly at Davis, who might become suspicious if he recognized Clark from the previous evening. At the moment, Davis's powers of observation appeared to be dull. Judging from the way he kept rubbing his head, he was fighting a hangover.

Within half an hour, the men who had arrived with Davis wandered into the lobby and joined him at the table. Clark had trouble overhearing their conversation, partly because they were not saying a lot. They worked their way through a meal, mostly in silence. The food seemed to improve their disposition. By the time they were done eating, they looked more like the group that Clark originally had spied upon.

Davis was clearly the leader. He spoke the most and laughed the loudest, and the others appeared to defer to him. They talked about the fall of Fort Sumter and the possibility that Maryland might secede—it was obvious that they supported the attack in Charleston and hoped that legislators in Annapolis would withdraw from the Union. "That would leave Washington all by itself, like a peach that's ripe for plucking," said Davis. His gang roared its approval.

The men eventually rose from their chairs. As they shook hands, Clark could tell that the group was splitting up. Two of them made for the door, leaving behind Davis and Stephens. For a moment, Clark thought about following the men who had departed, but he decided it was smarter to remain near Davis. He was the one to watch.

Back in their seats, Davis and Stephens seemed to relax. They even ordered drinks. Clark began to wonder if they were going to waste their night. Yet the two men limited themselves to a single drink apiece. When these were gone, they stood and stretched.

"Tomorrow we scout," said Davis. "But tonight is ours. I know how I want to spend it."

Stephens chuckled. "Yeah, me too!"

They exited through the hotel's front door. Clark waited a minute, set down his newspaper, and chased after them.

The afternoon had passed more quickly than he had realized. The shadows were growing long, and dusk was preparing to settle onto the city.

On the curb of Pennsylvania Avenue, Clark watched a horse-drawn omnibus kick up a small cloud of dust as it pulled toward Georgetown. For a moment, he feared that Davis and Stephens had hopped on board and that he had lost them. He would not be able to catch up to the vehicle without calling attention to himself. Then he spotted the duo on the other side of the street, walking by the vendors outside of Central Market.

Clark immediately had a notion of where they were heading, but he wanted to be sure. He stayed on his side of the Avenue and kept pace. They passed Eighth Street, then Ninth Street. They paused at the corner of Tenth. Davis seemed to indicate a desire to turn. Stephens pointed up the Avenue but quickly relented. They went left, walking south, and soon dropped out of Clark's sight.

This took them into the heart of Murder Bay, a section of Washington that was both built up and run-down. It was possibly the most dangerous part of the city—a lair of pickpockets, con men, and worse. Unlike other areas of the city, there were no wide-open spaces in Murder Bay. The streets were cramped by two- and three-story structures that stood in various states of disrepair. Many of them housed drinking establishments, though Clark was fairly certain that Davis and Stephens were not trying to quench a liquid thirst. They did not have to leave Brown's for that. Murder Bay was also a popular destination for gamblers, so perhaps they would try their hands at a game of chance. Yet Clark suspected that they sought a different sort of recreation.

Clark hustled across Pennsylvania Avenue and stood on the same corner, at Tenth Street, where Davis and Stephens had had their quick debate. He spotted them half a block away. Davis removed a wallet from his pocket, opened it, counted his cash, and handed a few notes to Stephens. The two men looked at each other and grinned, then entered an establishment called Madam Russell's Bake Oven.

With that, Clark knew how Davis and Stephens intended to spend their second night in Washington. He had never been inside Madam Russell's Bake Oven, but he knew that nobody visited it for the cooking.

* * *

Beneath a clear sky full of stars and a moon that was nearly full, Portia slipped into the stables carrying a small sack. She saw nothing out of the ordinary. The only noises she heard came from the horses.

A moment later, another person shuffled into the stables. Portia dropped to a crouch. She rose again when she saw that it was her grandfather. Lucius saw her too. They quickly embraced.

"Thanks for bein' here," said Lucius.

"I don't wanna let you down."

"I know—and I know you won't."

Lucius let go of her and made a quick search of the building. Every individual stall received a short inspection. While this was going on, Portia stuck her head outside. She was disappointed not to see anybody.

"There ain't much time," said Lucius when he was done. He reached inside a pocket and pulled out the photograph.

"Here it is," he said, handing it to her. "This is the whole reason for what you're gonna do."

Portia strained to see the photograph, but it was too dark. She stuffed it into her bag.

"What else is in there?"

"Just some food."

"Lemme see."

Portia opened the sack.

"That's enough for two people. I don't want you goin' hungry, but that's gonna slow you down. You can find food on the road."

"I just wanna be prepared."

"All right," said the old man, warily. "Let's make this short so you can get goin'. I'm gonna set you up with a horse. You'll wanna stay off the main roads and travel at night, and it'll take a couple of nights."

Lucius described a route to Charleston that would keep her on some less-traveled roads.

"When I get to Charleston, what do I do?"

"You remember Nelly?"

"Sure I do. She works next door to Mr. Bennett's."

"That's right. She asks about you all the time. She knows someone who can help slaves get to the North. I don't know who it is or how it works. Nelly's a talker, but the truth is, she usually knows what she's talkin' about."

Just then they both heard the sound of a foot scraping at the doorway. Lucius froze in place, but Portia jumped up. She ran over to Big Joe and put her arms around him. Then she took him by the hand and led him to her grandfather.

"What's goin' on?" asked Lucius.

"Big Joe is comin' with me."

"That ain't a good idea, Portia."

"I want him to come."

"This is trouble. There'll be two horses gone instead of one and twice as many tracks to follow."

"Grandpa, he's comin' with me."

Lucius shook his head. "I'm hopin' to get through the whole day tomorrow without anybody thinkin' too hard about where you're at, Portia. I can cover for you much longer than I can cover you and him together. Tate will start missin' Joe early in the mornin'. Bringin' him is a big mistake."

"Grandpa, he's comin' with me."

"Joe, have you told your mother about this?"

Joe didn't say anything right away, and it suddenly occurred to Portia that he had not actually agreed to escape with her. Maybe he was here to tell her that he was staying put.

"Your mother is gonna be a mess. Have you thought of that?"

Portia still held Joe's hand. She squeezed it.

"Yep," said the big man. "I'm goin' with Portia." He squeezed her hand back.

"Mr. Bennett's gonna send dogs after you. Chasin' two people is a whole lot easier than chasin' one."

Portia and Joe did not say anything. For the first time, Lucius saw their clasped hands. It occurred to him that if they were caught, their motive could be explained as a crazy elopement. They would still be punished, though perhaps not as severely. The reputation of Joe's jealous mother would make the story credible. Everybody knew about Sally.

"I'm not gonna change your minds, am I?"

"No," said Portia and Joe at the same time.

"We could talk about this all night, but that's only gonna slow you down." He looked at Portia. "Have you told him why you're doin' this?"

"He knows."

"And Joe, do you understand why that picture needs to get to Abe Lincoln?"

"Yeah, I get it."

"OK. Let's send you two off to Charleston. When you get there, find Nelly. She'll take care of the rest."

Portia watched Lucius and Joe move to the center of the stable and discuss which horses to take. They picked a pair, saddled them, and led them to the door. Joe held the reins while Lucius stepped outside to make sure the runaways would not be seen.

"Thank you for doin' this," whispered Portia. She gave Joe a quick kiss on the cheek.

Lucius came back in. "Looks clear. There's a light comin' from the manor, but I don't think you'll be seen. Ride quiet till you hit the main road, and then follow my directions. Be careful, too. Don't travel too fast. It's easy to go the wrong way in the dark."

They led the horses from the stables. Lucius helped Portia onto hers and then put his hand on Joe's shoulder.

"You take good care of her."

"Don't worry, Lucius. We're a team now."

Lucius looked at his granddaughter. "If you're caught, destroy the photo. If Mr. Bennett hears about it, he's gonna get madder than we've ever seen. From now on, there's only one person who should see that picture, and that's Abe Lincoln."

X

Friday, April 19, 1861

The parade of visitors would arrive soon. Faintly through the door, he could hear one of his secretaries lecturing a couple of them in the waiting room. These high-class beggars would march in and out of his office twenty-four hours a day for four whole years, he supposed. Sitting down with each individual petitioner, hearing him describe his important connections in dull detail, reading his reliably flattering letters of introduction, and listening to him grovel for a minor office—some days it made him little more than the national appointment-maker, the commander-in-chief of a vast system of political patronage. The party hacks would have liked nothing better than for the president to devote himself exclusively to this task. They seemed more concerned with pestering him about the postmaster of Marshall, Michigan, than with letting him concentrate on the disaster in Charleston. There might be a crisis of union—but they had friends and relatives who needed jobs!

Sitting in a high-backed chair, with his feet propped on his desk, Abraham Lincoln decided to wait a few minutes before beginning the revue. He gazed across his room in search of a distraction. Maps were good for that, and three hung on the east wall. The one of Charleston Harbor, all the

way to the left, would have to come down soon. It had been
the first one up, and he had spent many hours studying it.
He knew its markings so well he hardly needed to look at it
anymore. Little Sumter, surrounded by forts and batteries,
never stood a chance. Now the map annoyed him. It was a
symbol of his first failure in office, though it was true that
he had inherited the problem from the previous administration. Perhaps there was nothing he might have done to prevent Fort Sumter from falling, short of permitting Southern
secession. Whatever the circumstances, this was his watch.
He would have to take final responsibility for what had
happened there. He would order that map removed this
very day.

The next map, to its right, displayed all the Southern
states, from Virginia to Texas. They were starting to call
themselves the Confederate States of America, but Lincoln
insisted that nobody in his government use that name. They
were still part of the Union because secession was unconsti-
tutional. This was an important legal point, even though it
did not conceal the obvious fact that it was a map of enemy
territory. Lincoln had it on his wall for a military purpose. In
just a few hours, his cabinet would announce a naval blockade of the Southern ports. This was General Scott's idea,
and Lincoln agreed that a successful blockade would put a
strangling pressure on the region's export-dependent economy. Weeks would pass before it took full effect, but the decision to do it would provide a signal to the public that the
president now believed the national emergency would last
into the summer.

This thought led his eye to the right, where a third and
final map was tacked to the wall. Here was northern Vir-

ginia, from Harper's Ferry in the west to the widening of
the Potomac in the east, where it flowed into the Chesapeake Bay. Washington sat about midway between these two
points, and Lincoln worried about its vulnerability from every direction. If Virginia assembled an army soon, it might
seize the capital without much of a fight. The city was almost completely defenseless against a few boats floating up
the river for a bombardment too. Fort Washington, on the
Maryland shore, was essentially unmanned. Alexandria, the
port on the Virginia side, probably would welcome the raid-
ers and supply them. Lincoln believed he needed more soldiers in a hurry.

In one gangly motion, the president grabbed a brass
cylinder from his desk, swung his feet to the ground, and
rose. There was a window just to his right, stretching almost
from the floor to the ceiling. From this second-story vista, he
could see for miles to the south. He twisted the brass tube,
and the thing expanded to three times its original length.
It was a telescope, and Lincoln now raised it to his eye for
a long look. He spotted the buildings of Alexandria in the
distance. The docks on the waterfront were busy, as usual.
The city was a rail terminal for the whole South—travelers
destined for Washington by train would end up here, where
they could get on another train and cross the Long Bridge or
take a ferry to the wharves on Sixth Street. Lincoln could see
one of these boats approaching Washington now. He might
have watched it come in, except for the knock on his door.

"Yes?" called out the president, wearily. John Hay, his
young secretary, stepped inside.

"Mr. President, perhaps we should get started. The
lines will only grow longer today, especially if we don't get

through a few of these people before your other meetings this morning."

"I guess somebody has to keep me on time, no matter how badly I want to avoid these office seekers," said Lincoln with a forced smile. "All right, Hay, send one of them in."

Lincoln returned his spyglass to its place on the desk. If he had continued to look through the window, he would have observed the *George Page*, a ferry steamer that shuttled people between Alexandria and Washington. On this trip, it was moving in Lincoln's direction. The ship stopped at a dock and unloaded a handful of passengers.

The last person to disembark was a man who had made it to Alexandria only the day before, after spending the night in Richmond. He slipped a bank note to a porter and asked him to look after his trunk—he would send for it in a few hours. Unencumbered, the man now turned his sights to the city spread before him.

Mazorca had arrived.

* * *

Lucius awoke before anybody else in the Bennett manor. Truth be told, he had hardly slept after watching Portia and Joe ride away. Nerves had kept him up for long stretches. Even when he dozed fitfully, his head was full of questions and worries: Where were they now? How far had they gone? What if somebody saw them on the roads? It occurred to him that he might never know their fate. If Portia and Joe were caught between here and Charleston, they would be brought back. That would probably happen in the next few days, if it were to happen at all. If they were captured outside of South Carolina, their fate would depend on whether they revealed who owned them. They would be held in prison until they confessed or someone claimed them. If neither came to pass, they would be sold at auction.

If they actually made it all the way to Washington, thought Lucius, he probably would not hear about it. Confirmation simply would not come. They did not know how to write, and he did not know how to read. Even if Portia and Joe had somebody do the writing for them, there was no chance of Bennett letting a note pass through to him. So Lucius figured no news would be good news—or at least it would not be bad news. He would have to learn to cope with the anxiety of not knowing.

A rooster crowed in the distance. Lucius barely noticed as he wandered around the mansion. He moved with the careful silence of a thief, avoiding the squeaky floorboards. The house sometimes seemed empty during the daytime, with no family in it. Now it was desolate. Bennett only occupied a fraction of its rooms—mainly a study, the dining room, and his bedroom. Yet he insisted on having the whole place kept up, as if it were full.

Lucius paused in front of a portrait hanging above the mantle in the dining room. The picture showed Bennett sitting in a chair, with one son on either side. The boys must have been ten or twelve years old when it was painted. Lucius remembered when they sat for the artist, and how hard it had been to keep them still for more than a few minutes at a time. Bennett had a warm look of satisfaction on his face—something Lucius had not seen much since the boys' death in Kansas.

That was the real reason the Bennett home seemed so lonely. Most plantations had large clans of white folks living

on them. There were sometimes three or even four generations' worth, and lots of visiting relatives besides. Children
were almost always around too. Whenever Lucius accompanied Bennett on a social call to another plantation, he never
failed to notice how the white kids and slave kids played in-
discriminately. It had been that way on the Bennett farm as
well, when Bennett's boys were growing up. But there came
an age when the white folks insisted that the play stop, usually around the time the slave children could start perform-
ing useful chores. Before that moment, though, these kids
were innocent of what separated them. This was one of the
things that prevented Lucius from hating white people—he
thought they were not born bad, but made bad.

The other thing, of course, was his relationship with Bennett, however much slavery stained it. When he told Portia
that he could not do what he was asking her to do, he only
told part of the truth. He was certainly too old to attempt
any kind of escape. But neither could he envision life away
from Bennett. The very idea of it was inconceivable. Where
would he go? What would he do? Slavery was not something
he enjoyed, but he frankly could not imagine improving his
lot. For Portia and his other grandchildren, of course, the
matter was entirely different. They had many years to live,
and he wanted freedom for them.

He remembered the night Lincoln was elected, and all
of Bennett's bitter cursing. For months he had listened to
Bennett lecture on the horror of Lincoln, and he realized
during one of these little speeches that this politician from
the North represented hope. Lincoln was the subject of
much whispered talk in the plantation fields and anywhere
else black people gathered away from white ears. Nobody

knew very much about him, but many, like Nelly, had come to view him as a savior. Lucius was not comfortable going that far, though he did suspect that if the plantation owners hated Lincoln, then he was probably someone to like. It was this half-formed conviction that inspired Lucius to send Portia on her journey.

He wondered where she was at that very instant. Had she hidden in the woods now that the sun was coming up? Would she try to sleep? What would they do with the horses?

Lucius stepped from the dining room to the foyer, opened the front door, and walked onto the front porch. The sky was clear of clouds. The first slaves were already in the fields, with more on their way. He heard Tate issue instructions to a group of young men in the distance. Hammers clanged in the direction of the blacksmith's shop. Smoke billowed from the kitchen chimney. Then he looked down the long lane to the main road. This was the path Portia and Joe had traveled just hours before, and the last place he had seen them. They had left at a trot. Lucius recalled his final view of Portia, how she turned around and waved to him just before slipping into the darkness. He closed his eyes and remembered the image.

"Good morning."

Lucius nearly fell off the porch at the sound of Bennett's voice.

"I didn't mean to startle you, Lucius," said his master.

"Sorry, sir. I didn't hear you."

"What are you looking at? I've been watching you from behind for a couple of minutes."

"Oh, nothing. It's just a nice day."

"Indeed it is!" said Bennett. He joined Lucius at gazing into the distance. "I was thinking that later this morning you would join me on a little expedition to the slave quarters. We need to distribute the new clothes we brought from Charleston. I haven't been down there in months. It will be good to do some visiting. I can't be a stranger on my own plantation, after all."

"No, sir," said Lucius.

Bennett tapped him on the shoulder and smiled. "And I can't wait to see your granddaughter."

* * *

As Rook passed through the front door of Brown's, he tried to remember the last time he had dressed out of uniform. It had been at least a month, since before the inauguration. It felt awkward. On the walk to the hotel, he had hoped that none of his fellow officers would spot him. He did not want to have to explain himself to Scott.

A lunchtime crowd filled the lobby. Rook moved away from the door and toward a wall, where he would not call attention to himself. He scanned the lobby for Clark. The corporal was seated in a chair by a column and looking straight at him. Rook nodded slightly and then left through the front door. He crossed Sixth Street and stood on the brick pavement outside the National. From this vantage point, he could watch the entrance to Brown's and try to blend in with the loiterers on the sidewalk. It was harder than he had anticipated. Most of the people standing around him were slaves, waiting for their owners to finish their business inside. But not all of them were, and Rook was glad not to draw any suspicious glances. After about five minutes, Clark emerged from the hotel.

"Any sign of our friends yet?" asked Rook in a low voice.

"Davis is down here right now. Stephens will show up soon."

After about thirty minutes, the Southerners exited Brown's. Davis was big and tall, with black hair, dark eyes, and skin tanned from hours in the sun. Stephens was his opposite: short, scrawny, fair-haired, and ruddy. On Pennsylvania Avenue, they headed southeast. Rook and Clark followed about fifty feet behind. The tailing was easy. Davis and Stephens made no attempt to see if anybody was tracking them.

"It looks like they know where they're going," said Clark as they approached Second Street.

"Right for the Capitol," said Rook.

As they left the commercial stretch of the Avenue, Rook and Clark were able to drop back a bit further and still keep Davis and Stephens in sight. The Capitol did not appear much changed since the inauguration. Rook wondered if any work had been done on it at all. As they circled around to the east side of the building, the colonel noticed the grounds were still a mess, littered with piles of coal and wood, marble blocks, and columns in various states of assembly. Several statues stood amid the clutter, waiting for someone to put them inside the unfinished building. One was a big sculpture of George Washington that made the first president look like a Roman general.

When Davis and Stephens reached the wide steps on the eastern front of the building, they paused. A handful of soldiers sat near the top smoking pipes. They did not appear to be on duty. Rook assumed that because they were new to the city, they would not recognize him.

The two Southerners seemed uncertain about what to do. They exchanged a few words and looked around. As Rook and Clark approached the foot of the steps, Davis and Stephens began to climb them. At the summit, they turned around to take in the view.

Rook raised his hand to his mouth so nobody could read his lips. "Keep moving forward," he said.

He and Clark walked past the stairs. Now their backs were to Davis and Stephens. If the Southerners were testing them, turning around would blow their cover. If they kept walking, however, they might lose their quarry for good. Rook knew he had to make a decision. He casually stuck his hand in a pocket and found a penny.

All of a sudden, he halted and bent over. "Look at this," he said, trying to sound surprised as he touched the ground. He made a great show of holding up the penny, as if he wanted to study its design in the light. From the corner of his eye he was able to see the top of the steps. He could see the soldiers, but not Davis and Stephens. Rook and Clark raced up the steps, taking two at a time. "This isn't going to be easy indoors," said Rook when they arrived at the top.

They passed through a doorway and almost immediately were in the Capitol's rotunda, which was open to the sky. A massive wooden scaffolding rose from the center of the room, reaching toward the hole where the dome was supposed to rest. More than a hundred feet above his head, Rook could see a few men clinging to the planks and moving a giant crane. They were continuing the slow work of construction. President Lincoln had insisted that their efforts not stop, because they held symbolic importance to a divided nation.

As Rook gazed at the scene overhead, he saw one of the workers move off the scaffolding, grab a rope attached to a cornice, and lower himself to the ground in a matter of seconds. To the colonel, it was an incredible feat of acrobatics. He had seen it before, but it still impressed him. Others in the room had become used to it. Just a few feet from where the fellow had landed, a group of soldiers did not even look up from their card game. Elsewhere, men occupied themselves by reading and napping.

Rook studied the scene for a moment but did not see Davis or Stephens immediately. "There they are," whispered Clark. "On the far side of the scaffolding."

Davis was running his hand along a thick beam supporting the crane. He pointed upward and said something to Stephens. It appeared as if they were thinking about climbing the steps that spiraled up the middle of the scaffold. Then Davis shook his head. The Southerners studied the rotunda for a few more minutes. Rook tried to stay out of view. Then he realized they were not looking at people. They were examining the room itself. When they were done, they exited through an opening on Rook's left, which led toward the House of Representatives, on the south side of the building.

Rook did not want to follow them too closely, so he stood still for a moment and then moved cautiously toward the passageway with Clark. When they got there, Rook stood to one side, gestured for Clark to stay back, and peered down a long corridor. Soldiers were hammering wooden boards into place along both sides of the hall, apparently to protect the statues that lined it. Rook could see all the way to the House doors, but Davis and Stephens were nowhere in sight. Could they have gone so far in so little time?

Before Rook had a chance to wonder where they went, he heard the patter of footsteps on his right. In his haste, he had overlooked a small doorway that led to a curving staircase. Davis and Stephens must have used it. But had they gone up or down? He could not tell. He supposed it was even possible that they had separated. Rook knew from previous visits to the Capitol that up led to congressional offices and down led to the basement. He went up and ordered Clark down.

Compared to the grand space of the rotunda and the long hallway to the House of Representatives, the staircase was cramped. Rook could see only a dozen or so steps in each direction before they curved out of view. He climbed cautiously, not wanting to bump into Davis and Stephens. He also treaded lightly, not wanting to make a sound.

The staircase led to new opening, where a private stood at attention. He was the first soldier Rook had seen that day in the Capitol who actually appeared to be on duty. He could not have been a day older than twenty years.

"Excuse me," said Rook, "did a couple of men come this way just now?"

"No, sir," said the soldier. "It's been quiet up here for a while."

Rook offered a swift word of thanks, turned around, and descended the winding staircase. A moment later, he was with Clark in the Capitol basement. A long hallway stretched to the right. On their left, a large room occupied the space directly below the rotunda. It was full of thick support columns. The light was poor. They heard someone talking in a part of the room they could not see.

"…and they're planning to build a set of bakery ovens over here."

Rook recognized the voice of Lieutenant Easley, a man assigned as a liaison to the troops housed in the Capitol. He knew that Easley was working with architects to find suitable places for building ovens that would serve the troops. Rook was about to step forward and ask Easley if he had seen anyone pass when a deep Southern accent stopped him cold.

"So your deliveries will come in over here?"

Easley, still out of sight, answered that they would and added that they were going to stockpile flour in a warren of rooms nearby. It sounded as if he were giving Davis and Stephens a guided tour of the basement. Sometimes Rook could hear what they were saying; other times their words fell out of earshot. This went on for several minutes. Then came silence. Either they had left the room or the conversation had ended. Rook was about to step forward when Easley, heading straight for the staircase, nearly bumped into him.

"Pardon me," said Easley.

"Good afternoon, Lieutenant."

Easley looked up. "Colonel Rook? Is this an inspection? You're not in uniform."

Rook would have preferred not to encounter Easley at all. He wondered if he could bluff his way through a conversation.

"Why, yes, that's exactly right. When I'm dressed up, sometimes I worry that I'm not seeing things as they truly are—you know, everybody standing at attention and acting as they think they should rather than as they usually do."

"Very clever, sir," said Easley as he straightened his spine.

"Who were those men you were just with?" asked Rook.

"They are traders. I found them walking around the basement. They looked lost. People don't come down here much, except for soldiers. When I asked if they needed help, one of them asked a bunch of questions about selling flour and produce to the troops."

"They asked about food?"

"Yes. They wanted to know how much the soldiers would need, who would pay for it, where they might deliver it. They aren't inspecting things with you, are they, sir? I answered their questions as best as I could, which probably wasn't very well."

"Oh no, they're not with us. Don't worry about that."

Rook asked Easley to show him where the men went. The lieutenant led him through the big room beneath the rotunda, around one of its thick columns, and pointed toward a portal on the left-hand side. "They went that way, to the west front of the building. They can't be more than a couple of minutes ahead of you."

"Thank you very much, Lieutenant. You may be on your way."

As Easley left, Rook opened the doors and looked out. Trees dotted the landscape between the Capitol and the other buildings of Washington. Their branches were just starting to bud. Several hundred feet in front of them, walking straight toward the Avenue, were Davis and Stephens.

"Do you really think they're traders?" asked Clark.

"They're either traders or traitors," said Rook.

Rook and Clark continued their pursuit. They stayed far behind Davis and Stephens, but always in sight. When they reached the Avenue, they picked up their pace slightly, remaining a couple of blocks behind the two men. Rook expected Davis and Stephens to return to Brown's, ending their jaunt from where it had started. But when they reached Sixth Street, they kept walking. They had somewhere else to go.

As they marched up the Avenue, crossing street after street, Rook and Clark closed the gap. By the time they reached Willard's, at Fourteenth Street, they were just half a block behind the two men. At Fifteenth Street, however, the massive Treasury Department prevented them from continuing in a straight line. They turned right and slipped out of sight.

When Rook and Clark reached the corner, Clark glanced backward for a quick view of the Capitol, more than a mile away. For a moment, he imagined what the scene would look like when the dome was finally finished and Pennsylvania Avenue properly paved. It would present a grand vista for the nation—a commercial street framing the country's chief political building.

"It's odd how the Treasury stands where it does," said Clark. "It blocks the view between the White House and the Capitol."

"The city's designers originally had planned an unobstructed view," said Rook. "But twenty years ago, Andrew Jackson insisted on the construction of the big building right where it is. And so it went up."

Davis and Stephens were back in sight, moving north on Fifteenth. They crossed F street and then G street. They turned left, rounding the State Department and heading for Lafayette Park. They cut through it diagonally, right beneath the statue of Jackson. At the northwest corner of the park, they paused for the first time since leaving the Capitol. They seemed indecisive. Davis pointed one way, Stephens another.

Suddenly, they began walking on east on H Street, along the northern edge of the park. They stopped at the intersection of H Street and Sixteenth Street. Again, they paused. Stephens appeared to want to go back in the direction from which they had just come. Davis, however, pointed to a building on the north side of the street. He crossed H Street and Stephens followed. They marched up the steps and knocked on the front door. A moment later it opened and they entered.

Rook could not see who let them in. The building was a private residence. He did not recognize it. He ordered Clark to stay put and walked to the corner of H and Sixteenth streets for a better look. It stood three stories tall, with a facing of red brick, a black door, and a series of dark windows. Nothing about it was especially distinctive. To Rook, who did not appreciate the finer points of architecture, it was just another fine home in the best section of the city. He did not want to pass right in front of it, for fear of someone noticing him, but he approached close enough to check the home's address.

Rook walked back to Clark, who was not alone—Springfield was with him. The sergeant had been carrying out his orders of keeping a watch on the area and its inhabitants.

"Do you know who lives in the building they entered?" asked Rook.

Springfield squinted in the direction of Sixteenth Street. "Exactly which one did they go into?"

"The address is 398 Sixteenth Street."

Springfield nodded. "I suppose that's not much of a surprise," he said.

"Why not?"

"That's the home of Violet Grenier."

* * *

Mazorca had seen impressive mansions before, and the White House was not one of them. Compared to several that he knew, it was a modest country house—a big box of a building whose plain shape was broken only by a columned portico jutting from the structure's north side. After a moment, Mazorca realized it had the architectural effect of making the two-story house appear much smaller than it really was. The president's home may not have looked magnificent, but it certainly was large.

People often stopped and stared at the White House. Mazorca, however, did not want to attract any special attention. He began a slow, clockwise walk around a circular gravel driveway that swooped by the portico, where he saw visitors coming and going as they pleased. There were a couple of soldiers by the front door, beneath the overhang. They stood against the wall like sculpted bas-reliefs and did not move to prevent a single person from entering. Mazorca wondered what they thought they were guarding, because he could not tell.

For a moment he considered going into the building. It would have been easy. He had read that the building was more or less open to the public. The cheap guidebooks to Washington that he had been reading sometimes described the custom as a testament to the strength of American democracy. Whatever it was, Mazorca thought it was a weakness.

Maybe he could just walk in right now. Then he reminded himself that the purpose of this visit was simply to have an initial look at the White House exterior. He counted the windows: there were eleven facing north on the second story, all in plain sight except for one on the left, which was obscured by a tree. Smaller trees covered the view of most of the windows on the first floor. A decorative iron fence stood between the driveway and the house, with an open gate in front of the portico. The black fence was so short that any able-bodied person might have hopped over it without much trouble. It seemed even less useful than the guards.

Small sheds flanked the White House. A conservatory was on the right. A bronze statue of Thomas Jefferson, with his right hand placed over his heart, stood before the mansion in the middle of the driveway. Bright flowers surrounded the granite pedestal block. They were freshly planted, judging from the overturned soil.

A soldier approached from Pennsylvania Avenue. He was a private. The man was about to pass Mazorca when they both heard a loud commotion coming from the portico. Dozens of men poured out the front door. They were a rowdy bunch, whooping and boasting and knocking each other around. Mazorca stepped onto the grass to let them go by. The soldier did the same.

There must have been a hundred of them. Many had pistols stuffed in their belts. Others had big knives. When they reached Pennsylvania Avenue, they turned right, turned right again on Fifteenth Street, and eventually disappeared behind the State Department and Treasury.

As they left the White House grounds, the soldier turned to Mazorca.

"Are you one of Jim Lane's men too?" he asked.

"Excuse me?"

"I suppose not. You don't really look it." The soldier pointed toward the vanishing horde. "The 'Frontier Guards.' At least that's what they call themselves. They're more like a mob. They arrived yesterday from out West and spent the night here. They couldn't have been more out of place. There are a lot of them—two or three times the number that just passed by. They say they're here to protect President Lincoln."

The bluecoat apparently was a talker. "And they're all in the White House?" asked Mazorca.

"They've turned the place into a bivouac. I've never seen such a rabble. But the truth is we need every man we can get these days. We're short of soldiers all over the city, and those fellows look ready to fight."

"At least the president is safe."

"I suppose. With the soldiers on duty here, plus Lane's men, I think we could hold off a small group of attackers. I'm sure you've heard all the rumors of kidnapping plots and that sort of thing."

"It seems as though people move in and out of the building with ease."

"Mr. Lincoln has insisted on keeping the house open at all times. He talked to us the other day about it and said that when he was a congressman during the Polk years, the house was shut to the public. He said it created an appearance of aloofness, and he wanted no part of that."

"Interesting."

"I definitely see his point. But sometimes I wonder how safe he really is in there. He calls it 'the people's house,' but it's his house as well. I sure don't want any harm to come to him."

"I'm sure you don't."

"What's your business here?"

"Just looking."

"Have you come for a job?"

Mazorca narrowed his eyes. "You could say that," he replied.

The soldier thought nothing of it. "That's what most of the people who come here are doing," he continued. "They're asking Mr. Lincoln to give them jobs in the government."

"I see," said Mazorca. "Well, right now I'm just looking."

"Good to meet you, mister," said the soldier. He walked into the house.

Mazorca watched him go. "I've already got a job," he said, to no one but himself.

* * *

When Violet Grenier heard the Irish girl marching up the stairs, she rose from her chair and smoothed her dress. The door opened, revealing a plain-looking girl in a plain-looking dress. Polly was perhaps seventeen years old, and she possessed precisely what Violet wanted in a servant: an appearance so thoroughly ordinary that none of Violet's male visitors would notice her. If there was one thing Violet Grenier was good at, it was securing the attention of men.

"Mrs. Grenier, you have visitors," said Polly, in a meek brogue.

Violet already knew. She had been writing a note at her desk when she glanced out the window of her second-floor study, looked across Sixteenth Street to St. John's Church on the other side, and saw two men walking straight for her front door. She had not recognized either of them.

"They called themselves Jeff and Alex," continued Polly. She seemed unsure of herself, which was normal except that now she seemed hesitant even by her own standards. "They didn't give last names, and they said it didn't matter because you wouldn't know them by their names but by a phrase. They made me memorize it: 'Wide is the gate and broad is the way that leadeth to destruction.'" The girl's face, usually expressionless, showed a flash of distaste.

Violet recognized the words immediately. It surprised her to hear them. She asked Polly to repeat the line. The girl closed her eyes and spoke it again.

"Tell our guests that I will join them presently," said Violet.

Polly nodded and left. Violet stayed behind and paused before a mirror. She was one of those women who was not beautiful at first glance but became so as a man studied her. She was tall and slim, with olive skin that flushed into color on her face, thick eyebrows crowning brown eyes that somehow sparkled, and just a touch of gray in her black hair, which was parted straight down the middle and drawn back tightly despite a current fashion calling for rings and curls. Her beauty was the kind that comes with maturity, a confident pose of female experience that younger women could only hope to achieve one day. She also had a good figure— one that few women could duplicate even in their youth.

At the age of thirty-nine, Violet had never felt better about herself.

There was a time when she would have thought feeling good about herself was impossible. Just six years earlier, she had become a childless widow when her husband died on a business trip to California. The news came to her in a telegram. She had read it in this very room. For months she was despondent. Her husband had left her with enough money to remain comfortable, but also more grief than she thought she could bear.

Slowly but surely, however, Violet overcame her sadness. It had been like recovering from a long convalescence. Yet when it was gone, it was gone for good—and Violet once again threw herself into the Washington political scene as a high-powered hostess whose guests came from the ranks of cabinet members, military officers, and foreign diplomats. When her friend James Buchanan was elected president in 1856, she achieved even greater levels of prominence. An invitation to dine at her home had become a prized mark of social success.

Although Violet had no shortage of suitors, a widowed woman in possession of a good fortune does not necessarily want a husband. Violet enjoyed her newfound prestige and decided that she would rather entertain senators than marry one. She met most of them in drawing rooms and across dinner tables, but these were by no means her only places of congress. They were not even the most important ones.

Violet had discovered a talent for bewitching men. At first she deployed it for her own amusement. Before long, however, she realized that her paramours were willing to share their intimate knowledge of Washington politics—

she heard what was said behind the closed doors of committee rooms, which public men were to be trusted under
no circumstances, and who aspired to high office but would
never get there because of a drinking problem. Sometimes
men confided in Violet because they wanted to impress
her. Other times they did it because they just wanted to
talk and she was willing to listen. Their motives hardly mattered to Violet, who realized that she occupied a unique
and privileged position. And she saw it as an opportunity
to exploit.

Personal ambition was only a part of her motive, and it
was not even the biggest part. Instead, Grenier had become
radicalized by the times. Between North and South, there
was no question about her own loyalties.

She had grown up in Maryland, about two dozen miles
from where she now lived, on a small plantation that grew
tobacco and wheat. The entire operation depended on
slave labor. As Violet grew up, it had not occurred to her
that slavery might be unjust. Quite the contrary, she viewed
it as the natural order of things and felt that slaves often
were not sufficiently appreciative of the lives they were allowed to live.

This particular sentiment owed much to a family tragedy. When Violet was a girl, her father spent a dreary afternoon at a local tavern. In the evening, it started to rain hard.
Violet's father passed the hours by continuing to drink.
Shortly after midnight, the rain stopped and he decided
to leave. He was intoxicated and barely able to mount his
horse. His manservant, a slave called Jacob who often traveled with him, helped Violet's father onto his steed. They
departed together.

Violet's father never made it home. Somewhere along the way, he suffered a fatal head injury. Jacob insisted that he had fallen from his horse and struck a rock. The slave thought that perhaps the horse had slipped in the mud, causing its rider to lose his balance. A doctor who arrived on the scene confirmed that the wound came from a blow to the head but speculated that perhaps it had been delivered after the fall—in other words, that the slave had finished off his master. There was a trial, a verdict, and a hanging. Violet was too young to remember the details, such as the fact that Jacob was judged by an all-white jury and could not call character witnesses. Yet she grew up thinking that her father had been murdered by a slave and believing that the sons and daughters of Africa deserved bondage and should be more grateful for it.

As a widow in Washington, she knew any number of figures who supported freeing the slaves. She even liked a few of them. But that was on a personal level, and she despised their opinions. For a time, she kept these views to herself. Debating political or moral issues was not considered proper behavior for a society lady. Yet it became increasingly difficult to keep opinions bottled up, even in settings that were supposed to be filled with conviviality. Abolitionists from the North started refusing to break bread with slaveholders from the South, and vice versa. When the two sides did meet, often the best a hostess could hope to achieve was a frostiness that kept everyone's manners in check. The dinner party had been an essential feature of life in the capital because it allowed politicians from different parties, regions, and branches of the government to meet outside the halls of formal power, and hostesses like Violet provided an essential service. When the Republican Party nominated Abraham Lincoln for president and the Democrats splintered into hostile factions, however, it broke down completely.

Over the years, Grenier had made a habit of sharing the information she had obtained by her various methods with favored politicians. Most were from the South, but a few, such as Buchanan, were Northerners who were amenable to the South. Sometimes she merely repeated what she had heard verbatim, but she was not above planting false rumors when she thought these would serve a purpose, such as harming the chances of a certain congressman's winning a prized committee seat. Buchanan once called her "the Lady Macbeth of Washington." He meant it as a joke; Violet considered it a compliment.

In 1860, as it became apparent that Lincoln would win the election, Violet began telling acquaintances that no matter what happened, she would remain in Washington. She told her most trusted friends that she would be willing to serve as the eyes and ears of those who could not be there with her, either because they felt they had to leave or because they already lived elsewhere. Furthermore, she let them know that she would be glad to participate in plans to undermine the Lincoln administration, whether it meant merely making observations about cabinet deliberations or collecting data on local troop strength—or perhaps even something more extreme. The milk of human kindness was not her way. Lady Macbeth would have understood.

Violet and her far-flung network did not believe that they could communicate in the open, so they developed a system of codes and techniques that would allow them to make contact under watchful eyes. She kept a few ciphers in her desk drawer, as well as other materials that helped her send and receive messages to contacts in Richmond, Montgomery, and elsewhere. One of her correspondents was Langston Bennett of South Carolina, whom she had met through her husband some years earlier. Yet it was not to him that her mind turned when Polly delivered the message from her visitors. She thought of someone else entirely.

Several months ago, on a day when her anger at Lincoln's victory was particularly intense, Violet had discussed an extravagant plot with a New York merchant whose livelihood depended on his ability to transport slave-produced goods from Southern ports to European cities. When their conversation was done and the man gone, Violet reflected upon it—and concluded it was complete nonsense. There was no way the man could accomplish what he had proposed. It was simply too bold. But she also remembered how he had picked up a Bible on her shelf and flipped to the book of Matthew. "You will know my agents by the thirteenth verse of chapter seven," he said. Violet followed his finger down to the black letters: "Wide is the gate and broad is the way that leadeth to destruction."

She decided that she had spent enough time looking in the mirror. She was not sure that associating with these men was wise, but now they were here and they spoke the words from the book. It meant that no matter how much Violet might have wanted it otherwise, they already were associated. She decided at least to meet with them for a few minutes.

Violet walked down the steps and moved to the front of her home, where a pair of small red parlors stood side by side. A crimson silk curtain separated the rooms, hanging from a wide doorway. Gold candle sconces and small portraits of prominent statesmen decorated the walls. Several were familiar to anybody who kept abreast of federal politics: Senator Stephen Douglas, Secretary of State William Seward, and the late Southern political giant John Calhoun. A large tête-à-tête sat in the parlor by the front door, and a rosewood piano with pearl keys dominated the parlor in back.

Grenier moved silently beside the piano and watched her two guests, who had their backs turned to her as they stood and looked at the decorations in the front parlor. She could not see their faces, but their clothes were well-worn and lacking in the finery that most of her visitors displayed. One of the men was a good deal larger than the other.

"Good afternoon," said Grenier as she passed into the front parlor. She spoke in a voice that was meant to convey a cool formality rather than a warm hospitality.

Both men spun around. At first, they said nothing. Their eyes ran up and down Grenier—a habit of many men, and one that Grenier occasionally even enjoyed, especially when she was making an effort to impress. Yet these two men were coarse. Grenier wished they would simply announce their business.

"How may I help you?" she asked, hoping that one of them would speak.

The larger of the two gave her a mischievous grin. "Wide is the gate and broad is the way that leadeth to destruction," he said.

"So I have heard."

"Our employer suggested that we meet with you," he said. "My name is Davis, and this here is Stephens, except that those aren't our real names."

"Then why do you bother giving them to me?"

"Our real names aren't important. These are the ones that we're using as we pursue our current project." Davis raised his eyebrows, seeking some kind of acknowledgment from Grenier. She did not give him any. "You do know about our current project, don't you? Wide is the gate and broad is the way that leadeth to destruction?"

"You have already said that," replied Grenier. "I've met with your employer, and I think I know what you are planning. It is certainly ambitious."

Davis and Stephens began to smile, but their smiles vanished as Grenier continued.

"I'm also concerned that it's the wrong approach for right now. Sumter has fallen. Here in Washington, the government is confused and in disarray. What you are planning could create sympathies where none now exist."

"All of this has been thought through," said Davis. "We are beyond the point of reconsideration. I was told that you were consulted on these plans."

"I wouldn't use the word 'consulted.' But I was certainly made familiar with what you are intending to do. Perhaps you will succeed. My concern is that the risks are great and the price of failure is enormous. Events are going our way right now, all across the land. A mistake could change that."

"We won't make a mistake."

Grenier did not respond immediately. She was distracted by the smaller of the two men—Stephens, the one who had not spoken. He was rubbing his fingers on a pale Romanesque bust that decorated a table.

"Please don't touch that," said Grenier sharply. "You're supposed to look at it, not play with it."

The reprimand jolted Stephens. He moved away from the statue and placed his hands behind his back. He did not even apologize, leading Grenier to believe that he had been sworn to silence. Davis wanted to do all of the talking.

"Please excuse us," said Davis with a phony smile. "We are not men of great elegance. We have come to Washington with a single purpose. Upon the instructions of our employer, we have come here to seek your blessing and your advice."

Grenier thought she had already delivered the advice to stop. But apparently this was not an option.

"It is more important that you not fail than that you succeed. There is a difference, you know."

Davis laughed. "Don't worry, we won't fail." Stephens let out a chuckle as well.

An uncomfortable quiet then filled the room. Grenier wanted the men to leave. She thanked them for coming and politely pushed them toward the door. A moment later, they were gone. This is a clumsy plan and these are clumsy men, she thought. Grenier was perfectly willing to support radical action in Washington, but radical action also had to be intelligent.

The most intelligent man she had ever met was Langston Bennett. She had not heard from him in a few weeks. Yet she knew that he was planning something bold because they had corresponded in the fall about the problem of a Republican president and the lengths to which they might go to prevent him from taking action against the South. Nothing was ruled out of bounds. For such an important assignment, he would not associate himself with low-rent ruffians. He would work only with the most capable of men.

* * *

I can't wait to see your granddaughter. The words tormented Lucius all morning. Did Bennett know she was gone?

The old slave stood outside the front door of the manor, waiting for Bennett to finish writing a few letters and come out. A couple of younger men had just loaded several boxes of new clothes onto a cart. As soon as Bennett joined them, they would make their way to the slave quarters.

There was no way he could know, Lucius kept telling himself. Bennett had gone to bed before Portia and Joe had even arrived at the stables, and he had just gotten up when he made that troubling comment. It seemed impossible that he could know. And if he did know, would he play this kind of mind game? Lucius doubted that too. That was not like him. Bennett was a blunt man. He did not concern himself too much with runaways either. He generally let Tate handle those details. Yet Bennett had always taken a special interest in Portia. Would he treat her escape differently?

That was probably the real reason Bennett had mentioned Portia on the porch: she was a favorite. Her position had much to do with the fact that she was related to Lucius, but it was more than that, too. Portia had been an adorable girl growing up, with bright eyes and a precocious mind. She loved the company of adults and was a constant source of amusement for them. Since then she had grown into a striking young woman. There was not an unmarried male slave on the plantation who was not attracted to her, thought Lucius, and a few of the married ones must have desired her too. Over the years, Bennett had become quite fond of her, though his attentions were more innocent. He just seemed to like Portia. Everybody did.

I can't wait to see your granddaughter. Perhaps there was nothing suspicious behind those words at all. Lucius again looked down the lane where the runaways had slipped off the night before. He knew he would eventually have to cover for Portia. He had not expected that moment to come so soon, though. He would have preferred for a day or two to go by before Bennett or Tate started asking a lot of questions. But Lucius knew that he could not avoid a reckoning. Every hour between now and then counted. Lucius determined he would try to keep Bennett's curiosity about Portia to a minimum. It would be a real accomplishment, he now believed, if he got through the entire day without anybody realizing she was gone.

Big Joe was another matter. There were probably a few people wondering about him already. He was the sort of worker whose presence would be missed soon. Lucius still believed it was a mistake for Joe to have joined Portia on her flight, but he felt that the two of them had forced his hand the night before. What else could he have done, call the whole thing off and recruit another runaway? That would take a few days to arrange at a minimum, and Lucius was not sure how much time he had to spare. It had been more than a week since he had seen Lincoln's would-be killer in Charleston. It might already be too late to stop him. Besides, Portia really was the best choice—she was smart, she had been to Charleston before, and she knew Nelly. It made sense for her to be the one. Joe might even come in handy on the road. Unfortunately, his absence on the plantation probably would cause a search party to begin a hunt sooner than if Portia had gone by herself.

There was still no sign of Bennett in the manor. Lucius looked at the fields. Normally they would be full of slaves at this time of day. Now they were empty. He spotted Tate in the distance making his way toward the slave cabins. The overseer had spent the last half hour telling the field hands to pause in their work and assemble for Bennett's visit. Lucius wondered if Tate supposed that Joe was missing. With so many slaves on the plantation, it was not likely he would notice on his own, at least not right away. A slave might have reported it to him, though. Tate had plenty of informants on the plantation, and reporting a runaway was an easy way to keep in the good graces of the overseer. Another one of the overseers—there were four besides Tate—might have noticed Joe's absence too.

Lucius thought that if he could somehow prevent the news of Joe's disappearance from making the rounds until later in the day, or perhaps into the evening, then he might buy the runaways another night before a group of slave catchers went out after them. He just was not sure how to do it.

"Hello!" said Bennett as he emerged from the house. He sounded cheerful. The master of the plantation loved these gift-giving excursions to the slave quarters. Perhaps twice a year, he handed out blankets, clothes, shoes, and other items to the slaves. These were not gifts, actually. They were necessities, and somebody would have to supply them if Bennett did not. But Bennett took great pleasure in handing out these items personally. It allowed him to play the patriarch. He also believed it made him more popular among the slaves. He wanted them to think he was a good master.

"Let's go," said Bennett, heading in the direction of the slave quarters. He descended onto the gravel driveway with the cautious steps of a man owning a wooden leg, yet it might have been said that there was a spring in his step. Lucius walked beside him. The cart with the boxes followed. A few minutes later, when the slave cabins came into view, they saw a big gathering of men, women, and children. The group let out a few whistles and claps. Tate was standing to the side. He immediately approached. It was clear that he had something on his mind.

"Mr. Bennett," he said. "May I have a quick word with you?"

"Certainly."

"Big Joe isn't here," Tate said in a low voice.

Bennett stopped in his tracks, about fifty or sixty feet away from the cabins and the assembly of slaves. Lucius ordered the cart to halt. "Really?"

"That's right. I heard this morning that he hadn't shown up where he was expected. I didn't think too much on it—this is Big Joe, after all, and he's never given us any trouble. I figured on seeing him here with the others. Well, he's not here. I've asked around, and nobody seems to know where he is."

"That's odd. You don't suppose…" Bennett's voice trailed off.

"It's not like him," said Tate. "But you just never know who's going to get the notion in his head."

Lucius knew that if he was going to intervene at all, this was the time. He hardly knew what he was going to say when he spoke up. "Excuse me," he said. Bennett and Tate snapped their heads in his direction. They were not accustomed to being interrupted by a slave, even if it was Lucius.

"I woke up early," he continued, speaking slowly and choosing his words with care. He was making this up as he went along. "I saw Big Joe walk by the house and waved to him. He came up to me and said a tool had broken and he needed to borrow one from the Wilson farm. So I suppose that's where he is. He's probably on his way back now. I guess I assumed he'd gotten a pass from you, Mr. Tate."

Lucius could not tell whether he had convinced them. He worried that he was not a very good liar.

"He definitely didn't speak to me," Tate said, "and he knows the rules. If he wants to leave the plantation for any reason—even if it's to fetch a tool from down the way—he needs to talk to me first. He didn't do that and he certainly didn't get a pass. He knows better than this. Besides, we can fix tools here."

Tate spoke as if he were accusing Lucius. The old slave shrugged his shoulders.

"What tool did he say was broken?"

"I don't think he said which one. He just said a tool. That's what I remember. We talked about other things."

"What other things?"

"The weather. His family. Things like that."

Tate looked at Bennett. "I'm not so sure about this."

"Well, if Lucius says he saw him, then he must have seen him. Don't worry about it now, Mr. Tate. Give him a little while longer. He'll probably be back soon," said Bennett, starting to walk again toward the slaves. "You can speak to him then about the rules and handle this situation however you please."

"Oh, I'll handle it," said Tate, casting a look at Lucius and tapping his whip. "I'll definitely handle it."

* * *

Rook studied the exterior of Violet Grenier's home. He wanted to be inside listening to these men who called themselves Davis and Stephens as they talked to a lady about whom he felt he needed to know much more as soon as possible.

"Why would a couple of fellows who seem to be up to no good want to meet Grenier?" It was a rhetorical question. Neither Clark nor Springfield tried to answer it.

They backed away from H Street to a place in the park where they could keep an eye on Grenier's front door without making themselves obvious.

"The first step in figuring out why they would want to see Grenier is to figure out why they're in Washington in the first place," said Rook. He briefed Springfield on how he and Clark had followed the men from Brown's to the Capitol and then to here.

"The most peculiar thing is their interest in the Capitol's basement," said Springfield.

"Yes, and it worries me," said Rook. He was silent for a moment. "Have either of you heard of Guy Fawkes?"

The two men looked at each other. They did not know the name.

"Let me give you a little history lesson," said Rook. He described the Gunpowder Plot of 1605, in which Fawkes tried to pack explosives into the cellar of the British Parliament and blow it up on a date when the king was scheduled to visit. Before Fawkes could commit his crime, however, he was betrayed: the authorities arrested, tortured, and killed him.

"Do you really think these guys want to destroy the Capitol?" asked Springfield.

"I have no idea what to think," said Rook. "But I don't want to rule out anything either. Davis and Stephens concern me. They have come to Washington with assumed names, we have overheard them say provocative things, and they've traveled through a part of the Capitol that would have interested Guy Fawkes if he were a secessionist today. Now they're meeting with Violet Grenier, whose antipathy toward the Union is well known. It doesn't take a lot of imagination to suspect that trouble may be afoot."

They discussed the possibility that Davis and Stephens were targeting the Capitol. How many explosives would it take? Where would they have to be placed? What could they possibly hope to achieve?

"If they actually bombed the Capitol," said Clark, "it would wipe out any sympathy there is in the North for the South."

Rook considered this. It seemed plausible. "They would probably ignite a war," he said. "But maybe a war is what they want, for whatever foolish reason."

The door to Grenier's home opened. Davis and Stephens emerged and walked in the direction of Brown's and the Capitol.

The soldiers had discussed what they would do when Davis and Stephens reappeared. Springfield stayed put. His job was to monitor Grenier's home for further activity. Clark walked briskly to Brown's, ahead of Davis and Stephens, on the assumption that this was where they were going. Rook waited for them to pass. When they were a couple hundred feet ahead of him, he followed.

Davis and Stephens walked down Fifteenth Street and turned left on Pennsylvania Avenue. They seemed unaware of the fact that anybody might be tracking their movements, which made Rook think that they were possibly overconfident. Or perhaps, he thought, they really are not plotting anything at all. They could be visitors from out of town who wanted to see the Capitol and an old friend. Rook knew that he lacked any real evidence against them. All he had were a few vague suspicions and wild speculations. Was he too rash to think of Guy Fawkes? He could hear General Scott berating him for wasting his time in this pursuit and Locke snickering in the background.

But Rook did not intend to tell Scott about today's activities. He would not include it in his next briefing at the Winder Building. He would mention other things: troop positions, activity on the bridges, reports from Virginia—anything but this.

Rook knew he could not spend many more days tracking the likes of Davis and Stephens. If he did, Scott would find out somehow. Easley already had recognized him at the Capitol. Rook doubted that he could survive the general's wrath, not after the explicit order to quit surveillance. He would have to do something quickly to learn more about Davis and Stephens, or to force their hand in some way.

Two blocks from Brown's, Rook paused. As he had expected, Davis and Stephens walked straight to the hotel. By now, he figured, Clark would be there. He could take over observations for a few minutes.

Meanwhile, Rook examined the storefronts on his side of the Avenue. He was standing almost directly in front of what he was looking for: Brady's National Photographic Art Gallery. In addition to serving as a studio for Mathew Brady, the up-and-coming photographer, it sold small pictures of famous people. Rook wanted to buy one of the president. Then he would have a chat with Davis and Stephens.

* * *

With help from Lucius, Bennett stepped onto the cart. "Greetings," he said, with outstretched arms and a big smile. The slaves erupted in approval. Their noise energized Bennett, who now laughed with joy at the reception they gave him. "It's good to be here." More cheers. Someone in the front replied, "Welcome back, Mr. Bennett."

"Thank you very much," said the plantation master. "Yes, it's good to be back. And it's good to see you. All of you look wonderful." There were a few scattered handclaps. "I'm returning a little bit later this spring than I had intended. There is much ado in Charleston this year!" He paused, seeming to expect another outburst, as if he were addressing a convention of slaveholders. Instead, there almost was no response at all.

"Good to be back, yes, good to be back," he said, almost to himself. Then he recovered. "Shall we see what I've brought from the city?"

This met with a better reception—the applause returned, and so did Bennett's smile. He reached into the box and pulled out something big and brown. He fumbled with it for a moment and then announced, "Trousers!" He looked at the crowd. "Who would like a new pair of trousers?"

A balding man who appeared about forty years old stepped forward. His own pants were shredded at the bottom of their legs. There was a hole at one of his knees. "Willie! It's good to see you, my boy," shouted Bennett as he tossed the trousers to him. "Looks like you could use a pair!"

Willie caught the pants. "Thank you, Mr. Bennett," he said.

Bennett continued with more trousers and went on to a box of shirts. Then shoes. Then belts. Then hats. There was no method to how he went about it. He just moved on to the next box and reveled in the task of passing out each item individually. Tate tried to make sure the goods went to the slaves who needed them the most, and he had to settle a few small disputes over who received what. Bennett went on interacting with each of the recipients, albeit briefly, and made sure to say a slave's name every time. Lucius noticed that Bennett missed a few of the names, using one incorrectly or having to be reminded of it. In years past, he had almost never made a mistake.

Bennett was most of the way through the boxes when it happened. He lifted the top off the next one and announced, "Dresses!" He pulled out an attractive maroon garment, and a few of the women stepped forward in anticipation. "Ah, yes," said Bennett, admiring the piece of clothing. "This one is for Portia! Where's Portia?"

Lucius looked down at the ground and kicked the dirt.

"Portia? Where are you?"

No one came forward.

"Portia?"

There was now a general commotion among the slaves. When it became clear that Portia was not among them, they threw suspicious glances at one another. Most of them said nothing. A few cupped their hands and whispered into the ears of their neighbors.

"Portia?"

Lucius peered into the crowd, pretending to look for her. Then he caught the eye of Sally, Big Joe's mother. She was staring right at him. It was a hard look, full of anger. Her eyes narrowed, and she shook her head back and forth, almost imperceptibly. At that moment, Lucius knew that she knew.

"Lucius, where is Portia?"

The old slave looked up at his master, still standing on the cart holding the maroon dress.

"I'm sorry, sir, what were you saying?"

"Where's Portia?"

"My granddaughter?"

Bennett raised his eyebrows. "There's only one Portia on this farm."

"Yes. Of course," said Lucius. "I'm sorry, sir. She told me she wasn't feeling well this morning and wanted to take a little walk. I should have told you. I forgot to do that. I'm sorry, sir."

Bennett said nothing for a moment. He just stared at Lucius.

"A little walk this morning? Why isn't she back?"

"Maybe she took a nap. She didn't look very well."

"I see. That's peculiar. She's a healthy girl, isn't she?"

"Yessir. Most of the time anyway."

"And you forgot about this, even though we spoke about her just a little bit ago?"

"I'm sorry."

Bennett dropped the maroon dress onto the floor of the cart. "Mr. Tate," he cried, "please help me down from here." The overseer hurried to the cart and assisted his boss. "Thank you, Mr. Tate. I am getting a bit tired. Perhaps you will finish this business for me?"

Tate hopped onto the cart and grabbed the maroon dress. He handed it to a woman standing almost right beside him, and then he went back into the box for more.

Bennett walked over to Lucius. "Something isn't right."

"I'm sure she'll be back soon, sir."

"I'm not talking about Portia."

Lucius was dumbfounded. This was all beginning to unravel too quickly. What a mistake he had made. What a terrible, dreadful mistake.

"Listen here," said Bennett. "You've been working long hours for me the last few days. I want you to take the rest of the day for yourself. Stay down here and visit with your family. I can get by until morning."

"Thank you, sir," said Lucius. "But I don't think that's necessary."

"You will do what I say."

Bennett spoke with a sharpness Lucius did not often hear directed his way. The tone troubled him. Surrender seemed the only course. "Yessir," he replied, bowing his head. Lucius felt like an exile. He watched Bennett amble away toward the manor. The distance between them was growing, in more ways than one.

Bennett walked up the path and disappeared from the view of the slaves. He was tired. An activity like this used to take almost nothing out of him. Now he could hardly complete it. He might have gone on, but he was disappointed to hear about Portia. Two of his favorite and most obedient slaves were absent, and Lucius seemed to be the only one who knew anything about where they were. The implications were obvious, but he did not want to think about them. He decided to take a nap and not to worry about the situation until later in the day. Perhaps he had been too irritable with Lucius. A rest might do him good. Surely Portia and Joe would be back by then. This mystery would solve itself soon enough.

He was almost to his house, his mind set squarely on his bed upstairs, when he heard a woman's voice calling him from behind.

"Mr. Bennett! Mr. Bennett!"

He turned around. It was Sally, Big Joe's mother, and she was coming toward him at a jog.

"Yes, Sally?"

"Oh, Mr. Bennett, I'm so glad I can speak to you alone like this," she said. "I need to tell you something."

* * *

After leaving the White House grounds, Mazorca wandered around the city. He had memorized details from guidebooks, but studying maps and reading descriptions only went so far. Nothing provided as clear a sense of place as being there. His immediate concern was to find somewhere to stay—a base of operations.

He roamed up and down Pennsylvania Avenue and explored its intersecting streets. The south side of the Avenue—the part called Murder Bay—was full of shady saloons and brothels. Things improved to the north, but Mazorca did not want to check in to one of the large hotels that lined the Avenue. He wanted something smaller, a room at a place where he might come and go without having to pass through a crowded lobby. He eventually found what he was looking for at a boardinghouse several blocks north of the Avenue, between Sixth Street and Seventh Street.

The address was 604 H Street. It was a three-story building squeezed between two others. More important, though, was its location near the city center but not so close as to be a part of it. Mazorca watched it for a few minutes from across the street. In the middle of the day, it was impossible to tell how many people it housed—they were probably all at work. But he did see a woman bustling around the first floor. He figured she was the proprietress.

"Good afternoon!" she said when Mazorca walked through the door. "My name is Mary Tabard. Are you looking for somewhere to stay?"

She was a large woman, tall and heavy. A frumpy dress covered her shapeless body. Her pale brown hair was held in a bun. Mazorca guessed that she was fifty years old.

"Yes. I expect to be in the city for a few weeks. I would like a place where I may have a bit of privacy."

"You will definitely find that here!" said Tabard. Mazorca got the feeling that she would have said the exact opposite if he were to have remarked that he wanted a boardinghouse where all the guests became boon companions. That kind of salesmanship probably would have gone on anywhere, though. Still, he wanted to make a few things clear to her.

"I'm glad to hear that," he said, acting relieved. "Sometimes I find that the people running these boardinghouses just suffocate their guests with attention. I can tell already that you aren't the nosy type."

"Oh no! Not me!"

"Wonderful. I have some business in the city. I'm not sure how long I'll be here—but I'm willing to pay for a month's room and board right now if you can promise me a door with its own lock."

"I've got six rooms total—and exactly the right one for you. Every room has its own key."

They quickly agreed on a price for a second-story room. A window looked onto H Street. For a name, Mazorca told her that he was called "Mr. Mays."

Tabard offered to call for his trunk, and then she had the good sense to leave him alone. There was no avoiding that they would become familiar, thought Mazorca as he pulled up the right leg of his trousers and unbuckled a holster from his calf. He assumed his habits would become apparent to some of the other guests as well. They might come to know that he kept odd hours. Mazorca had no intention of showing up for meals, even though he had paid for them. This would cause them to whisper too. Yet Mazorca believed he could keep plenty of secrets from them. He found that preferable to engaging in conversation around a table, where he might have to concoct elaborate cover stories—and perhaps arouse suspicions that would otherwise lie fallow. After a week or so, they would probably come to regard him as a harmless recluse. If they showed too much curiosity, Mazorca had a few options available. This final thought passed through his mind as he removed a small derringer pistol from the holster and inspected it.

His trunk arrived within an hour, and a muscular black man carried it to his room. When he was alone again, Mazorca pushed it under the window. He unlocked the trunk and lifted its lid. The shirts and trousers were still stacked in neat piles. On the left-hand side rested a coiled brown belt, with the buckle facing away from him. A large knife lay beneath it with the cutting edge turned toward him. On the right-hand side was an upside-down book, with the spine facing away. Everything appeared as he had left it. Satisfied by this, he began removing the contents. When he had burrowed about halfway down, he found what he was looking for.

Mazorca reached into the trunk and removed a rifle. It was a Sharps New Model 1859 breechloader—a deadly weapon that could hit a target from a good distance. Right away, he started to clean it.

* * *

Rook walked through the front door of Brown's to find the hotel lobby in the lull of the middle afternoon, between the busy periods of lunch and dinner. About two dozen people milled about, some in conversation, a few reading newspapers, and two or three seeming to do nothing at all. Clark stood near a bar and caught the colonel's eye. He nodded toward the back of the room, where Davis and Stephens nursed drinks. Rook headed straight for them. He took a seat at their table and gave a big smile. It was not returned.

For a few seconds, Rook just stared at one man and then the other. Davis narrowed his eyes at Rook. He looked menacing. "What can we do for you?" he finally asked in a tone that suggested he did not want to do anything at all for Rook.

"That depends," replied Rook, affecting a slight Southern drawl.

"Depends on what?"

"It depends on why you're here."

"Our affairs are not your affairs."

"Perhaps not. But then again, perhaps they are. I'm intrigued by the fact a couple of boys like you would show up right now in our nation's capital." Rook inflected those last three words with sarcasm. "Where are you from? Alabama? Mississippi?"

Davis and Stephens said nothing. Clark took a seat at a nearby table, with his back to this conversation, and opened a copy of the *National Intelligencer*.

"Well, it hardly matters where you're from exactly," continued Rook. "I'm just interested in where you're from generally. There aren't many Southerners arriving here nowadays. There are even fewer calling themselves Jeff Davis and Alex Stephens."

Davis raised an eyebrow. Rook sensed an opening.

"Gentlemen, it does not take a genius to read a hotel registry," said Rook. He smiled again and took a small palmetto brocade from his pocket and placed it on the table. "Understand something. The number of people who think the way we do dwindles by the hour around here. Guests check out of Brown's these days, rather than check in. So your arrival is conspicuous. Most of those of us who remain behind are planning to get out soon. In my case, I must attend to some unfinished business."

Rook reached into his pocket again and pulled out the Brady photo of Lincoln. He put it on the table beside the brocade and made sure both Davis and Stephens saw what it was. Then he took the pin of the brocade and stabbed it into Lincoln's face. He twisted it around, carving a small hole where Lincoln's head had been. Rook let the brocade and defaced photo lie before Davis and Stephens for a moment. When he thought they had taken a good look, he collected both items and returned them to his pocket.

"As I said, I must attend to some unfinished business," said Rook. He was pleased to see that Davis and Stephens had dropped their threatening looks. Rook leaned into the table and spoke in a hushed voice. "And I'm always on the lookout for new business opportunities."

Stephens glanced at Davis, in a clear sign of deference. The big man did not budge. He still stared at the table, looking at the place where the defaced photo had rested. Finally his eyes moved to Rook.

"I appreciate the invitation, Mr.—?"

"Bishop," replied Rook.

"Mr. Bishop. Very well. I wish you every success, Mr. Bishop. I really do. But it appears as though we are working toward different ends, despite our shared sympathies. You have your intentions, and I have mine."

"What better intention could you have than this imposter who calls himself president?"

"I didn't say I had a better intention, just a different one. We may serve our interests best simply by staying out of each other's way."

"I don't think it's that easy," said Rook. "If one of us succeeds, the other surely will find his task much more challenging. Security is weak across the city, but it won't stay that way forever. Your hints intrigue me, Mr. Davis. They raise an important question: should one of us assist the other? I am native to this city and have resources at my disposal that you may find invaluable."

Davis tapped a finger on the table. "I will consider your offer," he said at last. "But it is too early for anything more. I'm waiting for a shipment to arrive, and it won't get here until the morning. Meet me in this place tomorrow evening. Perhaps we can talk in some detail then."

"If you need help on the Potomac docks with unloading a shipment, I can gather some men—"

Davis chuckled. "No, the shipment will not arrive by the river."

"Then at the train depot—"

Now Davis laughed, and Stephens with him. "Mr. Bishop, the shipment will not arrive by river, and it will not arrive by rail. Or even by road. Let's leave it at that. I do not seek your assistance with the shipment. Not now, anyway. We can meet again tomorrow night. Good day, sir."

Rook nodded and rose from his chair. He walked straight for the door and was gone from the hotel within a few seconds. Davis and Stephens watched him depart.

"I thought we were going to be gone by tomorrow night," said Stephens. "I hope you don't mean to change our plans."

"Of course not. I suspect Bishop himself may not even make the meeting we've just arranged. There will be so much commotion in this city tomorrow night, nothing will go as intended. If Bishop is smart, he will realize what has happened and who is responsible. He can show up here if he wants, but he'll wait a long time before he sees either of us again. We'll be miles away, and Washington will be gripped by terror."

A few feet away, Clark continued to stare at the pages of his newspaper. He heard every word.

* * *

"Sally, what would you like to discuss?" asked Bennett.

"It's about my son, Joe. He's the one everybody calls Big Joe."

"Of course," said Bennett, his interest suddenly aroused. "I know Big Joe. He is a fine young man, with a solid reputation around here. Mr. Tate praises him quite highly."

"He's very good, Mr. Bennett. Even when he was a little boy, he was very good, always listenin' to his mother. He never gave me any trouble. Never! You don't always see that around here."

"I know what you mean. I can't think of a single time Joe has given us any difficulty. I must say, though, there have been some questions raised about him this very day."

Sally broke eye contact with Bennett. She had been looking straight at him, but now she gazed at the ground.

"Mr. Bennett, I don't want you to hurt him."

"Is there something I should know?"

Her eyes were back on him, and Bennett saw that they had started to fill with tears.

"Mr. Bennett, please tell me you ain't gonna hurt him."

"Oh, Sally," said Bennett, trying to achieve a comforting tone in his voice. He put his arm around her. "I don't want to hurt anybody, but I don't think I can promise anything until you tell me what you know."

"Maybe there's one thing you can promise me," she said as she pulled up her apron and wiped the tears from her eyes. "Please don't do to him what you did to Sammy last fall. You remember Sammy? He's Roberta's boy."

Bennett had to think for a moment. He did recall Sammy—a real troublemaker who required the constant attention of an overseer before he would do any work. It was quite a shame too, because Sammy was a strong one who might have made a contribution to the farm if only he had put his mind to it. But when he ran off and hid in the woods last year—and then Tate caught him two weeks later stealing chickens from one of the coops, after several had already disappeared—that was the end of it. Bennett ordered him put up for auction. Sammy was sold to a buyer from Georgia for a bit less than what Bennett thought he should have gotten, but he was glad to be rid of the problem. Attitudes like Sammy's had a way of spreading like a contagious disease if they were not confronted, he believed. Sometimes a plantation master must set a clear example, even at the cost of breaking up families.

"Yes, I do remember Sammy," said Bennett, at last.

"Please tell me you won't sell Joe! It just broke Roberta's heart when Sammy left. I don't know how I could go on if Joe were to leave."

"It sounds to me as though he may have left already."

"Yes," sniffled Sally. "I do believe he has."

"What can you tell me about it?"

"Oh, Mr. Bennett, I just want him back. Please just bring him back to me. I promise you, I'll give him a good, hard talking to the way only his mother can! He won't leave again! Please just bring him back and tell me you won't sell him off!"

She was sobbing now, and Bennett gave her a moment to collect herself.

"Sally, don't worry about Joe getting sold. Sammy's situation was very different from Joe's. I'll be honest with you. When we get Joe back, we're going to have to deal with him in some fashion. I don't know what that will be. It will depend on what happens between now and then. It may also depend on how much you cooperate with us. The fact that you are speaking to me right now, however, is a great comfort. I want to get Joe back too. In all my years of running this plantation, I have learned one thing about runaways—they're best caught early. The longer they stay missing, the harder they are to find. So it's important to get started on this immediately. Perhaps you can help me figure out where he's headed. I received a report this morning that he might be going to the Wilson farm. Does he know anybody there? Maybe there's a girl he wants to see. He's at that age, you know."

"There's a girl, all right, Mr. Bennett. But she ain't one of Mr. Wilson's."

"This is a good beginning, Sally. Come with me inside the house. We can sit down and relax. Then you can tell me everything you know."

They went into the dining room of the manor and sat at the table. It occurred to Sally that she had been in this room only a couple of times in her whole life, and certainly not to sit down with Bennett. When one of the house servants asked Bennett if he would like something to drink, she was astonished to hear him ask her if she wanted something too.

A minute later, a pair of tall glasses of iced tea rested before them. It was the most delicious drink Sally thought she had ever tasted. She did not know what to say, and Bennett initially saved her from saying anything at all.

"There you go, Sally. Make yourself comfortable and tell me your story."

"Thank you, Mr. Bennett. I'm gonna tell you everything."

"Please do."

"Yesterday morning, I was cooking in the kitchen, like I do almost every day. I started feeling a little queasy. I don't know why, I just did. Margaret told me to go lay down and she would cover for me. So I did. I was there in my bed for about twenty minutes and already startin' to feel better when I heard Joe through the window. He was talkin' to someone, a woman who was beggin' him to run off with her. I listened for a spell. She said her grandfather wanted her to deliver some kind of photograph to Mr. Lincoln in Washington."

"A photograph?"

"You know, one of those real-life pictures?"

"I know what a photograph is," said Bennett. "But I'm puzzled why someone of your class would care about one."

"It sounded so crazy, Mr. Bennett, I hardly believed it. But that's what they were talkin' about—gettin' all the way to Washington. Joe wasn't saying yes, but he wasn't saying no. I ran outside and broke them up. Joe wouldn't promise me that he wasn't going to run away. He kept sayin' that he had to get back to work before Mr. Tate wondered about him. I finally got him to promise that he wasn't going anywhere, but I wasn't sure he was tellin' the truth. I think he was just tryin' to put me off. He avoided me the rest of the day, and then I didn't see him at all last night or this morning. I do believe he's gone, Mr. Bennett, and I just wanna get him back here where I know he's safe."

This took a moment to absorb. Bennett took a sip from his drink and set it back on the table.

"First of all, Sally, thank you very much. Your cooperation is very helpful. With it, I'm certain we'll get Joe back soon."

Sally perked up at this. She was gratified by Bennett's response. He did not seem angry. That possibility had worried her. She always thought Bennett was a good master—better than all the other ones in these parts. But she had seen him mad too, and even the best masters could be cruel.

"I do have a few questions, Sally."

"Yes?"

He tried to comfort her with a smile, but the anger inside him was mounting and the effort strained.

"Who was the woman you heard talking to Joe?"

"It was Portia."

Bennett felt his rage begin to swell. The pleasant demeanor he had tried to present to Sally vanished as he barked out more questions.

"Did either Joe or Portia mention the Wilson farm?"

"No. Not at all."

"Did they discuss how they intended to get to Washington?"

"I didn't hear nothin' about that."

"And they planned to take a photograph to Mr. Lincoln?" He spit out the name with obvious distaste.

"Yes, Mr. Bennett."

"Do you know what was in this photograph?"

"From the way it sounded, it was a picture of a person. Someone who was gonna hurt Mr. Lincoln."

"Did you see the photograph?"

"No, sir."

"Didn't they have it?"

"No, sir."

"Damn it, Sally, what do you know?"

The slave woman lowered her head. She began to shake with sobbing. Bennett knew he was pushing her hard. He had done a good job of winning this woman's trust, and now he saw it slipping away. His mind faulted his approach. Yet he was too furious to stop. He forged ahead.

"Sally, look at me!" he shouted. He saw the tears in her eyes when she lifted her face. "Where was the photograph when you overheard them?"

"Someone else had it."

"Who?"

Sally looked away from Bennett. She knew he would not welcome the answer. At this point, though, she had made her decision to confide in him. She could hardly hide it.

"Lucius."

Bennett shot up from the table and thrust his chair backward with such force that it gouged the wall behind him. In the same motion, he grabbed his walking stick, which had been resting against the table, and let out a roar. His eyes fell on the half-full drink in front of him. He raised his cane and whacked the glass. It shattered into a hundred pieces, spraying across the room. Sally screamed and covered her face in her hands as several house servants hurried into the room. Bennett pointed to one of them. "Get me Tate!" he growled. The slave immediately sprinted out of the manor.

Bennett gripped his cane in both hands now, so tightly that his knuckles turned white and his hands trembled. Then he stumbled out of the dining room, pushing one of the slaves out of his way as he lurched into the foyer and then through the front door and onto the porch. He started pacing back and forth. His peg leg pounded against the boards like a hammer.

Sally staggered out a moment later. She fell to her knees in front of Bennett and clasped her hands together, as if in prayer. "Please don't hurt my Joe, Mr. Bennett! Please don't hurt him!"

Bennett stopped in front of her and picked up his cane. For a dreadful few seconds he held it there, as if he were thinking about bashing it into her. Sally shut her eyes, expecting the blow.

"Get up," he ordered at last. Sally rose to her feet. "Get out of here."

As Sally ran down the steps crying hysterically, Tate raced toward the manor. In a minute, he was on the porch in front of Bennett. "Yes, sir, Mr. Bennett?"

"We have two runaways, Tate, and also a conspirator who's still on the farm."

"Big Joe and Portia?"

"Yes."

"And who did they leave behind?" Tate asked. The corners of his mouth turned upwards ever so slightly. He seemed to take a perverse pleasure in this development.

"Lucius." Bennett could hardly have spoken the name with more venom.

"I will gladly take care of him," said Tate, beginning to unfasten the whip at his side.

"No, I will handle him," said Bennett. "Come with me."

The two men walked through the front door and made their way to Bennett's study. The old plantation master sat down at his desk and scribbled a short note. He handed it to Tate. "Have this delivered to Mr. Hughes right away. I'm asking him to rush over here as soon as possible. Then fetch Lucius. Take him to the shed. I will be there shortly."

"Yes, sir."

Tate turned to go, but Bennett stopped him. "One more thing, Mr. Tate," said Bennett, pointing to the lash dangling from Tate's hip. "That's the least thing Lucius needs to worry about."

* * *

In Lafayette Park, about ten blocks from Brown's Hotel, Rook wondered how long it would take for Clark to arrive. They had agreed to meet here, and the colonel grew anxious about being out of uniform for so long. It was the middle of the afternoon. He would have to blaze through his rounds.

He sat beneath the bronze statue of Andrew Jackson mounted on a rearing horse. Many people believed that Jackson was the best man the country had produced since Washington. Rook knew that Scott was no admirer, but it was hard to avoid regarding Jackson as anything but a hero. As a general during the War of 1812, he saved the country's honor by winning the Battle of New Orleans. Then he became president and opposed South Carolina in the first secession crisis, a generation before the current one. Rook thought that the country needed a new leader like Jackson, someone who could rally the South for union. Looking at the White House, he wondered whether Lincoln had what it would take. He was not optimistic.

Clark came into sight as he passed the State Department on the corner of Fifteenth Street and Pennsylvania Avenue. He took a seat on the bench beside Rook.

"Whatever they're planning to do," said Clark, "they're planning to do it before tomorrow night." He described what he had heard following Rook's departure.

"This is strange," replied Rook. "We're missing a piece. The thing that really gnaws at me is the comment about how the shipment is supposed to get here. It won't arrive by river, rail, or road? That's doesn't make any sense. It's like a riddle."

"It's as if he wants us to think something will fall from the sky. His comment makes me wonder whether there really is a shipment at all. Maybe he was trying to throw you off."

"There's more to this. Davis is too satisfied by his own cleverness. He and his men are leaving clues all over the place, from their false names to where they go and what they say. They're convinced that they can fool us."

Rook didn't give voice to his next thought: And so far, they are succeeding.

* * *

Tucker Hughes galloped hard to the Bennett manor. It was difficult to see in the dark, but he knew the roads well.

When he turned onto the lane leading to Bennett's home, he spurred the beast into a full dash, like a cavalry soldier charging an enemy line. The horse's speed exhilarated him. So did the uncertainty behind the summons. Bennett had never requested his presence as urgently as he had in the note Hughes still carried in his pocket. He pulled up just short of the front porch. Hughes was not even off the horse when a pair of slaves appeared out of nowhere to take the reins. Tate was right behind them, holding a torch.

"Is Bennett in his study?" asked Hughes as he dismounted.

"No. He's down in the shed."

"What's he doing there?"

"A little disciplining. Come with me."

The two men walked briskly. They passed the kitchen and then went between two rows of small buildings. Soon they descended into a small hollow. Hughes heard the groans before he saw the shed. The sound was jarring, and Hughes only recognized it as human because he had heard it before, on his own plantation. It was the animal noise of deep pain, a strange mix of moans and whimpers. Bennett shouted something, but the only words Hughes could make out were "betrayal" and "traitor." Then came the sound of a whip whooshing through the air and ripping into flesh, followed by a miserable yelp and more of Bennett's yells.

Tate halted outside the door. "Let's wait here a few minutes."

The shed was not a shed at all. That was just what everyone called it. It was actually one of the older buildings on the farm, a brick structure that had gone up decades earlier, when the first generation of Bennetts came to this place. It had been used for storing tools and other equipment until Bennett's father replaced it with some of the newer buildings closer to the manor. It had remained in disrepair ever since, even as it gained a new use: this was where Bennett and the overseers meted out punishments to slaves. If somebody on the Bennett plantation was "taken to the shed," it meant he was beaten here.

"Why is Bennett doing this himself?" asked Hughes.

"He's mighty upset about something," replied Tate. "I never thought I'd see him do this to Lucius."

"Lucius?" Hughes was stunned. "He likes that slave more than he likes a lot of white people."

"I don't think that's true anymore."

The door of the shed flew open, and Bennett stomped out. Inside, Hughes could see Lucius on his knees, with both wrists held above his head and chained to an iron ring mounted on a post. It almost looked as though he were genuflecting, except that he was obviously slumped over. He was breathing, so he was still alive. Yet his neck and back were streaked with blood. Hughes knew something of whippings, and this looked like a thorough one.

"What took you so long?" barked Bennett when he saw Hughes.

"Good evening to you too, Langston."

"We have a big problem here," snapped Bennett, ambling by Hughes and Tate and heading toward the house. The two younger men fell in beside him.

"What's the trouble?"

"Two of my slaves have run off, and they've got something we need. That turncoat Lucius told me everything."

Hughes waited for an explanation, but Bennett did not elaborate. They walked back to the manor. Bennett stopped in front of it.

"It is of the greatest urgency that we track down the two fugitives," said Bennett. He pointed at Tate. "You may do nothing more important for me during your employment here than this. In fact, if you succeed in this task, I will double your salary for the next three months."

"You can count on me," said Tate.

"Unfortunately, I'm afraid we don't have time to organize a whole party. The two of you will have to leave immediately."

"That shouldn't be a problem," said Tate.

"I didn't think so. Now, Mr. Tate, I would like a word with Mr. Hughes."

"I'll need a few minutes to get the dogs." The overseer hurried away.

"I'm confused," said Hughes. "What does this have to do with me?"

"The runaways—Portia and Big Joe—have a photograph of Mazorca in their possession."

"What?"

"You must get it back."

"Lucius told you this?"

"No. Somebody else told me. But Lucius confirmed it. He actually helped take the picture in Charleston, the day we met with Mazorca."

Hughes didn't reply. Bennett just glared at him, making sure Hughes understood what it meant: this trouble might have been avoided entirely but for the photography session that Hughes had arranged.

"How did he do it?" asked Hughes.

"The details hardly matter. Suffice it to say they have a photo, and we must get it back. I don't care if you catch them or kill them—just get that photo back."

"It's against the law to kill a slave."

Bennett shot him a nasty look. "Just get me that photo. I don't care how you do it."

"Are you certain that Portia and Big Joe are traveling together?"

"Yes. They're on horses headed for Charleston. Lucius says he doesn't know what they'll do when they reach the city—or if he does know, he isn't saying. But that's where they're going. That ought to give you enough information to find them."

For a moment, Hughes said nothing. He was thinking about Portia and his recent encounter with her.

"You mentioned Portia. Is she the one—?"

"Yes. She's the one you offered to purchase from me only two days ago. If you catch her, you can keep her and do with her as you please."

Hughes smiled. "I may very well do that."

Just then, Tate arrived with the dogs. Bennett's overseer was an experienced slave catcher. There were a few professionals in the area, and Bennett had hired them from time to time. But Tate was their equal on the chase. Hughes knew what he was doing too. He had once remarked to Bennett that chasing runaways was like a sport to him. "No other hunting compares to it," he had said. "I never grow bored with it, for the quarry has courage and cunning. Runaways are the most exciting game—the most dangerous game."

When they set off, Bennett walked into the manor and went to his study. He looked at the clock. It was a few minutes to midnight—much later than he liked to be awake. He sat down at his desk and took out a piece of stationery. He wrote in a clear cursive and left wide spaces between the lines.

> *April 19*
>
> *Dear Violet,*
>
> *Please accept my apologies for waiting so long to write since my last letter. The developments in Charleston have kept me busy. I am quite hopeful for the future, though.*
>
> *Do you remember Lucius, my old manservant? I'm sorry to report he has recently suffered a terrible bout of something—it's so hard to say what—and may not last the night. I will miss him so.*
>
> *Sincerely,*
> *Langston Bennett*

When Bennett finished composing these words, he put down his pen and ran his fingers along the left-hand side of his desk. They paused about halfway across and then pulled on something. It was a hidden compartment. Among the items Bennett removed from the little drawer was a tiny brass key. He set it on the edge of the desk. Next he touched up the letter he had just written, addressed an envelope to Violet Grenier in Washington, and sealed the letter inside. In the morning, he would order a rider to take it to the postmaster.

Then he took the small key and unlocked a drawer to his right, on the front of the desk. He put the key back in its hidden compartment and opened the drawer he had just unlocked. He reached inside and pulled out a pistol. He turned it in his hand and admired its design. Then he opened the chamber to confirm that it was loaded.

About ten minutes later, everybody on the Bennett plantation heard a single shot echo through the night. It came from the vicinity of the shed.

XI

Saturday, April 20, 1861

Mazorca had wanted to look inside the narrow brick house at 398 Sixteenth Street, but the pair of first-floor windows was too high off the ground and the shutters were closed anyway. If he had not known better, he might have assumed that the house was locked and abandoned, like so many others in Washington. But about an hour earlier he had watched its two occupants descend the steps and walk toward Lafayette Park. Mazorca then slipped into an alley about halfway down the block. A door in the back was locked, but a window next to it was not. Mazorca pulled himself through and began to inspect the three-story home.

Now that he was in, he wanted to look back out. He went to one of the tall windows on the front of the house, pushed the shutter slats open, and peeked through. A carriage rolled by on Sixteenth Street. Across the street sat St. John's Church, a yellow building with Doric columns. He glanced to his right, across Lafayette Park. Mazorca knew that President Lincoln's mansion lay within rifle range, at least for a very good marksman, but the angle from here was too severe to see much of it. It was not a good view.

Upstairs, he searched a library and several bedrooms. A curled-up cat slept on one of the beds. It looked surprised to see him, but not so alarmed that it failed to fall back asleep a few minutes later. Mazorca checked the view to the south from the windows on these top floors. As he expected, their lines of sight were no better.

In the library, stacks of correspondence indicated the woman living in the house was a prolific letter writer, or at least a person who received many letters in the mail. A large collection of maps suggested an interest in cartography, except that they were all local and many were marked. If there really was an interest, it was not academic.

Mazorca did not read any of the letters or study the maps. Instead he returned to the red-walled front parlor and sat down in the tête-à-tête, positioning himself in the part of the S-shaped couch that faced the doorway. The room did not let in much light with the shutters closed, so at first he just sat there. He did not want to turn on the gas lamp beside him.

Patience was a virtue in his line of work. The prospect of sitting in the parlor an hour or two did not bother him. He was only a few minutes into his wait, however, when he decided to reach for a pair of books resting on a table next to his seat. He had noticed them earlier, but their spines were turned away and he could not see their titles. Pulling them into his lap, he opened to their title pages: *A Treatise on Field Fortifications* by Dennis Hart Mahan and the first volume of *Infantry Tactics* by Winfield Scott.

He returned the Mahan book to its place and began to read the one by Scott. He hoped it might provide some insight into the mind of this legendary general, but the book was a dry text for military officers. Mazorca had an interest in these matters, however, and decided to pass the time with

Scott's thoughts on drills, maneuvers, and drum signals. He adjusted the book to catch what dim light came in from the shuttered window. As he flipped through its pages, however, his own thoughts kept drifting back to the question of why a woman—and one described to him as a socialite, no less— would choose to read the words of Mahan and Scott. It was a peculiar pursuit, even in these troubled times.

An hour later, Mazorca heard shoes scraping on steps outside the front door. He put the Scott book back on the table. A key scratched against a lock and found the keyhole. The door squeaked back on hinges that needed oiling. It let in a blinding light but was shut almost immediately. Mazorca could see clearly again in the shadowy room. Someone had entered. He watched her from just a few feet away. She was by herself and did not see him.

Grenier stood by the door and let her eyes adjust to the poor light. Mazorca could not tell when she first saw him. She did not jump in surprise or even flinch slightly. Instead, she just cocked her head to one side, trying to recognize the uninvited guest who sat cross-legged on her couch. Her composure was remarkable.

"Good morning, Mrs. Grenier."

"Do I know you?"

"We haven't met."

"You've chosen an odd way to make my acquaintance, sir."

"These are odd days, Mrs. Grenier."

"And you appear to be an odd man. I would like to know what you're doing in my house."

Mazorca rose from his seat slowly. He did not want to appear threatening, even though Grenier seemed unusually difficult to startle. From a pocket on the inside of his coat, he removed an envelope and held it out. "This may answer your question," he said.

She did not reach for it. She did not even look at it. Instead she simply stared at Mazorca as he stood with his arm outstretched. Then she took a couple of steps to his side. Her eyes roamed up and down. She noticed his ear but said nothing. She was taking his measure.

Grenier finally nodded at the envelope. "What is that?" she asked.

"A letter from a mutual friend."

"I have so many friends. Which one is also yours?"

"Langston Bennett of South Carolina."

Her eyebrows arched on hearing the name. She shifted her gaze from Mazorca to the envelope. "Langston Bennett is a great man," she said. "I will read the letter."

Grenier took the envelope and studied it. The flap was sealed shut. She opened the drawer to a small table and pulled out a letter knife. As she thrust it in a hole at one end of the envelope, she gave Mazorca a quick look. "Please, have a seat," she said, motioning to where her visitor had been sitting. Then she ripped open the envelope, unfolded the letter, and started reading. Mazorca already knew what it said. Before leaving Charleston he had steamed open the envelope, read the undated contents, and then resealed it.

> *My dear Violet,*
>
> *Some weeks ago I wrote to you about an important project, whose nature we need not mention here. The man bearing this letter will execute our plans. He is a stranger to Washington and may benefit from your intimate knowledge*

*of it. Please provide him with whatever assistance he seeks,
in the interest of our vital cause.*

*Yours most affectionately,
Langston*

Below the signature, the bottom of the letter was sheared off. Grenier set it down and left the room. Mazorca heard her open and shut a drawer. She came back with a small piece of paper in her hand. One of its edges was ripped. She held it beside the letter from Bennett. They matched perfectly. Grenier smiled and placed both pieces of the letter into the envelope.

"What is your name?" she asked with disarming sincerity.

"I'm called Mazorca," he said.

"It is a strange name. A little mysterious, too."

"No more strange and mysterious than a woman who reads books on infantry tactics and fortifications."

"They are in the front windows of all the bookstores."

"And ladies are buying them?"

"Last year I couldn't tell the difference between a flanking maneuver and a casement carriage. Now I'm able to carry on whole conversations with federal officers about their work. I'm able to learn things which I may then pass along to others who find such information useful."

"You sound like a spy."

For the first time since entering, Grenier smiled. It brought warmth to her features. "We all have our secrets," she said, circling around the tête-à-tête and sitting in the seat opposite Mazorca, even though the parlor contained several chairs. "Perhaps, like your name, it is something we best leave a bit mysterious. I am Violet Grenier, and I am pleased to make your acquaintance, Mazorca."

"Likewise. But I'm curious about something. An hour ago, two of you left this house, but only one of you returned."

"You've been watching me?" She sounded more flattered than offended. "That was Polly, who helps out around here. She has several hours off. I had thought that I would be alone in the house. Then you turned up."

She leaned toward Mazorca and touched his arm gently. Just by watching her look at him, Mazorca understood what Bennett meant when he called Grenier the most persuasive woman in Washington.

"Your ear is terribly scarred," she said. "What happened?"

"It's an old injury, acquired far from here during a disagreement."

"Something tells me that your adversary lost more than a piece of skin."

"He did not fare well."

Grenier smiled. "I have entertained presidents in this very spot," she whispered.

"What about the current one?"

She pulled away from him, as if the mere thought of Lincoln was physically repulsive. "No. Never. He is the Mammon of Unrighteousness. I believe this is a subject upon which Langston Bennett and I are in complete agreement."

"That would seem to be the case."

"And that is why I'm willing to help you," she said, drawing near again.

"I would appreciate it if you simply told me what you know about Lincoln and his circle."

"The abolitionists are pathetic. Because of them I cannot now look upon the Stars and Stripes and see anything but a symbol of murder, plunder, oppression, and shame."

Her face had twisted into a scowl, but the expression vanished just as quickly as it had appeared. "I certainly understand the importance of consorting with them," she continued. "I'm friendly with some—quite friendly, as a matter of fact. I receive detailed reports on cabinet meetings, troop movements, and the like. I'm often aware of what the president intends to do, and I know it before Congress or the newspapers do. It requires me to spend a considerable amount of time in the company of people whose opinions I find repellent. Yet it is all in the service of a cause greater than us. Wouldn't you agree, Mazorca?"

"It will serve your purposes and mine if you can share some of what you know with me, Mrs. Grenier."

She smiled sweetly and touched his arm again. "Please, call me Violet."

"What can you tell me about the president, Violet?"

"I will try to be objective," she said, taking a deep breath. "I have despised him ever since he came to prominence in those debates with Stephen Douglas, when they were campaigning for the Senate three years ago. He is a buffoon from the backwoods of the far frontier. Much of Washington and even many of his supposed friends consider him a coward—first for the way he sneaked into the city in the middle of the night before his inauguration, and then for taking the oath of office under armed guard. There are soldiers everywhere nowadays. We're used to seeing them in Washington, of course, but today they have a greater presence than ever before. The president wants more of them still.

Some of my friends say he is worried about an invasion from Virginia and Maryland. He should be, considering how his policies are driving half the states to secession. By preparing for war, however, he makes it impossible for people to believe he is a man of peace. I think he wants to assemble an abolitionist army and intends to rule the Southern states with an iron fist."

"How does he spend his time?"

"Mostly in the mansion. He has long lines of visitors seeking favors. There are cabinet meetings. You may have noticed that he has turned the place into a military camp, with those vile men from the West arriving just the other day."

"You mean Jim Lane's men?"

"Yes, they're the ones—and they're more evidence that Lincoln is yellow. If he really were a man of the people, why would he place so many soldiers between himself and the public?"

"Does he ever go out in public?"

"Not often. I actually haven't seen much of him."

"When he's out, does he have guards?"

"A few. He is less secure outside the White House than in it. He's often in a crowd, though. The man may never be alone. Yet there are fewer soldiers around him when he leaves the grounds of the mansion than when he stays inside its walls. I'm told that some of the officers on General Scott's staff are not pleased by this state of affairs. They believe the president is vulnerable in these moments. They are so worried about his life they would rather lock Lincoln in a bank vault than so much as let him peep out a window. I have this on exceedingly good authority."

"What does General Scott think?"

"General Scott!" she chuckled. "Have you seen him? He is the fattest man in the country. He's a traitor too. The other sons of Virginia are rallying to defend their homes, like Robert E. Lee. But fat Scott won't have anything to do with it. That would probably require him to get on a horse and ride south—but there's no horse that could support his bulk."

She laughed again and then turned serious. "Yet this is not what you asked me. I know Scott well—he has called on me here—and I know he is a spent man. His finest days are far behind him. He will do what Lincoln tells him to do, perhaps offer a few ideas, and little more. He certainly won't challenge any of his orders, as much as a few of the younger officers on his staff might like him to. There is a Colonel Rook who presses him to be more aggressive."

"Do you know Rook?"

"Rook is an enigma to me. Most of the officers in Washington always worry about their prospects. They pass up no opportunity to mingle with the cabinet and Congress. They would like to win favors as much as battles. It is a wonder they find any time at all to think about war and prepare for it. Yet Rook is not like them. He avoids society. I do not predict that his career will flourish."

"I'm less concerned about where he is in the future than what he's doing now."

"Of course. He may be a man to watch—and to beware. Scott put him in charge of the president's security, so it is Rook who was responsible for that extravagant military display at the inauguration. It is hard to believe, but he apparently thinks that Lincoln is under protected."

Grenier rose from the couch. "But enough about Rook. There is something I would like you to have, Mazorca," she said. She walked into the other parlor and returned with a key in her hand. "This was given to me by a friend who has left the city. It is to a home located at 1745 N Street. I am to look in on it occasionally while he is gone. He has not yet decided whether to sell or rent, though it is probably impossible to do either right now. You may use it as a safe house. Do not go there unless you must—it would appear odd if you were seen to be coming and going all the time—but also know it is there for you in a time of need."

She returned to her seat on the tête-à-tête and handed Mazorca the key. "I'm here for you too," she said in a low voice. "Let me know if there is anything you need." She leaned across the couch and kissed Mazorca lightly on the lips. "I mean anything."

A moment later, she led him upstairs.

* * *

Joe and Portia had never felt so tired. Two nights had passed since leaving the Bennett plantation. The physical effort was exhausting, and the nerve-wracking knowledge of what lay in store for them if they were caught only made matters worse.

Portia even found their general direction unsettling: all her life she had understood the promise of freedom lay to the north. In the night sky, she looked for the Big Dipper— or the Drinking Gourd, as she knew it—and spotted the two stars in that constellation that pointed toward the North Star. When she gazed up at the clear sky that first night, though, she realized she was heading the opposite way. This was intentional, of course: their destination was Charleston, which lay to the south. It just seemed unnatural.

She might have banished the thought from her mind if she and Joe had avoided simple blunders and made more progress. On their first night, however, a wrong turn had cost them a substantial amount of travel time. Neither Portia nor Joe was sure how far they had gone in those first hours, but they knew it was not far enough. At daybreak they retreated to the edge of an isolated meadow and ate most of their food. They tried to sleep, but it was a fitful effort for both of them. Their horses had wandered off. They could not take the risk of searching for them, so they would have to finish their journey on foot.

After the second night, the dim light of dawn had found them near a large plantation, where they observed a few field hands beginning their chores. Portia and Joe were not sure whether any of these slaves had spotted them, but they knew for certain that they had to find a new hideout for the day. A stand of trees rose about half a mile from the plantation, and they hustled into it. Leaves and branches concealed them from view.

"Do you think we're safe here?" asked Portia.

"Safer than if we were still on that road," replied Joe. "As soon as a white person sees us out there, we're done."

They were too anxious from their journey to sleep right away. They fed themselves from the small supplies of food that remained and cleared an area for lying down. This chore was just about finished when a dry branch cracked nearby. They looked toward the noise: a slave boy was coming toward them from the general direction of the plantation. He was perhaps thirteen or fourteen years old.

Joe pulled out his knife and went right for him. The big man was swift for his size. He raced forward, grabbed the boy by his collar, and threw him to the ground.

"Who're you?" he demanded, holding his knife in front of the boy's face.

The boy shook with fear. "Jeremiah," he said in a quivering voice. "My name's Jeremiah."

Joe patted Jeremiah's clothes to see if the boy carried weapons. There were none.

"Where you from, Jeremiah?"

"I live on the Stark plantation."

"Oh no!" said Portia.

Joe looked at her. "What's the matter?"

"I've heard of it before. We wanted to be at least this far after the first night."

Joe returned his attention to the slave lying on his back. "How far to Charleston?"

"I don't know."

"Don't mess with me, boy," said Joe, flashing the blade.

"I don't know. I ain't never been there."

"What should I do with him, Portia?"

"Don't say our names!" she scolded.

"Sorry."

"Let him up," she said.

Joe took a step back and signaled for Jeremiah to sit on a log.

"What're you doin' here?" she asked.

"Just lookin' around."

"What are you lookin' for?"

"I saw you comin' down the road this mornin'."

"So?"

"You seemed real nervous, the way you kept lookin' at Mr. Stark's house."

Portia forced a laugh. "And what makes you think we been nervous?"

Jeremiah did not answer immediately. Then he asked, "You're runaways, ain't you?"

"No, we ain't!"

"You got passes?"

"Yeah."

"Lemme see."

"No."

"I think you're runaways, and I wanna help you."

"You'd get yourself in big trouble for somethin' like that."

"Nobody knows I'm here."

"Were you the only one who saw us?"

"I don't know. I think so. Lemme show you a better hidin' spot than this."

Joe looked at Portia. She shrugged. "I say let's go," she said.

"OK," agreed Joe, who then turned to Jeremiah. "But if you try anything funny, boy, I'm gonna carve you up with this knife."

"Don't worry," said Jeremiah. "Just follow me."

A smooth-running creek ran about two hundred feet from where they started. It was so quiet Portia and Joe had not even known it was there. They paused for a moment to drink.

"We're going to walk in the water," said Jeremiah when they were done. "It will confuse the dogs."

Portia and Joe had not mentioned dogs to each other since leaving the Bennett plantation, but the topic was not far from their minds. Slave catchers always worked with dogs—fierce beasts the size of wolves. They were trained with meat. They would kill their quarry unless they were called off. Slaves feared the dogs far more than they feared the slave catchers. When a chase was coming to an end, it was common for runaways to consider the slave catchers not as their doom but as their salvation. They would do almost anything to keep from being mauled by the dogs.

As they waded down the knee-deep creek, Portia knew they were covering their scent. She also understood the dogs were smart enough to recognize this trick and patient enough to follow along both sides of a stream for long distances in order to pick up the smell again.

After a while, their creek ran into a slightly bigger one. Jeremiah turned into it and started heading upstream. "If the dogs come this way, they'll go downstream first," he said.

"How do you know your way around here?" asked Portia.

"This is where my brothers and I come lyin' out," he said. "We only do it for a couple of days at a time. But we ain't been caught yet."

"Ain't you whipped for that?"

"Not enough to stop us from doin' it again."

They walked upstream for a few minutes. Suddenly Jeremiah stopped. There was a high bank on one side of the creek. "There's a hollow behind there," he said, pointing. "Anybody lookin' for you is gonna be comin' from the stream or the main road." He indicated the direction of the road, on the side of the stream opposite the bank. "You'll see 'em before they see you—and you'll hear 'em before that."

"This is kind of you," said Portia. "Have you helped others like this before?"

"Yes."

"They been caught?" asked Joe.

"I'm two for five," said the boy, with a big smile. "Five times I've helped, and two times they've gotten away from here without being found out."

"That makes you more of a failure than a success," said Joe.

"It's not always my fault," protested Jeremiah. "One time the people I helped stayed here at night and they were dumb enough to light a fire. They got caught."

"The runaways that weren't caught—what made them different?" asked Portia.

"They were smart."

"How were they smart?"

"They traveled alone."

Portia looked at Joe.

"That's one reason I want you to succeed," said Jeremiah, oblivious to the effect of his words. "I want you to be the first group I've helped get through."

"We'll try not to let you down," said Portia.

"You hungry?"

"As a matter of fact, we are."

"Then I'll go now and bring some food. I may be an hour or two, but I'll be back." Jeremiah splashed into the stream, crossed it, and then ran into the trees.

"You're right about one thing: if we can't trust him, we're done," said Joe. "It just seems to me there was one way of makin' sure he doesn't tell anybody about us."

"Joe!" said Portia. She wanted to think they had found a friend.

"Our lives are at stake, Portia."

She frowned. "I think we can trust him—or else why would he have led us here?"

"I hope you're right."

Joe picked up a skipping stone and whisked it into the stream. It bounced three times and sank. He tossed a few more without better results. Then he and Portia decided to rest. They would need to save their energy. They would leave again at dark, whether or not Jeremiah returned.

* * *

As he approached Lafayette Park, Springfield yawned. He wanted a cup of coffee. Across the park, about a city block away, was Grenier's home on Sixteenth Street. When it came into view, he did not expect to see anything. To his surprise, the door opened and a man stepped out.

Springfield looked away quickly. He was in uniform for a change and did not want to be seen staring, even from a distance. He slowed his pace and strained to keep the man in his peripheral vision. Was it one of the fellows from yesterday? Springfield hoped so, if for no other reason than it would provide him with new information for Rook.

Grenier's visitor walked in the same direction as Springfield, but on H Street, which bounded the park on its north side. As the man reached the edge of the park, where it touched Vermont Avenue, Springfield shifted into pursuit. He remained about half a block behind the man, who stayed on H Street as he passed Fifteenth Street, Fourteenth, Thirteenth, and kept going.

Seeing the man only from behind, Springfield could not get a good view of him—except to become certain that he was not one of those who had visited Grenier a day earlier. He was sandy haired and clean shaven. To get a better view, Springfield walked to catch up and soon was about twenty feet behind the man. He crossed Twelfth Street, Eleventh, and Tenth at a steady pace. At Eighth Street, he turned his head, and Springfield saw the man's face in profile. He did not recognize it, but he knew he would not forget it: the man's right ear was half missing.

Grenier's visitor kept moving, now across Seventh Street. Before arriving at Sixth Street, however, he slowed down and entered a building on his right. Springfield had dropped back from his closest approach and could not tell what it was. He lingered at the corner of Seventh and H Street, waiting to see if the man would come out again. After about five minutes, Springfield decided to proceed down H Street. He made certain to note the building in question. It was a boardinghouse, addressed 604 H Street.

At Sixth Street, Springfield turned to the right and took about a dozen steps before stopping. The boardinghouse was around the corner and out of sight. He thought about what to do next. Rook had wanted to meet near Brown's, but should he stick around, trying to learn more about Grenier's guest?

It occurred to him that the only reason this new visitor to the Grenier residence intrigued him was the fact that yesterday she had received different visitors whom Rook had regarded as potentially significant. Was there any connection between the two? He had no basis for thinking so.

He walked south on Sixth Street, in the direction of Pennsylvania Avenue. On the way, Springfield thought about coffee.

* * *

It was late afternoon when the sound of Jeremiah wading through the stream woke Portia and Joe. He arrived with a pot of stew in a satchel. He sat as they ate, and then he cleaned the pot in the stream.

"I've got one more thing for you," he said. "Grave dust."

Portia and Joe knew immediately what he was talking about. Some slaves believed that wiping feet with cemetery soil—grave dust—removed all traces of scent and made it impossible for dogs or trackers to continue a search. The runaways watched Jeremiah pull a bag from the satchel. It was full of dry, gray dirt.

Joe looked at Portia. "Do you believe in this?"

"One time I asked my grandfather if ghosts were real."

"What did he say?"

"He said, 'Don't pretend that such things can't be.'"

Portia took a handful of grave dust and wiped it on her feet and legs. She smiled at Joe, who was not sure whether she was doing this for their benefit or Jeremiah's. The boy certainly seemed to view the grave dust with great seriousness. He had saved it for last—after leading them to the hideout, after giving them food. It was his parting gift. Joe thought that perhaps he should take some just as a courtesy.

Suddenly in the distance, the three slaves heard a sound that made them shiver: barking.

"Well, I'm ready to become a believer," said Joe, reaching for the bag of grave dust. "We're gonna need all the help we can get."

* * *

When Rook wanted to concentrate on a difficult problem, he liked to go for a stroll—not to a quiet place, but a noisy one. For whatever reason, the commotion of a crowd encouraged fresh thinking. And so he found himself at Center Market, the busiest commercial hub in the city. It was a sprawling structure that took up two entire blocks on the south side of Pennsylvania Avenue between Seventh and Ninth streets. Farmers and fishermen from across the region descended on it every morning before sunrise to sell their wares. Rook walked beside dozens of wagon stands outside the building, only half aware of the salesmen shouting their prices and the customers who haggled with them.

It did not hurt that Center Market was near Brown's Hotel—the site of the puzzle that had vexed him since the previous afternoon, and where Springfield and Clark were monitoring Davis and Stephens. *Not by rail, river, or road.* What could it possibly mean?

Rook wandered down the market's crowded aisles, trying to ignore the overpowering stench of fish that came from the stalls piled high with bass and shad from the Potomac. Sellers stocked all kinds of food—venison, ducks, turkeys, oysters, and lots of vegetables—but the smell of fish drifted through the whole building.

He wondered whether he was right to defy Scott's orders. In a strict military sense, of course, he was in the wrong—it was always wrong to disobey a direct order from a superior officer. Yet Rook was convinced that Scott's judgment was mistaken. It bordered on dereliction of duty. The old general simply did not take the president's protection as seriously as he should. Rook was certain Davis and Stephens were up to something. He could not prove it in a court of law or to the satisfaction of Scott, but he had no doubt.

Reaching the end of a row of wagon stands, Rook found himself at Seventh Street—and with a clear view of Brown's Hotel. A horse-drawn omnibus waited outside the hotel as it took on several passengers. This was a popular form of transportation up and down the Avenue, between Capitol Hill and Georgetown. When the horse started pulling, Rook made a sharp right-hand turn into Center Market itself, where nobody on the street would be able to spot him.

Not by rail, river, or road. Didn't Davis mention a "shipment"? He might have used a different word, such as "load" or "delivery" or "consignment." But he said *ship*ment. That would suggest a cargo arriving on a ship, which meant over water, which meant by river. Yet Davis seemed to rule out that possibility. Rook told himself not to get snared in semantic games. Shipments might mean anything, even goods transported by train. He started to wonder. Maybe Davis and Stephens were playing games with him. Perhaps Scott was right, and it was all just a waste of time.

At the rear of the market, where a number of the seafood sellers kept their stalls, Rook found himself watching an old man train a boy in the art of fish cleaning—chopping off the head and fins, removing the guts, scraping the scales. It reminded him of a similar lesson his grandfather had taught him many years earlier. He watched with amusement as the boy struggled to perform the sloppy chore his employer could complete in a matter of seconds.

Not by rail, river, or road. The riddle forced its way back into his thoughts. Was there a way the shipment could arrive by land but not by road? Suddenly, a shout caught his attention.

"Colonel!"

Rook saw Springfield trotting toward him from the front of the building.

"What's the news, Sergeant?"

"Davis and Stephens boarded an omnibus a few minutes ago. Corporal Clark got on with them."

"Do we know where they're going?"

"They were headed toward Georgetown."

"I don't suppose you were able to communicate with Clark."

"Actually, I was. He nodded to me, very faintly—and he did not give the signal that he needed anybody to trail behind. I assume he's just going to follow them around. We'll get a report when he returns."

"If we had more men assigned to this operation, we would be able to send a whole team after them."

"At least one man is better than none."

"True. Perhaps Clark will come back with more information. I just can't get Davis and Stephens out of my mind. They are an enigma."

"What do you mean, sir?"

"This business about rails, rivers, and roads confounds me. How can something possibly arrive here if it doesn't come by rail, river, or road?"

"It's quite a riddle, sir. In a lot of other cities, it wouldn't be much of a problem. But here it's a stumper."

Rook arched his eyebrows. "What do you mean?"

"I was thinking about this. Most of the cities on the East Coast aren't on rivers, or at least not ones that link them to the rest of the world. They're beside harbors or bays or other bodies of water. Boats come and go without ever touching rivers. Give me that same riddle in New York or Baltimore and the answer is easy—so easy it isn't even a riddle."

"That had not occurred to me," said Rook. "Of course, it's academic."

"Right. In this city, a boat must come up the river to get here."

Something in that sentence caught Rook's ear. He repeated it in his mind: A boat has to come *up* the river to get here. "The same thing is not true in some other cities," he said.

"What do you mean?"

"Take a place like New York City," offered Rook. "You're right that most of its water traffic comes from the harbor. Not all of it, though. Some actually comes *down* the Hudson River. So lots of boats must reach that city by river—they come not from the ocean, but the interior of the country."

"I suppose that's correct."

"But it's academic too. The Potomac is not navigable much past Georgetown. Even if it were, it would still be a river—and we would be no nearer to solving this riddle."

Their conversation sputtered to a halt. They looked at the two fish cleaners, the old teacher and his young student. They had just created a stack of filets. A mound of leftover fish parts sat in front of them.

"Customers don't want to see that," said the man, pointing to the heap of heads and guts. "We need to get it out of sight." He pushed the mess into a bucket with his knife. "This is full," he said, grabbing the bucket's handle and giving it to the boy. "Carry it around back."

The youngster took the bucket and left the stall. He passed in front of Rook and Springfield and walked through an open door. Sunlight fell on his head. He stopped in plain sight of the two soldiers, lifted the bucket, and dumped its contents, which splashed beneath his feet. Then the boy turned around and came back in, swinging his empty bucket.

"Do you have the same thought as me?" asked Rook.

Now it was Springfield who arched his eyebrows.

"Let's go!"

* * *

The dogs were getting closer.

Portia and Joe splashed down the stream, running with the current. They moved as quickly as they could. "Don't let your feet touch the bank on either side," warned Portia. The temptation to get out was strong. The water sucked at their heels with each step, making their run twice as strenuous as it would be on dry land. Yet the barking propelled them forward. Each yap was like the prick of a spur.

Jeremiah was still with them, but they knew he would not be for long. "Get in the water," he had yelled when they first heard the dogs. Portia had lost all track of time. Had their run started five minutes ago—or half an hour ago? She wasn't sure and didn't care. All she wanted was to get away from the dogs. The little brook seemed their single hope—the only thing that might cover their scent and keep them free just a little bit longer.

They could not tell how much ground lay between them and their pursuers. The trees and rocks played tricks with the sound and made it impossible to know. For a time, Portia had thought they might actually get away. The barking remained faint. Then it erupted. Then it stopped completely. For a while they heard nothing. The slaves even stopped racing at one point to listen, and the only sound they heard came from the trickling water of the creek. Portia's hopes rose, only to crash minutes later when the barking started again—and grew steadily louder. "They must've paused at our hideout," panted Joe.

When they reached a small meadow perhaps half a mile later, Jeremiah halted them. "This is where we gotta split up," he said. "You gotta go your way, and I gotta go mine. There's nothin' more I can do for you."

"You gotta promise not to say nothing about us," said Portia.

"I ain't gonna do that. If I did, everybody would know I helped you. I'm gonna say that I ain't never seen you."

"OK, and we won't say nothin' about you if we're caught."

"Here's what you gotta do: keep runnin' down the stream. After a while, get out and rush away as fast as you can. Don't leave no footprints in the mud. If we're lucky, the dogs can't smell us now—they're runnin' along the banks trying to pick up a trail they've lost. You gotta hope they miss you and keep on going. Then you can get back on the road tonight."

Somewhere behind them, the barking continued.

Jeremiah looked over his shoulder. "No more time for talk," he said. "Good-bye." He leaped out of the water onto a log. He walked its length away from the creek and took a big jump into the woods. Then he was gone. Portia looked intently but could see no physical evidence of Jeremiah having left the creek.

"I guess that's how it's done," said Joe.

The two slaves resumed their flight. For a while, the dogs did not seem to gain on them. Then the barking became noticeably louder. Suddenly Portia stopped. Joe nearly collided into her.

"We gotta do something," she gasped.

"They're gonna be at least a few minutes behind us. We should keep runnin'. No time for restin'."

"If we keep runnin', they're gonna catch us. We gotta get away from the river. We gotta make a move."

Joe saw Portia looking at a tree that had fallen into the streambed. Once it had stood tall, and now it lay long. The trunk had cracked near its base, but somehow the tree remained alive. Several young branches reached upward.

"OK, we'll do it here," said Joe. "Jeremiah left on a log. That's what we'll do."

Portia put a foot on the tree and was about to lift herself up when Joe stopped her.

"There's one thing I gotta ask you, and I'm only gonna do it once," he said. "Those dogs are bad news if they're set loose. I don't wanna see you hurt by one of them. We can still give ourselves up and make sure that doesn't happen."

"No way, Joe. They're gonna have to catch us."

"All right then," he said, helping her onto the trunk.

A moment later, they were both out of the water and darting through the woods.

* * *

Rook and Springfield sprinted out of Center Market and to the Winder Building. Ten blocks later, they arrived short of breath. "I hope this is worth it," huffed Rook as they waited for a private to retrieve their horses. "If their shipment isn't coming by rail, river, or road, then it must be coming by that canal."

"The Chesapeake and Ohio Canal."

"That's right. Washington gets almost all of its coal from barges on the C&O, plus lots of grain and lumber."

"What if Davis and Stephens are just picking up a few sacks of coal?" asked Springfield.

"I can't believe that's what they're doing. It must be something else. Maybe they have a shipment of guns coming in. The canal goes right by Harper's Ferry and the federal armory there."

"Didn't I hear something about Harper's Ferry?"

"Virginia troops seized control of it yesterday. Davis and Stephens would have needed some kind of collaborator up there a couple of days before that, assuming they are in fact carrying weapons down from Harper's Ferry."

"It would certainly explain why they're being so secretive. Maybe they're trying to arm rebels in the city, thinking they can pitch in if Virginia marches on Washington next."

The private emerged from the rear of the building, leading both horses over to Rook and Springfield.

"The only thing it doesn't explain is their 'scouting mission' of the Capitol," said Rook as he and Springfield mounted. "If Davis and Stephens were trying to arm an underground militia, why would they roam around the Capitol and ask about where to make food deliveries?"

"They could be planning an assault and wanted to become familiar with the building's layout and see where the soldiers were staying. They might have been counting soldiers too. The questions about food may have been their excuse for being there."

"I think there's more to it. I just don't know what."

Borne by their horses, they started north on Seventeenth Street, turned left on the Avenue, and took it to M Street. There they crossed the bridge over Rock Creek. Georgetown was on the other side. The busy thoroughfare of Bridge Street lay before them. As they passed an omnibus heading in the opposite direction, Rook slowed his horse and signaled Springfield to do the same.

"Let's not call attention to ourselves," said the colonel, speaking over the sound of hooves as they clattered against the hard surface of the bridge. "How far do you figure we're behind them?"

"Fifteen minutes or so."

The two soldiers rode a couple of blocks into Georgetown, dismounted, and tied their mounts to a post beside a store. Then they walked south on one of the streets intersecting Bridge. In a minute, they reached the end of the C&O Canal, the terminal point of a commercial waterway that began almost two hundred miles upstream.

At least a dozen wooden boats rested there, all of them remarkably similar in appearance. They were long, low, and narrow—more barge than boat. They did not move by mast or paddle but by mules that pulled on ropes from a towpath. At the stern of each boat was a rudder and small cabin, with steps leading down to a galley. On the opposite end, a shed housed the off-duty mules. In the middle, flat boards covered the hatch and took up most of the length of the boat.

Rook and Springfield studied the canal boats from the side of a building where they had a full view of the area but remained mostly out of sight. They saw every degree of activity, from boats where eight or nine men hurried to unload a cargo to a few that appeared empty. On one boat, children wore chain tethers as they pranced on top of the hatch covers. On another, a woman removed laundry pinned to a line stretching from one end of the boat to the other.

"There's one of them," said Rook. "It's Stephens."

About a hundred feet away, the wiry little man paced back and forth. He could not have been more than an inch or two above five feet tall. In the cabin of the boat behind him, Davis waved his arms and yelled something, as if he were in a bitter argument. Rook could hear his voice but was not able to make out the words except to sense they were full of anger. There were two other men in the cabin, but neither of them seemed to be the target of Davis's fury.

"I see Davis and two other men—they could be Mallory and Toombs, the men who left the other day," said Rook, pointing to the boat. He spoke in a low voice, even though there was no chance he could be overheard. "I wonder where Corporal Clark is."

Suddenly Davis broke off his tirade. He took a step to the left and Rook had his answer: Clark was sitting down, his face blank. Davis said something and the two others grabbed Clark by the arms, stood him up, and spun him around. Rook thought he saw them bind Clark's wrists behind his back just before they shoved him down a set of steps leading into the galley.

When Clark disappeared, the two soldiers pulled out of view entirely.

"They've got Clark below the cabin, and it looks like he's a captive," said Rook. "Davis, Mallory, and Toombs are still on the barge, and Stephens is on lookout right beside it."

"If there are others, they're in the galley."

"That could be, but there can't be much room down there."

"Did you see the cargo?"

"No. Whatever it is, it's in the hatch and not visible."

Springfield moved to the edge of the building and peeked around the corner. When he came back, he saw Rook examining a pistol. It was a Colt Army Model 1860 revolver, a .44-caliber gun with an octagonal barrel nearly eight inches long. Rook opened the chamber to make sure it was fully loaded. All six bullets were there. Satisfied, he put the pistol back in his belt. He looked at Springfield and gestured to the sergeant's holster. "You may want to make sure everything's in order," said the colonel. "I want to end this right now."

"It's two against four—maybe more," said Springfield. "Shouldn't we get some help?"

It was a smart question. Yet involving more men would mean involving Scott. Rook knew that would be a mistake. "I'm not sure we have time to call for assistance," he said. "Clark's in there and we have to help him. They may have taken him below for something worse than an interrogation."

"Very well."

"Give me five minutes, then walk up to Stephens," said Rook. "Engage in small talk. I'm going to circle around and try to get on that boat. Don't let Stephens see me, and be ready for action."

Rook went up the block toward Bridge Street and worked his way back to the canal from another alleyway. He looked at the boat holding Clark, this time from the opposite direction, where he had a better view of its stern. Davis leaned on the rudder and glared into the galley but did not move. Stephens continued to stand alongside the boat. Between Rook and these two men was another boat, and it did not appear to have anybody on board.

A team of mules sauntered by, and Rook fell behind them. He walked in a crouch toward the deserted boat. When he was right next to it, he hopped on board. An empty mule shed at the other end of the boat kept him from seeing Davis, but had a clear view of Stephens. The little man did not appear to have noticed him. His eyes instead were locked on Springfield, who now strolled toward the Southerner from the other way.

"Hello?" A voice from the galley startled Rook. The colonel reached for his gun as he heard a foot hit the steps leading upward. "Weaver? Is that you?"

A black-haired man in a white shirt and brown trousers came up from the galley. "Hello?" he said again. Suddenly he stopped, seeing Rook squatted down and pointing a pistol at him. The man raised his hands above his head, and Rook put a finger to his lips. The man froze in place, but his eyes shifted to his right and down. Rook followed the man's gaze to a rifle leaning against the wall of the boat's cabin. Rook knew he had to act quickly.

"Are you for Union?" whispered Rook.

The man nodded. Rook weighed his options. He assumed the man was from western Maryland because that was where so many of the canal workers came from. The C&O Canal cut right through their territory. The people of western Maryland generally were unionists, and many of them supported the Lincoln administration even though they lived in a slave state.

"Then in the name of the Union, either get back down in the galley or take your rifle and come with me," said Rook, rising to a full stand. He was glad to be in uniform—he thought it would help win the man's confidence.

The man thought for a few seconds and then picked up his gun. "My name is Higginson," he said, holding out his hand. Rook grasped it and introduced himself.

"We have a potentially dangerous situation here," he said. "A man's life may be at stake."

"Just tell me what to do," said Higginson.

"Is there anybody else on board?"

"No. We unloaded this morning, and everybody's gone for the afternoon."

"Very well. Then it's you and me. I'm hoping that we won't need to fire these guns, but I'm certain we'll have to show them."

A minute later, they scrambled the length of the boat, each in an awkward hunch. Reaching the mule shed, they remained in a stoop and paused. Rook could hear Springfield talking to Stephens.

"...so as I was saying, I've always been fascinated by how the locks work on the canal. It's really ingenious how you fellows get up, down, and around the rapids and falls."

Then Rook heard another voice, coming from the cabin. "Is there a problem here, Officer?"

It was Davis. Rook could not see him, but he pictured the scene: Stephens and Springfield on the edge of the canal, Davis looking at them, and two others below with Clark. With the collaborators separated and distracted, now was a good time to strike, he thought.

Rook drew his gun and looked at Higginson. "Ready?" he asked in a whisper.

Higginson gripped his rifle. He looked nervous but nodded. "Let's do it."

Both men hopped onto the roof of the mule shed. Rook now had a plain view of Davis. There was a gap of about seven or eight feet between the end of Higginson's barge and the start of Davis's. Rook took a few steps and hurtled himself across, crashing into Davis. The big man slammed into the floor of the cabin. He took a bad blow to the head. Rook fell down too, but he regained his balance quickly and stuck his gun in Davis's face. The commotion caused Stephens to turn around, which forced his attention away from Springfield just as the sergeant shoved him into the canal. Higginson remained standing on the mule shed of his boat, with his gun trained on the steps leading into the galley.

As Stephens thrashed around in the water—"I can't swim!" he hollered—Springfield boarded the boat. Rook pointed to Davis. "Guard him," he ordered. Then the colonel ran to the galley steps. Mallory was starting to climb them from below, but Rook kicked him in the face, knocking him backward.

The colonel scurried into the galley. It was small and dark, but he saw Clark sitting in a corner with Toombs hovering over him. "Hands up," shouted Rook, pointing his gun. The man obeyed. The whole encounter, starting with Rook leaping onto the boat, had lasted about fifteen seconds.

* * *

"The dogs have found something," said Tate, holding the end of a long leash.

"I think we're getting close," said Hughes.

The overseer knew the fugitives were nearby—the marks in the mud along the riverbank about half a mile back, where Portia and Joe apparently had rested, were fresh. The dogs had become ecstatic when they stumbled on that spot too. But then they fell silent and prowled around for a scent that suddenly had gone dead.

Tate suspected that the dogs' barking had warned the runaways, who then raced into the creek. There was no way to tell whether they had gone upstream or downstream, though. Downstream seemed the likelier path, because upstream led to the plantation he and Hughes had seen from the road. So they set off downstream, leaving behind their own horses, which were too big to be of much use in the forest. Ahead of them on leashes, a dog raced along each side of the creek checking for the right smell.

One of the hounds stopped at a log beside the stream and yapped with excitement. The other splattered across the water to join it. Both sniffed at the fallen tree with great care, pacing up and down its length several times.

To Tate, the dogs appeared hesitant. If the scent of a slave led out of the stream, they would take it. If it did not, then they would continue following the flow of the water in the hope of picking it up soon. Yet they appeared torn between these two choices.

"Why do they seem so confused?" asked Hughes as the dogs continued investigating the log.

"I don't know," said Tate. "If these were younger dogs, I'd say a fox was distracting them. But these two are experienced. They're onto something, and they don't know what to make of it."

One dog finally moved away from the log and into the woods. It had only gone about ten feet, however, when it turned around and barked. Its companion did not follow. Instead, it jogged back to the bank of the stream, pointed its snout in the direction they had been traveling, and barked a reply.

"They're having a disagreement," said Tate. "One wants to go into the trees and the other wants to stay with the stream."

"Then it's obvious what has happened," said Hughes. "The slaves have split up. They must have panicked. I suggest we split up as well. You go into the woods because that's where your dog wants to go, and I'll follow the creek. We'll have them soon!"

"I'm not so sure. It might make more sense to stay together—to catch one, and then the other."

"Nonsense," said Hughes. "It could take a couple of hours to track down just one of them. By then we would have allowed the gap between us and the other runaway to widen. I want to get them both, Tate. This is not a suggestion—it's an order."

Tate scowled at that comment. He did not care for orders coming from someone other than Bennett, though he understood Hughes to be Bennett's man on this chase. Why had Bennett insisted that Hughes join him on this jaunt? He had spent the early part of their pursuit wishing one of the other overseers was with him instead.

"Very well," Tate said at last, and he crashed into the trees.

Hughes watched him go. The man was good, he had to admit, even if there was a whiff of insubordination about him. Splitting up was the right thing to do, though. Capturing just one of the slaves rather than both was not necessarily half a success—it might very well be a total failure. What he needed was that picture. Only one of them could have it. Or perhaps each of them carried a copy. Whatever the case, Hughes knew he had to find both Portia and Joe. There was no other way to be sure an image of Mazorca did not fall into the wrong hands.

He continued down the stream, letting his dog dart from side to side. The animal had picked up the pace a bit. It sensed that success was at hand, and so did Hughes.

About twenty minutes after leaving Tate, Hughes and his dog came upon another big tree that had fallen into the creek. It lay horizontal but was not dead. Branches reached upward for the sun.

The animal let out a yelp and looked back at Hughes. It seemed eager to rush into the woods. When Hughes did not respond immediately, the dog issued a torrent of barks. "So you think it's time, do you, boy?" said Hughes, unhooking the long leash. The dog did not budge, but Hughes could see the excitement in its eyes. He smiled. "Get 'em!" he snapped, and the dog zipped into the trees.

Hughes examined the young branches on the fallen tree and noticed that one of them had cracked near its base. Beneath the bark, the wood was pale yellow. This was a fresh wound. Somebody had stepped on the tree.

Hughes could not match the dog's speed, but he followed its barking. He half expected Portia or Joe to run his way begging for deliverance from the sharp fangs and claws of a fierce dog whose first instinct was to cripple its prey. The young man walked up a small rise and along the edge of an open field, always following the sound of the dog. When he reentered the woods, he heard the barking grow more intense. It probably meant that the dog had spotted a slave. Hughes jogged in the direction of the noise.

In a couple of minutes, he was there. His dog was running in circles and barking like mad at the foot of a tree. About eight feet off the ground, on a low-lying limb, quivered Portia. She kept her eyes locked on the dog. She was paralyzed by fear.

Hughes could not keep from smiling. "Hello, my dear."

* * *

A few minutes later, everyone was gathered in the cabin. Davis held his head in his hands, still dizzy from being bowled over; Stephens, having been yanked out of the water by Springfield, was soaked and coughing. Mallory held a towel to his bloody nose. Toombs was unscathed but twitched with nervousness. They were all disarmed and sitting. Higginson continued to watch over them from his boat. Clark described how he had followed Davis and the others from the hotel but was recognized and forced on board the boat at gunpoint.

"What's the cargo?" asked Rook.

"I don't know," said Clark.

"Let's find out."

Rook and Springfield left the cabin and removed the hatch cover closest to them. Below it was a pile of coal. They yanked off the next cover, with the same result. Removing the third panel exposed even more of the stuff.

"This doesn't look good," muttered Springfield.

"We're not done yet," said Rook.

One by one they tore off the hatch covers, always finding coal beneath. Finally, with just two panels remaining, they discovered something else: a dozen wooden kegs.

"What do you suppose that is?" asked Springfield.

"I have an idea," said Rook. "Wait here." The colonel went back to the cabin and found a hatchet. When he returned, he broke open the top of the keg. Black powder spilled out.

Rook examined the other kegs and searched between them. When he saw what he was looking for, he reached down and pulled up a white coil of string. He set it on top of a keg and hacked it in half. A fine black powder poured out of the string too.

"Do you know what this is?" asked Rook.

"No."

"It's a fuse. These kegs are full of blasting powder."

* * *

Hughes whistled loudly, silencing the dog and compelling it to sit still. He thought that Portia would be relieved to see him, but instead she seemed to panic. She grabbed a branch above her head and prepared to pull herself higher into the tree.

"You should be happy to see me, Portia," he said. "I'm the only thing that stands between you and this vicious creature Mr. Bennett forced me to take along on our little romp in the woods."

Portia spit in his direction. A big dollop of dribble landed on his forehead.

Hughes was stunned by her act. Why did she refuse to come down? He removed a handkerchief from his pocket and wiped his brow.

"This is silly, Portia. I mean you no harm. I merely want to take you back home, where you belong."

Portia frowned. "Get away from me," she said and then spit again. This time Hughes was ready and her aim not as good. The projectile landed on the ground near his feet. The dog, still sitting at attention, growled.

"Really, Portia. I'm sorry it has to come to this, but you leave me little choice," said Hughes, pulling a pistol from his holster. "Come down right now, or I will use this, as much as I would regret doing so."

Portia did not move immediately. Her alternatives were few. She could climb higher, but that would not stop Hughes from shooting her. Jumping at him did not seem like a good idea either—she was more likely to break her own bones than to hurt him. She scanned the other trees nearby but saw nothing to encourage her. Only one option made sense. She remembered something her grandfather once told her:

When you don't have a choice, you don't have a problem. That was a bleak bit of advice, but it seemed that surrender probably was her only real choice. She eased herself down from the branch. A minute later she was on the ground. Hughes put his gun back into his belt, and Portia turned to face her pursuer.

The dog rose to its feet. It was on her left. She glanced at it nervously, and Hughes let the animal frighten her for a moment. "Back off," he said finally, and the dog sat down again. It continued to stare at her, though.

"I don't know why you're trying to avoid me, Portia," said Hughes. "I want to be your friend. I think you would like me if you simply tried."

He stepped toward her. She might have taken a step away, except her back was already to the tree trunk.

"I can be good to you."

Hughes now stood directly in front of her. He caressed her cheek with the tips of his fingers. "Very, very good to you." Portia closed her eyes. Hughes brushed his hand against her neck. She swallowed hard. He moved his hand lower and cupped one of her breasts, feeling its curve and sensing its mass through her shirt. He massaged it lightly. The sensation aroused him. He lowered his hand again, keeping his eyes on her face. She was gorgeous. He had noticed this before, of course, but the difference between recalling her features in his mind and actually seeing them—and touching them—was enormous. He wanted her badly. Hughes hoped that she would not resist.

Portia opened her eyes, and Hughes saw the hatred. He wanted her to want him, but he wanted something else more, and so he just returned the gaze with a blank expression. She broke away from it a moment later, though, and glanced to her right. Hughes heard a commotion nearby and turned his head just in time to see Joe lunging at him with a knife. He must have been hiding behind a tree, Hughes realized—though he barely had time to complete the thought.

The big slave slammed into Hughes, driving his blade deep into the white man's shoulder as they both tumbled to the ground. Hughes fell flat on his back and let out a terrible groan. Blood began to soak his shirt immediately. Joe ripped out the knife and jumped to his feet. He was preparing to thrust it again when the dog hurtled toward him. Joe raised his arm to block the animal. Its teeth clenched his forearm with the strength of a vise. Its claws raked Joe's body. Joe managed to force his arm through this thicket of legs and drive the knife into the dog's abdomen. It released his arm and howled. On its way down, Joe slashed upward and sliced its jugular. The dog was dead before it even hit the dirt.

Joe paused long enough to make sure the dog did not move, and then he stepped toward Hughes, still lying on the ground. Just as he was about to lean in and deliver a fatal blow, Hughes rolled to his side and pulled a pistol from his holster. He fired a single shot into Joe's chest.

Portia screamed at the blast. The force of the impact knocked Joe backward. He tripped over an exposed root and fell—a sudden drop that caused Hughes's next shot to miss. Now Joe lay prone on the ground, and Hughes stood up, but with difficulty. His left arm was lame from the wound to his shoulder. He struggled to remain steady and looked down at the large and growing red stain on his shirt. Then

Hughes turned his attention to Joe, lying motionless nearby. He hobbled over to the slave and pointed his gun.

"Don't shoot! Oh please, don't shoot him!" cried Portia, who had barely moved since coming down from the tree.

Hughes looked at her. She could see that he was not all there. His eyes were bleary and his face was pale. His lips moved as if he wanted to say something, but no words came out. Then he collapsed, falling to the ground just a few feet from Joe.

Portia did not move for a moment. After the earsplitting fury, the ensuing silence was eerie. Not even the birds chirped. She looked at the two bodies in front of her. She saw that the chests of both men rose and fell. They were alive.

At the thought of Joe breathing his last, she rushed over to him. The wound to his chest was enormous. It appeared fatal. That was obvious even to someone like Portia, who had never seen a deadly gunshot wound before. When she touched his face, though, his eyes opened and the corners of his mouth tried to curl into a smile. "Portia," he whispered.

"Joe! Don't leave me! You can't leave me!" she wailed, tears dripping down her cheeks. She started to sob.

"Portia…"

The effort to speak even these two syllables was an enormous strain. Portia gasped when he closed his eyes. Was this the end? He opened them again and seemed to summon all that was left in his failing body to utter a single word. "Go."

Portia moaned and raised her head to the sky. "Why? Why? Why?" she pleaded. She looked back at Joe. He mouthed the word once more. This time he could give it no voice. *Go.*

Portia knew there was nothing she could do for him. She kissed his mouth lightly and touched his brow. "I love you," she said. He closed his eyes. Portia sensed that he would not open them again. A minute later, his breathing stopped. Portia rose to her feet and looked at Joe for a long minute or two. She wanted to imprint his face in her memory forever. Then she checked her pocket for the photograph her grandfather had given her—it was still there—and escaped into the trees.

* * *

"Miners use blasting powder in coal country," explained Rook. "There's enough here to blow up something big, and I think we know exactly what they were intending to destroy."

Springfield, Clark, and Higginson listened to the colonel describe how a few barrels of blasting powder in the basement of the Capitol—perhaps delivered in boxes labeled as food and later on moved to strategic locations—could turn the building into a pile of rubble.

"That must be why Davis and Stephens visited there yesterday," said Springfield. "They were studying the foundations."

Davis finally came to his senses during this discussion. "You have no proof of that, Bishop—if that's even your real name," he sneered.

"It's just as much my name as Davis is yours," replied Rook.

"You've got no business being here," yelled Davis. "It's not against the law to possess blasting powder!"

"As far as you're concerned," snapped Rook, pointing his finger in Davis's face, "my word is the law."

With Clark and Higginson keeping their guns trained on the men in the hold, Rook hopped off the barge. Springfield followed him. "What are we going to do with these fellows?" asked the sergeant. "He's got a point. Have they actually committed a crime?"

"Let me worry about that," said Rook. "Late tonight, when the streets are dark and quiet, we'll take them to the Treasury and confine them to one of those rooms in the basement, far away from the main corridors. I don't want anyone who doesn't need to know about them to hear them or even to suspect that they're locked away."

"Sir?"

"What, Sergeant?"

"This seems unusual. Why don't we take them to the new prison at the Old Capitol?"

"Let me worry about that. Just go to the Treasury and prepare a place for them. Keep all of this to yourself."

* * *

It took Tate nearly an hour to arrive on the scene. His own pursuit had led him in exactly the opposite direction, and there had been plenty of distance to cover. Hearing the gunshots compelled him to give up his own chase immediately. In his experience, slave hunts rarely ended with violence, except perhaps where the dogs were concerned. Slave owners generally wanted their slaves returned alive and without serious injuries, and certainly without gunshot wounds that would make them less productive or harder to sell. Because the shots were unexpected, Tate believed his top priority now was to find his companion and see if he needed help. Besides, his trail was a hard one. His dog seemed to have trouble following the scent, pausing several times or doubling back on a path it already had taken. This was the mark of a slave who knew how to evade capture, Tate thought—and it was a trait he had not believed Portia or Joe to possess.

His dog found the remains of the bloody encounter before he did. It howled in a plaintive whine Tate had not heard it make before. He soon saw why. Three bodies lay motionless on the ground. The dog was obviously dead. No person or animal could have survived the huge wounds it had suffered. Tate's dog sniffed at the carcass, let out a few miserable squeals, and sat down with its head resting on its front paws. This must be how dogs grieve, thought Tate.

The overseer figured the fates of Joe and Hughes were no different than the dog's. He examined the body of the slave first, and it did not take long to see that it was without life. The big gunshot wound in the chest probably was responsible, even though there was also a gash on the side of the head, a little above and behind an ear. Tate wondered if someone had clobbered the slave there, but then he noticed a small patch of blood on an exposed root a few inches away. Joe must have hit it on the way down.

Hughes lay a few steps away, and Tate initially assumed that he was a corpse too. But he saw that Hughes was actually breathing, albeit slowly. The blood had congealed around the stab he had taken from the knife. The wound was not a clean one, but Tate thought it might heal in time. It helped that Hughes had gone unconscious on his back. This stroke of luck probably saved him a good amount of blood and perhaps even his life. Tate poured water from a small canister into the injured man's mouth. Hughes swallowed.

In the meantime, Tate would have to make a few decisions. Their slave-hunting party had been effectively reduced from two to one—Hughes would need days or weeks to recover—and now Tate could account for one of the two runaways he sought. A dog was dead too. Tate wondered about Portia. Had he been on her trail earlier? That was possible, though he had his doubts. And if that was not her trail, whose was it? Where was hers? Perhaps she had split off from Joe much earlier. Or maybe she was nearby, looking at him even now from some hidden spot. This thought forced him to examine his surroundings, spinning around like a slow-moving compass as he studied the area. There was nothing. He inspected the trees too, and there was still no sign of Portia. He did notice, however, that the sun lay low in the west. Twilight would come soon, and then darkness.

Tate determined that he was in no position to continue a pursuit that might very well fail. He did not think it was a good idea to abandon Hughes either. He knew that Bennett appreciated Portia far more than many of his slaves. As an attractive young female, she was a valuable commodity. It occurred to him that much of what he liked about her, though, was her connection to Lucius—and this was a tie that Bennett might now scorn. There was the very real possibility Portia would be caught by somebody else and returned for a bounty, too. Tate knew he was not the only person who could bring her home.

This was the proper course, he decided: save Hughes and let Portia go, at least for now. And so he quit the chase.

* * *

Violet Grenier stood on her porch and watched her final guest trudge up Sixteenth Street, turn right on I Street, and disappear from view. It was almost midnight. Clouds obscured the waxing moon. Behind her, inside the house, she could hear Polly straightening the foyer. The girl could be quite efficient late at night, when she knew that only a few chores stood between her and sleep.

Grenier wondered if the senator would turn around and wave as he sometimes did, but she was not surprised when he did not. She knew he was frustrated. He had lingered, waiting for the other guests to leave. When they were finally alone, she had pressed him for information about the president's meeting with the governor of Maryland and the mayor of Baltimore earlier in the day. She had hoped he would know something about it and what impact it would have on the movement of soldiers as they approached Washington.

The senator was normally a reliable source of information. He was from a Northern state, but he was sympathetic to the Southern cause and certainly had no fondness for Lincoln. His usual talk about committee deliberations would have bored many women, even in Washington. Yet Grenier listened to every word. She never took notes while he was talking, but she often wrote down his observations and comments when he was gone, passing them on to friends in Virginia and points south. Sometimes she was able to do this an hour or two after he first knocked on her door. Occasionally, though, she had to wait until morning before he was gone. The senator was one of her more familiar acquaintances.

On this night, however, Grenier had rebuffed his gentle advances. The day had been long. Although she was often full of energy as the hour grew late, she longed for sleep. Besides, she had already shared her bed today.

Would she see Mazorca again? She knew that she might not. If he actually accomplished his mission, she would be more than content never to lay eyes on him again. Yet she also recognized that she would enjoy more of his company. She had almost forgotten what it felt like to be attracted to a man. The ones she knew nowadays, such as the senator, were merely useful. Mazorca was different. He was satisfying.

Grenier lingered outside her front door, breathing the crisp air. She thought that perhaps she would sit by an open window upstairs as she jotted down a few notes. Then she could sleep and dream.

She had turned around and stepped through her front door when she heard a noise coming from H Street. A group of soldiers shuffled into view, their boots scraping across the dirt-filled street. There were three of them, heading east, and they surrounded four other men who were not in uniform. Grenier could see that these men were prisoners, their hands bound behind their backs. Their mouths appeared to be gagged as well. This detail made her curious. She had seen prisoners marched through the streets before, but they had not been gagged as these were.

As they passed by, about fifty feet from her doorway, none of them appeared to see her. The light from inside her house was weak and apparently did not draw their attention.

Besides, they were preoccupied with their prisoners. When one of them glanced up Sixteenth Street, she recognized his face. It was Colonel Rook. She doubted he would involve himself with criminals who had committed petty offenses.

A disturbing thought entered her mind. She looked at the prisoners more carefully, wondering who they might be. Was Mazorca among them? It was difficult to see much in the blackness, and now their backs were turned to her as they crossed Sixteenth Street and continued along H Street. She could not rule it out. As they passed St. John's Church, Grenier hustled across the street and into the church's courtyard.

A bush snagged her petticoat. If she had not been trying to move in silence, she might have cursed it. Instead, she quickly pulled it loose, not bothering to inspect the damage, and darted between the columns on the front of the church. Peering around the side, she saw the entourage of soldiers and prisoners about a block ahead of her. As they turned right on Fifteenth Street, she raced into Lafayette Park. If people had seen her running, they might have thought she was fleeing an assailant. Yet the park was empty. Nobody saw her as she flitted through, emerging on the corner by the State Department, a little brick edifice across the street from where she now stood.

From this vantage point, on the short strip of Pennsylvania Avenue that ran between the White House and Lafayette Park, Grenier could see a portion of Fifteenth Street. The soldiers had not yet come around the block, but she could hear their footsteps. She hurried across the Avenue, behind the State Department. Its windows were dark. She sidled along its exterior, turning a corner and moving forward until she came to a spot where she could crouch down and hide as the group came into view.

Rook was in front. She could tell right away that Mazorca was not among the prisoners who followed him. They were too big, too small, or the hair was wrong. She breathed a sigh of relief and scolded herself for embarking on a pointless excursion. Had she really gone this far in order to disprove that Mazorca was captured? If so, it would suggest that she was not thinking straight about him. That was a problem.

She did not budge from her spot because the men were still coming toward her. As they approached, she was able to study their faces—and she recognized Davis. What a fool, she thought. His plans were larger than his abilities. She knew it almost from the moment she had met him. Now he was caught. Stephens was with him as well. She wished that they had not come to her house. It was a shame that they had even come to Washington at all.

In a moment, the men passed by. She kept watching them, expecting a turn to the left, away from the barricaded Treasury Department. But when they turned, they actually went through the barricades and into the building.

For several minutes, Grenier did not move. She had not harbored high hopes for Davis and Stephens. She was disappointed in them as well as for them. Even worse than the disappointment, however, was the confusion: why would Rook take prisoners to any place besides the new prison in the Old Capitol?

She went back to her house, scribbled a few notes, and tried to sleep. But her mind was racing.

XII

Sunday, April 21, 1861

Portia stopped at the edge of a field and realized suddenly that the morning had arrived in all its brightness. She had stumbled through the night in a daze of walks, jogs, and mad dashes. The last fifteen hours were a blur. She had fled from a scene of horror and tragedy—the spot where a man she loathed tried to take her by force and where a man she loved gave his life so that her own might go on. For a long while she had simply crashed through the woods, desperate to get away from that place and not concerned about where she was headed.

Shortly before dark, she had found a road. She took it south, plodding onward, step by step. She had no idea how far she had traveled or how near she was to Charleston.

Her feet throbbed. She considered removing her shoes and going barefoot. The penny-sized holes in her soles made her partially barefoot as it was. But she worried about stepping on a sharp stone that she could not see in the dark. As painful as it was to keep pushing forward, she was determined not to give up.

The daylight caught her by surprise because the road had run through a forest for a couple of miles. Now a plantation complex lay before her. In the distance she could see the manor. Behind it were all the outbuildings, including the slave quarters. She wondered why nobody was in the fields. With the sun up, there should have been plenty of activity. Was it abandoned? Then she remembered: this was Sunday morning.

This realization filled Portia with a powerful sense of relief. Slaves often left their plantations on Sunday to visit friends and relatives who lived nearby. She thought she might pass as one of these innocent travelers. Of course, slaves who left their plantations even on a Sunday carried passes signed by their masters or overseers, and Portia had no pass. Just about any white person could demand that she present one. For the first time in many hours, Portia tried to make a plan. She did not know what lay ahead, and she feared that pursuers were somewhere behind her with their hounds. The possibility of curling into a bed of leaves and sleeping through the day tempted her. Yet this was not necessarily the safest course.

She sat down in a spot where she could keep a watch on the road and the plantation but where nobody was likely to see her. It felt good to get off her feet. She removed her shoes and noticed the blisters for the first time. If she walked much further, she thought, they might force her to stop.

Portia reached into her pocket and removed the photograph her grandfather had given her. Was Joe's life worth this little picture? The thought of Joe brought tears to her eyes. She had managed not to think of him much since he had told her to leave. Now the memory of him closing his eyes forever made her shake with sorrow. Then she welled up with anger. Holding the photograph in her hands, she thought about ripping it into pieces. She imagined herself doing it.

Then she remembered the last thing Joe had said to her: "Go." He knew the stakes. He knew the risks. He did not want comfort as he drew his final breaths. He did not want her to make a heroic last stand. He wanted her to go on. She had started this journey because of her grandfather. Now she would finish it because of Joe.

Portia was still undecided about whether to walk in the daylight or to get some rest when she heard the sound of a horse-drawn wagon rolling down the road. It came into view through the trees a moment later. A black man drove it, pulling a load of burlap sacks. He was probably a slave on his way to Charleston for the Monday market. She wondered how long it would take him to get there. How nice it would be to hitch a ride. She could get to the city without maiming her feet any further and perhaps even shut her eyes for a spell.

Portia never understood why she did it—the chance of being noticed seemed too great—but she rose from her spot as the wagon passed. A moment later, she fell in behind the cart, placed her hand on its back end, and kept pace for twenty or thirty feet. When it hit a pothole and bounced, Portia threw herself onto the pile of bags. She studied the driver. He did not move. The wagon continued on its leisurely course. Portia wiggled beneath a few of the bags, which were full of rice. She adjusted several of them and settled into a hiding spot that was not exactly comfortable, but it would do. Her aching feet felt better almost right away. And then she closed her eyes.

* * *

Walking through Lafayette Park in the morning sun, Mazorca decided there would be nothing tentative about his visit to the president's house. He would stride up the driveway, pass the guards under the portico, and enter the building like someone with legitimate business there. If anybody asked, he would say that he was seeking an appointment with the president. That was even sort of true.

Scouting the White House on the previous day had convinced him he could get in without raising suspicions. Perhaps the security on the inside was tighter than what he had seen on the outside. Perhaps he would have access only to a couple of the big rooms on the first floor. There was one way to find out. He had many basic decisions to make over the next few days—choices about when, where, and how. What he needed now was information to help him make these decisions. These details could not be found in books or conversations.

As Mazorca crossed Pennsylvania Avenue toward the White House, he watched a group of Jim Lane's men assemble on the front lawn. There were a good number of them, and they looked like a ragged bunch as they tried to herd themselves into neat rows and columns. Military drill was obviously not a specialty. These were men to have on your side in the chaos of a barroom brawl, thought Mazorca, but not necessarily on a battlefield, where preserving order was vital.

He did not pause to observe them as he neared the house. Two guards stood under the portico again, but they were more interested in watching the spectacle on the lawn than the approaching visitor. Neither took his eyes off Lane's men, and it was not until Mazorca had passed through the short gate and grabbed the knob on the front door that one soldier bothered to give him a quick glance. Mazorca was ready to explain himself when the bluecoat delivered a slight nod and turned his attention back to the lawn.

"A fine spot we'll be in if we're forced to stand by these men under fire," he said with the slight brogue of an Irish immigrant.

Mazorca almost replied, but then he realized the guard was not talking to him.

"Say what you will, O'Malley, but these roughnecks are better than nothing—and right now they're all we've got," remarked the other guard.

They were letting him pass. Mazorca did not hear the rest of the conversation. Instead, he pushed the front door open and stepped into the White House.

He found himself in a foyer stocked with plain furnishings and badly in need of a paint job. A small chandelier drooped down from the ceiling. Through a glass screen held in place by an iron frame, this entranceway merged into long hall that ran left and right. A soldier sat on a wood bench against one of the walls. His eyes were closed.

Mazorca entered the hallway and turned to his right. He knew the East Room, presently occupied by Lane's men, was located in the opposite direction. He saw a grand staircase at the west end of the hall. At the foot of the steps stood three well-dressed ladies listening to a man conclude a short lecture.

"Does anybody have a question?" asked the man.

"Let's move on, Senator," replied one of the ladies. "I'm anxious to see the portrait you mentioned earlier."

"Then we shall continue our tour in the State Dining Room."

With that, the little group filed into a room just to the left of the staircase. When they were out of sight, Mazorca reached the base of the steps and peered into the room they had entered.

He was surprised at its small size, perhaps thirty feet by twenty-five feet. An elegant table with fourteen chairs sat in the middle. Mazorca wondered if the president ever entertained more than a few diplomats, cabinet members, and congressmen at one time. He had thought about this dilemma only for a moment when the senator, standing before a fireplace, began a new speech.

"And here it is, above the mantel: the famous painting of our first president, by the extraordinary Gilbert Stuart."

The picture was almost life-sized, and it showed a white-haired, red-cheeked George Washington dressed almost entirely in black. His face was expressionless. He held a sword in his left hand, and his right one appeared to beckon.

"You all know the story," said the senator. "As the British marched on our capital almost half a century ago, the brave Dolley Madison refused to leave her mansion until she received assurances that this portrait would not be left behind. When unscrewing it from the wall took too long, she ordered the frame broken and the canvas removed. This heroic little woman got away just in time—and she saved a national artistic treasure from redcoats who would have been happy to see it swallowed in flames."

One of his listeners let out a sharp gasp. Mazorca turned and walked away. At the opposite end of the hallway lay the East Room, and he made for it. He passed by a few closed doors on his right. On his left, he went by the entranceway where he had come into the building, and then a small stair-case leading upward.

The East Room was large, with high windows on three sides. It was perhaps twice the size of the state dining room and appeared both majestic and worn out. The ceiling's white paint had chipped in one corner, and a panel of grimy yellow wallpaper sagged in another. The signs of for-mer grandeur were everywhere: three massive chandeliers, a detailed floral carpet, several marble fireplaces with tall mirrors hanging above them, thick maroon curtains cover-ing the windows, and regal blue chairs. Gold trim seemed to decorate everything.

The most striking features, though, were the East Room's occupants: the so-called Frontier Guards. About thirty of them lounged around playing cards or snoozing. They had transformed the room into a campground. A pile of backpacks rested to one side, and rifles stacked upright formed teepees beneath the chandeliers. The men were not responsible for the room's faded appearance, but their presence had faded it further. The carpet wore a coat of dry mud. Pipe smoke drifted upward. Mazorca figured the dilapidation here was like the growth of a plant: too slow to watch minute by minute, but rapid enough to measure over the course of days.

After observing this scene, Mazorca left the East Room and returned to the stairs by the doorway. He began to climb them, half expecting to be stopped by a soldier. The man-sion's security—or, more accurately, the almost total lack of it—astonished him. He had visited capital cities in other countries before and had seen official residences. He was not sure he knew of a single one that was open to the public, let alone one that permitted the free movement he enjoyed here. Some Americans, he knew, would applaud this as a praiseworthy feature of their democratic nation. Mazorca believed it was sheer foolishness.

He arrived in an office vestibule on the second floor. There was nobody in it, but he observed a small population of men lined up in an adjoining hallway, which he could see through a pair of glass doors. There were probably fifteen of them, all civilians. To his left was an open doorway into another room. Just as he was about to enter it, a tall, skinny man appeared on the threshold. He turned around, his back to Mazorca, and said, "When may I expect to hear something?"

"That is impossible to know, Mr. Meadors," came a voice from inside the room. "Please be patient. We will inform you as soon as possible."

"Thank you again, Mr. Hay."

Then Meadors nearly collided into Mazorca. He quickly apologized and departed into the hallway, where the crowd began to pepper him with questions. Mazorca paid them no heed and walked into the room Meadors had exited.

There was a window at one end and two doors along each side. It resembled a short corridor more than an office. By a desk in the middle stood a young man with a thin mustache, studying a set of papers in his hand. When he saw Mazorca, an expression of irritation crossed his face.

"I thought I told everyone to stay in the hallway until you were called," he scolded.

"Please excuse me," said Mazorca, "I thought—"

"Oh, never mind. The last one just left. But you probably know that. I'm John Hay, the president's secretary."

Hay held out his hand, and Mazorca shook it. Then a bell rang. Hay seemed to expect it.

"He's ready," said Hay. "You can expect to have about five or ten minutes. Come this way."

Hay stepped to a mostly closed door on the north wall, pushed it open, and walked in. Mazorca followed. Before he even knew where he was, he heard the secretary say something he scarcely believed.

"Mr. President, your next appointment is here."

* * *

Tate walked to the stables at the Stark farm, near the scene of the previous day's violence. He had spent the night there with Hughes, who remained bedridden on the orders of a doctor summoned in the middle of the night. The young man would recover, but it would take time. Tate now wanted to get back to Bennett and let him know what had happened. It was a grim task, but he was determined to do it.

As he approached the stables, with his dog by his side, one of Stark's slaves saw him.

"Jeremiah," he shouted over his shoulder, "get Mr. Tate's horses."

A boy emerged with a group of horses: the one Tate had ridden, the one Hughes had ridden, and the two taken by Joe and Portia, which they had picked up along the way. A large sack drooped over the back of one animal. Inside of it was Joe's cold body. Tate thought it made sense to have it buried on Bennett's land.

Tate paid no heed to Jeremiah until the dog sniffed him and let out a yelp. Then it started barking wildly at Jeremi-

ah. Tate hollered for silence. The dog obeyed but continued to stare and flick its tail. Tate thought the dog's behavior was a clear sign of recognition. He studied the boy and
wondered.

"What's your name?" asked Tate.

The question startled Jeremiah. He was not used to
white visitors taking an interest in him, except to scold. Tate
repeated the question, and Jeremiah answered it.

"Have I seen you before, Jeremiah?"

"I don't know," said Jeremiah, a bit tentatively.

"Have you seen me?"

"Before today? I don't think so."

The dog remained agitated. It grumbled and refused to
take its eyes off the boy.

"Do you know anything about runaways? If you know
what's good for you, answer truthfully."

"I haven't seen any."

Tate liked to think he could spot a liar just by looking at
him—it was an essential skill for an overseer. With Jeremiah,
however, he just could not tell. Rather than shiftiness or defiance, he saw fear in the boy. It meant that either he really
did not know anything about Portia and Joe or he was an
above-average deceiver. Tate was tempted to put Jeremiah
in shackles and quiz him.

But what would that solve? Hughes was badly hurt,
and Tate did not want to alienate the Starks. Portia was
long gone. It made sense to get back to Bennett's. The
overseer got on his horse and left. The horses followed
Tate to the road, and the dog did too. But the dog also
kept turning around for another look at Jeremiah.
When the boy disappeared into the stables, the dog

let out a final bark. Then it stayed by Tate's side all the way home.

* * *

The basement of the Treasury was so dark and dank that if Rook had not known better, he might have thought it was a medieval dungeon. A king of old Europe might condemn a prisoner here and throw away the key. These were helpful atmospherics, thought Rook, but best of all was the obscurity of the place. Almost nobody ever came down here— the only reason Rook had learned of it was because he had inspected the building several weeks earlier, when he was assessing its value as a defensive structure. The place was a warren of rooms filled with everything from dusty financial records to pieces of broken furniture. In one remote corner, however, was a short corridor of empty chambers that were little more than glorified closets. It was here that Rook had taken his four prisoners from the C&O Canal, placing them in separate rooms.

Through the night, Rook, Springfield, and Clark had taken turns grilling Davis, Stephens, Mallory, and Toombs. The interrogations had not gone well. Rook had a long list of questions: What were their real names? Where were they from? Why had they walked around the Capitol? Why had they visited Violet Grenier? What were they planning to do with the blasting powder?

After a while, it became apparent that Mallory and Toombs did not say much because they did not know much. Yet even they held their tongues on simple questions about their identities. Davis and Stephens seemed to have more to hide, but they did not budge either. Rook could think of no easy way to compel them. Out of sheer frustration, he had kicked Davis in the gut and threatened to do worse, but to no avail. Rougher techniques were an option though he did not feel confident about resorting to them—at least not yet.

"What are we going to do with these men?" asked Springfield.

"Right now, we're not going to do anything with them," said Rook. "We know they can't do any harm here. After a day or two of sleeping on the floor and hoping that we'll bother to feed them, they may prove more cooperative."

The colonel wished he could summon someone with more expertise at asking questions and obtaining answers. Unfortunately, he didn't know anybody in the city with these skills. An even more fundamental problem than finding the right person, however, was Rook's desire for secrecy. He was running a rogue operation without General Scott's knowledge or approval—a clandestine program that, as he saw it, was necessary in order to counteract the complacency of his superior officers. Asking around for personnel would merely draw attention to what he was doing.

He suspected that he could keep Davis and the others locked up for at least a few days without anybody noticing. Perhaps time would break their resolve. There would be logistical matters, such as providing them with food and water, though Rook did not feel particularly inclined to give them much of either. Hunger and thirst might erode their willpower as well. Would he have to post a guard outside their doors? He was tempted not to. Right now, only he, Springfield, and Clark knew of the prisoners. He wanted to keep it that way. But could he? What if somebody happened to wander through the basement? What if the prisoners sensed that they were alone and yelled for help? Would someone hear?

How all this would play out remained unclear. For now, Rook told himself that he had achieved his most immediate objectives: determining that Davis and company were an actual threat, and then preventing them from carrying out their plans. For the time being, perhaps this was enough of an accomplishment.

"This will be difficult to keep hidden," said Springfield.

"Let me worry about that," said Rook. "If it becomes a problem, I'll take the blame."

"Just tell me what to do."

"We aren't going to learn anything from these fellows, at least not now. We should try to learn more about the people they're working with. There must be others. Violet Grenier may be the key."

On hearing her name, Springfield remembered his excursion of the previous morning, when he'd followed the stranger from Grenier's home to the boardinghouse on H Street. He told Rook about it, including the detail about the man's ear.

"Do you think he's connected to Davis and the others?" asked the colonel.

"It's impossible to say. He's definitely connected to Grenier, and she's definitely connected to them."

Rook ordered Springfield to keep Grenier under watch for the rest of the day. The colonel himself had to rush around the city making appearances at several posts—he had neglected his rounds yesterday and could not afford to do it again. Clark, meanwhile, would stand guard over the prisoners.

As Rook and Springfield left the Treasury and walked into the sunlight, the colonel issued a final order. "Whatever you do," he said, "don't let anyone spot you."

"I won't, sir."

"You can always hide behind that mustache of yours."

* * *

John Hay handed a clutch of papers to Abraham Lincoln and quit the room. He closed the door, leaving Mazorca alone with the president.

"Hello," said Lincoln, who sounded slightly bored. The two men shook hands. Mazorca was struck by the president's long fingers and firm grip. Lincoln gave Mazorca's torn-up ear a quick second look, as so many people did. He gestured to a short chair. Mazorca parked himself in it, and the president began to rustle through the material Hay had given him.

As Lincoln read, Mazorca glanced around the room. The president's office was functional rather than grand. A modest desk sat in a corner, near one of the room's two windows and beside a fireplace. Above the mantel was a portrait of Andrew Jackson. The opposite wall displayed a pair of maps. A long table dominated the middle of the room. It was big enough for a cabinet meeting, thought Mazorca. A small lamp rested in its center, amid a mess of documents. A black gas line ran up from the lamp to a modest chandelier above it. Sunlight from the room's big windows and yellow wallpaper brightened the space. Next to the president, a cord dangled from the ceiling. By pulling on it a minute earlier, Mazorca assumed, the president had rung the bell in the waiting room.

Lincoln himself was all angles. His knees and elbows made sharp points as he sat with crossed legs, hunched over the papers. His face looked as though an ax had carved it from a block of wood, with jagged edges and severe lines. The deep creases were distinctive but not conventionally handsome. Lincoln's eyes were a light blue fading into gray, and they sparkled with intelligence from deep sockets. Messy hair and a beard running low along his jaw framed his countenance. Mazorca thought Lincoln was one of the oddest looking men he had ever seen.

"You have a letter here from your congressman, plus notes from a few of my local supporters." Lincoln continued shuffling the papers. "One of these men even seems to think that he alone is responsible for my election," he said, more to himself than his guest. "And now this immodest fellow expects a reward for getting me into this fine fix." The president emitted a sound that was half grunt and half chuckle. Then he looked at Mazorca. "So, Mr. Collins, tell me why you want to become a lighthouse keeper in New Jersey."

Mazorca tried not to look surprised. "Somebody must offer protection against the reefs and shoals."

"We must all steer clear of them—ships of sea and ships of state."

"Indeed."

Lincoln waited for more of a response, but Mazorca did not want to say too much. He had not planned to be in this position, and he did not like to do anything he had not planned. But neither did he want a good plan to get in the way of an excellent opportunity. He knew his assignment required seizing every advantage handed to him. Here was Lincoln, seated before him and ignorant of any personal danger. They were alone.

At last the president decided to carry on. "Lighthouses have always intrigued me, Mr. Collins. When we see a light shine in the darkness, we are invariably drawn to it, like the proverbial moth and flame. The light attracts us. It invites us to come closer. And yet in the case of lighthouses, the light is often a warning. Its message is to stay away. If we approach, we perish."

"It is important to know what things to avoid."

Lincoln closed his eyes, leaned back in his chair, and tilted his head upward. He was trying to remember something. "Confess yourself to heaven," he said. "Repent what's past; avoid what is to come."

He opened his eyes to a blank expression on Mazorca's face. The president smiled. "Never mind me—just a little Shakespeare. I reread those lines in *Hamlet* only a few nights ago."

An uncomfortable silence settled between the two men. Mazorca assumed that Lincoln had grown accustomed to guests who did nothing but beg favors. "I suppose you wish there were lights to guide you through the darkness now, in these troubled times," said Mazorca.

"I surely do," replied the president. "But I would also want to know whether the lights come from a harbor calling me in or a reef warning me away."

"Some things are not as they seem. The trick is to know which is which."

Lincoln's eyes narrowed. "How many legs would a dog have, Mr. Collins, if you called his tail one?"

Mazorca paused at this riddle. He wanted to say five but knew that could not be the answer. "I'll guess four, because calling his tail a leg would not make it one."

The president smiled. "You are a clever fellow. Most people don't get that one."

"It's an easy mistake."

"A careless one, too. It reminds me of a story. One day, a farmer was working around his property when his son—a boy of about ten years—came rushing up to him. 'Pa,' he shouted, full of excitement, 'come quick! The hired man and sis are in the barn, up in the hayloft. He's pullin' down his pants and she's liftin' up her skirt!'"

Lincoln paused, barely able to suppress a big grin. It appeared as though he had told this story many times and took delight in watching it fall on fresh ears.

"'Pa,'" continued Lincoln, in the earnest voice of the boy, "'they're gonna pee all over our hay!'"

Lincoln howled at this line, doubling over in his seat. As the president wiped an eye with his sleeve, Mazorca smiled politely and tapped his foot. He felt the holster strapped to his calf. The possibilities buzzed through his mind. All he would have to do was pull up his pant leg and remove the gun. He had thought the deed might be accomplished from a distance, with a rifle. Now he wondered if it could be done up close. It would be easy, unbelievably easy. But then, this was always the easy part. The hard part was the escape.

Mazorca found himself enormously tempted to take advantage of this extraordinary moment. He looked at the window but knew from his earlier observations that the drop to the ground was too far. He would probably break a leg, or worse. The sound of the shot would set off an alarm through

the whole house, too. Hay would burst in immediately, followed by the men waiting in line in the other room. Some of
them were sure to have weapons. Mazorca thought he might
hold them off for a moment with his pistol, but he knew
a gunfight was not in his interests. Scores of Lane's men
would swarm the White House and its grounds in seconds.
They would spot a man running across the south lawn and
begin a chase—and a chase was the thing he most wanted to
avoid. The way to escape after killing a target was not to become a target right afterwards. That meant creating uncertainty about where the shot came from and who pulled the
trigger. Ideally, he would walk away calmly from the scene of
an assassination.

"I have received several other inquiries about lighthouses
in New Jersey," said Lincoln, when he finally stopped laughing. "You are by no means the first and may not be the last.
I have not made any decisions yet and will give your request
full consideration."

Mazorca realized he was being released from the inter-
view, but he wanted this bizarre meeting to continue. He
nodded at the portrait of Jackson. "I did not take you to be
an admirer of his."

"Doubt my credentials, do you?" smiled the president. "I thought doubting credentials was my job." He
gave a short laugh, a high-pitched hee-haw, and looked at
the picture. "Many people assume that a Republican like
me wouldn't hang his picture. It was here when I moved
in—a remnant of the previous administration. I had
hoped it might bring me some success in my own dealings
with South Carolina. I suppose that's what Mr. Buchanan
wanted too. It didn't help either of us much, did it? Presi-

dent Jackson had a little more luck with that state than we did."

Lincoln paused for a moment and made eye contact with Mazorca, who sat motionless. "It does remind me of another story, which comes from that old revolutionary war hero Ethan Allen. Do you have time for a short one?"

Mazorca nodded his approval. Sometimes a fruit appearing ripe on the outside could be rotten on the first bite. He decided to let Lincoln survive this accidental encounter. Their next meeting would be different.

"Allen was visiting England, sometime after our country had secured its independence," said Lincoln. "His hosts enjoyed poking fun at Americans, so they put a picture of George Washington in the most undignified place they could imagine—the back room, you know, where they kept the toilet. They could hardly wait for their guest to see the picture and were delighted when Allen excused himself for a moment. His hosts were bursting with anticipation while he was away, and they guessed at what Allen might do or say when he returned. They were startled, though, when Allen came back in with a huge grin on his face. He did not appear even mildly annoyed. One of his hosts finally asked, 'What did you think of the décor?' And Allen replied, 'Very appropriate. In fact, I cannot think of a better place for an Englishman to hang a picture of General Washington than above the can.' The reply confused everybody, so the host asked, 'Why is that?' And Allen replied, 'Because there is nothing in the world except the sight of General Washington that will make an Englishman so quick to shit!'"

Lincoln roared at the punch line, slapped his knee, and rose from his seat. Mazorca did not quite grasp the point of the story, but he stood up too and understood he was being dismissed for good. Maybe that was the point.

Lincoln put a hand on his shoulder as they walked to the door. "You are a man of few words, Mr. Collins. That is probably a good quality in someone seeking out the loneliness of lighthouse work. You also seem to have a talent for riddles. I'll see what I can do for you. Good day."

* * *

Looking out the window for Hughes and Tate made Bennett feel helpless. Years ago, he would have led the pursuit of Portia and Joe. Now, every glance made him tense. This was no pursuit of ordinary fugitives. Portia and Joe had something in their possession that he desperately wanted to have returned.

Bennett tried to reason his way out his anxiety. The odds of these two slaves making it all the way to Washington were incredibly low. Even if they did make it, they might not arrive in time. Mazorca would strike at some point. Bennett did not know when or how, but he knew it would happen. Anything the slaves did after that would come too late. And even if by some miracle they made it to Washington and also made it in time to interfere with Mazorca, there was the very distinct possibility that nobody would take them seriously. They would have to convince the right people in government that their photograph contained important information. Yet they were nothing but a pair of runaway slaves who could not even write their names on a scrap of paper.

It was early in the afternoon, following a small lunch he had eaten alone in the dining room, when Bennett finally saw something. In the distance, a man on a horse turned onto the path leading up the manor. Behind him were three horses without riders. Was that Tate?

Bennett walked onto the porch. He saw that it definitely was his overseer. But why was Tate by himself? Where was Hughes? What was that big sack draped across the back of a horse? Its shape and size troubled him. His mood darkened as Tate approached the steps and stopped.

"What is going on here, Mr. Tate? Where is Mr. Hughes?"

"I have some very bad news to report, Mr. Bennett." Tate explained what had happened.

When he was done, Bennett summarized what he had just heard: "So Hughes is hurt, Joe is dead, and Portia is missing. I presume this is Joe's body you have here?"

"I thought we should bury it here at the plantation."

"Remove the body from the horse immediately and put it on the ground right here."

"I thought I would take it directly to the slave cemetery, sir, and gather Joe's relations for a quick funeral. We really should get this body in the ground soon."

"Did you hear me, Mr. Tate?" yelled Bennett. "Do it now."

Tate was baffled by the request, but he and a slave lowered the body to the ground. The stiffness made it difficult to manipulate.

"Remove the wrappings," commanded Bennett.

They uncovered Joe's corpse. Its skin had assumed an ugly gray pallor. The stench was strong. Tate took a step back.

"Search the clothes."

Tate was puzzled. "What am I looking for?"

"Just do it!"

The overseer knelt beside the corpse and began patting it. He stuck his hand in the pant pockets. From one he removed the crumbled remains of a biscuit. In another he found a small slingshot and several round stones. He placed these beside the body.

"Take them off."

"Sir?"

"The clothes. Remove them from his body. I want them thoroughly searched."

Tate did not move right away. He considered this a strange request. "It would help to know what you're looking for," he said.

"I know what I am looking for, and I will recognize it when I see it. That is all you need to know."

Tate began to take off the clothes, piece by piece. The shirt was the hardest to remove, having become crusty with dried blood. The whole experience was humiliating. Tate not only resented having to perform this indecent chore. He also resented having to do it where a number of slaves could see him. This is a story that will spread fast, he thought. He worried about what this desecration would do to his reputation around the farm. Certainly it would not make things any easier for him.

When Joe's naked body lay exposed before Bennett and it was clear that no more searching could be done, Tate looked up at his boss. "Will that be all, sir?"

"Damn it, Tate. He does not have what I want. You should have followed Portia."

Bennett stormed up the steps to the manor. The door slammed shut behind him with a loud bang.

Nobody had moved from the scene. Tate took command. He ordered a slave to lead all but one of the horses
to the stables. He told two others to dress Joe again, wrap
him up, and put him on the back of the remaining horse.
He sent a final slave to fetch a few shovels. When the body
bag was in place and the shovels in everybody's hands, Tate
took the reins of the horse and began to walk to the slave
cemetery. This was on the edge of Bennett's property near
the road. It was a fairly large section of land, having been
in use for several generations. The graves were unmarked.

The most direct route from the manor required Tate
to walk by the slave quarters. As he approached them, a
crowd began to gather. They whispered among themselves.
Before anybody called out to ask what had happened, Sally
appeared on the scene. When she saw Tate, she dropped
the pot she had been holding. It cracked when it hit the
ground. Soup sprayed everywhere. She ran toward Tate.
"Oh Lord, don't let it be true," she screamed. "Please don't
let it be true."

But it was true. Joe had come home, and he would never
leave again.

* * *

The cat startled Violet Grenier when it jumped onto her
desk. She rubbed the black-and-white animal behind its
ears, listening to it purr. "That's a good boy, Calhoun," she
said, in a baby-talk voice. The cat was named after John
Calhoun, the South Carolina politician who had served as
a vice president, a cabinet officer, and a senator. He had
died a decade earlier and since then had achieved an iconic

status among Southern partisans. When the cat made an
appearance at one of her parties, Grenier loved to tell her
guests its name. She especially enjoyed teasing Northerners
who stroked its fur. "See how easy it is to please him?" she
would say. "That's what I like about cats. They demand so
little—just a bit of freedom."

At the thought of this barbed comment, Grenier smiled
and leaned back in her chair. She felt a cramp in her back
and realized that she had been sitting for too long. It was
time to take a break. She set down her pen and rose from
the seat where she had composed letters for much of the afternoon. The most important of these letters had been the
most difficult to write. She had saved it for last because she
was unsure of what to say.

The adventure of the previous night, when she had followed the soldiers and their prisoners to the Treasury Department, had left her confused. One plot was now foiled.
This was no loss. Yet she wondered exactly how it had been
defeated. How much of the conspiracy was compromised?
Would the prisoners talk to their captors? How much would
they say? Would her acquaintance in New York become exposed? Would she find herself implicated?

If they mentioned visiting her, she could expect to face
difficult questions. She could deny knowing them, or at least
deny knowing their plans. The fact that she was a woman
could prove advantageous—the chivalry of her interroga-
tors might coax them into believing her professions of total
innocence. She could confess to holding the Southern sympathies for which she was already well known. "But no lady
in my position would associate herself with the schemes of
ruffians," she said grandly, as if practicing for the occasion.

Calhoun looked up at her and meowed. "I'm glad you approve," she said. She stroked his neck.

Her wiles might help, but Grenier appreciated that perhaps she was falling into some danger. What were her choices? Leaving Washington was an option, though one she did not want to take. She was needed here. A man could put on a uniform and fight in a battle. Grenier knew that wars were not always won by strength of arms. Generals needed reliable information almost as much as their troops needed ammunition—and Grenier understood that she was in a unique position to provide information about federal activity that perhaps nobody else could obtain. Men were willing to die defending the rights of the South. Grenier was determined to help them win in any way she could. This cause was bigger than any man—or any woman.

A Bible rested on her desk, propped open to Matthew. It helped her compose her letter to New York: "A stranger recently told me that 'Wide is the gate and broad is the way that leadeth to destruction,'" she had written. "Success, however, is a strait gate—and the one he had hoped to pass through is now shut." She thought perhaps it said enough without saying too much. It would mean little to anyone but its recipient, and to him it would convey an important piece of news. How he used this information would be his own concern. For her part, Grenier felt that he at least deserved to possess it.

She tucked the letter into an envelope and sealed it. Her thoughts turned to Mazorca, as they had done so many times since the day before. She had given herself to him freely—something she had not done with a man in quite a while. Her trysts always involved some kind of transaction, as she sought to extract a fact or obtain a favor. Mazorca was different. She had wanted nothing from him but the pleasure of his company, and she indeed had found it pleasurable.

Mazorca had not said anything about a second visit. There may not be a reason for one, she realized—or at least not a professional reason. They had not spoken directly about why he was in Washington. Yet she knew what task lay before him and understood the importance of discretion. He needed to keep a low profile. Still, he had given her his address at Tabard's, for use in an emergency. Or was it an invitation?

Grenier gazed out her window. Her eyes settled on a man standing at the corner across the street, in front of St. John's Church. He seemed to be doing nothing in particular, as if he were waiting on a friend. A loiterer was not remarkable, especially with Lafayette Park nearby. Yet something about him looked familiar. Had she seen him before? She thought that perhaps she had spotted him several hours earlier. That big mustache was hard to miss. Mustaches were fashionable these days. Only the oldest men, impervious to the latest trends, seemed able to shirk them. Mazorca, too—that was one of the things she liked about him. Yet the whiskers of the man outside her window achieved an astonishing thickness.

"Calhoun," she said, turning away from the window and toward the cat. "Let's keep an eye out for this fellow."

* * *

Portia did not know how much time had passed when she woke up, but the shadows had grown long and the sun was plunging into the horizon. For a few minutes she did not move. The driver sat just a few feet away from her. She had not gotten a good look at him before hopping into his cart and burrowing beneath his rice sacks. If he had detected her, she probably would have known by now.

Could she trust him? All Portia could see was the back of his head. The gray flecks hinted at someone getting on in his years. He was humming a familiar tune, but Portia could not quite place it. The simple fact that he was alone and far away from his plantation suggested a strong loyalty to his master and a demonstrated ability to travel distances and always come back. Portia knew that some slaves would take an interest in helping her make it to Charleston, as Jeremiah had done. She also knew that others would seize opportunities to win the favor of whites by betraying runaways. She worried that this man was such a slave.

As Portia squirmed out from under the rice sacks, the soreness in her feet rushed up her legs. She winced. Sleep had provided a reprieve but not healing relief. Her blistered feet seemed to hurt worse than before.

The sun continued to sink. Portia lifted herself up and immediately recognized the sight in front of the wagon. She had seen it before when she was just a girl: the huddled mass of buildings, a skyline dominated by church steeples, and water in the distance. They were minutes away from entering Charleston.

The slow pace of the wagon made her anxious. Portia knew her real destination lay well within the city. As buildings began to appear on both sides of her, she wondered when she should make a move. Her head told her to slip out of the wagon soon. Her feet urged her to stay put.

The farther the wagon went into the city, the more crowded the streets would become. She started to hear voices and other vehicles passing them. It was important to get away without being noticed by the driver or anybody else. How long could she wait?

The wagon made a turn, and still Portia didn't move. As the sky grew darker, she kept telling herself that she had to do something. The noises from outside the wagon began to fade. They were in a quieter part of the city now. She heard the driver's humming again. She knew the tune from somewhere, but the words continued to elude her. Suddenly, the wagon stopped. So did the humming. Had she waited too long?

"Get out."

She sat up straight, not sure where the voice had come from. The wagon was on some kind of side street. All was quiet. There were no people around except for her and the driver. He still faced away from her, but the command only could have come from one place.

"Get out before I change my mind."

It was definitely the driver talking to her. Portia crawled over the rice sacks to the rear of the cart and lowered herself to the ground. She did this with care, but her feet still burned with pain. She limped to the side of the street and propped herself against the wall of a building. The wagon started to move again. The driver turned and nodded. She only saw his face for a moment, and there was kindness in it.

"Good luck."

The wagon traveled another block, turned, and vanished from sight. Had he known the whole time that she was there? She could not be sure—her deep sleep had lasted the better part of the day. Now it hardly mattered. He was gone, and it was a detail. She had to find her way to Nelly's, by the Battery. It was at the end of a long street that cut through most of the city, she remembered. She hoped she could find it.

After walking about half a block, however, she had to stop because of her feet. She slipped into a narrow alleyway and sat down. A troubling thought came to her mind: what if the wagon driver really wanted her caught? Perhaps he had dropped her off only to inform the local authorities of her presence. Why would he let her go only to see her captured? It made no sense. Portia told herself not to panic. She wasn't thinking clearly.

Then she remembered the words to a song she had known for years. It was a secret song, one that slaves sang when only slaves were present—and never in the fields where a white person might overhear.

> *Master sleeps in the feather bed,*
> *Slave sleeps on the floor;*
> *When we get up to Heaven,*
> *There'll be no slaves no more.*

This was the song the wagon driver had hummed. She got up and started walking again. This time she hummed it too.

* * *

When Rook arrived at the Winder Building, a soldier posted outside said the general was in the big room near the back of the building. Normally they met in Scott's office—this other place was reserved for larger groups, such as the general's whole senior staff. Rook had attended a few of these gatherings, but he had not heard about this one. It must have been called at the last minute. Was there news of war?

Officers filled the room. Rook noticed that Scott had dressed himself in full regalia, the way he did when he had a meeting with the president. The colonel wondered why. Lincoln wasn't here. Then he saw a man with wavy hair and a sharply angled nose that looked almost like a snout. It was William Seward, the secretary of state—the man who nearly had received the Republican nomination for president the previous year. If Lincoln had not grabbed it from him, in fact, Seward probably would be president today. Some people said Seward was the real leader of the administration. Others believed he was ferociously jealous of Lincoln.

Rook ignored the officers who milled around and went straight for a chair at the large table. A moment later, Scott's booming voice interrupted all conversation.

"Please be seated, gentlemen. Let's get started."

Everyone found a chair.

"You have probably noticed that we are joined today by a distinguished guest," said Scott. "Welcome, Secretary Seward." The general bowed his head slightly, and men grunted greetings from around the table.

"Thank you very much, General Scott," said Seward. "This is a difficult moment for our country, but we in the administration are comforted to know that the protection of the capital and the president are in your capable hands."

"Thank you, Mr. Secretary," replied Scott. "Let us proceed now to our reports. Where's General Johnston?"

Heads bobbed around the room. Quartermaster General Joseph E. Johnston should have been at the table, but he was missing. It did not take much thinking to realize why: he was a Virginian and believed to hold secessionist sympathies.

"Unfortunate, but not unexpected," mumbled Scott. The big general turned to his assistant, Colonel Locke. "When this meeting is concluded, find out where Johnston is and whether he has resigned."

Locke scribbled a note to himself, and Scott continued. He spent the next several minutes describing recent events. It was one alarming piece of news after another. On Friday, federal troops passing through Baltimore on their way to Washington had sparked a riot. It was not clear who fired first. Either way, the results were grim: thirteen people killed, including four soldiers.

Rook leaned over to the captain beside him. "Nobody died at Sumter," he whispered. "If there's a war, then these men in Baltimore are its first casualties."

The next day—yesterday—Baltimore's rioters cut telegraph lines and destroyed railroad tracks coming into the city from Pennsylvania. This halted Washington's mail and newspaper deliveries from the North. Trains continued to run irregularly from Washington to Baltimore, and they were packed with people trying to escape from the capital. Even more left by foot or carriage. The slow exodus of recent weeks was picking up. And word had come just hours before the meeting that the commandant at the Norfolk navy yard had ordered his garrison burned, his cannon spiked, and most of his ships scuttled. It was one defeat after another—first Sumter, then Harper's Ferry, and now the clash in Baltimore and the capitulation at Norfolk. Rook worried that things would get worse before they got better.

"Let us proceed with the business at hand," said Scott. "We all know what happened in Baltimore on Friday, but today we have with us Colonel Edward F. Jones of the Sixth Massachusetts. His men are bunking in the Senate. He will give us a full report of what transpired."

A lanky colonel stood. He described arriving in Baltimore by train and drawing a crowd as his men marched across the city. At first, agitators shouted insults. Then they began hurling bricks and stones. The troops kept their composure but grew aggravated. Finally, a shot went off—almost certainly from the mob and possibly from a musket that was stolen from one of the soldiers after he was hit in the face with a rock. "I have four dead soldiers and more than thirty injured to prove that our harassers were armed and willing to open fire," said Jones. "We had no choice but to fire back." They fought their way to the depot, boarded a train, and made it to Washington.

Seward stood up. "You fought bravely and well, Colonel," he said. "On behalf of the government, let me say that we are all grateful for your sacrifice."

Rook did everything he could to keep from rolling his eyes. Seward might be a cabinet secretary, but at heart he was a politician. Like so many other politicians, he enjoyed hearing himself speak and ingratiating himself to his listeners. He looked at soldiers, but he did not see warriors. He saw voters. Even so, Rook began to think that Seward's presence today might prove useful.

"We are under siege and isolated, gentlemen," said Scott. "We are all that stands between the preservation of the Union and its ruin. Yet we do not possess an adequate force to defend Washington from an attack of any significance."

"Will reinforcements come?" asked Seward.

"The New York Seventh is supposedly on the way. It cannot get here soon enough."

Scott rattled off a series of orders. He told the officers already in charge of organizing armed citizen groups and marshaling provisions to redouble their efforts. He demanded stronger picket lines around the perimeter of the city and better intelligence on military activity in Maryland and Virginia. He insisted that sandbags be placed around the Treasury Department—if war came to the streets of Washington, it would become a military headquarters and a refuge for the president. The general reviewed evacuation procedures, including a scheme to escort the president from Washington if the city's capture was imminent. He wanted a plan for everything and gave everybody something to do. Rook was responsible for monitoring the bridges and locating facilities for additional soldiers, should they ever come.

"Are there any questions?" asked Scott.

When nobody had any, Rook spoke. "General," he said. "I might make a comment."

"Yes, Colonel?"

"Last Friday's incident demonstrates the wisdom of President Lincoln's decision to pass through Baltimore in the middle of the night rather than risk the fury of a mob. He has been greatly criticized for it, even by his friends and allies. It is said that he regrets having done it. Now we have fatal evidence showing that he was sensible to have been cautious."

Seward leaned forward in his chair, which Rook viewed as an encouraging sign. Perhaps the secretary's presence would force Scott to make a concession.

"We also have a better understanding of the enemy's level of commitment and resourcefulness—and the knowledge that we have perhaps underestimated it," continued Rook. "We're responding effectively to the external threat. What about the internal threat? We know this city is full of secessionists—"

Scott interrupted. "What are you driving at, Colonel?"

"We can surround the Treasury with a wall of sandbags soaring above our heads, and it won't do any good if a handful of secessionist vigilantes storm the president's mansion. At the very least, we must improve our surveillance of likely instigators."

A few heads nodded in agreement. An equal number did not move at all. Colonel Locke scoffed. Seward narrowed his eyes.

"I thought we had already discussed this matter," said Scott. "Our focus now is on military operations. Sneaking and snooping won't do us any good when Lee comes marching into northern Virginia at the head of an army."

Seward raised his hand, stopping Scott's commentary. "How serious is this problem, Colonel?"

"I would definitely call it serious—and made more so by a failure to recognize its potential. We just learned a painful lesson in Baltimore about not appreciating the lengths to which some people will go in opposing our aims. We must avoid making the same mistake here."

Scott could not restrain himself any longer. "Mr. Secretary, you must understand that this colonel"—he emphasized the rank, as if to show it compared poorly against his own—"is making an old argument. We've gone over this many times before, and still he persists. Frankly, Colonel, it is beginning to smack of insubordination—and your desperate attempt to show off in front of the secretary here is embarrassing to me and all the other officers sitting around this table. You are now in charge of sandbagging the Treasury Department. You will devote yourself to this project exclusively. Others will assume your previous responsibilities."

The meeting went on for another half hour. The only part Rook would remember was how Locke smirked and Seward stared for the rest of it.

XIII

Monday, April 22, 1861

Portia opened her eyes to a small room she did not recognize. Light seeped in from a half-closed doorway, revealing white walls, a low ceiling, and not much else. She was lying on a hard bed. It made her wonder where her own bed was and why she was not in it. The answers did not come quickly to her groggy mind.

She remembered lumbering down a city street in Charleston. The need to rest her aching feet overcame her every block or two. Between her hampered gait and the frequent stops, it had taken half the night.

The street finally ended where the waves lapped against a seawall. When she turned around to look at the way she had come, Portia recognized that she was in the Battery. Water bounded it on two sides. Houses lined the rest of the park. They were big homes with white columns and cast-iron balconies. Packing them together so tightly made them look smaller than they really were, but Portia knew they sprawled on the inside. Most were three stories high. The Bennett home was on the opposite side, its ground floor lit by gaslight and visible through the trees. Nelly lived next door.

It was too late to knock, not that she would have tried it, even in daylight. What if Nelly had left for a plantation?

The thought sent a shiver through Portia. Nelly was supposed to spend all her time in Charleston. But things could
have changed. If she was gone, Portia did not know what she
would do.

No lights shone through the mansion's windows. Portia entered an alley. There was a single door in the rear of
Nelly's house. She thought about trying the handle. Instead,
she sat down and rubbed her feet. The ache receded after a
few minutes. Portia was not sure what to do next. It was easy
to do nothing at all. She was exhausted. Her eyes began to
droop. She fought to keep them open but felt herself losing
the battle. Part of her actually wanted to lose it. A comforting blackness washed over her.

That was the last thing she remembered before she
woke. Suddenly, a heavyset woman walked through the
door. Even from the dim glow from the hallway, Portia recognized Nelly.

"You're awake," said Nelly. She reached for a damp rag.
"Lemme wipe this grime off your face, child. It looks like
you ain't been clean in days." She rubbed lightly at first,
then dipped the rag into a bucket by the side of the bed and
scrubbed a bit harder.

"You're a pretty young thing," she said. "But you're
feelin' a little cold. I'm gonna get you one more blanket."
She twisted around and called out of the room, "Benjamin!
Gimme that green blanket!" Then she turned back to Portia and gave her a warm smile. "Everything's gonna be all
right."

"Do you remember me?" asked Portia.

"I remember a cute little girl from the winter season
eight or nine years ago. I know how you've grown because

your grandfather keeps tellin' me about you—or at least he answers all the questions I ask. I've known that man for years, and you're the first and only grandchild of his that I've met. Of course, I can't see people in my own family as much as I'd like. Anyway, I know Lucius has a lotta kin. You're just the only one who has been this way before."

"How did I get here?"

"I can't answer that question, honey," said Nelly. She put down the washcloth and started to fuss with Portia's hair. "I found you sleepin' by the back door, right after sunrise. I spotted you through a window and walked outside to kick you awake. We don't want no vagrants around here. But somethin' about you looked familiar. The shape of your face is the same as your grandfather's. I also knew it was you because years ago I saw the woman inside the girl. So I pulled you in here and set you down on this bed. It's a good thing Mr. Jenkins ain't around. He wouldn't lemme skip all this work and take care of you. He'd insist that you go next door to the Bennett place, even though I would tell him there's nobody there right now. Of course, the fact that nobody's next door makes me wonder what you're doin' in these parts."

Benjamin walked into the room just as Nelly quit talking. He was a skinny boy of perhaps eight years. He carried a green blanket folded over both arms and gave it to Nelly. "Thank you, Benjamin," she said as she took it and began spreading it on top of Portia. "This is my own grandson," said Nelly. "Mr. Jenkins is lettin' him stay with me through the summer."

It took Portia all this time to absorb the question Nelly had asked a moment earlier. What was she doing here? Then the reason why struck her. She bolted upright, tossing off the blanket and shoving her hand into a pocket. Nothing was there. She checked another pocket and found what she was looking for.

"My goodness, girl, somethin' has gotten into you," said Nelly. "What's that you've got there?"

"It's nothin'."

"It's somethin', all right. You don't gotta tell me. I understand secrets. Just lemme peek."

"Sorry, Nelly. I'm not tryin' to hide nothin' from you. In fact, it's you I been lookin' for. My grandfather sent me. He said you would help."

"Helpin' the granddaughter of Lucius. Now that's somethin' I would gladly do. Your grandfather is a good man. There ain't a thing I wouldn't do for him."

"He said you can help me get to the North. He said you knew people here in Charleston who can do that."

Nelly stood up. She looked at Benjamin as if she were about to dismiss the boy because of the conversation's direction. Before she could do anything, though, Portia spoke up.

"I've run away, Nelly. I left the farm and came here. I gotta get to the North."

"We all wanna do that, honey, every one of us slaves."

"This ain't the same thing. There's somethin' I need to take there—somethin' that will help all the slaves."

"You gonna tell me what it is?"

"I shouldn't. It's somethin' my grandfather gimme. He says I gotta hand it to Abe Lincoln. He said you could help me do that."

"You're in Charleston, child, and Washington is a long way off. We slaves can't just buy tickets and hop on board the next boat."

"That's why I need your help. You know how it can be done, don't you? You know how I can get to Washington. My grandfather said you did."

Nelly did not reply. She crossed her arms and stared at her grandson. The boy had been riveted to their conversation, his head flicking back and forth between Portia and Nelly as they spoke.

"Do you really think you're gonna meet Abe Lincoln?"

"I gotta. Please help me. It's about our freedom—and his freedom too, Nelly." She pointed to Benjamin.

"Everybody says he's gonna free the slaves. But you're askin' for a whole lot, maybe even a miracle."

"There won't be no miracles if you don't help me."

"I can't promise nothin'. If somethin' went wrong, I'm not sure I'd ever be able to look at your grandfather again."

"He sent me to you. He would say it's better to try and fail than not to try at all."

Nelly thought it over. "When your grandfather said I knew people, he spoke the truth. I know some people right here in Charleston who hate slavery, who would like to see all the slaves have their liberty—and I'm not talkin' about no colored folks. There's some white folks who are real quiet about it. But I know how to get to them. Maybe there's somethin' we can do."

"Thanks, Nelly. That's what my grandfather wants."

"If I had known your grandfather was gonna send me one of his favorite grandchildren, I never would have said nothing to him. This ain't a burden I wanted. There's a good chance this ain't gonna work, Portia."

"It's gotta work. If I'm gonna be punished for runnin', I want to be caught goin' north, not by givin' up."

Nelly said nothing for a few moments. She barely even moved. Benjamin's head swiveled between the two women. Portia wondered how much of this he really understood.

Nelly finally broke her silence. "Benjamin, do you remember that store we been walkin' by, where they take the pictures of people and put them in the front window?"

The boy nodded.

"I want you to run over there right now. Find the owner. Tell him I have an extra-special package for him. He'll know what it means. His name is Mr. Leery."

* * *

After visiting Clark in the recesses of the Treasury Department's basement, Rook actually looked forward to supervising the sandbagging of the building's exterior. It was a lonely assignment for the corporal. Davis and the others still refused to talk. The good news was that nobody had come near Clark or the prisoners. They were secure, at least for the time being.

Outside, Rook spent a few minutes watching a crew of men pile sandbags along Fifteenth Street. Their wall stood at three feet and was growing, layer by layer. By the end of the day, they would have a rudimentary barricade.

Up the street, Rook spotted Springfield standing by the State Department. He had no idea whether the sergeant had been there for long, but Springfield clearly wanted to talk to him and had the good sense not to approach. The last thing either of them needed was for Springfield to be seen in plain clothes doing something other than piling sandbags.

Rook glanced at his crew of men and decided they could spare him for a few minutes. A wagon loaded with more sandbags had just arrived. It was enough to keep them busy for a little longer.

A few minutes later, Rook and Springfield were sitting beside each other on a bench in Lafayette Park.

"I didn't want to approach you while you were sand-bagging," said Springfield. "I heard what happened at the meeting."

"I got sandbagged all right."

"It's a shame, sir."

"Don't worry about it. Technically, as one of my men, you're supposed to be over here piling bags too. But I don't care what Scott thinks. I want you to keep doing what you're doing."

"Yes, sir."

"What do you have for me?"

"I started intercepting Grenier's mail. One letter caught my eye because of who sent it."

Springfield removed a letter from his pocket and gave it to Rook—it was the April 19 letter describing the loss of Lucius, signed by Langston Bennett. Rook skimmed it.

"I knew Bennett in Mexico," said Rook. "I didn't know him personally, but by reputation. He was an officer during the war. He lost a leg and returned home. I haven't heard his name in ages."

"It comes from South Carolina."

"Yes, that's where I believe he was from. That's all?"

"He must be a secessionist."

For a moment Rook thought that perhaps Scott had a point after all. It looked like a harmless piece of mail. Were they spending too much time obsessing over conspiracies?

"I don't think there's much to it," said Rook.

Springfield must have had the same thought. "I'll let it go through," he said.

"Anything else, Sergeant?"

"No, sir."

"What about that visitor she had?"

"I haven't seen him."

"You will soon. I've got a plan to learn more about him."

* * *

It was late afternoon when Mazorca returned to his room at the boardinghouse. He had risen before dawn to examine the bridges leaving Washington, one by one. Originally he had planned to rent a horse for the day, but with so many the people leaving the city following the catastrophe in Baltimore, horses were hard to come by and exorbitantly priced. He had the money for it but did not want to be seen as having the money for it. So he walked. There were four bridges in all, and Mazorca wanted to see how long they were, how well they were guarded, and what the other side of the river looked like. He did not actually cross any of them, because turning around and heading right back would draw notice, especially if the sentries at one bridge were to compare notes with the sentries at another.

First he went all the way to the Chain Bridge, to the west. Then he proceeded eastward, observing the bridge in Georgetown and the Long Bridge south of downtown. The last bridge, spanning the east branch of the Potomac, interested him the most. It was the only one leading into Maryland. The other side of the river was technically a part of the District, but Maryland lay just beyond, across an invisible

line in what appeared to be sparsely populated countryside. Soldiers at the other three bridges were on the lookout for military activity in Virginia, and there were enough of them posted at each to hold off an advancing column until reinforcements could arrive. The last bridge, however, was different. An attack from Maryland wouldn't come from across the bridge. There were few guards. Mazorca liked what he saw.

Back in his room, Mazorca opened his trunk and removed a pile of maps. He searched through the small stack until he found the one he wanted. It was of southern Maryland. He unfolded it on the floor. A few small towns were sprinkled around the region, though for the most part it seemed to be a mixture of rural farmland and swampy wilderness. Coves, creeks, and inlets pockmarked the Potomac. It looked perfect.

Mazorca knew from experience that the information contained on maps often required verification. There was a big difference between studying an area on paper and visiting it in person. Doing it properly, he realized, would require a horse, even at some expense.

But that was a problem for another day, and this one was coming to an end. He was happy with what he had learned. He was one step closer to an escape plan. Now he needed to think about a plan that would make his escape necessary.

He had purchased a copy of the *Evening Star* on his way back from the bridge. The small type on its front page described the news and other events, but his eye drifted over to the right-hand columns, full of little advertisements. One in particular caught his eye. It was for French & Richstein, a bookstore at 278 Pennsylvania Avenue. The proprietors proudly announced the arrival of "the first elegant household edition" of *The Pickwick Papers*, by Charles Dickens.

Mazorca had heard of the popular British author. He decided to buy a copy of this new book. But he had no intention of reading it.

* * *

James Leery had not moved to Charleston specifically because he wanted to free its slaves. He had arrived there from New York in 1859 to open a photography studio. After working as an apprentice for three years in his native city, he wanted to succeed on his own. But the picture business was fierce, and he feared failure. Then his father, an indulgent man who supported his son's fascination with this newfangled technology, made a vital connection.

The elder Leery was a trader who dealt extensively with commodities from the South. He came into frequent contact with men from the region and learned much about life in a part of the country he had never seen with his own eyes. It gave him tremendous sympathy for the Southern cause. One day a conversation with a visitor from Charleston turned to photography—and it did not conclude until after they had walked to the shop where the young Leery coordinated sittings for customers and took photographs that were ultimately credited to the owner of the studio. Within a week, the three men had settled on a plan: the father and his friend would invest in the son, who would start a new studio in Charleston, which had not yet embraced photography with the enthusiasm of Northern cities.

At first, James did not want to go. Unlike his father, whose livelihood depended on a thriving Southern economy, James detested the South and its culture of forced servitude. He believed slavery was immoral, corrupting both the lives of those in bondage and the souls of the men who kept them there. He attended abolitionist meetings and subscribed to William Lloyd Garrison's newspaper, *The Liberator*. He felt a strong sense of guilt over the fact that his prosperous upbringing—which included a good home, an expensive education, and the ability to shirk his father's profession in favor of the photographic arts—had been made possible, in part, by the product of slave labor. The idea of living in the South to provide a service to the people who cracked the whips did not appeal to him.

Yet his love of photography was strong, and the opportunity to run his own studio proved too tempting to resist. He resolved that he would indeed go to Charleston and take pictures of planters and their families—but that he would also work against the slave system. His business thrived from the start. Leery resolved to use the money the planting class threw at him to purchase the freedom of young slaves whose whole lives lay in front of them. This was how he came to know Marcus, his studio assistant. He bought him at auction, took him back to the shop, announced to the startled boy that he was free—and offered him a job.

Leery's reputation for charity spread quickly through Charleston's large community of free blacks. It later became known to many of the city's slaves that he was a friend. When a runaway knocked on his door late one summer night, he consented to give the man some money. A few weeks later, another runaway showed up and Leery agreed to harbor him for a few days. To the whites who ruled Charleston, Leery was an eccentric Northerner who provided a unique service. They had no idea of what else he did—and he was always cautious about doing too much.

Through the grapevine of slave gossip, Nelly heard a story about Leery buying a one-way boat ticket to Boston for a light-skinned runaway who was able to pass as a white person. She did not know whether to believe any of it. She wondered whether Leery really worked in cooperation with local slave catchers with the aim of spreading rumors among the slaves and drawing out the fugitives. Yet such a trick would work only once or twice before Leery was exposed as a fraud. So far, that had not happened.

Then something incredible took place. One day, Leery was standing at the doorway to his studio as she walked by with Benjamin. The photographer called her over and struck up a conversation. Nelly was shocked because outside the immediate circle of people she served, no white person had ever done this before. Leery brought her in his shop and showed her his equipment and samples of his work. She was suspicious but interested—and then astonished when he asked her whether Benjamin might be purchased for the purpose of setting him free. Would she inquire with Mr. Jenkins and let him know?

That would have been about three weeks ago—and Mr. Jenkins was still out of town, probably not returning except for a brief visit in May or June. In the meantime, her view of Leery clarified. There must be something to the stories about him, she realized. Nelly had known that there really were white people who opposed slavery. Abraham Lincoln was one of them. She had heard that some white Southerners wanted to see the slaves let go—mainly small farmers who resented the power of the large plantation owners. She had even heard how a handful of white people actually helped slaves escape to the North through something called the Underground Railroad. But she had never actually met any of these people—or at least, did not think she had met any. Until she met Leery, that is.

And so she took Portia to Leery. They arrived in the afternoon. Leery was busiest in the autumn and winter, when Charleston's social season was in full swing. He had a few jobs now, but not many. Much of his current income came from selling small reproductions of South Carolina's secessionist heroes, such as P. G. T. Beauregard, the man who had opened fire on Fort Sumter earlier in the month. Images of Jefferson Davis were popular as well.

When Nelly and Portia arrived, Leery rose from behind a desk where he had been cleaning lenses.

"To what do I owe the pleasure of this visit? Benjamin mentioned a package, but I wasn't sure what he meant. Have you had a chance to speak with Mr. Jenkins?"

"No, and I don't expect to see him for a few weeks."

"If you prefer, Nelly, just let me know when he's back and I'll approach him myself."

"Yes, sir, Mr. Leery. Thank you very much."

"So what brings you here?" he asked, looking at Portia.

"This is my friend, Portia," said Nelly. "She's in a bit of trouble."

Leery glanced out his storefront window. Nobody was there. "What kind of trouble?"

"I've run away," said Portia.

"I see," said Leery, rubbing his chin. Nelly could see he was trying to decide how much he could reveal about himself.

Portia spoke up. "I can't stay here in Charleston. I gotta get to Washington, and I gotta get there fast."

Leery raised his eyebrows in surprise. It was an extraordinary request.

"Something like that takes time and planning—and it's a long way to go and very hard to get from here to there without being caught. Washington isn't the best destination either. They allow slavery there, you know. It would make more sense to get you on a boat to New York or Boston. You could try to settle in one of those cities or even go to Canada."

"No, Mr. Leery, Washington is where I gotta go. I have a message to deliver to somebody there, and getting it there quickly will help all the slaves."

"Well, this is a first," said Leery. "I've done a few small things to help slaves here and there. I know there are a few stories about me going around. Many of them are nothing more than fairy tales, though a few of them approach the truth. I'm sure Nelly has told you what I'm about. They are modest measures, Portia, and they're the only things that help me tolerate the sale of these obnoxious little mementos." He pointed at a display holding the pictures of Beauregard, Davis, and the others. "There is a kind of poetic justice in thinking that the sale of these images will help me free people kept in bondage."

Leery snickered at the thought of this. "But you are not asking me to purchase your freedom," he continued. "You present a different type of problem. I wish I could just give you a horse and tell you to be on your way. The boats are fast, but I wouldn't recommend stowing away right now—certainly not a woman on a ship full of men. But even if that were a risk worth taking, I don't think it would work. With all this talk of a naval blockade, the ships heading out of port are crammed full of goods—there probably isn't a nook or cranny anywhere in their holds for a person like you."

"Ain't there somethin' we can do?" asked Nelly.

"I'm thinking," said Leery, staring at Portia. "You're not very big, are you?"

"What do you mean?" said Portia.

"You're not a big person. Have you ever heard the story of Box Brown?"

"Who?"

"Henry 'Box' Brown, a slave who lived in Richmond, Virginia, about ten or twelve years ago."

"No."

Leery looked at Nelly. "I haven't either," she said.

"His story hasn't been told very much down here. That's because the white people don't want word of it leaking out. Box Brown is pretty well known in the North, though. He lived with a cruel master who sold Brown's wife and children to another owner far away—Brown had to watch them march off in chains with the knowledge that he would never see them again. That experience convinced him to escape. He didn't think he could evade the slave hunters, so he came up with an ingenious plan. He met with a carpenter that he knew he could trust and they manufactured a special box, two feet by two and a half feet by three feet. They lined the inside with a thick cloth, punched a few small holes in the sides, and loaded some provisions. Then 'Box' climbed into his box. The carpenter nailed it shut, wrapped it with a few hickory hoops, and shipped his human cargo to Philadelphia. One day later, Brown emerged from his container in the offices of an antislavery society."

"He was alive?"

"He was worn out and sore—but definitely alive. I think he lives in England now."

"You tryin' to say somethin', James?" asked Nelly.

"A package leaving here by train this evening probably would need until Wednesday morning to make it to Washington. You can never tell for sure how long it will take. This is only worth doing, Portia, if you're absolutely certain that you want to go through with it. I would estimate that the risks are quite high and failure a very real possibility. But I've actually got a box in the back room here that might do the trick…"

Portia watched him go through a doorway on the back wall, chattering without stop. For the first time in days, she smiled. She knew her blisters were not going to get any worse.

XIV

Tuesday, April 23, 1861

The bookshop of French & Richstein sat on Pennsylvania Avenue, just off Twelfth Street and in the heart of the downtown business district. In addition to books, it sold stationery, pens, ink, and just about anything having to do with the written word. Periodicals were an important part of the business too, especially newspapers from New York. These were generally regarded as better than the ones produced in the capital. They arrived by train each day and went on sale by late afternoon, in time for people to buy them on their way home from work. Yet no papers from New York had passed through Baltimore since the weekend, putting a nasty dent in French & Richstein's revenue flow.

As Philip French unlocked the door to his shop early in the morning, he wondered if a train would make it through before the sun went down. Fewer people had bought books since the start of the secession crisis. Many more of them, however, were buying the daily and weekly publications. These sales did not make up the difference, but they certainly helped. French did not welcome the prospect of these falling off as well.

Lots of businesses had suffered in recent weeks. There had been a flurry of economic activity around the time of

Lincoln's inauguration, when the city swarmed with members of the new Republican Party celebrating their victory and trying to get jobs in the government. Each day since then, the city had seemed a little emptier. There were soldiers, but they were not customers. The departing long-time residents nevertheless provided a unique opportunity for French & Richstein because many of them decided to sell their book collections. French's partner, Norman Richstein, had spent a good portion of the last several weeks appraising and purchasing the libraries of people leaving town. The sellers essentially bet against Washington, or at least Washington's continued normal existence. French & Richstein gambled in its favor. This made Philip French nominally for the Union, though his feelings were not strong. He was perfectly willing to stock secessionist newspapers from Richmond in his shop as long as there were buyers for them. He just wanted to continue selling books, and he was for whatever made that possible.

As the day's first customer walked through the front door, French hoped the morning would get off to a good start. The tall, sandy-haired man headed straight for the bookshelves and started to examine titles. French became hopeful. This was the best sort of customer for a business that relies on repeat visits: a new one.

French knew that book buyers were often shy people who would rather read a printed word than exchange a spoken one. Strangers made them feel especially uncomfortable. He wondered if his new customer was that sort of person. The man had made only the briefest eye contact when he entered the store. Still, the proprietor wanted to extend some kind of greeting. "Please let me know if I may be of service," he said at last.

Mazorca looked up from an open volume. "I will," he said, flipping through the rest of the pages of the book in his hand and putting it back on the shelf. He ran his finger along the spines beside it, settled on another thick tome, and slid it off the shelf. He tested its weight and studied it from several angles. He pulled back the cover and appeared to assess the texture and strength of the individual pages.

French watched Mazorca do this with several volumes. He thought it was one of the most unusual book examinations he had ever seen. It was not obvious to him that his customer had even read the titles of the books. He certainly wasn't reading the words on the pages. He seemed to be judging the books by their material quality instead of their literary content, which, he thought, was rather like judging the taste of a wine by the shape of its bottle. Yet his customer accumulated a small stack of books under his arm. French was grateful for that.

After about twenty minutes, Mazorca approached the counter.

"Did you find everything?"

"Yes, thank you."

Mazorca placed five oversize volumes in front of French. Four were in excellent condition. The last one was in dreadful shape, with a cracked binding and loose pages stuffed between its covers. French was a bit embarrassed to see that it had been sitting on one of his shelves. It was a copy of Schiller's plays and criticism, in the original German.

"Sorry about the condition of this one," he said as he totaled Mazorca's bill. "I don't believe we have another copy."

"I've been looking for it," came the reply. "I would have taken it in any condition."

French was a bit surprised by Mazorca's choices. In addition to Schiller, there were two Bibles, a lavishly illustrated guide to American birds, a novel called *The Mysteries of Udolpho*, and a copy of the new Dickens book. French liked to comment approvingly on his customers' purchases, even to the silent types. When he added the Bibles to Mazorca's tally, he settled on something to say.

"Ah, yes. The good word."

Mazorca smiled, though French was not sure it was for his benefit. "The last word," he muttered, looking at the book rather than its seller.

French totaled the bill and Mazorca paid it. "Thank you very much. I hope we will see you again," said French, really meaning it.

"You may," said Mazorca, walking to the door. Before stepping out, however, he turned back to French. "By the way, I thought I might try to have the Schiller book repaired by a bookbinder. Can you recommend one?"

"Of course," said French. "Try Charles Calthrop. He's just a few blocks away."

French gave Mazorca the address and directions. A moment later, Mazorca was gone. French did not notice a man with a bushy mustache standing across the street. Neither did Mazorca.

* * *

Portia tumbled onto a hard surface—and nothing had ever felt quite so good. After spending the first leg of her journey upside down, she at last lay on her side. She had not planned on comfort while pressed into her small crate, but she had expected the porters at the railroad station in Charleston at least to have seen the words Leery marked on the outside of her box in big black letters: "This side up." There were even arrows pointing in the right direction in case the loaders could not read. Whether they failed to see Leery's instructions or simply ignored them hardly mattered now. It just felt good to be off her head.

She knew it was daytime because a thin ray of light streaked though a tiny hole in her box. But she had no idea whether it was morning or afternoon, or even where she was. Leery had told her that she probably would be loaded off and on trains a couple of times before reaching her destination—he had mentioned Wilmington and Richmond, but these names meant nothing to her.

Nelly had raised plenty of objections—starvation, suffocation, and so on—but Leery had an answer for each one. When Nelly finally consented, he packed Portia into a crate with a sack of water, a dozen biscuits, and a pillow. He also bored a few small holes around the box to ensure that she would have enough air to breathe. He even gave her a gimlet in case she needed to create more holes. He sealed the box so that she could open it from the inside.

For Portia, the decision to follow the example of Box Brown was easy. It represented her best chance of getting to Washington in a short amount of time. It carried obvious risks—discomfort, delay, discovery—but so did the alternatives. Portia had heard stories about slaves in places like Maryland and Kentucky running through the woods to freedom in the North, but they really did not have very far to travel. From South Carolina, an overland trek would be long and hard, and the odds of success incredibly slim. Not only would Portia risk getting caught, but she would also risk arriving in Washington too late. A refusal to take chances guaranteed failure. And so she had gone into the box.

Portia could not have been off the train for more than a few minutes when she felt herself moving again. Then her box was lifted and placed down somewhere else. It was not long before she heard a train whistle and felt that same sensation of momentum that she had experienced upon leaving Charleston. She was cramped and sore, and the light through her hole had disappeared. Yet she did not care— this time, at least, her handlers had paid attention to Leery's instructions. Portia was right side up.

* * *

Charles Calthrop knew he was out of place in Washington. Most of the country's high-quality artistic bookbinders were in New York, where they operated close to major publishing houses and the center of national wealth. For three decades Calthrop had labored among them, restoring frayed family Bibles and designing ornamental covers for the vanity books of socialites who mistook themselves for poets. Work was everything to him, and he was proud of what he did. He often signed his volumes in a discreet place when he was particularly satisfied with a result, as if he were a painter.

By the late 1840s, a growing portion of Calthrop's business was coming from Washington. It had started with a single senator who wanted to collect several of his own speeches and writings in attractive volumes for friends and supporters. Through word of mouth, Calthrop eventually became Washington's favorite bookbinder, even though he did not live there. Over time, Calthrop decided to move closer to his clientele. So the gray-haired bachelor moved to Washington and opened a small shop on the second floor of a K Street building, near the corner of Fourteenth Street, in 1855.

For Calthrop, a busy day was when a visitor climbed the stairs to his shop and he also received an inquiry through the mail. That was fine with him. Bookbindery was a lonely occupation that required a tremendous amount of patience. Calthrop enjoyed nothing more than the solitude of several quiet hours spent fixing small cracks and waiting for glue to dry before proceeding to the next step. The arrival of customers often bothered him because they interrupted his work—even though he knew they were the people who provided him with the ability to continue doing what he loved most.

When Mazorca walked into the shop with an armful of books just before lunchtime, Calthrop set down a tiny blade he had been using on an old volume of Gibbon's *Decline and Fall of the Roman Empire,* owned by a cabinet secretary. He hoped this man would be the day's only business.

"May I help you?" sighed Calthrop, not moving from his seat behind a table.

"Your services have been recommended to me. I have a book that would benefit from restoration."

Mazorca placed the Schiller book beside Calthrop. The old man picked it up and cradled it gently. He flipped it over several times. Then he opened it and studied the pages.

"You have good taste," he said. "I am a great admirer of Schiller's. There aren't many other people in Washington who know much about him."

Mazorca simply nodded.

"*Sprechen sie Deutsch?*" asked the bookbinder.

"Excuse me?"

"Do you speak German? Apparently not."

"No, I don't. This book is for an acquaintance."

Disappointed, Calthrop returned his gaze to the book and sighed again. "Its condition looks worse than it really is," he said. "A few minor repairs should do the trick. Unfortunately, I'm a bit behind on several projects right now. I'm not sure how soon I could give it attention."

"I was thinking about trying to fix the book myself. Would you be willing to show me what needs to be done and sell me the tools? I'd be happy to pay you for your time as well."

Calthrop thought it was an odd request. He did not want an apprentice peering over his shoulder. He did have some spare tools, though. He always had more tools than he needed. Selling them to this fellow might not be a bad idea—and getting paid for a short lesson on top of that made additional sense.

The bookbinder studied the Schiller volume again, this time more intently. "Here is how I would approach the problem," he said, outlining a strategy that would take three days to complete. For a half an hour, Calthrop described what to do and showed his student how to use several tools. When they were done, Mazorca had a small pile of knives, glue, and ribbon. They settled on a price—one that Calthrop found extremely pleasing.

"Please come back with additional questions as the need arises," said Calthrop, surprising himself with the offer.

"I'm sure that won't be necessary. You've told me everything I need to know, Mr. Calthrop."

"Well, feel free to return."

"I will," said Mazorca, turning to exit.

"There is just one more thing, sir."

Mazorca turned around. From his look, Calthrop could tell his customer desired to leave. But a question nagged him. "Are you from Cuba?"

"Excuse me?"

"I'd wager that you're from Cuba."

Mazorca froze. "What makes you say that?"

"I can hear a touch of Spanish in your accent, and specifically a Cuban dialect."

"You are mistaken," said Mazorca, coldly.

"Have you at least spent time there, or somewhere else in Spanish America?"

"No." This time Mazorca was more insistent. "Not Cuba." He pursed his lips. He looked annoyed.

Calthrop felt a need to explain. "I'm very sorry. I was a musician in my youth, and my ear catches small variations in sound. I would still be a musician today, except that I heard music better than I played it. I'm left with this ability to pick up tiny differences in the way people pronounce words. I've made guessing where people are from into a little hobby. I'm usually pretty good at it. I'll feel better if you tell me you've at least spent some time in Cuba."

"Where I'm from is no concern of yours." Mazorca's glare unsettled Calthrop.

"I didn't meant to offend…"

Mazorca was gone before Calthrop could finish his sentence. The old man was glad this customer had purchased supplies rather than dropped off a book. He did not want to see him again.

* * *

"What's this?" asked Rook, pointing to the stack of books piled next to Springfield on his bench in Lafayette Park. The colonel had slipped away from his sandbagging command for a short meeting. He bent over and looked at the spines. There were five copies of the same book: *The Pickwick Papers*, by Charles Dickens.

"I didn't take you for a reader," said Rook before Springfield could respond. "I took you for a vile and calumnious man."

Springfield leaped to his feet, startled by the colonel's comment. "Excuse me, sir?"

"I meant that in a Pickwickian sense."

"A what?"

"Well, that proves it."

"Proves what?"

"That you aren't a reader."

"I'm confused, sir."

"Me too. You're sitting here in the park with five copies of *The Pickwick Papers* beside you, and you don't understand an elementary reference to them—a humorous one, I might add. If I say you're vile and calumnious *in a Pickwickian sense*, then I mean the exact opposite. I've actually paid you a compliment."

Springfield furrowed his brow. "Thank you, I guess. I haven't read these books, sir."

"Obviously not. What are they doing here?"

"I bought them this morning."

"A good selection. But I hope you realize each copy is the same on the inside—you might have saved yourself some money buying only a single copy. An experienced reader would know that."

"Right. Except saving money wasn't the issue. Spending it was. I've been gathering information all morning on one of our secessionist friends. The price for some of it was five copies of this book."

"Perhaps you had better start from the beginning," said Rook, taking a seat on the bench. He gestured for Springfield to sit down as well, and the sergeant complied.

"You wanted me to learn more about the fellow seen leaving from Violet Grenier's on Sunday, so this morning I did," said Springfield. He described waiting for his man outside the boardinghouse on H Street, following him to the bookstore and the bookbinder, and finally trailing him back to the boardinghouse.

"After he returned, I went back and interviewed the storekeepers. He bought five books at French & Richstein and some supplies from Calthrop the bookbinder."

"Did you get the titles of the books he bought?"

"French didn't want to tell me. He mumbled something about proprietary information, but it turned out not to be so proprietary that he couldn't be persuaded to share it."

"You bribed him?"

"It depends on how you define 'bribe.'" Springfield tapped the stack of Dickens books. "These were displayed prominently near the front of the store, and I've heard that Dickens is a fine writer."

"Very clever. So what did French tell you?"

"He gave me the names of the books our man purchased." Springfield removed a slip of paper from inside the front cover of the top Dickens book and handed it to Rook.

"Ann Radcliffe is an intriguing selection."

"I didn't know of your interest in Gothic novels."

"That's not what interests me—what interests me is the range. Our man is an eclectic reader: German plays, American birds, an English novel, and two Bibles."

"French said the same thing."

"What about the bookbinder?"

"That's where our man went next. The owner is an older gentleman named Charles Calthrop. He doesn't seem to get many visitors—I was apparently the very next person to stop by, even though it had been at least an hour since our man had been there."

"What did Calthrop say?"

"He didn't want to say much, and he grew agitated at my questioning. It seems our fellow took a short lesson on how to repair a damaged book—one of the books he had bought from French was in rough shape. Calthrop gave him a few tips on restoring it and sold him some supplies."

"Sounds reasonable."

"Then something weird happened. Calthrop said he thought he detected a slight accent in the man's speech—

a Spanish inflection, and in particular a Cuban dialect of Spanish. So he asked his customer where he was from. The guy clammed up, said he wasn't from Cuba, and that Calthrop should mind his own business."

"He likes privacy, though I suppose the behavior is a little odd."

"More than a little, figures Calthrop. He thinks the man gave him a threatening look on the way out, after what Calthrop describes as an otherwise pleasant encounter."

"Perhaps. But perhaps innocent. What we seem to have learned is that our man likes to read, wants to fix a damaged book he bought, and doesn't like people asking about his background."

"I suppose that sums it up."

"Have you interviewed the person who runs his board-inghouse? We don't even know this man's name."

"I'm worried that talking to her might strike a bit close to home."

"Maybe that's for the best. If he's stayed with her for a long time, she could be loyal to him, which means she'd tell him we're watching. Winning her over might cost a lot more than five books."

Rook wished he knew more about the man, but the re-sources for surveillance were limited essentially to the time of Springfield and Clark, plus whatever Rook could devote to it. There was also the question of their prisoners.

"For now," said Rook, "turn your attention back to Gre-nier. We'll watch her for at least a few more days, and then we'll reassess what we're doing."

"I think that's a terrible idea, you ugly lout."

"Excuse me?"

"I mean that only in a Pickwickian sense, sir."

* * *

There was no year. That was the first thing Violet Grenier noticed about the letter.

Sitting behind the desk in her second-story study, Grenier held a single piece of paper dated April 19, with no year attached to the date. It could have been written just four days earlier, a year and four days earlier, or a decade and four days earlier. She might not have spotted the incomplete date on another missive—lots of people left the year off their correspondence—but on this one she had looked for it right away. That was what she did whenever she received a note from Langston Bennett. It was a signal.

The script was familiar and the letter brief. Langston said he was very busy and commented on the passing of a favorite servant. None of it interested Grenier. Everybody was busy nowadays, and she could hardly care less about some slave in South Carolina. If anybody else had written to her this way, she would have wondered why its author was wasting her time with such nonsense. With Bennett, however, nonsense was the furthest thing from her mind.

Grenier set the letter on her desk and walked to a table by the wall, picked up a candleholder, and returned to her seat. Light poured through the big window next to her desk. She had read Bennett's letter by it and did not need the candle to aid her eyes. Yet she removed the glass cylinder enclosing it and lit the wick. A small yellow flame began to burn.

Taking the letter in both hands, she held it just above the candle. At first, it looked like she wanted to burn the paper. Then it became clear that she meant to expose it to as much heat as possible without singeing it.

Tan splotches began to appear between the lines of Bennett's letter. Soon they darkened and assumed distinct forms. More shapes became visible as Grenier rotated the letter above the candle. The faint smell of something burning began to rise up, but Grenier barely noticed. After several minutes of this, she pulled the letter away and blew out the candle. Then she placed it squarely in front of her and read its hidden message between the lines of the original script.

> *I assume you have met Mazorca by now. Warn him to halt his mission immediately. His existence has been discovered. Future missions like his will be jeopardized if he fails. He must stop at once.*

Grenier read the letter several times. Then she set it down and leaned back in her chair. Who had discovered Mazorca? How would Bennett have learned about it? The whole matter was puzzling. Mazorca had revealed himself to her just two days ago. And now Bennett was announcing everything a failure. His letter had been composed before she had even met Mazorca. How could the plan have failed so utterly?

She looked at the clock. It was later than she had thought. She would have to reflect on this message and decide how to proceed. But reflecting and proceeding would have to wait. In the meantime, she had to prepare for an important guest.

* * *

After returning to his room at the boardinghouse, Mazorca seethed at Calthrop. He knew he risked something every time he interacted with another person. The old man had gone a step too far with that comment about Cuba.

Mazorca put the encounter out of his mind. The books he had purchased at French & Richstein's were stacked on the floor next to his bed. He removed the beat-up Schiller volume from the pile. The others he lined beside each other, a few inches apart on the floor. They were all a bit larger than the average book. One by one, Mazorca repeated the inspections he had given them at the bookstore, now going over them with greater care. He ran his hands over the covers, checked the quality of the binding, and tested the strength of the pages—everything a person might do to a book short of reading it.

When Mazorca was done examining the five tomes on the floor, he went to his trunk and removed a small revolver plus half a dozen bullets. He dropped the bullets into a pocket and checked the gun's chamber. It was empty.

He returned to the books on the floor and knelt in front of them. He flipped back the top cover of the first one and placed the gun in the center of its title page. Then he leaned over the book and stared down at it, judging the gun's distance from the margins of the page. After studying this scene, he took the gun back in his hand, closed the book, and rested the gun on the floor beside it. He lowered his head to the floor and closed one eye, comparing the width of the gun to the thickness of the book. He repeated this process with the other three books. When he had finished examining all four, he removed two from the lineup and put them off to the side, by the discarded Schiller volume.

Mazorca began his inspection all over again with the two books still on the floor, reviewing their covers, binding, and pages, and then placing his revolver on and around them. After several minutes of this, he finally paused. For a little while longer he did not move. He simply gazed at the two books before him. At last he took one and placed it on the pile of other books nearby.

He stared at the one still on the floor, studying the stylized lettering on the black cover: The Holy Bible, written in shiny gold. He remembered his conversation with the bookseller that morning. The last word. It made him smirk.

Mazorca set it back on the floor. He collected the items he had purchased that morning from Calthrop and laid them beside the book. Then he lifted the cover and turned in about hundred pages, partway through Exodus. He positioned the revolver on the open page, with the barrel running parallel to the spine and aiming upward, toward the top of the page. He looked at the gun for a moment, adjusted it slightly, and then looked at it some more. When he was satisfied, he marked the page in several places, removed the gun, and picked up one of the miniature bookbinder knives.

Just as his blade began to touch the page, a few words from the book caught his eye: "Let my people go." They stung him, but he was not sure why. He removed the gun, flipped a few more pages, and set it down again. This time he read a different line: "There was a great cry in Egypt; for there was not a house where there was not one dead." It struck him as possibly appropriate, but he really did not know what to make of it. The Bible was not something he had ever studied. He did not know its stories or its characters. He certainly did not believe they were anything more than fables. At least, he did not want to believe that they were. Whenever the topic of religion entered his mind, he tried to change the subject—and he always succeeded.

He read nothing more from that page or any other page that afternoon. Instead, he cut.

* * *

Working at his books under a gas lamp all day made Calthrop unaware of the night falling outside. Twilight had faded to black before he realized the lateness of the hour.

It was not unusual for the bookbinder to lose track of time, and so he was hardly surprised that he had missed the sun's disappearance a few minutes before seven p.m. The incident reminded him, once more, of how much he enjoyed his trade. He might have been old and he might have slowed down, but he would not give up what he did until he could do it no more.

Calthrop looked over what he had to do in the morning. He arranged a few items on his desk and rose to leave. He closed the door to his shop, locked it, and descended the staircase. He stepped onto the sidewalk and bolted another door. Light still glowed from the establishment on his immediate left, the one that sat directly below his own little shop. Calthrop knew it would shine for several more hours. The business of Madame Costello, a professional astrologist, began late in the afternoon and ran into the evening. "Reader of the Stars," said the words painted on her window. "Consultations of Past, Present, and Future Events."

Calthrop looked to the sky. There were no stars to read. Clouds obscured his view of the heavens.

He walked a block to a small pub and ate a light dinner. By the time he was heading home, the streets were desolate. Parts of the city remained alive well into the night, but he did not pass through them. Once he was away from the pub, he did not see anybody else except for a couple of soldiers who passed him and a man walking in the same direction he was going, but about a block behind him. It was a lonely scene. Only a few of the homes in his neighborhood had their lights on. In the others, people already had gone to bed or nobody was home because the occupants had fled the city.

On the doorstep of his home, on B Street just south of the Capitol, Calthrop struggled with his key. He had to wiggle it around before it finally released the lock. It had been causing too much trouble lately. He would have to get it fixed.

Calthrop opened the door to his home and stepped inside. Before he could close the door, he was pushed into the unlit hallway. He fell down and heard the door shut. Someone was in the house with him, but he could not see anything in the blackness.

"Good evening, Mr. Calthrop."

"What do you want? Is this a robbery?"

"No, I'm afraid it's something else entirely."

"Who are you?"

"You disappoint me. A man with your keen ear and you don't know who I am?"

"You're the fellow with the Schiller book. I can tell by your voice."

"How perceptive. It's a remarkable ability you possess. A little too remarkable, unfortunately."

"I don't understand. If it's money you want—"

"Money is the last thing I need from you, old man."

"What do you want, then? I've done nothing to you."

"That's not quite true. You have done something to me. You learned a piece of information about who I am. It may not sound like much, but we can't pretend it didn't happen. I really did enjoy our time together this morning. You were quite helpful. Everything was going well for both of us until you made that remark about Cuba."

"What are you talking about? You said you weren't from Cuba."

"I did say that. Did you believe me? It hardly matters. The fact is you know too much."

"How can I know too much? I don't know who you are. I don't even know your name."

"I'm called Mazorca."

Calthrop paused for a moment. It was an odd name. "You didn't have to tell me that," he said. "Please, sir, I mean you no harm. What do you want with me?"

"I've come to give you a piece of advice."

"What's that?"

"You should have stayed in the music business."

In the dark, Calthrop could discern only the outline of a figure moving toward him. Then he saw a flicker of light in the man's hand. It was the glint of a knife. It was the last thing Calthrop saw.

* * *

"So you say Scott held an emergency meeting Sunday night?" asked Violet Grenier. She thought the pleasantries had gone on for long enough. Now it was time to get down to her business before she let her guest get down to his.

"It was called in a great hurry. Fortunately, I was able to make it."

"Well, you are one of the sharpest men in town," said Grenier, staring wide-eyed at the man in the facing seat of the tête-à-tête in her parlor. "What did General Scott discuss?"

"He's in a panic over what happened in Baltimore, and especially over losing the telegraph wires. The general devoted most of the meeting to the defenses of Washington. He ordered the perimeter of the city strengthened and the major buildings barricaded. You've probably already seen the result of that."

"It's hideous. They're turning the city into a fort."

"It's for everybody's protection. If we're attacked, these preparations will be vital to our defense."

"But people are supposed to live here too. It won't be long before there's nothing left to defend—everyone will have gone away."

"You're right, Violet. That's a big problem. Too many people are evacuating the city."

"What else did General Scott talk about?" she pressed, trying to sound like an excited schoolgirl—inquisitive, but innocent.

"He's desperate for more troops to arrive—specifically, the New York Seventh. There was also some discussion of what to do with the president in the event of a Southern attack on the city."

"Was anything decided?"

Grenier's visitor hesitated. She put her hand on top of his and began to rub gently.

"There is a whole plan," he said at last.

"A whole plan? To protect the life of the president?"

"We've tried to consider every contingency."

"What is the plan? What will happen to Mr. Lincoln if the city is attacked?"

Again her guest seemed reluctant to answer. Grenier pulled her hand away from his and pouted. "You're distant tonight," she said. "It's not like you."

"I'm sorry, Violet. It's just that this is privileged information. We don't disclose everything to the public, in the interests of security. You must understand."

"Am I the public? Are you and I together in the public? No, we are not, my love. We are private—very private. This is a discreet relationship. I certainly privilege you. Why won't you privilege me in return?"

"There's no reason you need to know any of this."

"It depends what you mean by need. Now you've made it a challenge, and I need you to tell me," she said, folding her arms and putting on a pout. "I can't think of a reason why you shouldn't."

"I don't know, Violet. Your sympathies lie with the South—"

"And yet I lie so often with the North."

Her visitor understood the pun. Grenier was glad, because sometimes she thought he could be a little dim. She noticed his eyes drop to her low-cut dress. It was not the first time this evening they had done so, but it was the first time she had detected something other than desire in them.

There was judgment in them too, as if he were calculating risks and rewards. She raised her hand and began fidgeting with her necklace. The move blocked his view. Her other hand returned to his. She gave it a slight squeeze.

"This is a test," she said when his eyes met hers once more. "I'll probably forget it all in a few minutes. But I want you to tell me because I want to know everything about you."

Grenier removed her hand from her necklace and lowered it a few inches to the edge of her dress, exposing part of her bosom again. Her visitor did not fail to notice.

"Oh, very well. You are right, Violet. There is no harm in telling you."

Grenier lifted herself off her seat and gave her guest a quick kiss on the lips. "I'm so happy you see it this way," she said, making sure her breasts brushed his arm. "It makes me feel close to you." She kissed him again, this time a bit longer, and pulled away. She was ready for the information.

Her visitor smiled. "If the city is attacked and the fighting is intense, the president will be removed from the White House and placed in the Treasury."

"He wouldn't flee from the city? Not even in the middle of the night, the way he did when he arrived here?"

"That certainly was embarrassing, wasn't it?" chuckled her guest. "No, he won't flee except in the most desperate of emergencies. He felt the sting of criticism in February from some of his friends. I don't think he cares to feel it again."

"That makes sense. He definitely seemed like a coward the way he came here."

"There is at least one member of our council who would have him become a coward again."

"Really? Who is that?"

"Colonel Rook."

"The man who was in charge of security for the inauguration?"

"Yes. He's also been involved in the defenses of Washington, including the personal safety of the president."

"How would he have Mr. Lincoln become a coward again?"

"At the meeting, he said recent events in Baltimore justified the president's decision to pass through that city unobserved in February. Today he would practically confine the man to the White House. It's quite an overreaction, but that's not even the worst of it. He would additionally have the military wage a major spy campaign against the citizens of this city."

"A spy campaign?"

"He apparently believes that the secessionist element here presents such an enormous threat that our soldiers should quit guarding the bridges and start monitoring the activities of people like you." Grenier joined her guest in laughing heartily at this comment. He continued, "To think that he considers you a bigger threat to the republic than Robert E. Lee!"

Grenier roared with laughter. "You delight me with these tales. What did General Scott say to the colonel?"

"He was completely dismissive and was quite sharp with Colonel Rook in front of the whole group. I'm not sure that man has much of a future in the military."

"Apparently not."

"This is a real victory for people like you, Violet. It's no secret that you hope secession prevails. But there is a matter of decency at stake here. Gentlemen do not spy on ladies."

"So there is no surveillance?"

"No. There is none. Scott has specifically forbidden it."

"That's welcome news," said Grenier. "Shall we retire to my chambers?"

Upon hearing that suggestion, her guest jumped out of his seat. He had a big grin on his face. "What a splendid idea," he said.

"You know the way," said Grenier. "You lead and I'll follow."

Her enthusiastic visitor was halfway to the next floor before Grenier even made it to the staircase. She paused at a window, pulled back a curtain, and peeked onto the street. It was dark outside, except for a few gas lamps. There, on the corner, she saw him: the same thick-mustached man who had stood outside the day before. He was looking right at her house.

"Are you coming, Violet?"

What a fool, Grenier thought as she let the curtain fall back in place.

"Here I come, dear."

Even fools sometimes deserved rewards.

* * *

If there had been a better way to disguise the murder of Charles Calthrop, Mazorca would have pursued it. Several plans had come to mind, from pushing the bookbinder down the steps of his second-story shop to disposing of him in an alleyway in what might have been made to look like a robbery that turned fatal. But Mazorca rejected these as too hazardous. The astrologer or one of her customers might hear the fall. Anything on the streets involved the risk of discovery. Mazorca had chosen instead to follow the old man home. Seeing that Calthrop lived alone had made the decision easy.

Now he was left with a body—and the problem of what to do with it. Still in the dark of Calthrop's short hallway, Mazorca weighed his options. The simplest thing would be to leave the body alone. By killing Calthrop, Mazorca had accomplished his main goal. Everything else was secondary. Yet the body would be found at some point, and when that happened the stab wounds would show that an assailant had murdered him. Mazorca wanted to make sure that no investigation into the bookbinder's death pointed in his direction. He was certain that nobody had spotted him tailing the old man home. The only clues of any interest to the authorities would be found at the crime scene.

How long would it take before anybody came in search of the old man? The bookbinder did not conduct much business. Perhaps several days would pass before his failure to open the shop would draw attention. The next day was Wednesday. Thursday or Friday might arrive before Calthrop's failure to come to work seemed unusual, and maybe a day or two beyond that before anybody thought it was sufficiently unusual to start looking for him. Arousing curiosity was one thing, and provoking scrutiny quite another. Maybe a whole week would go by.

That was probably too much to hope for. There was at least a good chance Calthrop's body would be found the very next day, perhaps even by the early afternoon. Mazorca considered how he might confuse the people who would search for Calthrop.

The body lay twisted on the ground, in one of those contorted positions that only a lifeless form can take. The bookbinder's clothes had absorbed most of the blood. The body could be moved and nobody would be the wiser. Stashing it somewhere in the house entailed the fewest immediate risks. Yet this would not prevent discovery. The house was small, and stink would soon fill it.

Dumping the body somewhere in the wilderness was a more attractive option—Calthrop's remains might never be found. Yet the risks were far higher. Mazorca did not care to be seen in the company of a bag that was the shape and size of a corpse. There was no way he could cross one of the bridges into Virginia without drawing the attention of a soldier. That left Maryland, which he could enter discreetly, but it did not solve the more fundamental problem of unfamiliarity with the area. He simply was not sure where he could go to get rid of the body and avoid detection. And he knew soldiers were on patrol.

Perhaps there was a closer option. Mazorca was aware of his approximate location just south of the Capitol, but he had not explored this part of the city. He needed to get his bearings. From his pocket he pulled out his small guidebook and consulted its map. He had forgotten about the canal. It was closer than he had realized.

In a bedroom, Mazorca removed a blanket and sheet from a neatly made bed. He wrapped the corpse in them and decided to wait a couple of hours, when the streets would be even more desolate.

XV

Wednesday, April 24, 1861

The sun's rays had just started to touch the crane poking through the top of the half-built Capitol dome when Nat Drake heard the whistle blow. He always looked forward to the overnight train pulling in from Virginia at dawn. The load was sometimes big, and he was usually tired from hours of work, but its arrival marked the end of his shift. He could go home and sleep as soon as this last chore was done. This morning, the train was a little ahead of schedule. Nat hoped he would be walking toward his bed before the whole Capitol building was lit.

When he arrived on the platform, though, Nat frowned. Two members of his crew had not yet appeared. They were on the day shift, and they were supposed to show up in time to help unload the Virginia train. Nat knew what they were doing because they had done it plenty of times before: they were choosing to come in late. They would get away with it too, because they were white. Nat and the other night-shifters were black.

Nat understood that there was no point in complaining. He might have been a free black man, but that did not make him as free as the white people. He accepted this reality even as he did not like it. When the day shifters failed to show up on time, Nat just had to finish his job without them. He only wished they would treat him with the respect he thought he deserved as a fellow worker.

As the four members of his crew waited silently for the train to pull in, Nat remembered the morning, about two months earlier, when Abraham Lincoln had arrived. Nat was scheduled to work a double shift that day to prepare for the president-elect's arrival in the afternoon, but the man appeared on a Baltimore train first thing in the morning. Instead of the celebration that would have greeted Lincoln later in the day, a handful of somber-looking men escorted him away from the train station and into the city without fanfare.

Nat did not know what to expect from the new president. He had heard all the talk about Lincoln freeing the slaves—it was something his neighbors discussed almost daily, though never in the presence of a white person. When Nat set his eyes on Lincoln that morning, a part of him wanted to quit what he was doing and applaud the man who had become the symbol of so much hope. But Nat kept on working, partly because he did not want to draw attention to himself and mostly because he was a natural skeptic. He worried that Lincoln was just another white man who did not show up at the station on time.

The Virginia train was fairly empty, as it had been for weeks. His crew opened a car that normally would have been full of cargo only to discover that it was mostly vacant.

"Gimme a hand with this one, Martin," said Nat when he saw a square box in the corner. "It's kind of bulky."

Another man came over and they lifted the box together. Nat did not think it was too heavy, but the weight of it seemed to shift around inside. He was glad someone was helping him carry it out.

"I think this is the last one," said Martin as they moved the box off the car. "Unloadin' is quick when nobody wants to come to Washington. I could get used to this."

"You could also get used to not having a job," said Nat. "If this keeps up, there won't even be a train station here."

Nat thought he felt the weight of the box shift around again. "Hey, Martin, keep this thing balanced," he said.

"What're you talkin' about? You're the one who can't hold it straight."

"It's not movin' around because of me. That leaves you," said Nat as they lowered the box onto the platform.

"Give it up, Nat." Martin let go of his end of the box when it was still a foot off the ground. Nat could not prevent it from dropping hard onto the ground.

"Ouch!"

Nat thought the box had landed on Martin's foot, but Martin had already stepped away. Then it occurred to him: the voice came from inside the box. He stood up and looked at it for a moment. Was he hearing things? He shook his head and started to walk off.

Then he heard a sharp knocking sound. He spun around and listened. It was definitely coming from the box. Something inside was trying to get out.

"Martin, get over here," he yelled.

As Martin approached, he heard the knocks too. The top of the box started to budge. All of a sudden, it burst into the air. Beneath it stood a small woman in crumpled clothes. She arched her back, spread her arms, and groaned loudly.

Nat was dumbfounded by the scene in front of him. The woman squinted. "Is this Washington?" she asked.

"Yes it is," replied Nat.

Portia smiled briefly before a look of pain crossed her face. She twisted around, trying to loosen her muscles from the long trip.

"Who are you?" demanded Martin.

Portia did not answer. She stepped out of the box, almost falling over. Her head whipped around, looking for an exit. Then she stumbled off and disappeared from view.

Nat and Martin looked around the platform, then at each other, and finally at the empty wooden box. Apparently nobody else had seen the woman. They were not even sure they had seen her themselves.

"Don't say a word about this," said Nat.

"I don't think anybody would believe me if I did."

* * *

Grenier leaned into her back door and pressed it closed. She let out a deep sigh. Finally rid of him, she thought. At least he was worth the effort. The men who came into her bedchamber were rarely there because of Grenier's raw attraction to them. The only thing that drew her to this latest bedmate was his willingness to provide details on the inner workings of the government. This was plenty. He was an exquisitely well-placed source.

Her informant must have recognized her keen interest in his work. She was constantly asking him questions about it. The key, of course, was that he provided the answers. Sometimes it took a bit of enticing, but he never failed to give her what she wanted. He got what he wanted in return. Grenier wondered if he even knew their relationship was based on a transaction. It was conceivable that he did not know, and that his vanity kept him from understanding her actual motives. Or he could have been willfully blind—vaguely aware of his own recklessness but refusing to confront it because he enjoyed the reward so much.

Whatever awkward justifications went on inside his head were of little interest to Grenier. If he kept providing information, she would keep arranging rendezvous. As far as she was concerned, they could go on like this for as long her friends south of the Potomac found it helpful—and so far they had found it extremely helpful.

Unless somebody tried to stop them. Before last night, surveillance of her activities had been nothing more than a theory—the knowledge that it might happen. Now there was actual proof: her recent guest's information about Rook's interests and her own observation of the man who was watching her house.

Grenier was not a woman to ignore a problem. She locked the back door and headed for the staircase. This morning would be dedicated to solving problems, she decided.

Her cat squeaked a greeting as Grenier entered the second-floor study. The animal was on her desk, sprawled across loose papers. She rubbed his head and listened to his loud purr. With her other hand, she yanked a piece of paper from under the cat's paws. "This letter has weighed on me all night, Calhoun," said Grenier, glancing over the Bennett correspondence once more. "I don't want to call off Mazorca. What good would come of that? I want him to succeed. It took months of planning to get him here, and we can't afford to let more time pass while we search for a replacement."

She put down the letter and walked to the window, looking out toward the president's mansion. "If Mazorca fails, then he fails—and we are no worse off than we would be if we terminated his assignment. And if he succeeds..." Her voice trailed off, and her lips curled into a smile. "I have an idea," she said, settling into her chair by the desk. "I will write two letters." The cat sensed that it was time to leave. Still purring, it hopped to the floor. Grenier removed two small envelopes and some stationery from a drawer.

On the first envelope, she wrote "Mr. Mays" followed by Mazorca's address at the boardinghouse. Then she scribbled a short note:

> *I have reason to believe Rook is watching me. You may be in danger as well. Proceed with extreme caution.*

She folded the paper and stuffed it into an envelope. Then she placed the second envelope in front of her. For a moment, she stared at its blankness. Finally, in a careful script, she wrote the name of its intended recipient: General Winfield Scott.

* * *

Nat Drake finished unloading the other cars on the Virginia train, but he could not stop thinking about the woman in the box. When his crew was just about done, he returned to the open box. A cloth lay inside, along with a gimlet, some crumbs of bread, and an empty pouch that probably had contained water. He could not believe that this small space actually had enclosed a whole person. From the slight stench, he could tell that she had been in it for a while. He shook his head in disbelief.

The lid of the box rested a few feet away, upside down. Nat flipped it over. It was addressed to "H. Brown, Washington City." The name sounded familiar, but he was not sure why.

Then it dawned on him: H. Brown was short for Henry Brown, which was the proper name of Box Brown, the slave who had escaped to the North in a box. Nat had heard the story many times. He recalled the abolitionist leader Frederick Douglass criticizing its notoriety. Douglass thought the method should be kept secret, to prevent publicizing a successful method of liberating men and women from slavery.

Nat figured the woman was a slave. The only thing that made him wonder was the address on the box. Slavery was still legal in the District of Columbia. Box Brown had been shipped to Philadelphia, in the free state of Pennsylvania. That made sense, even if it was not foolproof. Fugitive laws covered the whole country, meaning that slave owners could reclaim their escaped slaves in states that did not permit slavery. There was no truly good place for runaway slaves to go except Canada or Europe, which many of them actually did. But free states were better destinations than slaveholding ones. Why would a boxed-up slave from the South allow herself to be taken to Washington when Philadelphia was only a little farther away? Nat could not think of a good reason. The box and its former occupant continued to puzzle him.

John J. Miller

He decided that although he might not know the motives of the woman in the box, he might be able to protect her, assuming she was in fact a runaway.

"Martin!" he called out. Martin was carrying the last crate off the Virginia train. He set it down and came over to Nat.

"What, boss?"

"Did you mention this to anybody?" said Nat, pointing toward the box.

"No. I haven't done anything but unload."

"Let's keep it to ourselves. I don't think any good will come from it if we start talkin'."

"Do you think that woman was a—"

"Stop right there. We should forget it even happened."

"Whatever you say."

"Go home now. See you tonight."

When he was gone, Nat put the lid in the box and moved them off the train platform. He was not sure where to put them, but just about anywhere was better than leaving them where they had been unloaded, in plain sight. He carried them out of the depot. The first thing he saw was the Capitol. He headed toward it.

Before long, Nat was in a construction yard. There were piles of coal and wood. Columns in various states of disassembly lay strewn about, plus blocks of marble, keystones, and iron plates. He set the box down by a pile of rock chips and grabbed a small ax lying by a wheelbarrow. He pried and chopped until only a pile of scrap wood remained.

Leaving the work area, Nat thought he heard a foot scrape against the ground behind a tool shed. He hoped that nobody had seen him. When he heard the noise again, he went around to the back of the shed. There she was: the woman from the box. She was crouched low, with her arms folded across her chest. She was not well dressed for the brisk morning weather, and she shivered a bit at the cold. Had she followed him here? Nat was not sure. He could tell she was exhausted and confused. This did not surprise him, considering what she had just gone through. How long had she been in that box? One day? Two days? More? It was amazing she had even survived.

Yet her ordeal was not over. For a moment Nat considered leaving her there. As a free black, he knew his position in Washington was tenuous. He was not a slave, but helping one escape would make him lose what few rights he did have. It was a problem he did not need or want.

Just then, some life appeared in the eyes of the woman. She looked up at Nat. Her lips parted and her voice was weak.

"Please help me."

* * *

Grenier's guest slipped through an alleyway behind her house. He moved with a mixture of caution and speed, pausing in the shadows but also determined to get away as quickly as possible. The last thing he needed was for somebody to recognize him here. It would lead to questions he did not want to answer. He wished he had left when it was still dark.

At least it was early. The day had only barely begun. At Seventeenth Street, he stood in the gap between two houses and waited. When he was certain that nobody was on the

street, he turned left and walked toward H Street. There
he made another left. He tried to act indifferent to his surroundings, but at the corner of Sixteenth and H he could
not resist a glance toward Grenier's house.

He did not love her, but he imagined that it would be
nice if she loved him. Sometimes he even let himself believe that she really did. It would have struck him as roman-
tic to see her peering from her bedroom window, hoping
to catch one more look at him. Perhaps he would risk a
little wave, something to make her smile as he set off for
another day of important meetings with top officials in the
government.

No such luck. The curtains were drawn. The front of her
house was as blank as the others nearby.

He crossed the street and entered Lafayette Park. He sat
on a bench, aware that he had some time to pass before his
first appointment of the day: a security meeting with General Scott and his top advisors.

Grenier's desire to know about the inner workings of
government was peculiar. He had never known a woman
with such an interest. But what harm was there in telling
her? She was merely curious. Why should he deny himself
the opportunity to be in her good graces? What a pleasure
it was to know such a woman, and in such a way. Already he
wanted to go back to her.

His mind churned with ideas of how to make that possible and how soon it might happen, but he found it difficult to concentrate. That dark-haired beauty had a grip on
his imagination.

A young man walked by—a civilian, probably a clerk
at one of the government agencies. His footsteps snapped

the man on the bench to attention. If the bureaucrats were already on their way to their offices, he thought, then he should be on his way as well. General Scott did not appreciate latecomers.

He rose from his seat and looked once more toward Grenier's home.

"You'll be hearing from me soon," he whispered. "Very soon."

He decided to send her a note promising more secrets the next time they were together. She would have it by morning—and he would have her again too.

* * *

The conference in the Winder Building was drawing to a close when Scott turned to Rook and gave the colonel a devilish grin. Right away, Rook did not like it. He had barely spoken during the meeting. Roughly the same cast of characters was present as compared to the previous day—Seward, Locke, and all the rest. Rook just wanted it to end without incident. The general's look suggested that he would not get his wish.

"So, Colonel Rook," said Scott, pausing for effect. "We haven't heard much from you. How goes the sandbagging?"

Locke snickered, but Rook ignored him. He kept his eyes fixed on Scott. He despised the question, but his goal of getting out of the meeting remained unchanged.

"They're piled high, sir. I'd be happy to give you a tour if you want to inspect them yourself."

"That won't be necessary, Colonel. I have faith in your ability to get this job done."

The exchange was infuriating, but Rook let it rest. Earlier, they had discussed serious matters. Washington's latest security troubles included another suspension of train service from Baltimore. The reason for the interruption was unclear, though probably the result of sabotage. Whatever the cause, it meant that no mail or newspapers from New York or Philadelphia would get through. The lines to the South remained open, at least for the time being. When Scott had shifted his attention away from these developments and toward sandbags, Rook assumed that their meeting was about to break up.

He was correct. Moments later, Rook walked from the room. In a corridor, he passed a private who was moving in the opposite direction, toward Scott. Rook thought nothing of the soldier, who was little more than a boy, and continued on his way out of the Winder Building.

Behind him, the private stepped inside the room and saw that Scott was occupied with several farewells. It took a few minutes for the room to clear. Seward was the last to depart.

"It's very good of you to come again," said the general, shaking Seward's hand. Although decorum normally would have called for Scott to be standing, he remained planted on his chair. Seward did not seem to mind. Everybody made accommodations for the weighty general.

"Thank you for your hospitality," said the secretary of state. "It's good for a member of the president's cabinet to attend these gatherings. I just hope that before long the purpose of our encounters won't be quite so pressing."

When Seward finally left, the private approached Scott and stood at attention. The general examined him for a moment. His back was nicely arched, chest out, arms straight, heels together. This was a well-trained soldier who knew how to present himself to a superior officer. Scott let him stand this way for a few moments—long enough for his unnatural pose to grow uncomfortable. It would build the boy's character. At last he spoke.

"Yes, Private?"

"Sir, this just arrived for you." He held out an envelope.

The general took it. The outside read, "Gen. Scott—personal and urgent." He ripped the seal and unfolded a piece of stationery. The script was delicate and elegant. As he read it, he grew angry.

> *Dear General:*
>
> *I hope this note finds you well. I know you are busy—perhaps too busy to know what some of your men are doing. Surely you would not order anybody to keep watch on my home, as if I were a common criminal. The current crisis is far too important for you to concern yourself with a lady's dinner parties and visits to church.*
>
> *You may want to discuss the matter with Col. Rook. You may also want to inquire as to why he puts prisoners in the Treasury Department.*
>
> *Apparently I have enemies, so I can't possibly sign my name to this letter. To have my name attached to a scandal would be ruinous.*
>
> *Yours in desperation and hope,*
> *A Friend*

Scott read the letter a second time, then a third. Part of it felt like an insult—the implication that he did not know what his own men were doing. That irritated him. But the rest of it enraged him—an accusation about surveillance and a question about prisoners. He knew what he had to do.

Scott looked up at the private and barked an order: "Get me Rook!"

* * *

Mazorca woke late and tumbled downstairs. Tabard was sitting in the dining room, hunched over a copy of the previous day's *National Intelligencer*. A steaming cup of coffee sat on the table beside her. She looked up as he approached. "Good morning, Mr. Mays," she said. "I'll get you some coffee."

The woman is efficient, thought Mazorca as he sat down. He began to reach for the newspaper when she came back with his coffee. "You were out late last night," she said.

It was not a question. Mazorca wondered whether this was an innocent attempt at small talk or the kind of inquisitive behavior that he could not tolerate. His first task was not to arouse her curiosity any further than it already had been.

"Yes, I was," he said with a smile. "I started playing cards with some new business acquaintances. We lost track of time. I'm a little embarrassed, actually. I tried to keep quiet coming in."

"Oh, don't worry about it. I'm an early riser."

That was true enough, Mazorca knew. "Do you mind?" he asked, gesturing to the newspaper. "Not at all," said Tabard, pushing it toward him.

Mazorca opened the pages, using it as a shield to hide his face from the woman. It stopped their conversation, which he had hoped it would, but it did not end his concern about her curiosity. He gulped down his coffee, continuing to hold the paper but not reading its words. When he was done, he folded the paper, set it on the table, and stood.

"Anything interesting in there?" asked Tabard. Mazorca wished she had not asked, but at least the question fell squarely in the category of small talk, rather than nosiness. "Not really," he said, smiling once again. "Thanks for the coffee."

Back in his room, Mazorca turned his attention away from the conversation downstairs. He collected the knife and a few items from his trunk and placed them in a bag.

When everything was ready, his thoughts returned to what had transpired in the dining room. It was probably nothing, he assured himself. But he wanted to be certain. Once he was gone, Tabard could unlock the door and scour his room from floor to ceiling.

With the tips of his fingers, Mazorca combed through the hair on the crown of his head. When he had isolated a single strand, he yanked it out. The hair was short, light in color, and slightly curled. Mazorca opened his trunk and positioned the hair inside, on the edge of a folded shirt. If intruders went through his belongings, they would almost certainly knock it out of place.

When this was done, Mazorca gave his room a last glance. If the previous night was late, he knew that the one ahead was likely to be even later. In fact, he was not sure when he would return.

As he descended the steps, Tabard was still sitting in the dining room. Mazorca kept his eyes trained on her the whole time, but she did not look up. She was keeping to herself. He considered it a good sign.

Less than ten minutes after Mazorca had departed, a boy carrying Grenier's message knocked on the door of the boardinghouse and handed it to Tabard.

* * *

Rook knew he would reach the Naval Observatory well ahead of Springfield. He did not like to spend his time waiting around, but he had been so desperate to get away from Scott and the Winder Building that it was a relief to stand alone with his horse. He held the horse's reins and rubbed its muzzle. The black ball above the observatory would not drop for several more minutes.

When Rook saw Springfield, he was surprised to see that the sergeant was not alone. A lieutenant walked with him—it looked like Lieutenant Fick, who had graduated from West Point within the last year or two. Rook had attended a handful of meetings with him but did not know him well. He and Springfield approached at a rapid pace.

"Sir, General Scott demands to see you immediately!" said Fick, still walking toward Rook and almost shouting the sentence.

"I was just with him not half an hour ago," said Rook.

"He's very insistent," said Fick. "He dispatched half a dozen of us to track you down."

"Why?"

"He didn't say. We're just supposed to get you back to the Winder Building as quickly as possible."

Rook looked at Springfield. "Do you know what this is about?"

"No, sir," said the sergeant, shaking his head. "Lieutenant Fick spotted me a couple of blocks from here and said he needed to find you. I told him to come this way."

"That's strange. The general hasn't had much use for me recently."

"Sir, we really should get to the general," said Fick, sounding impatient.

"Before we go anywhere, I have some business to discuss with Sergeant Springfield."

"Forgive my impertinence, sir, but the general is likely to become angry at any delay."

"Calm down, Lieutenant. You only found me a minute ago. It sounds like General Scott is mad enough to begin with. I can't see how another minute or two will make a difference. If you like, go back to the Winder Building and tell everyone that I'll be along shortly."

"Sir, I'm not supposed to let you out of my sight."

"Then by all means keep a steady gaze on me. But please allow me to have a private conversation with Springfield," said Rook. When Fick did not quickly back away, Rook raised his eyebrows in mock irritation. "And Lieutenant, that's an order."

The young man was unsure of how to respond. He crossed his arms and took a few steps back. Rook and Springfield turned away from him.

"You really don't know what this is about?" asked Rook.

"No, but I doubt it's good."

"Lately, none of my meetings with Scott have been good. Anyway, what intelligence do you have for me?"

"Not much. Grenier had a visitor last night. He wasn't there for a meal."

"Could you identify him?"

"Afraid not. It was late when he walked up the steps to the door. I wasn't close enough to get a good look."

"Was it our friend, the bibliophile with the bad ear?"

"I don't know."

"How do you know he wasn't there for a meal?"

"He arrived alone, and he stayed long past any hour of decency."

"Did you see him leave?"

"No. I gave up waiting at about three in the morning. If I hadn't, I swear I would have fallen asleep on a park bench."

"All right, Sergeant. I'm not sure what that proves, but it may be helpful. See what you can learn about Grenier's friend, the one you followed to the boardinghouse."

"Okay."

"I'll check in with you later, if General Scott hasn't bitten off my head."

Fick stood about fifteen feet away—not close enough to hear anything they had just said, and still struggling with the question of whether he should have tried. Rook saw his uncertainty. The lieutenant's earnestness was impressive.

Rook mounted his horse. "I'll see you back at the general's," he said, leaving at a trot. Fick ran behind, trying to keep up.

* * *

Portia slurped at the soup, enjoying the taste but more interested in filling her belly. Her meal was gone in a few spoonfuls. The last part of her journey from Charleston had been hard. She had grown cold, sore, and hungry. There were moments when she wanted to push out of her box, give up, and go back home, whatever the consequences.

A blanket covered her shoulders and another wrapped her legs. Beneath them, she wore the clothes of the man who found her behind a shed. He sat a few feet away from her. His own bowl of soup was still mostly full.

"I'm not sure I've ever seen anybody down my soup so quickly," said Nat. "Keep that up, and you're gonna make me think I'm a good cook."

Portia smiled. She was weak, but not so weak she could not appreciate a joke—especially one coming from a man who may have saved her.

"Want more?" asked Nat, nodding toward her empty bowl.

"Yes, please."

As Nat took her bowl and ladled soup from a pot in the next room, Portia reached into her shirt for the picture her grandfather had given her. She knew it was there because she must have felt for it a hundred times during her train trip. But she had not actually laid eyes on it since she was in South Carolina. It was a little more crinkled, but essentially the same: a black-and-white image of a man she had never seen.

Nat turned around just as she was thrusting it back into her shirt. She hoped he had not seen it.

"What's that?" he asked as he handed her a steaming bowl.

"What's what?"

"You put a piece of paper into your shirt. I see the corner stickin' out."

Portia looked down, and there indeed was the corner. She pulled out the picture and flashed it.

"It's just a picture. Nothin' important."

She put the picture back in her shirt, this time making sure none of it was exposed. She was irritated with herself for letting Nat have a look. She was grateful to him for what he had done, but she did not know whether she could tell him about her real purpose for being in Washington. Her grandfather had said only Lincoln was to see that picture, and she intended to follow his instructions.

"This soup is wonderful," she said, wanting to change the subject.

"Tell me about yourself," said Nat. "The only thing I know is your name and that you jumped out of that box on the platform."

"Maybe that's all you should know."

"Does that mean I'm gonna get in trouble if somebody finds you here?"

"Maybe you shouldn't ask questions. You've been very kind, and I don't want to make a problem for you. I won't be here long. I have somewhere to go."

"You look tired. Get some sleep here, and then you can be on your way."

When they finished eating, Nat collected their bowls and went into the other room. He was gone for just a minute or two, but it was long enough. When he returned, Portia was lying on her back with her eyes closed, breathing heavily.

As Nat tried to adjust her blanket, Portia rolled onto her side. The photo fell from her shirt. Nat stared at it a moment. Then he picked it up.

* * *

"Shut the door," snapped Scott when Rook walked into his office. "It took you long enough to get here."

Rook had not even removed his hand from the doorknob. "I came as soon as I heard you wanted to see me," he said.

"You were quiet at the meeting this morning."

"My mind has been focused on sandbagging. I've discovered that it's a contemplative activity."

"Knock it off, Rook, or that's what you'll spend the rest of your career contemplating." The general reached for a piece of paper on his desk. He held it up in one hand and pointed at it with the other. "What do you have to say for yourself?"

Rook took the letter. It was printed on cream-colored paper. The contents startled him. His secrets were secrets no more. Inexplicably, the letter seemed to have been written with knowledge deeper than what would come from mere observation. There was more to this.

"I would say that the author is Violet Grenier and that she is correct: some of your men have been keeping a watch on her. And I've locked four prisoners in the Treasury."

"Damn it, Rook. I brought you into this position because I thought I could trust you. Now I find that you're breaking orders and running rogue operations. How far has this gone?"

Rook felt he had no choice but to come clean. He described his activities going back to a week earlier, when he first took an interest in Davis and Stephens. He told of their walk around the Capitol, their visit to Grenier, the riddle that led him to the canal, the discovery of blasting powder on the boat, and his decision to imprison the collaborators. By the time he was done recounting these events, he felt better about them. He might have broken a few rules, but it was difficult to argue with the result: a group of dangerous men was now behind bars.

"Why didn't you ever tell me about any of this?" said Scott.

"I didn't believe you were taking the security threat seriously. One incident led to another, climaxing in the discovery of these men and their explosives. Since their capture, I've been trying to learn more about their plans and who they're working with—so far without much success, though I hope at least one of them will break soon. We haven't had them down there for long. It was never my intention to keep this hidden from you, but I was waiting for the right moment to reveal everything."

"Unfortunately for you, it was revealed to me before you were ready."

"I'm sorry about that, sir. But based on what we have here, I'm sure you'll agree with me about the significance of all this."

"It's certainly significant, Colonel—it's a significant blunder on your part."

"Again, sir, I'm very sorry. Please tell me how we can get past the blunder and do right by this government."

"I've already taken care of that. I'm ordering the release of the men you've been holding."

"You're letting them go?"

"They've committed no crime. You thought they looked suspicious, so you followed them on a tour of Washington and found a few barrels of blasting powder on a canal boat. I don't consider this compelling proof of a sinister plot. Colonel Locke will see to their release."

"It's enough blasting powder to take down half the Capitol!"

"Or to use in a mine. We can't go around arresting people on mere hunches."

"This is a grave mistake. Those men are part of a broader conspiracy. They were in contact with Violet Grenier, a known secessionist…"

"Don't get me started on her again," interrupted Scott, pointing his finger aggressively at Rook. "Their contact with one of Washington's society ladies convinces me of nothing except their good taste. Violet Grenier hosts parties for members of the Lincoln administration and Congress. She is an acquaintance of mine too. Are you going to toss me into the cellar of some building as well?"

Rook was flabbergasted to hear this. For a moment, he was tempted to tear the insignia off his uniform and quit. He could tell Scott that he was done trying to protect the president, only to have his best efforts blocked by an old man who would fail to see a threat if a gun were pointed directly at Lincoln's head. Yet Rook knew that if he exploded in anger here, he would make a bad situation even worse. He resolved not to lose his temper.

"Tell me," said Scott in a calmer voice, "what do you think you have learned from your surveillance of Grenier?"

Rook wondered if the general was giving him an opening. He described what he had learned: the discovery and pursuit of Davis and Stephens, the monitoring of Grenier, and the observation of her guests as they came and went from her home and moved around Washington. Scott listened to the report without interjecting.

When Rook was done, the general shook his head. "So you're spending your time following people into bookstores?"

"The way to uncover a conspiracy is to track down every lead, even the ones that seem trivial."

Scott shook his head and let out a deep sigh. "I ought to fire you for insubordination. I appreciate your enthusiasm, but you must stop the surveillance immediately. Take the rest of the day off. Get some sleep and come back in the morning. If I'm in a good mood, I'll let you keep your job."

* * *

Clark opened his eyes when he heard the voices. They did not belong to Rook or Springfield, which meant that for the first time since he had started guarding the prisoners in the basement of the Treasury, someone else was approaching—many people, judging from the number of footsteps.

"They must be this way," said one of the men he could not yet see. They were getting closer. This sounded bad.

Clark jumped out of the small cot in the hallway. There was not much to do on duty, so he had spent a lot of time napping. He was awake instantly, aware that he was posted to this place for a moment precisely like this one. The main threat did not come from the prisoners, who were safely locked up. It came from their discovery by others. Clark needed to prevent it.

"Over here," said an officer as he turned into a corridor and spotted Clark, who saw that the officer was a colonel.

Five soldiers followed behind him. "What are you doing down here, Corporal?"

His confident tone suggested that he already knew the answer to his own question. Clark nevertheless pointed to a pile of boxes in the hallway. "Trying to find some old records," he said. "There's supposed to be some information about the construction of the Treasury. It's wanted for defensive information."

"Is that so? Don't you think this is a strange place to store such valuable documents?"

"I just do what I'm told, sir. They haven't been found elsewhere."

"Who sent you down here?"

"Colonel Rook."

"Ah, yes. Well, Corporal, my name is Colonel Locke, and I'm down here in this godforsaken place to find something too. Do you know what I might be looking for?"

"No, sir."

"Are you sure about that? I would hate for you to be in a position that requires you to lie to an officer. You may be interested to know that Colonel Rook is in an enormous amount of trouble."

Clark swallowed hard.

"Why don't you just tell me where they are?"

Clark realized that it was useless to maintain the ruse. "Come this way, sir," he said, resigned to defeat. He led Locke and the other soldiers through a door that led to a short passage lined by several other doors. "They're in here," he said.

Locke pointed to a door. "Open it," he said.

Clark removed a key from his pocket. Inside the small room, Davis sat in a corner.

Locke entered the room. "It's your lucky day," he said. "You're free to go."

* * *

After crossing the bridge into Maryland, Mazorca turned south on a dirt road that followed the course of the Potomac River as it flowed toward the Chesapeake Bay. He passed Fort Washington around the middle of the day. Just as Fort Sumter was supposed to protect Charleston from attack, Fort Washington was supposed to defend the capital city from enemy warships that sailed upriver. The entrance gate was closed, and there did not appear to be anybody inside the fort's walls. The fort was not ready to defend anything.

A little to the south, a path broke off from the main road and tunneled through trees and bushes to the river. Mazorca stopped his horse and looked over his shoulder. He saw nobody. For a long minute he sat motionless, listening for the sound of anyone who approached. He heard nothing. Satisfied that he was alone, Mazorca followed the trail as it sloped down to a muddy shoreline. A small rowboat was pulled out of the brown water and tied to a tree.

Mazorca smiled. He had planned to spend the afternoon searching the riverside for a boat, and here was one in the first place he had looked. He dismounted his horse and examined the boat. Except for a couple of oars, it was empty. The boat was weather-beaten, but it looked seaworthy. It would suit his purposes well enough.

He scanned the river and saw a single ship about a mile downriver, headed away from him. There was no way anybody on board could spot him. Across the river sat a col-umned house. Even from a distance, Mazorca could see that its white paint was peeling. The roof needed shingling. A lawn in front was ragged and unkempt. Mazorca realized that this must be Mount Vernon. Its famous owner had been dead since 1799. It appeared as though nobody had taken care of the home in decades. Mazorca was not surprised to see it in a state of disrepair. In the city, Washington's mon-ument was incomplete. In the country, his old home was falling apart. This was how America honored its heroes. No wonder the young nation was coming undone.

Mazorca fixed his horse to a tree. Then he removed a saddlebag and placed it in the boat. Next he untied the rope that secured the small craft to the shore. He shoved the boat into the water and hopped inside. The oars slipped easily into their locks. Mazorca began rowing north, against the Potomac's slow current. He stayed close to the shore— so close that a few low-hanging tree branches brushed his hat. After rowing for several hundred feet, Mazorca found a small break in the foliage.

Maneuvering toward it, he heard the boat scrape its bot-tom. Mazorca got out and pulled the boat from the water, dragging it onto the land until it was a dozen feet from the Potomac. Behind the trunk of a large tree, he turned the boat upside down and covered it with branches and leaves. Then he walked back to the shoreline and studied his work. It was just barely possible to make out the contours of the rowboat, but only because he knew it was there. A casual observer almost certainly would not see it.

Mazorca figured that if the boat's owner bothered to hunt for his missing craft, he would assume either that it was stolen and long gone or that it had broken loose and drifted downriver. The possibility of it being both nearby and hauled onshore just a bit upriver probably would not occur to him. Yet it was now positioned perfectly for Mazorca, who wanted to make sure he could have free access to water in reasonably short order.

Mazorca removed his shoes, rolled up his pant legs, and tossed the saddlebag over his shoulder. Then he splashed into the river and waded back to his horse. He was pleased to think that he was well ahead of schedule. There was one more thing he wanted to do before leaving Maryland.

* * *

A block from Tabard's, Rook told Springfield about the drubbing he had just received from Scott. "I'd like to know how Grenier came to write to Scott about me and those men from the canal. We've been watching her, but it seems like she's been watching us."

"Am I supposed to quit monitoring this fellow?" asked the sergeant, gesturing in the direction of the boardinghouse.

"He ordered me to stop the surveillance of Grenier. That's all."

Springfield smirked. "I suspect you're living by the letter of the law, rather than its spirit."

"At the moment, the spirit is moving me to learn more about Grenier's friend," said Rook. "Tell me what you know."

After his meeting with Rook, Springfield had walked over to Tabard's boardinghouse. He observed it for a little while. He concluded that the tenants were at work and that Mrs. Tabard was alone.

"So I knocked on the door," he said. "When she answered, I introduced myself as Mr. Jones and inquired about a room. She said that she had one available on the third floor and offered to show it to me. Once we had looked it over, we sat in her dining room and chatted for several minutes. I made some gentle inquiries about her boarders. Thankfully, she's a talker. I'm convinced that our man goes by Mr. Mays—he's a new lodger, with a room on the second floor. It's right at the top of the steps. She was reluctant to say much about him, but I could tell that she actually craved the conversation. She allowed that Mays is quite private and keeps strange hours. Sometimes she's not even sure whether he's in or out."

"Do we know where he is right now?"

"He's definitely out. She saw him leave this morning."

"Does she know where he went?"

"No. As I said, his movements are a mystery to her."

"The more we learn about this man, the more he intrigues me. It's too bad we can't take a look at his room."

"Colonel, you're much too pessimistic."

"What do you mean?"

Springfield grinned. "Well, I got her to start talking about her son, who is in the navy."

A puzzled expression crossed Rook's face. The sergeant continued. "She wanted to show me a picture of him. So she retrieved it from another room." Springfield paused and smiled even wider.

"Yes?" asked Rook.

"She was gone for a minute or two. I know it doesn't sound like a long time, but when you think about it, a minute or two can seem like quite a while."

Rook only let a few seconds go by before he prompted Springfield. "Please go on."

"You can get a lot done in a minute or two."

"That's certainly the implication. So what did you get done?"

Springfield reached into his pocket. He jingled its contents. When he took his hand out, it held a key. His smile grew wider.

* * *

Portia woke to the sound of Nat snoring in a rocking chair. She sat up, stretched her arms, and yawned. Lying in bed all day had seemed to rejuvenate her.

The room was full of shadows, cast by the dim light coming from a window. She saw Nat stir, in the last stages of sleep. He had told her that he worked nights. When he left, she would be alone again, in the dark.

Perhaps this would be a good time to make her getaway. By giving her protection and food, Nat had done plenty for her. He did it at some risk to himself, too. Portia had not told him in so many words that she was a runaway, but what else could she be? Nat had to know. Leaving now would remove a danger from his midst. The problem was that she still had to find the White House. She had no idea where to go or even what it looked like.

Nat shifted around in his chair again. Maybe he could tell her. Then Portia could leave.

She yawned again and slipped her hand into her shirt to check on the photo. She had become so accustomed to its presence that she was only half aware that she was doing it. This time, however, her hand felt nothing. The failure to touch it startled her. In an instant, she was fully awake, patting down her clothes and searching through her blankets in a panic. She looked all over the bed, under it, and on the floor nearby. The picture was missing. Her mad scramble to find it had turned up nothing.

But it did wake Nat.

"Lookin' for somethin'?" he asked. She did not care for his tone of voice. It sounded as if he already knew the answer to his question.

"I had somethin' here, but it ain't here now," she said.

Without a word, Nat reached to a table beside him and lifted the photo for Portia to see.

"Gimme that!" shouted Portia, leaping to her feet. She tried to grab the picture, but Nat pulled it away. He held it with both hands from the top, ready to rip it in half if she took a step toward him. Portia froze in place.

"Just tell me what this is," he said.

"I can't believe you took that from me."

"I didn't take nothin' from you. All I did was pick it up from where it fell."

"Well, it's mine, and I want it back." Portia held out her hand.

"Put your hand down," snapped Nat. He spoke with an authority that reminded her of an overseer. She obeyed. "Now sit back down," said Nat in a lower voice. She obeyed that order too.

"I brought you here knowin' the risks," he said. "That was my choice. I'll also help you get on your way to wherever it is you need to go. The worst thing for me would be for you to get caught two minutes after leavin' because you didn't know what you were doin'. I'll give you help, but there can't be no secrets. You've been hidin' this photograph ever since you come here. Maybe you think it ain't my business, but when I brought you here, fed you, and let you sleep, you made it my business."

Portia's voice held a note of desperation. "That picture's the whole reason I'm here. You've helped me this much, Nat. You gotta give it back."

"Tell me about it."

"Let me ask you somethin' first."

"Okay."

"What do you think of the president?"

"Abe Lincoln? He's causin' a lot of fuss around here. Right now, nobody seems to know if there's a war comin' or not. I sort of wish things were back to normal."

"Are you for him or against him?"

"I've never thought of it that way. Nobody has asked me. I don't get to vote, you know."

"Where I'm from, everybody's against him. All the white people are, anyway. They say he's gonna free the slaves. That makes me for him."

"I ain't no slave, Portia. I don't wanna see nothing happen that's gonna make me one. Abe Lincoln's givin' people worries, and I'm not sure I'll be better off when it's over."

"Does that mean you're against him?"

"No, it don't mean that. It would be good if Lincoln freed the slaves. But it's not somethin' he can just do. It's more complicated than that. He'd have to fight a war, and that ain't in my interests. If an army from Virginia were to come marchin' into Washington, things wouldn't look so good for me or my kind."

"Don't you want to see him succeed?"

"I don't want him to mess up."

Portia didn't reply immediately. Could she trust him with the information he wanted?

"What does any of this gotta do with the picture?" asked Nat, looking again at the photo.

Portia decided she had no choice but to trust him. "Nobody's supposed to see it except the person I'm bringin' it to."

"And who's that?"

"Abe Lincoln."

"You're tryin' to get this picture to Abe Lincoln?" Nat was incredulous. He looked at the photo again. "Why?"

"It's just somethin' I gotta do. I made a promise."

"Why would Abe Lincoln want to see this?"

"I can't say. I just gotta find him. Can you tell me where he's at?"

"There ain't no way you're gonna get near him. He's the president of the United States, and you're just a runaway."

"The whole purpose of my bein' here is to find Abe Lincoln and give him the picture. If you just tell me where he is, I'll go. You won't have to worry about me no more."

"All right, I'll walk you there tonight before I gotta start work. But once I point to his house, I'm gone and you're on your own."

* * *

Ten minutes. That was how long Springfield said he could detain Tabard. From across the street, Rook watched the sergeant enter the boardinghouse. He could hear him greet her. The plan was to tell Tabard that he wanted to look over the unwanted room a second time. On the third floor, he would run through a series of questions about everything from the price to the condition of the floorboards. Meanwhile, Rook would enter the building and quietly examine the second-story room belonging to Mays.

Rook's gaze locked on the upper-story window. Soon, he saw Springfield standing just inside of it. That was his signal to move. He crossed the street, opened the door, and walked in. Then he passed through the foyer and carefully climbed the steps. At the top was a door. He pushed the key into its lock and turned. It opened easily. Rook slipped into the room and closed the door.

The curtains were only partly drawn. An envelope rested at his feet. He noted its position on the floor and picked it up. It was addressed to "Mr. Mays, 604 H St." Rook tried to lift the flap, but it was sealed shut. A corner was loose, however, and Rook slid a finger into the gap and gently ran it along the edge of the flap. The seal began to give. Rook thought he could open the envelope without damaging it. Suddenly the flap ripped in half. Rook cursed under his breath. It would be obvious that someone had tampered with the envelope.

The damage having been done, he figured there was no harm in ripping open the envelope all the way. He pulled out a piece of stationery, made from the same creamy stock that Grenier had used in her note to Scott. Rook read the note: "I have reason to believe Rook is watching me. You may be in danger as well. Proceed with extreme caution."

Rook folded the note and stuck it in his pocket. Given its condition, he figured that it was best for the note to vanish entirely.

Much of the rest of the room was plain, with a bed positioned lengthwise along a wall and a trunk beneath the window. A pile of thick books attracted Rook's attention. They were stacked on the floor and in various states of disrepair. Bindings were slit and pages were removed. Paper shavings sprinkled the floor. Rook noticed the titles: these were the books purchased from French & Richstein's. Behind them, Rook found scissors, knives, a ruler, glue, and a few spools of colored ribbon. These would have come from the bookbinder. He had no idea what it all meant.

The bed was bare, except for a blanket and pillow. Nothing was hidden beneath it. The only thing left to investigate was the trunk. Rook raised its lid and peered inside. He saw shirts, pants, and socks, all neatly folded. Kneeling down, he pulled out a few items and sorted through the rest to see what they covered. At the bottom of the trunk, he found a rifle—a Sharps New Model 1859 breechloader. This was a preferred weapon for marksmen. A proficient shooter could hit a target at fifteen hundred feet. Rook pulled it out. The gun was clean and well maintained. It was also loaded.

The fact that a man would keep a gun in a trunk did not startle Rook in the least. Yet he was still concerned that Mays owned a sniper's weapon. Mays was connected to Grenier, who was connected to those canal conspirators. Perhaps Scott could dismiss this mass of circumstantial evidence. Rook remained convinced that something lay beneath it all.

His ten minutes had just about expired. Rook put the gun back in the trunk and then returned the clothes, arranging them as he had found them. He took one more look around the room. Nothing else jumped out at him. Upstairs, he imagined Springfield quizzing his hostess about what kind of ceiling paint she preferred. He knew it was time to go.

A moment later, the lid to the trunk was shut, the door to the room was locked, the key to the room was dangling from the hook in the kitchen, from where Springfield had plucked it—and Rook was walking down H Street, away from the boardinghouse. Scott had told him to take the rest of the day off. Rook would put the time to good use, going over his options and thinking about going over the general's head.

* * *

The sun was sinking below a stand of trees when Mazorca finally turned his horse onto a short lane that led to a small cabin. He had observed the house for two hours when the light was still good and decided that its single occupant, an elderly man, lived alone. Perhaps he had once shared his home with a wife and children, but there was no evidence of them now. In all likelihood, the wife had passed on and the children had grown up. Several acres of farmland sat behind the house, but the man probably rented them to a younger neighbor. It looked like he scratched out a modest existence from combining this income with whatever he raised in a nearby pigpen.

Yet this was all guesswork. What mattered to Mazorca was the apparent fact that the man was in the house by himself and that nobody else lived nearby. Riding up and down the dirt road, Mazorca had discovered that the nearest house was about a mile away. Further on there was a crossroads tavern that catered to travelers moving between Washington and southern Maryland. But the cabin in front of him was about as isolated as anything he had seen in the region that day. Mazorca dismounted. He would perform the test here.

The smell of a warm dinner drifted through an open window. The old man must have heard Mazorca because he appeared at the door. Until now Mazorca had seen him only from a distance. This was his first close look. He was of average height, on the skinny side, and stooped at the shoulder. Much of his hair was gone, and what remained of it had turned gray. He had not shaved for several days. Mazorca figured him for at least sixty years old, maybe seventy.

"Hello," said the man in a tone more suspicious than welcoming.

"Good evening," said Mazorca, removing his hat and trying to reassure the man with a smile. "I'm sorry to arrive unannounced, so late in the day. It wasn't my intention to interrupt your dinner. May I trouble you for a minute?"

"If you're looking for the inn, there's one just up the way," he said, pointing in the general direction of the crossroads tavern.

"Thank you, but that's not why I'm here," said Mazorca, resting his hat on the horn of his saddle. "I have a simple question for you." He opened his saddlebag and pulled out a book. Its exterior was black, with gold letters on its front and spine. A pair of yellow and red ribbons dangled from the bottom. Mazorca approached the doorway and raised the book, displaying its cover. "Do you know what this is?"

The old man squinted for a moment, and then recognition filled his eyes. "Look, mister," he said. "I don't have time for your preaching. If you'll please excuse me…"

Mazorca laughed. "I'm not a preacher, and I'm not going to preach. It's the furthest thing from my mind, really. I was just hoping you could identify this book." He continued to hold it up, a few feet away from the old man.

"Well, it sure looks like the Holy Bible."

"Yes, it does look like a Bible," said Mazorca in a patronizing voice that a teacher might use to encourage a slow student. He now began rotating the book in his hands, so that the old man could view it from several angles. "But are you certain it's a Holy Bible?"

"Is this some kind of trick?"

"I prefer to think of it as a challenge."

"Mister, I don't know what you're trying to do here, but I'm in no mood for this."

"Very sorry!" said Mazorca, laughing again. "I see that I'm trying your patience. Let me make this simple. Please permit me to ask a direct question: you think this looks like a Holy Bible, such as a preacher might carry around?"

"Yes," said the old man, warily.

"Excellent. That's all I wanted to know. Thank you very much."

Rather than turning to leave, Mazorca now just stood in front of the doorway and stared at the old man. He held the book by the spine, in his left hand. No part of him moved, except for the thumb and index finger of his right hand, which gently massaged the red ribbon hanging from the book. His friendly look had vanished from his face.

"What is the meaning of this?" asked the old man.

"The exam is over," said Mazorca, taking a step forward so that he was an arm's length away from the doorway.

"Excuse me?"

"The book passed. You failed." Mazorca yanked on the yellow ribbon. Inside the book, something clicked. Then Mazorca pulled the red one. The book banged. The old man crashed backward through the doorway, clutching his neck. He was dead before he hit the floor.

Still standing outside, Mazorca examined the top of the book. A wisp of smoke rose from a small puncture that was newly visible in the pages between the two covers. He chuckled to himself. "It was a Holy Bible, and now it's a Bible with a hole in it."

He tucked the book under his arm and sniffed the air. The smell of the gunshot was strong, but not enough to mask the aroma coming from inside the house. Mazorca moved through the doorway, stepping over the corpse that lay on its back in a widening pool of blood. A pot of soup boiled on a stove in the fireplace. It was time for dinner.

* * *

In the White House, Rook watched John Hay descend a staircase. He was glad to see that Lincoln's personal secretary still wore a bow tie. It indicated that the young man had not yet gone to bed, even though it was approaching midnight. He had not seen Hay for several weeks and was not entirely sure how he would be received at this odd hour.

Given the events of the afternoon, he did not know where else to turn.

"Good evening, Colonel," said Hay before he had even reached the bottom step. "This is a pleasant surprise." He sounded like he actually meant it. The two men shook hands.

"I'm sorry to bother you, especially so late."

"No trouble at all," said Hay. "I was helping the president with correspondence until just a little bit ago."

"Has the president retired?" asked Rook. A part of him was relieved to learn that Lincoln had made it through another day without encountering a mysterious rifleman.

"About half an hour ago, and not a minute too soon," said Hay. "The man needs rest—he has spent too much time convinced that a secessionist army is about to plunder our city. If he slept more, he might worry less."

Hay described how the president's day had been full of routine business—writing letters to public officials, listening to job seekers beg for federal appointments—and how his mind kept drifting off to the subject of the Seventh Regiment. Where was the army that was supposed to defend the capital? With the telegraphs to Maryland severed, nobody knew. Washington remained cut off from news except from the South. At a meeting with troops who had arrived in advance of the missing soldiers, Lincoln was downright gloomy. "I don't believe there is any North. The Seventh Regiment is a myth," he had said. "You are the only Northern realities." Hay added that he was glad there had been no cabinet meeting that afternoon, because the president clearly needed a break.

"I hope he gets a long night of sound sleep," said Hay. "He could use it."

"It sounds as though the only real cure will be for the Seventh Regiment to arrive," said Rook.

"That's probably true. But I've rambled on for too long. You came to see me. What can I do for you?"

Before Rook could respond, the two men heard a loud commotion down the hall in the direction of the front door. Half a dozen members of the Frontier Guard burst in. Two of them held a black boy by the arms. The captive struggled to break free from their grasp. The other guardsmen gripped pistols and rifles. All of them hollered curses and threats, but Rook could not make out what anyone was saying. At the other end of the hall, several of their comrades emerged from the East Room, brandishing their own weapons. The ruckus sounded like a gigantic barroom brawl.

Rook sprinted down the hall, hoping he could quiet the little mob before somebody actually pulled a trigger inside the White House. "Stop!" he yelled, trying to raise his voice above all the others. The Frontier Guards were rowdy mavericks, but they also recognized the authority of Rook's blue uniform and fell silent as the colonel reached them. Their captive, however, continued to thrash around and scream, "Lemme go! Get your hands off me!"

The voice did not belong to a boy, but a small woman. With a violent kick, she planted her foot in the groin of one captor. He bent over in pain and released his hold on the woman. Three more guards jumped to replace him. Each grabbed a limb, and a moment later the woman was suspended above the ground, looking as if she were about to be drawn and quartered. Even in this state of helplessness, she still squirmed and howled.

"Set her down!" roared Rook, pushing his way to the woman. "And you," he said, pointing his finger in her face, "shut your mouth!"

His aggressive behavior had the desired effect. The guards released the woman's legs. She stood up straight between a pair of large men who continued to clutch her arms. All eyes turned to the colonel.

Rook's own gaze settled on one of the guards who seemed older than the others. "Tell me what's going on here."

The man said that he and several guardsmen had spent the day patrolling along the river, looking across the water for signs of military activity on the Virginia side. They quit at the end of the day but went downtown for dinner instead of returning to the White House. Rook could smell alcohol on the man's breath and figured the group must have spent several hours drinking. That probably would account for their boisterousness. He let the man continue his story.

"When we came back here, Tommy"—he nodded his head in the direction of a young man who was having some difficulty standing at attention—"went to one of the bushes by the gate." The man now paused to reflect upon whether a late-night visit to the bushes needed further explanation. He decided it did not. "When Tommy got there, he found this woman hiding behind them. She tried to run, but Tommy tackled her before she could get away. The rest of us apprehended her, sir, because suspicious activity on the grounds of the White House cannot be tolerated." Proud to have made this report, the guard arched his back and puffed out his chest. He tried to suppress a hiccup and failed.

Rook turned to the woman. She was slim and not much more than five feet tall. She certainly seemed to have a lot of energy, but she did not appear to pose a threat to anybody.

"Who are you?" asked Rook.

"My name is Portia."

"Were you on the grounds of the White House?"

"Yeah."

"Were you hiding behind a bush?"

"Yeah."

The way she had resisted the guards proved that she was feisty. But now Rook noticed her tremble. She was afraid.

"Why were you hiding?"

"I gotta see President Abe Lincoln."

By now, nearly two dozen members of the Frontier Guard had emerged from the East Room. When Portia announced her desire to see the president, they exploded in laughter. "Do you have an appointment?" mocked one, prompting louder guffaws. Several of the guards swore loud oaths that she would never lay eyes on him. "Did you think you were going to find the president behind a bush?" demanded one of them. The others hooted their approval.

"Silence!" shouted Rook. "Let the woman speak."

"I got a message for President Abe Lincoln," said Portia in a tone of despair. "I was goin' up to the house when I heard these loud men comin' up, singin' their songs. They frightened me. So I ran behind a bush. It was the first thing I could find."

"And when you were found out, you tried to run away?"

"Yeah. I ain't here to talk to them. I come for President Abe Lincoln."

The guards continued their chortling but hushed at the sound of a tinny voice from down the hall.

"Who wants to speak to the president?"

The guards parted to make way for the tall, bearded speaker, who wore a robe over a nightshirt. He halted before Portia and Rook. John Hay stood just behind him.

"Sir," said Rook, "perhaps you should let us handle this matter—"

"So that I can go back to sleep?" said Lincoln. "Ha! Nobody can sleep through this racket. Now, who wants to speak to the president?"

Hay shrugged. "You had better just tell him, Colonel," he said.

"This woman, sir," said Rook. "Her name is Portia. We don't know anything about her except that she was found in the bushes outside."

"I see," said Lincoln. "Tell me, Portia, what is it you would like to discuss with the president of the United States of America."

Portia narrowed her eyes. "You're President Abe Lincoln?"

"I've been called much worse."

Portia did not say anything immediately. Lincoln smiled, trying to put her at ease.

"I've come a long way to give you somethin'," she said, reaching into her pocket.

As she made this move, one of the Frontier Guardsmen raised a pistol and pointed it at Portia. "No tricks," he warned, moving the gun closer to her than was probably necessary. He looked as though he would enjoy shooting her. Portia froze in place, her hand hidden beneath her clothes.

"Calm down," said Rook sharply.

"She's just a stupid slave girl," sneered the man. "She doesn't even deserve to be in this house."

Everyone tensed. Rook thought about pulling out his own pistol to protect Portia, but he hesitated just long enough for Lincoln to speak up. "Whenever I hear anyone arguing for slavery, I feel a strong impulse to see it tried on him personally."

The Frontier Guards broke into laughter. Their trigger-happy comrade looked embarrassed. "Why don't you lower that gun," said the president. The man obeyed. Rook was amazed at the effect.

"Now, Portia, what do you have for me?" asked Lincoln.

Portia looked around nervously. From her pocket, she removed a small piece of paper and turned it face up. The light in the hallway was weak, but Rook could see that it was a photograph. Portia held it out.

Lincoln took the picture and raised it close to his face, squinting at the image. He stared at it for what seemed like quite a while.

"I've seen this man before," he said, still looking at the picture. "He came to me for a job recently. I don't immediately recall his name. He was good with riddles." He handed the photograph to Hay. "Do you remember seeing him?"

Hay studied the image. "Yes. I recognize the ear, or rather the lack of one. I let him into your office. I'd have to look at the records to get his name."

"I know his name," said Portia. "It's Mazorca."

"An unusual name," said Lincoln. "I don't think that's what he called himself with me. Why are you showing me his picture?"

"The man in that picture is gonna try to kill you," said Portia. A murmur of voices rumbled through the hallway.

"Mr. President," said Rook, "we need to talk."

XVI

Thursday, April 25, 1861

A few minutes after eight o'clock, Rook walked into the meeting room of the Winder Building. Portia followed him in. All of the conversations between the officers immediately stopped. Those who were not already seated scrambled for their chairs, almost like schoolchildren who dashed to their desks upon the first sight of their teacher. The only sound came from the ticking of a clock.

The colonel had wondered what his reception would be like. He now realized that there would be no friendly greetings or informal pleasantries. The only exception was Springfield, who nodded almost imperceptibly at him. The two men had not seen each other since the previous day at Tabard's. Springfield never before had attended one of Scott's meetings—as a sergeant, his rank was too low—but Rook had sent him a note overnight requesting his presence. The colonel was counting on him to make an important contribution.

Portia's nighttime appearance at the White House had led to several important connections. Rook learned that she came from the Bennett plantation in South Carolina, carrying the picture of a man supposedly sent to murder the president. Langston Bennett corresponded with Violet

Grenier, a secessionist who seemed to sit at the center of a conspiracy. The pieces of the puzzle were beginning to fit together, even if the full picture remained unclear.

All eyes were on Rook, who remained standing. The colonel thought he detected a mix of curiosity and skepticism. At the opposite end of the room, sitting furthest from the door, was Scott. He looked positively hostile, with crossed arms. Locke sat to his left, trying to mimic the general's posture and expression. On the other side of the general sat Seward. Rook had not expected to see him.

Scott was obviously irritated. Having a good sleep interrupted for any reason made the general grumpy. Having it ruined the way it was just a few hours ago, when a messenger from the White House banged on his door in the middle of the night and delivered an urgent note whose contents seemed to undermine so much of what he had been saying over the last several weeks—that was downright humiliating. And Scott disliked few things more than personal humiliation.

Anybody who knew Scott even a little knew this much about him, and Rook had admired the tactful way in which President Lincoln phrased his note to his top general. There was no attempt to complain or disgrace. It was a simple order, issued delicately:

> *My dear sir:*
> *In the morning, you will be pleased to receive Col. Rook.*
> *He will convey information of the utmost importance.*
>
> *Your obedient servant,*
> *A. LINCOLN*

Rook was gratified to see it written and dispatched. At the same time, he knew that it left a lot unsaid. He understood that it would be his responsibility not only to say it but also to impress Scott and the others with its significance.

"Good morning, gentlemen," said Rook. Several of the officers mumbled responses. The general continued to glare in silence. "Let me bring you up to date on the events of the last day, culminating with an extraordinary encounter late last night at the White House."

Rook knew it would be difficult to summarize his recent activities and how he came to know what he knew. He did not want to attribute any blunders to Scott, at least not yet. A genuine threat against the president needed to take precedence.

"This is Portia, the little woman who is responsible for our meeting this morning," he said. He described her journey from South Carolina to the White House. He mentioned the photograph and how both Lincoln and Hay had recognized the man in the picture.

"It appears as though an assassin has been in the presence of our commander-in-chief," said Rook. "His name is Mazorca, and this is what he looks like." He removed the photograph from a pocket and held it up. The image was too small for everyone to see at once, so Rook handed it to a major who was seated next to him. "Please take a good look and pass it around."

The picture moved halfway round the table, with each officer plus Seward taking a quick glance, until it arrived at Scott's place. The general stared at it for a long time. Nobody had said anything since Rook began his report. All wanted the see the reaction of the general prior to forming their own opinions. Would he accept Rook's logic?

"So, Colonel," said Scott as he set the photograph on the table rather than passing it on, "you found it impossible to work underneath me and decided to go over my head."

"Sir, this is an amazing development that none of us could have foreseen—"

Locke broke in, almost shouting. "How do you know that this slave woman is telling the truth? She is a fugitive who ought to be returned to her rightful owner."

Around the table, a number of heads nodded in agreement. Several others, however, were visibly annoyed at the suggestion. Here was the question that divided the nation, writ small.

"She has no reason to lie," said Rook with agitation. "Let's remember the focus of this conversation—it's not about her." He gestured to Portia and then walked around the table and grabbed the photograph from the spot where Scott had set it down. "It's about him." He held the picture at arm's length, showing its image to the officers. "This man wants to murder the president. He may have come very close to doing it already. We must stop him from making a new attempt."

The room erupted into a chaos of voices as several officers spoke at once. Rook could barely hear what any of them said. Soon, however, he became most interested in the one officer who was not saying anything at all: Springfield had not taken his eyes off the photograph since Rook had held it up for the second time.

The sergeant rose from his chair, walked over to Rook, and asked for the picture. Rook gave it to him. Springfield looked at it intensely. He stroked his mustache. It was not long before everybody in the room noticed what he was doing. His deep interest in the photograph could mean only one thing, and everybody knew it.

"I've seen this man before," said Springfield. "I know where he lives."

* * *

Mazorca delayed his return to Tabard's boardinghouse until the middle of the morning. He had not lingered long at the cabin in Maryland. He had eaten a quick supper, dragged the body of the man he had killed to a nearby stand of trees, and left the scene. He had taken a roundabout route home, avoiding the bridge he had crossed in the morning, using less-traveled roads, and coming into Washington from the north. This was faithful to his plan of keeping his movements irregular. At dawn, as he approached the city, he decided to give his fellow boarders time to eat their breakfasts and leave for their jobs. The less contact he had with them, the better. When he finally walked through the front door, he was exhausted and ready to sleep.

Tabard was in the dining room, wiping the table with a rag. "Good morning, Mr. Mays," she said.

"Good morning," replied Mazorca. He headed straight for the stairs.

"You will find a letter in your room," said Tabard. "It arrived yesterday. I slipped it under your door."

"Thank you," called Mazorca without pausing as he made his way up to the second floor.

In truth, he was not at all thankful. He immediately regretted giving his address to Grenier. She was the only person who would have known it. He did not want to be contacted by anyone—even her. Then again, perhaps she had something important to tell him. Maybe she had learned an important detail about Lincoln's security or his whereabouts.

He unlocked the door, pushed it open, and looked at the floor. There was no letter. He shut the door and scanned the entire room. He saw nothing and wondered whether Tabard had slid the envelope under the door with such force that it had coasted to the opposite wall. He looked under his bed, behind his trunk, and below the window. The search turned up nothing. The letter simply was not in the room.

A troubling thought gripped him. What if Tabard had put it under the wrong door? What if one of the other boarders had opened it?

Mazorca examined the room again. Still no letter. Something was definitely amiss. He thought about the strand of hair he had plucked from his head and positioned in the trunk. He raised the lid of the trunk slowly, not wanting a sudden motion to blow the hair from its place. Peering inside, his clothes appeared to be where he had left them. But the hair was gone.

Mazorca marched down the stairs and into the dining room, where Tabard was arranging a new centerpiece for the table.

"Mrs. Tabard, what did you say as I walked up the steps a few minutes ago?"

A look of concern crossed her face. "I said that I had slipped a letter under your door yesterday. Is there a problem?"

"I don't know. Are you certain that you slipped it under my door and not somebody else's?"

"Yes, I'm sure."

"There's no letter in my room."

"Oh dear," said Tabard. She pulled out a chair and sat down. The news clearly troubled her. "It came in the morning," she said, trying to recall details. "You hadn't been gone for very long—just a few minutes, actually. I even looked out the doorway to see if you were in sight. I didn't think you would be, and you weren't, but that's how close the arrival of the letter followed your departure. When I didn't see you, I went straight upstairs and put it under your door."

Mazorca said nothing. A worried look appeared on Tabard's face. "I am absolutely certain of this," she said. "I recall it distinctly. I did not make a mistake."

Either she was telling the truth, or she was an adept liar, thought Mazorca. His instincts told him to believe her. So did the missing piece of hair.

"What can you tell me about the envelope?" he asked. "How big was it? What did it say on the outside? Tell me everything you remember."

Tabard did her best, but there was not much to report: it was a small envelope, off-white in color. It was thin and probably contained only a page or two inside, though Tabard could not say for sure because she had not opened it. She didn't recall any writing on the outside except his name and the address. Mazorca asked her several more questions but failed to learn additional details.

"I'm terribly sorry, Mr. Mays," said Tabard. "It sounds like a very important letter. I'll be sure to ask the other guests whether they saw it."

Mazorca thought about this for a moment. "I'd rather you didn't," he said as he turned toward the stairs. "There must be some other explanation. I'm going to search the room again."

He had no intention of doing that. He knew the letter was not there. And that meant he had a very serious problem on his hands.

* * *

The officers hushed when Springfield announced that he had recognized the man in the photograph. "I've seen this man in the flesh," he said. "The mangled ear—I am certain of it." He looked squarely at Rook. "Mazorca is Mr. Mays, the man we investigated yesterday at the boardinghouse."

"If he is our assassin, we can stop him right now," said Rook, looking directly at Scott. "Just give the order, sir."

The general took a deep breath. "Let me make sure I have this straight," he said slowly. "A slave woman has given us a photo that is said to contain the image of a man who wants to murder the president. The president himself has identified the man in the photo as a person who met with him recently, almost certainly under false pretenses. And now Sergeant Springfield says that he has seen this man and that the two of you know where he may be found."

For the first time that morning, Rook heard Scott speak with something other than irritation in his voice. He seemed to be genuinely contemplating what he had just heard. "Is there a connection to Violet Grenier?" he asked.

Rook was glad that the general had mentioned her name—he did not want to bring it up on his own. "Actually, sir, there is." He explained how their surveillance of Grenier had led them to the man at Tabard's, and how Grenier had received correspondence from Bennett, from whom Portia had escaped. "We don't know exactly how she is tied to all of this, but there is almost certainly a relationship."

"Where was she last night?"

Rook did not want to sound frustrated with the general whose very orders had made it impossible to answer the question he now asked. "We didn't have her under surveillance, sir," he said as plainly as possible.

"Right, of course not," said Scott, almost to himself, as he realized his mistake. He asked to see the photograph again and studied it with intensity. The mood in the room began to shift as the officers witnessed Scott reconsider his most recent judgments. Rook felt a tremendous urge to criticize the general—to accuse him of imperiling Lincoln's life by ignoring security concerns that had been brought to his attention. It was difficult to remain quiet, but Rook knew how important it was for Scott to arrive at the obvious conclusion on his own rather than having it thrust at him.

At last, with his eyes on Rook, the general held up the photograph. "We must find this man," he said, with a determination that Rook found gratifying.

There were nods of agreement around the room. Rook noticed that Locke was not among them.

"General," pleaded Locke, "this is really quite extraordinary. Colonel Rook is suggesting that Violet Grenier, a respected citizen of this city, is part of a ludicrous conspiracy. I smell a hoax. You are basing your conclusion on the testimony of a slave woman!" He spoke these final two words with utter contempt.

Portia recoiled, but only for a second. "I don't know who you are or why you think you're better than me, and

I don't really care," she said sternly. Rook thought about trying to stop her, but even if he could he was not sure he wanted to. "Me and a lotta other folks put it all on the line to get that picture here. I saw a friend of mine die. I ain't gonna see my family again. You can call me a liar, but you're a coward."

Locke jumped out of his chair. "That is no way for you to talk to me!" he hollered, his face red with anger. "That is no way for a fugitive negress to speak to a white man!"

Rook wanted to reach across the room and slug him, but Scott made sure this was not necessary. "Shut up, Locke!" roared the general.

Locke was astonished. Was Scott really taking the side of a runaway slave over his loyal aide? It was a remarkable turn of events.

"Now that you've shut up, sit down," sputtered Scott. "I don't care what you think about proper decorum. I find this woman's story credible, and we will act upon the information she has presented to us."

Locke dropped into his seat, crushed by the general's words.

"On behalf of myself and my officers, please accept my apologies," said Scott, looking at Portia. "The best way to make amends is for us to do our duty."

Scott let the words sink in. Then he began to develop a plan. A group of soldiers would immediately rush to Tabard's and place Mazorca under surveillance; if he had collaborators, Scott wanted to find them. Springfield would join them, but only after helping several other soldiers establish surveillance around Violet Grenier's. Rook would oversee all aspects of the operation.

The meeting began to break up when Scott spoke again. "One more thing," he said. "We should have additional copies of this photograph." He pointed to a lieutenant and told him to go to Brady's on the Avenue and order reproductions. "Before we're done, I suspect that we're going to have to learn a lot more about this man in the picture. It's a curious name, Mazorca."

For a moment, nobody said anything. Then Seward, who had remained quiet through the meeting, spoke. "I may know a man who can help us. Let me make an inquiry."

"By all means," said Scott. The gathering broke up. Before Rook walked out the door, however, the general called to him. "Colonel Rook, let me have a word with you."

* * *

Mazorca checked the room a final time to make sure that he had remembered everything. It was pointless to play against the odds that someone had been in his room while he was away. An intruder was the simplest explanation for the vanished letter. He had not planned on moving out of the boardinghouse, but now he did not have a choice. It was the safest thing to do.

He jammed a few extra items into the trunk alongside the clothes and rifle. He found room for a couple of guidebooks, the tools from Calthrop, and not much else. The books from French and Richstein were too big, and he did not want to carry them—except for his one remaining copy of the Bible. He would not abandon it.

Mazorca closed the curtains, darkening the room. Before he moved away from the window, however, he looked at the scene outside. Several people walked in either direction, going about their business. A figure on the opposite side of H Street drew his notice. He wore a brown frock coat as he ambled east, toward Sixth Street. Unlike the other pedestrians, who seemed to be heading places, he appeared to be out for a stroll. He would take a few leisurely steps, pause, and look around. Without fail, his eyes would stop on Tabard's. The man was trying to convey a sense of nonchalance, but Mazorca thought this was just a poor performance. He was, in fact, keeping an eye on the boardinghouse. He wondered how long this had been going on. What had he missed before now? He cursed himself for failing to take better precautions.

At the intersection of Seventh and H Street, Mazorca spotted a handful of soldiers in their blue uniforms. This was an ordinary sight in Washington. Yet he had not seen them in this particular place before, certainly not lingering. The fact that these men did not appear to be doing much apart from staring down H Street in the direction of Tabard's and the fellow in the brown coat aroused his interest even further.

He opened the door to his room and called down. "Mrs. Tabard? Would you mind coming up here? I have a favor to ask."

* * *

The one-on-one meeting with Scott had kept Rook from departing for Tabard's as quickly as he would have liked. He supposed it was worth it: the general wanted to apologize for questioning his loyalty over the last few weeks. "It

appears that you were right about the threats to the president's security," Scott had said. "I should have listened
to you."

Rook appreciated the effort. The general was a prideful
man. Apologies did not come easily to him. The two men
talked for several minutes, trying to repair the damage to
their relationship. Then Rook announced that he must be
going: he had an assassin to catch.

Leaving the Winder Building, Rook walked past the
White House, east on G Street. On Seventh Street, he turned
left. From a block away, he saw blue uniforms bunched
together at the corner of H Street. He hustled toward
them.

"Move out of the way," he said as he approached. "You
can't stand together and stare up the street. You'll be seen."

The men sauntered away from the corner. Scott had ordered them to begin an observation of Mazorca, but they
obviously did not know what they were doing. They were soldiers, not detectives. Rook was inclined to forgive their error,
but he wished they had used an ounce of common sense.

"This is no way to conduct surveillance," said Rook. "We
need men who are out of uniform, in places where they
won't be noticed. Have any of you thought about getting behind a window in a building across the street from Tabard's?
More important, where is Mazorca?"

A captain spoke up. "We believe he may be in Tabard's
right now, sir."

"Why do you believe this?"

"Just a few minutes ago, we spotted someone closing the
curtains to the window in his room. Either it was him, or
someone else was in there."

"Did one of you actually walk in front of Tabard's, in uniform, to see this?"

"We sent a fellow who wasn't in uniform down the street," said the captain, whose name was Leach. "Here he comes now." He pointed to a figure in a brown coat, walking toward them. Rook figured that he must have passed in front of Tabard's and rounded the block. The colonel did not recognize him.

"Who is he?"

"He files applications at the Patent Office. We knew that we needed someone in street clothes to get a close look at Tabard's. We didn't want to walk up there ourselves," said Leach. He hoped that Rook would congratulate him for having done something clever.

Instead, Rook rolled his eyes. "You recruited him off the street to do this?" He almost could not believe what he was hearing.

"I know him from one of the local militias," said Leach. "He's a Union man, and he's reliable. His name is Grimsley."

The militiaman stopped in front of Rook and the others. "Nothing new since the lady left," he said. "Shall I pass by again?"

"Before anything more happens, I need to know exactly what has occurred since you men arrived here," said Rook.

Leach said that they had rushed straight from the meeting with Scott and began watching Tabard's from a block away. They monitored the front as well as the rear, which led to a cramped alleyway. Leach spotted Grimsley on the street and pressed him into service. The clerk had walked in front of the building several times to determine whether anybody was inside. On his first pass, he saw the curtains close in a second-floor window—the one that the officers knew as Mazorca's. A few minutes later, a woman emerged from the front door. "None of us knew whether to regard Mrs. Tabard as an innocent or to suspect her of working in cahoots with Mazorca," said Leach. "So we put Lieutenant Hamilton on her tail." This had happened just a few minutes before Rook's arrival. Since then, they had continued to watch from a block away and Grimsley had passed by two more times, but none of them had seen any more activity.

To Rook, it was a series of mistakes: standing in plain sight a block away from Tabard's, sending a novice down the street, and failing to take key positions where they might observe without being observed. At least they had the sense to send somebody in pursuit of Tabard. If she was collaborating with Mazorca, then it was important to keep tabs on her.

And perhaps the officers' mistakes were minor. If Mazorca was in Tabard's, it meant that they had pinpointed his location and could apprehend him at any time.

The colonel barked out a series of orders. He placed officers at both ends of H Street but out of sight of Tabard's. He ordered another man down an alley to obtain backdoor access to a building across the street from Tabard's. He demanded a dozen soldiers to change out of their uniforms. Grimsley was dismissed. Within minutes, the assembly of bluecoats was broken up, with each man heading in a separate direction but with a common purpose.

For the first time since the inauguration, Rook felt as though he was in full control of presidential security. The release of the C&O men was an aggravating blow. Even so, Rook believed that he had seen the last of them. Justice might not have been done, but order was preserved, and that was more important.

The revelations of the last several hours had validated all of his warnings from the previous six weeks. He was no longer a Cassandra, uttering prophecies that others would ignore. As he stood just a few hundred feet from Tabard's, thinking about the deadly assassin who lurked inside, it was impossible not to feel vindicated. Even Scott had been finally motivated to abandon his dangerous complacency. This was an outcome Rook barely could have imagined a day ago, when Scott had come close to firing him. Now he stood on the threshold of defeating an ambitious and evil scheme. He knew that much remained undone, but for a fleeting moment he allowed himself to experience a sense of relief.

* * *

Mrs. Tabard isn't out for a casual stroll, thought Lieutenant Hamilton as he followed her south on Sixth Street. She walked quickly, never pausing at a storefront to look inside or stopping to talk to an acquaintance. Although Hamilton was careful to keep a distance, he did not have to deflect suspicious glances sent in his direction or disguise his own activity in any way. He simply got in the woman's wake and made sure that she stayed within view. All he had to do was keep up with her rapid pace. Tailing her was much easier than he had expected.

When she reached the Avenue a few minutes later, she halted and looked up and down the dusty street. Hamilton held back and watched her reach into a large bag. She pulled out something small. The lieutenant could not see what it was, but he did not have to wonder long. An omnibus pulled up, drawn by horses. She gave a nickel to the driver and climbed aboard for a ride in the direction of Georgetown.

Hamilton's impulse was to sprint, in order to arrive at the omnibus before it rolled away. But he fought the urge. He had plenty of time, at any rate, as the vehicle paused to let at least a dozen passengers get off and come on.

He was the last person to get on. As he reached into his pocket for loose change, he felt the eyes of the driver fall on him. The man was on a schedule and probably did not want to stay here a moment longer than necessary. Hamilton pulled a handful of coins from his pocket and saw that he did not have a nickel. He had four pennies. He shoved his hand back into his pocket and wiggled his fingers until they found another penny.

The vehicle was crowded, with riders either pressed against each other in their seats or standing shoulder to shoulder. Facing forward, Hamilton could not see Tabard. He figured she was in the rear. Right now, he wanted to avoid gawking. That might give him away.

About a minute into the ride, a wheel slipped into a rut on the Avenue, jolting the entire carriage. As passengers shuffled around, Hamilton craned his neck and allowed himself a brief glance over his shoulder. He still did not see Tabard, but he knew she must be back there. Too many people blocked his view. She was probably in a seat.

As the omnibus crossed Fourteenth Street, Hamilton made a show of looking at Willard's, on the north side of the street, as if he were admiring its architecture. Instead of concentrating on the hotel, however, he tried to spot Tabard peripherally. He still could not see her. A couple of riders obstructed his view of the other end of the omnibus. A wave of anxiety swept over Hamilton, but it was gone in a flash. He was certain that she was there. How could she be anywhere else? He had seen her climb aboard. She could not possibly have gotten off. Besides, only a ridiculous spendthrift would give up an entire nickel to ride less than a few blocks. People who boarded at Seventh Street usually were traveling all the way to Georgetown. He would spot her soon. He was certain of it.

* * *

Half an hour had passed since Rook's arrival at the intersection of Seventh and H Street, and the colonel was finally becoming satisfied with his surveillance of Tabard's boardinghouse. Men were positioned at key street corners within several blocks of where he stood, and most of them were now out of uniform. Behind a third-floor window, in a building directly across the street from Tabard's, three soldiers sat and watched the front of the boardinghouse. In an alleyway behind it, another had assumed the appearance of a drunkard. With a ratty coat covering his body and a half-empty bottle in his hand, he sat against a wall and kept an eye on Tabard's back door.

Rook was confident that nobody could enter or exit the boardinghouse without at least one of his men knowing it. He was also aware that surveillance could be tedious business—it might take hours of watching the most mundane activity before something happened. Boredom posed the biggest threat. It dulled senses that need to stay sharp, and the problem of sleep always loomed. Long stretches of idleness could lead to napping on the job. Rook had seen it plenty of times in the military with troops posted to the watch.

Because it was daytime rather than evening and the surveillance was young rather than old, Rook knew that he could let some time pass before he worried about these problems. Yet he knew that he might have to confront them eventually. He was already giving orders to prepare second and third shifts of men who could relieve those currently on duty. And at some point, he assumed, Mazorca would make a move. He would not stay caged in Tabard's forever. For now, however, Rook was content to wait—and remain alert.

He had just dispatched a courier to the Winder Building, to inform Scott of the situation, when Hamilton came dashing in his direction. He was almost out of breath when he stopped in front of Rook.

"She lost me," gasped the lieutenant.

"Mrs. Tabard?"

"Yes."

"What happened?"

"I followed her down to the Avenue, where she boarded a bus. I followed right behind. It was crowded, so I didn't have a good view of her. But I know she got on, and I never saw her get off. Halfway to Georgetown, though, I realized she wasn't there. She just vanished."

Hamilton's eyes dropped to the ground. Rook could tell the lieutenant was ashamed. But then, he deserved to be.

"She didn't vanish. You lost sight of her," scolded Rook.

"She must have gotten off the bus just as I was getting on. That's the only thing that makes sense. But that would mean that she knew I was following her, and I was certain that she didn't know. She never even looked in my direction."

Rook pondered this. He knew nothing about Hamilton's skills at shadowing subjects. He assumed they were unexceptional. But he knew that Tabard was a middle-aged woman who ran a boardinghouse. She was no savvy spy either. It was reasonable to suppose that Hamilton could keep tabs on her, as well as to suppose that even if she were to become aware of him, she would have trouble shaking him. Yet it sounded as if she had not only lost Hamilton but also that she had lost him with speed and efficiency.

"Very well, Lieutenant. Get some rest and report back here at midnight." That would be Hamilton's punishment: the late shift. Rook would find a role for him that did not involve following anybody.

As Hamilton loped away, Rook decided to get a better view of the boardinghouse. He walked to Eighth Street, almost two full blocks away from Tabard's, and crossed H Street. He allowed himself to steal a quick look in the direction of the boardinghouse. The distance was too great to see much of anything. He merely confirmed what he already knew: in the middle of the afternoon, Tabard's was no beehive of activity. The tenants would be at their jobs around the city.

Once Tabard's slipped from sight, Rook maneuvered around the city block and entered an alleyway. He passed the back side of several narrow buildings, finally entering one close to Sixth Street. It was an apothecary's shop. A sign on the wall promised "Remedies for All Ailments!" The shelves contained bottles of strengthening cordials for general heartiness, packages of cephalic pills for headaches, and something called "volcanic oil liniment" that guaran-

teed instant relief for painful sores. The proprietor waved as
Rook charged up two flights of stairs.

He reached the third floor and stepped into a small
room. The soldiers were seated. Two were positioned near a
pair of windows while the third smoked a pipe behind them.
All three rose when Rook entered.

"Nothing stirring, sir," said the smoker. "We haven't
spotted anything since we got up here."

"Sit down," said the colonel. Through a window he
could see Tabard's across the street, and looking downward
he had a good view of the front door and the window to
Mazorca's room—the one he had stood in just a day earlier.
The curtains were shut, just as Grimsley had reported.

"Have you had your eyes on those closed curtains the
entire time?"

"Yes, we have," said one by the window. "If there's a person in that room, he hasn't touched the curtains."

Rook continued looking out even though he did not
see anything in particular. "Don't get your faces too close to
the window or you might be seen," he said, mostly because
he wanted to fill the silence. He had already warned the
soldiers about this.

"Yes, sir. We know."

A few more moments passed quietly.

"What do we know about the druggist downstairs?"
asked Rook.

"He's a Union man," said the soldier with a pipe. "We
made sure of that before we came up here."

"Does he know Mrs. Tabard?"

"We didn't ask because we didn't want to give away our
purpose. We just told him we needed to watch the street for

382   *John J. Miller*

a few hours. He was agreeable, but I think he's curious to know what we're doing."

"That's understandable," said the colonel. "I'll try to have a few words with him later."

Rook considered the situation. The disappearance of Tabard troubled him. It suggested that despite appearances, she was no ordinary keeper of a boardinghouse. Perhaps she was in league with Mazorca. This led to another troubling idea. If Rook and his men couldn't keep track of Tabard, then how could they hope to monitor Mazorca? He might slip from their grasp just as easily as Tabard, even though he was striving to prevent this. Rook reviewed the possibilities. Mazorca could be in Tabard's right now. If he left, Rook's men could try to pursue him, but they might fail and it would be difficult to locate him again. On the other hand, they could try to seize him in the boardinghouse. This could hurt their chances of breaking up a wider conspiracy. Mazorca nevertheless appeared to be at the center of everything. He was the man in the photo. The notion of capturing him and putting an end to his machinations, while it was still possible, was appealing.

Rook kept looking across the street. He and the other watchers would have seen anybody who stood beside one of the windows or passed by it. The only exception was Mazorca's room, where the curtains were shut. They were open everywhere else.

Why were his closed? The day before, when Rook was in the room, they had been left slightly open. The only time Rook had ever closed a curtain in the middle of the day was to sleep. If Mazorca was dozing, he might be secured without a fight.

Rook mulled it over and decided to act on what his gut was telling him to do. "We're done waiting," he said. "Let's go in."

* * *

Polly brightened when the soldier waved to her on Pennsylvania Avenue, outside Willard's Hotel. She might have worked for Violet Grenier, who could say all kinds of terrible things about federal men, but Polly rather liked how they looked in their blue uniforms. The idea that one of them had actually noticed her made her heart beat a little faster.

"Hello, ma'am," said the soldier, a private who was about Polly's age.

Polly smiled coyly. "Hello," she replied.

"May I show you something?" He held out a card.

It was a peculiar approach, but she had no intention of complaining. She took the card and realized that it was not a card at all but rather a photograph. Polly owned several about the same size. They were mostly pictures of handsome actors who toured the country and occasionally came to Washington.

The image was not sharp. Polly could tell it had not been taken in a studio. It certainly did not appear posed. A man was in the center of it, viewed in profile. His ear was disfigured. It did not make him ugly, but he sure was not as fine looking as the men Polly had admired from the balcony at Ford's Theatre.

"Have you seen this man?" asked the private.

Disappointment washed over her. The soldier was not interested in her but in what she might know. This was not a casual rendezvous. That was all right, she realized, because he was not as handsome as her favorite actors either.

She looked down at the picture again. "No, I'm afraid not." She tried to hand it back to him.

"Keep it," he said. "I've got a whole stack, and I'm supposed to get rid of them all." Polly saw that he held about a hundred of them in his other hand. "Take it back home. Anybody who has seen this man should report to the Winder Building as quickly as possible. He may be dangerous."

"Okay," said Polly. She tucked away the photo. "You be careful," she said as she walked away.

"Yes, ma'am. I will," said the private. He winked at her and smiled.

Polly decided that he was not bad looking after all. She would have to find an excuse to walk down Pennsylvania Avenue again soon.

*   *   *

In the middle of a weekday afternoon, H Street did not exactly hum with activity—and Rook waited until it was positively deserted before he crossed it from the apothecary's shop. Six uniformed soldiers followed him, and they made directly for Tabard's boardinghouse. Anybody watching them would have understood that it was not a social visit.

The door to Tabard's was unlocked. Rook pushed it open, removing a pistol from his holster at the same time. The soldiers gripped their own guns. Even though H Street was empty, they had not wanted to draw their weapons until they were actually entering the building. To their backs, above the apothecary's shop, a pair of soldiers leaned out of a third-story window and aimed their Sharps rifles. Several other soldiers were positioned at the intersections of Sixth and Seventh streets, and a few more guarded the alley in the rear. The boardinghouse was surrounded by armed men.

The door swung open. The foyer was vacant except for a rug on the floor and a few small pieces of furniture pushed against a wall. Rook stepped inside and made straight for the staircase, without even a glance at the other rooms on the ground floor. This time, he did not bother with the key in the kitchen. There was nothing surreptitious about what he planned to do. Behind him, three soldiers spread out on the first floor. The other three went up the steps with him.

On the second floor, Rook positioned himself outside of Mazorca's room. He pressed his ear to the door and listened. No sounds came from within. All was silence except for the rustlings of the soldiers below as they moved around the first floor's dining room, kitchen, and Tabard's personal quarters. They were trying to keep quiet, but Rook could hear their muffled footfalls. They had orders to conduct a thorough search, opening closet doors, checking pantries, and looking beneath and behind curtains and anything else that might hide a person who did not want to be found.

When Rook heard one of them coming up the steps, he finally pulled away from Mazorca's door. The soldier looked at Rook and shook his head to indicate that they had found nobody. A moment later, a soldier who had gone upstairs came back down with the same report: the common areas were free of people.

With his pistol still in hand, Rook reached for the knob on Mazorca's door and gently tried to turn it. The thing refused to budge. The colonel took a step back, squared himself to the door, raised a leg, and kicked. The sole of his black boot crashed into the door, ripping its latch and flinging it open. His gun entered the room before he did, ready to fire upon anybody who wanted to put up a fight.

The light inside was dim. What illumination there was came from the edges of the closed curtains. He scanned the room rapidly, his head jerking around like a bird as it tried to spot predators. On the bed, a blanket covered a lump the size of a body. Rook had hoped to catch Mazorca napping. Yet he knew that nobody could have slept through the sound of the door smashing in.

The soldiers swarmed in after Rook. One of them opened the curtains. As light fell on the bed, Rook saw the dark stain. He leaned in for a closer look. It was red and fresh. One whiff and Rook knew it was blood. The body was a corpse.

The blanket was not tucked in. Instead, it had been tossed on top of the body in haste. Beneath it was Tabard. She lay on her right side, but her head was twisted unnaturally to the left. Her chin rested on her shoulder, and her face looked up at the ceiling. Her eyes were wide open. If it had not been for the huge gash in her neck, Rook might have thought that she was still alive. He could tell that she had not been dead for long. The blood glistened in the sunlight. It had soaked into everything—the blanket, the mattress, her clothes. Rook had seen men die in battle before. It always amazed him to see how many buckets of blood could fill a human body.

He pulled back. "Mazorca did this," he said to nobody in particular. "And we don't know where he is."

He told the soldiers to clear the entire building—to open all of the doors that were closed, to investigate the guest rooms, and even to check the roof. Rook's own attention turned to the trunk. He opened it and reached in. To his mild surprise, the rifle was still there, exactly as it had been before. Rook wondered why an assassin would leave behind his weapon.

Rook descended the steps onto the ground floor. From above, he heard knocking on doors, and then the bangs and cracks of forced openings. Yet he was not really listening. He walked into the dining room, passed through the kitchen, and entered Tabard's bedroom.

It was small and neat—the private chamber of a woman whose life had revolved around her guests. Rook imagined Tabard coming in here at the end of each day, worn out from hours of cooking, cleaning, and conversing, and collapsing into the cool sheets of her bed.

Across the room, a closet stood wide open. It appeared as though someone had ransacked its contents. A few dresses hung from a rack, but several others lay in a heap on the floor. Rook called for the soldier who had entered it just a few moments earlier. When he appeared, Rook pointed to the closet.

"Did you do this?" he asked.

"No, sir. I found it like this."

"Right," said the colonel. "At least it's one mess we aren't responsible for."

It was exactly as Rook had feared: his men had arrived in time to capture Mazorca, but Mazorca had outwitted them. Their failure to act sooner or more intelligently had cost Tabard her life—and now it might cost the president as well. They had gone from having the assassin within their grasp to having no clue about where he might have gone. He could be anywhere.

The colonel walked outside the boardinghouse. When he realized that he was still holding his pistol, he holstered it. Across the street, the sharpshooters were gone from the windows. A few other soldiers, sensing that something had gone wrong, made their way toward Tabard's from their posts. Rook knew that he would have to explain the events of the last few minutes and issue new orders. He would have several men gather whatever information they could from Mazorca's room, tell the boarders half-truths about why the doors to their rooms were smashed in and their landlady was dead, and question them in detail about Mazorca.

Those were the easy orders to give. The hard ones involved figuring out how to find Mazorca again. Rook wanted time to think about it. He wished he could talk to Springfield, who had been his confidant on these matters for weeks.

Just then, Springfield appeared from a block away. When he saw Rook, he broke into a sprint. He stopped in front of the colonel, panting from exhaustion and excitement. "You won't believe whose letter I found in Grenier's mail just now," he said. He held out a piece of paper.

* * *

Mazorca rubbed a hand against his cheek and felt the scratchy stubble of a new beard. He tugged on the shawl wrapped over his head, hoping to cover more of his face, but it was already pulled tight. The whiskers growing on his chin and jaw were pale in color and so not as immediately obvious as they would have been if he were brown- or black-haired. Yet anybody taking a look at his face probably would notice them. His disguise was not going to work for long. He knew that he needed to avoid eye contact and conversation. And that meant getting out of Center Market, where the crowds would swell as government clerks left their jobs for the day.

For now, however, the disguise would suffice. Mazorca was glad that Tabard had been a large woman. Her closet was full of clothes that fit him comfortably. Most were plain, which was to Mazorca's liking. He had chosen a dull gray dress that seemed especially ordinary. The fact that it was a little smudgy on its sleeves and slightly frayed at its bottom probably added to its authenticity. To the typical passerby who paid no special heed, Mazorca appeared as a woman who was trying to run errands and keep to herself.

Killing Tabard had been an unfortunate necessity, thought Mazorca. She was not guilty of a penetrating insight, like Calthrop, though there was the question of the missing letter. If Tabard had played a role in its disappearance, she probably would not have told him to look for it under his door. This seemed like a safe assumption. When Mazorca spotted the man with an unusual level of interest in the boardinghouse, however, even the safest assumptions seemed to have their risky elements. Mazorca needed to escape quickly. The idea of using Tabard's clothes as a disguise came to him immediately. He killed her because he wanted to move with speed, plus there was the possibility that she might say something unhelpful to his pursuers.

Mazorca did not regret the murder. He did not care whether Tabard lived or died. The inconvenience of having to silence her merely annoyed him. Her blood was splattered on the clothes he wore beneath the dress, and they would need replacing. The fact that he had not planned on her murder, however, distressed him. His plans were swerving off course. The government's security apparatus was onto him. He was no longer in total control.

Mazorca realized what a close call he had just been through. Agents were watching the boardinghouse. They had put a tail on him when he left. Fortunately for him, the tail was inept. Mazorca had spotted him almost immediately, saw him again in the reflection of a storefront window, and then watched him try to board the omnibus at the last possible moment. Just as he had gotten on, Mazorca had gotten off, slipping out from the rear of the vehicle. Then he had crossed Pennsylvania Avenue and darted into Center Market.

Now he wandered among the farmers and fishmongers. Their prices were rising, owing to the city's nervousness about its immediate future. The local cost of food was far from his mind. His real purpose in visiting Center Market was to confirm that nobody else was following him. After half an hour of maneuvering, he was convinced that he had escaped. Now he needed to get out of Center Market and out of Tabard's garments.

As Mazorca stepped outside, the sky was clear and the temperature was comfortably cool. He immediately noticed that quite a few people were standing along the Avenue, looking toward the Capitol as if in anticipation of something. The crowd thickened as others streamed out of buildings and lined the street. Mazorca had wanted to cross, but he decided to wait. A woman standing nearby spoke to a companion with excitement. "It's the Seventh! It's finally here!" Everyone seemed to be pointing and chattering. From a few blocks away came the sound of music and cheers.

A long column of soldiers marched toward the White House, complete with a band. Mazorca kept his shawl pulled and his head down, so he did not see much of the procession. But he learned that this was New York's Seventh Regiment. It had come into the train station following a difficult and delayed journey by train and ship. The soldiers had traveled through Annapolis to avoid another violent reception in Baltimore. "There must be a thousand of them!" said one awestruck spectator. "Abe Lincoln will love the sight of this," said another. "At last, we're safe!"

Mazorca listened and waited. As the troops strutted by, many in the crowd fell in behind them, on their way to what they imagined would be an enthusiastic reception at the White House. The president was sure to come out and say a few words expressing his gratitude and relief.

When the numbers thinned and the Avenue returned to normal, Mazorca moved on. He would skip the grand affair with Lincoln. His own appointment with the president would come soon enough. He would make sure of that.

* * *

Violet Grenier closed her book when Polly walked through the front door. The girl launched into a story about a soldier and a photograph. "He said this man is very dangerous and requested that I show this picture to everyone I know."

Her earnestness amused Grenier. "Well, you had better let me see it," she said.

Polly came over to where Grenier was sitting and handed her the photograph. A look of astonishment must have crossed Grenier's face, because Polly immediately sensed what Grenier knew. "Do you recognize him?" she asked in a mix of excitement and fear.

At first, Grenier was speechless. It was clearly Mazorca. How in the world had Polly obtained a photograph of him?

"Where did you get this?" she asked, making Polly repeat her story. This time, Grenier peppered her with questions about precisely what the soldier had said to her.

When she was done, Polly narrowed her eyes. "Who is he?"

"I have no idea," lied Grenier. "I've never seen him before."

Polly was suspicious. She did not dare contradict the woman who employed her. Yet she sensed that Grenier was hiding something.

"Have you seen him, Polly?" asked Grenier.

"Me? Oh, good heavens, no. I have not."

"Are you sure?" Grenier's voice was heavy with doubt.

"Never—I swear it," said Polly, nervously. "I'm just trying to do what the soldier asked. That's all."

The girl was flustered, which was just how Grenier wanted her.

"Okay, Polly. That's fine. If this man is dangerous, then we need to be very careful. I'm going to keep this picture. I'd like you to clean the white chair in the guest room. Calhoun has been napping on it again, and he's left it covered in fur. And you might dust the room while you're in there."

Grenier watched her go. She had done a poor job of masking her surprise but believed she had recovered adequately.

She looked at the image again, hoping it would somehow look different and contradict her first impression. Yet she grew even more certain that the picture was of Mazorca.

This was very bad news.

* * *

Rook heard Scott before he saw him. The big general's hearty laugh boomed through the Winder Building as he made his way to his office, where Rook was waiting for him.

"A glorious day!" roared the commander of the army. Rook stood up as Scott entered the room in full military regalia. An enormous, plumed chapeau sat on his head, making him seem even taller than his six foot four and one-quarter inches. His uniform was a crisp blue, with golden epaulettes strapped to his shoulders, their fancy fringes dangling down. A sword was fastened to his belt. Shiny black boots completed the outfit.

Rook never had cared for the pomp and circumstance of the military, but he had to admit that whereas another man might have looked ridiculous, Scott looked majestic. He was fat and old and never would use that sword, or possibly any weapon, in a real battle again. Yet he inhabited his flamboyant costume as perhaps no other American could.

Two other men came into the room behind him. The first was Locke, the general's ever-present shadow. He was trying to look his best too. His uniform was clean and crisp and its buttons shone. Rook thought he looked more prepared for the intrigues of a ballroom than the ferocity of a firefight. Scott could dress up and still look like a soldier, but not Locke. The second man was Seward, who seemed to be lurking around constantly these days.

"Colonel!" bellowed Scott when he saw Rook. It was both an announcement of surprise and a greeting. The general removed his hat and set it on a peg. "Did you see that marvelous procession?"

Rook knew that he was referring to the arrival of the Seventh Regiment from New York—he had heard the commotion and learned the full story of the regiment's sudden appearance from a lieutenant just a few minutes earlier. The influx of a thousand fresh men meant that Washington at last was ready for a fight. Lincoln and members of his cabinet, plus Scott and many of his officers, had come out for an impromptu rally.

"I didn't see the Seventh," said Rook. "I'm glad that it has arrived."

"That's too bad. You missed quite a parade. The best part was to see the president. He was relieved." Scott emphasized the final word and looked at Seward, who nodded in approval. "I didn't think this day could get any better," continued the general. "If you bring me good news, though, it may indeed do just that!"

"I'm afraid that I'm going to make it worse, sir," said Rook.

"I see." The smile vanished from Scott's face. He fell into a chair and gestured for Rook to do the same. Locke and Seward also took seats. The general's eyes narrowed to slits. "What do you have?"

Rook hesitated. "Sir, what I have to say might best be said to you alone," he said, casting a quick glance at Seward. The general saw it and seemed to consider Rook's request for the briefest of moments before rejecting it.

"That won't be necessary," he said. "Secretary Seward is fully aware of the Mazorca situation and will soon present us with a valuable piece of data. Isn't that right, Mr. Secretary?"

"Yes, General, in a few moments anyway." He made a motion to rise. "I could easily step out..."

"Nonsense, sir!" thundered Scott with such force that Seward dropped back into his chair. "We will have a frank discussion about the Mazorca operation. It is indeed fortuitous that we are all here." He looked directly at Rook. "Colonel, give us your report."

Rook described what had happened: the beginning of the surveillance, Mazorca's murder of Tabard, and the raid that had revealed the whole operation as a failure.

"No wonder you wanted to make your report to me alone. This is an embarrassment. We had him in our clutches, and you let him get away."

Rook bristled at the phrasing but let it pass. "The reason he got away is because he knew we were coming," he said.

The general raised his eyebrows in at least partial disbelief. Seward shifted uncomfortably in his seat.

"Mazorca has an informant—someone who may not know that he is passing information to a man who seeks to murder the president, but someone who nonetheless is doing it through his own sheer recklessness."

Rook paused. He wanted to read the general's face. Did he harbor any suspicions? Scott merely sat still. His face was expressionless. Seward pursed his lips and scratched his chin. Locke made no attempt to conceal his disdain: he rolled his eyes and let out a mocking sigh.

Scott broke the silence. "That is an extraordinary charge, Colonel. Do you have extraordinary proof to back it up?"

Rook reached into a pocket and pulled out the letter Springfield had given him. He unfolded it slowly.

"This may explain our problem," said Rook, handing the letter to Scott.

The general took the letter and read it in silence. Rook watched Scott's eyes widen in astonishment as he read a few lines and checked the signature at the bottom. He let out a little gasp. "This is an unwelcome development," he said. Then he read aloud, with disgust:

> *Dearest Violet,*
>
> *So much to tell you! I have an amazing story to relate about the insubordination of Col. Rook and a group of prisoners that I personally released, acting upon intelligence from an unnamed source. It appears that the unauthorized surveillance of ordinary citizens was much more extensive that I had originally believed. Expect me Friday night. I will keep no secrets from you. I desire to tell you all—and I desire you.*
>
> *Most intimately,*
> *Sam Locke*

Scott glowered at Locke. "Is there anything you can possibly say for yourself, Colonel?"

Locke buried his face in his hands. When he looked up, Rook could see his eyes turning red from tears. "Sir, it is an innocent mistake!"

"Your dealings with Mrs. Grenier do not sound very innocent to me," said the general, his voice rising in anger. "It would be bad enough if you were merely divulging sensitive information to a random whore—but here is the proof that you're giving it away to a woman whom we now know is in league with the enemy!"

"I'm sorry, I did not know," sobbed Locke. "She seduced me."

"Get out of my sight," sputtered Scott. "You are relieved of your rank and your duties. Leave this building and never come back."

As Locke rose and headed for the door, Scott turned to Seward. "This is a tremendous embarrassment. I personally guarantee you that I will get to the bottom…"

He was going to say more but became distracted when Locke nearly crashed into a new figure in the doorway— a short man with dark eyes, thick black hair, and skin the color of bronze. He wore black clothes as well.

Seward rose. "General, I believe that this man will have some answers for us."

* * *

Mazorca rolled the dress into a ball, tossed it into a half-empty closet, and shut the door. He hoped he would never have to see it again. The experience of wearing Tabard's clothes was humiliating, but it could have been worse. Nothing would have been more humiliating than the defeat he had so narrowly avoided.

His own clothes were ruined. A mirror confirmed it. Tabard's blood had streaked across his shirt and pants. There was no way he could go out in public. He was annoyed at himself for letting it happen. He could have killed Tabard more cleanly. She had not even put up a fight and probably did not know what was happening to her before she was dead. He had taken her completely by surprise.

The problem was that he had been caught by surprise as well. Someone had exposed him. He reviewed everything that had happened since his arrival in Washington. He had tried to cover his tracks, even murdering Calthrop when the smallest hint of possible detection surfaced. He wondered about whether Tabard was some kind of informant, but that seemed far-fetched. Then there was Grenier. Was she a weak link? Bennett had vouched for her. She must have been the author of that missing letter, because she was the only person who knew his whereabouts. He wished he could read it now. Had she tried to warn him of something?

Before he could plumb these mysteries, he needed a change of clothes. At least this problem had an easy solution. Beneath the mirror sat a dresser. Several of its drawers were empty, but others contained shirts and pants for a man. Mazorca dumped them onto a bed and sorted through the piles. The closet held a few coats and ties. Within minutes, he found all that he needed. He stripped and changed, then threw his old clothes into the closet beside the dress.

His next dilemma was only slightly less urgent. He was in the safe house at 1745 N Street that Grenier had recommended for a time of emergency. Was it truly safe? He could not be certain, and there were few things he disliked more than uncertainty.

From a window, he looked at N Street. People across the city were leaving their jobs and heading home. Three soldiers strolled by. Mazorca figured they belonged to the New York regiment. They must have broken ranks and obtained some free time to explore the city they had come to defend.

Mazorca left the bedroom and drifted down the staircase. In a closet by the foyer, he found a light coat with a pair of large pockets and a hat with a wide brim. A layer of dust covered them. Mazorca brushed them off and put them on. At the front door, he slipped his deadly book into one of the oversize pockets. He grasped the door handle and stepped onto the front porch.

After closing the door and locking it with the key Grenier had given him, Mazorca turned to walk in the direction the soldiers had taken. He collided with a red-haired boy who was running home with a loaf of bread from the market. The boy, less than half the size of Mazorca, tumbled to the ground.

"Watch where you're going," snapped Mazorca. He bent over and picked up his hat, which had fallen beside the boy. He placed it back on his head and continued on his way.

For several moments, the boy sat on the ground and watched Mazorca go. Then he stood, grabbing his bread and brushing off a few specks of dirt. His parents would never know that he had dropped it. But there was something else that he suspected he would have to tell them. He reached into his pocket and pulled out the photograph that the soldier on Connecticut Avenue had given him—the picture of "a very bad man who needed to be found as soon as possible."

* * *

Rook did not recognize the man in the doorway to Scott's office, but Seward clearly did.

"Thank you so much for coming, Ambassador," said Seward.

"My pleasure, Mr. Secretary."

Seward put an arm on the ambassador's back and swept the other one toward Scott and Rook, who also had risen. "Allow me to introduce Señor Don Luis Molina, the minister to the United States from the Republic of Nicaragua."

The men shook hands. Rook noted Molina's firm grip. In a moment, all four were seated, facing each other.

"I asked the ambassador to come here because he may have some information about Mazorca," said Seward. "Before this morning, I had not heard the name. It is certainly unusual. I repeated it over and over—Mazorca, Mazorca." He was enunciating the name, vibrating his tongue as he trilled the R. "I came to the conclusion that it sounded vaguely Latin, and specifically Spanish."

Here he paused, as if expecting a dollop of praise for his ingenuity. Nobody spoke, and he continued.

"So I sent a note to Ambassador Molina, whom I first met last month, when he was formally received at the White House by President Lincoln. He speaks Spanish, and more to the point, he knows a great deal about the affairs of Spanish America. But best of all, he is a great friend of the United States."

Seward paused again. This time he looked directly at Molina, who nodded in acknowledgment.

"So I sought the ambassador's wise counsel and asked if he had ever heard this name, Mazorca. He replied in the affirmative, and we arranged this meeting."

"It is good of you to come," said Scott. "What can you tell us about Mazorca?"

Molina folded his hands in his lap. "I have not encountered this name in some time, and I certainly never expected to rediscover it here in Washington."

The ambassador spoke with an accent, but his English was good.

"The name comes from Argentina. It is not my home, but I know something of it. Have any of you heard of Juan Manuel de Rosas?"

Rook shook his head. The name meant nothing to him. Scott did not seem to be familiar with it either. Finally, Seward spoke, with some hesitance in his voice. "Was he the ruler of Argentina?"

"That is correct," said Molina. "He was a rancher who became a dictator. He moved in and out of power, but he dominated the politics of Argentina for more than twenty years until he was finally ousted, once and for all, in 1852. Today, Rosas lives in exile, in London. During his reign, Argentina fought with its neighbors. Inside the country, Rosas ruled by fear. One of his instruments of terror was a secret police force—a gang of thugs and killers. Its members were fanatically loyal to Rosas. Within their ranks, they were so closely united that it was said they were like the kernels on an ear of corn."

Molina illustrated the point by pressing his fingertips together. He squeezed them so hard that they turned red.

"In your language, there is another word for corn," he continued. "You don't use it as much, but you know it. The word is maize. In my language, corn is called *maiz* and an ear is *oreja*. Put them together in an ear of corn, and you have *la mazorca*. This was the name that the secret police of Rosas used for themselves."

Seward straightened his back. "I see we've come to the right place," he said with obvious satisfaction.

"There is something else as well," said Molina. "Mazorca is a joke—what I think you call a play on words or..." His voice drifted off as he searched for the term.

"A pun," said Rook.

"Yes, a pun," said Molina. "*Mazorca* also means *mas horca*." He paused for effect. "*Mas horca* means 'more hanging.'"

"That is all very interesting," said Scott. "But what does it have to do with our man here in Washington?"

"I cannot answer with certainty. What I have said up to now is based on fact. It is all true. What I am about to say is speculative. But it is also reasonable."

"We're all ears," said Seward, who suppressed a chuckle when he remembered that this was no time for laughter.

Molina ignored him. "During the final years of the Rosas period, the *mazorqueros* were less active than they had been previously. Yet they maintained a horrifying presence. The most ruthless among them was said to be a foreigner—an American. He arrived in Buenos Aires shortly after your country's invasion of Mexico and conquest of Mexico City."

"We marched into Mexico City on September 14, 1847," said Scott. "The country had become ours in just six months."

"Yes," said Molina, replying to Scott. "It would have been shortly after that. It was always presumed that this most brutal of *mazorqueros* was a deserter or a criminal who had decided to venture south rather than return home."

"What happened to him after Rosas was deposed?" asked Seward.

"Again, I do not know for certain. But I have heard that after the fall of the Rosas regime, this man left Argentina and sought occasional employment from individuals who required special services—sinister services, if you will. I was given to understand that those who seek him must approach intermediaries in Cuba."

"How can you be sure of all this?" asked Scott.

"I am sure of nothing. But you will recall the recent history of my region—the internal strife that has plagued my country, combined with the external pressures of British colonialism and American filibusters such as William Walker. We have lived through turbulent times. We have known dreadful violence. And we have suffered from the acts of men who murder for money. If the Mazorca you are worried about right now is the same man who operated in and around my country just a few years ago, then I am truly fearful for the safety of your leaders."

"So our Mazorca is a professional killer—an assassin for hire," said Rook.

"I believe that is a sound assumption. It is certainly an assumption that will prevent you from underestimating him. He is most dangerous when he is underestimated."

Rook caught the eye of Scott, who quickly looked away. The general was chastened.

"Be warned," said Molina, leaning forward in his chair in order to emphasize his point. "This man is a destroyer of lives. He will let nothing stand between himself and those whom he has marked for death."

* * *

Beside the murky waters of Washington's oozing canal, a woman leaned her back against a wall. Mazorca could see her only faintly in the dark. She held a small box in her arms, and her shoulders trembled. When she raised a sleeve to her face, Mazorca assumed that she had sneezed and was wiping her nose. But she continued to shake. Mazorca realized that she was crying. For several minutes, he watched her take turns between looking at the box and raising her head upward, toward the heavens.

Mazorca stood motionless in a doorway, about thirty feet from where she wept. Eventually the woman suppressed her tears and approached the edge of the canal. The stench rising from the canal was strong enough to repel anybody who did not have a good reason for being there.

The woman dropped to her knees and raised the box to her lips. Its top was open. She kissed whatever was inside. Then she set it down beside her and adjusted its contents. She appeared to pull out a small, rectangular object, flip it around, and set it back in. She fidgeted with the box for a few more seconds and then placed it in the water. For a moment it bobbed up and down and Mazorca thought it might sink. Yet it appeared to steady itself and began floating with the lazy current. By the time it had drifted in front of Mazorca, the woman was gone.

Propelled by curiosity, Mazorca approached the canal and looked at the box. Tucked inside, swaddled in a blanket, was a newborn baby. The child's eyes were wide open, but it did not cry. At its feet, Mazorca saw the rectangular object that the woman had shifted: a brick. Actually there were two of them, and their grim purpose was apparent. It did not occur to Mazorca that he might reach into the water and pull the box out. As the baby meandered by, he felt nothing at all.

The child's mother was obviously a whore, thought Mazorca. She did what whores so often do after giving birth, in their loneliness. The baby's father might be a poor clerk or a rich senator. He had almost certainly vanished from the woman's life long ago, just as suddenly as he had appeared, and he was not aware of what their brief encounter had created. Or what was now floating toward its doom.

Such was the way of things in Murder Bay, the seediest part of Washington. It slouched between the malodorous canal and the business district on Pennsylvania Avenue to the north, in a triangular section of the city between Ninth and Fifteenth streets. The streets were grimy and narrow, the buildings dilapidated, and the inhabitants dissolute. For all of its drawbacks, however, the area offered a concentration of amusements and diversions that could not be found anywhere else in the city: drinking saloons, gambling halls, and dens of ill repute.

Early on, Mazorca had learned to avoid the place. Although he was not above partaking of its vices, he wanted nothing to get in the way of his objective. Murder Bay posed too many risks: its cheap hotels weren't safe, its alleyways were full of toughs and pickpockets, and its bars and bordellos were unwelcome distractions. Yet now he relied on the allure of its debauchery to help him reach his goal. Murder Bay was a magnet for certain types of men: young, far from home, unencumbered by the obligations of marriage and family. Soldiers were frequently all of these things at once. As day turned to night, they fell on Murder Bay in droves, intending to explore its decadent entertainments.

On this night, New York's Seventh Regiment contributed heavily to their numbers. Its members came from the upper crust of their city—they were the sons of bankers and shippers. They had endured a long journey, marched past the White House, and settled into rooms at Willard's and other fine hotels along Pennsylvania Avenue. In the morning, they were supposed to report to their new quarters in the House of Representatives, an empty chamber ever since the congressmen left town immediately following the presidential inauguration. Yet this evening was entirely theirs, and many of the New Yorkers were eager to pursue very particular forms of rest and relaxation.

Mazorca had watched them flock to Murder Bay. Some were loud braggarts who made no effort to hide their intentions. They boasted about their own prowess and the pleasures they planned to obtain. Others were less sure of themselves. Mazorca saw the guilt on their faces as they wandered about, battling their inhibitions as they contemplated entering establishments with names such as the Haystack, the Blue Goose, and Madam Wilton's Private Residence for Ladies. Sooner or later, they all went inside.

The problem for Mazorca was that the soldiers traveled in packs. He suspected that their officers had warned them to stick together, like herds of animals that sought safety in

numbers. It was good advice: Murder Bay was full of predators in search of prey. Most of them merely intended to separate the soldiers from their money. Occasionally, however, a
denizen of this squalid district wanted something far worse.
Murder Bay had not earned its nickname for nothing, and
its victims were not always babes.

* * *

Outside the Winder Building, ten-year-old Zachariah Hoadly
stood beside his father. He brushed aside his red hair, which
kept falling in his face. He needed to visit a barbershop.

"You're sure it's him?" asked Isaac Hoadly, repeating a
question he had posed perhaps a dozen times already.

"I'm pretty sure," said the boy, sounding less than fully
confident.

Isaac looked at the photograph. "And it's because of the
ear?"

"Yes, Dad," said Zack, annoyed at his father's doubts.

"And this is where they told you to come?"

"Uh-huh."

Isaac was building up the nerve to go inside when a man
in a blue uniform walked out the front door. "Excuse me,"
said Isaac. "Can you help me?"

Colonel Rook halted in front of the Hoadlys. He looked
tired and none too interested in helping anybody.

"My son came home with this picture," said Isaac. He
held up the photograph of Mazorca.

Rook's eyes lit up. "Please tell me you've seen him."

* * *

From a block away, Mazorca saw the sergeant walking along Tenth Street. Springfield was alone, which is what initially attracted Mazorca's interest—he was searching for a blue-coat who was not part of a crowd. He figured that as the night grew older, soldiers would stumble away from their card games, bottles, and prostitutes. Most would have entered Murder Bay with companions, but many would exit on their own.

Springfield was far from ideal. For starters, he was a burly man who looked like he could put up a fight. He was also sober. Mazorca's goal was to identify someone who was closer to his own size, and preferably drunk. Yet he decided to keep an eye on Springfield for at least a few minutes.

The sergeant's behavior quickly puzzled him. Springfield walked methodically from brothel to brothel. He would enter one, remain inside for several minutes, and come back out. Then he would go to the next one on the street. At first, Mazorca suspected that the ladies of the house Springfield had chosen were preoccupied. After he came out of the third house, however, Mazorca wondered if Springfield was picky about whom he would pay for companionship. Mazorca soon decided that something else was going on.

When Springfield turned onto C Street, Mazorca was only a dozen feet behind him. As the sergeant approached yet another bordello—it went by the name of Madam Russell's Bake Oven—another man approached him.

"Sir! Do not enter that house of sin!" he shouted.

Springfield stopped in his tracks and smiled. Mazorca halted as well, pretending to look through the window of a watering hole, as if he were searching for a friend. From the corner of his eye, he could see that the man who assailed Springfield was a bespectacled chaplain. He wore a broad-brimmed hat and a frock coat that extended almost to his knees. In one hand he held a cross and in the other a Bible.

"Walk through that doorway and abandon all hope of salvation," pleaded the chaplain.

"Don't worry," laughed Springfield. "I will commit no sin by entering the Bake Oven."

Springfield placed his arm on the chaplain's shoulder. Their voices dropped, and Mazorca could not make out what they were saying. The sergeant seemed greatly amused. The chaplain maintained an earnest look on his face, but soon he began to nod, as if Springfield had persuaded him of something. Then Springfield handed the chaplain a slip of paper, headed for the door of Madam Russell's Bake Oven, and went inside.

The chaplain began to look up and down C Street, apparently hoping to find more soldiers he might approach. His job must be a lonely one, thought Mazorca, and especially on a night like this and in a place like Murder Bay. Armies functioned because they built a sense of camaraderie among the young men who joined their ranks. The intensity of a battle might frighten them, but they would refuse to retreat because they did not want to let their buddies down. They preferred to take their chances against bullets and bayonets rather than risk the disappointment of the men who marched and fought beside them. Yet here was the chaplain, haranguing soldiers for doing what soldiers always have done. Mazorca realized that this chaplain might become attached to a regiment, but he never would be just one of the guys.

Mazorca made a snap decision: he whistled. The chaplain looked his way, and Mazorca gestured for him to approach.

In the dim light, Mazorca had not seen that the chaplain's coat was black, not blue. He noticed the difference in color as the man came forward but decided to speak to the chaplain anyway.

"I'm so glad to have found you," said Mazorca, pretending to be short on breath, as if he had been sprinting. "I just pulled a baby out of the canal."

"We must rescue the child!" said the chaplain.

With that, Mazorca made for Tenth Street and turned south. The chaplain kept pace with him, holding his hat to keep it from falling off.

"I didn't expect to find a man of God in these parts," said Mazorca as they ran.

"The Lord came into the world to save sinners," said the chaplain. "He is most needed in places like this."

They smelled the canal before they saw it—its powerful reek reached into Murder Bay even without the help of the wind. A moment later, they stood at its edge.

"You took the baby from the canal?" asked the chaplain.

"Yes, I removed it right away and carried it over to this alleyway," said Mazorca. He pointed to a dark passage between a pair of abandoned buildings.

A look of doubt spread across on the chaplain's face. "Why did you put the child there? Why didn't you bring it away from this dreadful place?"

It was a sensible question, asked with a tone of mounting skepticism. Mazorca had relied on the man's good heart and gullibility to get him to the canal. He figured he had no time to lose. In a fast and fluid motion, Mazorca whipped out his knife and sprang at the chaplain, who took an instinctive step backward but lost his balance when he tried to avoid plunging into the canal. He tumbled to the ground. Mazorca fell upon him, pressing his knee against the chaplain's chest and his blade against his neck.

The chaplain closed his eyes and started mumbling, "Our Father..." He continued to clutch his cross and Bible.

"Shut your mouth—if you want to live," said Mazorca.

In the silence, Mazorca looked up and made sure nobody had seen them. The track along the edge of the canal was desolate.

Rising to his feet but keeping his knife on the chaplain's neck, Mazorca pointed to the alley once more. "You will get up, you will walk over there, and you will do it quietly," he said.

The chaplain did as he was told. The alley was dingy and strewn with rotting garbage. A stray cat scampered away as they entered.

Several feet in, the chaplain stopped and faced Mazorca. "I forgive you," he said.

Mazorca scoffed. "Are you sure about that?"

"I'm absolutely sure of it."

"Your faith is pathetic. Do you think it will save you?"

"I'm not the one in need of saving."

"Whatever," said Mazorca. "Take off your coat."

The chaplain did not hesitate. He quickly set down the cross and Bible, unbuttoned, and removed the coat. As he handed it to Mazorca, the clouds overhead suddenly parted, exposing the moon. One night before, it had been full. Its bright beams lit Mazorca and the chaplain.

"Wait," said the chaplain, squinting at Mazorca. "You look like…"

He paused.

"What?" said Mazorca, with anger in his voice. "What do I look like?"

The chaplain sighed. He knew he should not have spoken.

"Tell me," insisted Mazorca. The knife was no longer pressed against the chaplain's neck, but Mazorca continued to point it at him. One wrong move and the chaplain would be dead. "Tell me now."

"There is only one way to confirm it," said the chaplain. "It's in the pocket."

He reached for the coat, but Mazorca pulled it away.

"What's in the pocket?"

"A picture."

"A picture of what?"

"Please just let me retrieve it," said the chaplain. "I don't care about the coat. You can keep the coat."

Mazorca wiggled the knife to remind the chaplain of its presence. "If this is a trick, you'll be dead before your corpse hits the ground," he said.

The chaplain nodded, reached a hand into his pocket, and pulled out a stiff piece of paper. He looked at it in the moonlight and then studied Mazorca's face. When Mazorca realized what he was doing, he dropped the coat and grabbed the photograph.

The image astonished him: the picture was a little fuzzy, but there was no mistaking it. Mazorca had never allowed a photograph of himself to be taken before. Where could this one possibly have come from? He had absolutely no idea.

"Where did you get this?" he asked. There was urgency in his voice.

"A sergeant handed it to me, just a few minutes ago."

Mazorca remembered Springfield's encounter with the chaplain, outside Madam Russell's Bake Oven.

"He had a handful of them," said the chaplain. "He was distributing copies to the women of this quarter, hoping that one of them might recognize the person in it. I didn't really want one. He practically forced me to take it."

"How many did he have?"

"I don't know—quite a few."

Mazorca looked at the picture again but remained mystified as to its origins. He appeared to be standing outside. But where? And when?

"Could be anybody, I suppose," said the chaplain.

Mazorca glared at him. Up above, the clouds moved in front of the moon. Darkness descended on the alley again.

"Just keep the coat," said the chaplain. "You can have the picture as well. I have a little money too."

He thrust a hand into his pants pocket. As he did, Mazorca struck, slashing the knife across the chaplain's throat. Blood spewed out, and Mazorca hopped out of the way as the chaplain collapsed.

He put on the chaplain's coat and hat and stuffed the picture into the pocket from which it had come. He thought about removing the chaplain's pants, but he decided not to bother. They were close enough in appearance to the ones he was wearing. He did, however, pick up the cross and the Bible. The dead man's neck was still seeping blood as Mazorca left the alley.

At the edge of the canal, Mazorca hurled the cross into the water. It splashed and sank. Then he tossed the Bible. It splashed and dipped below the surface before coming back up. Its dark cover was difficult to spot, but Mazorca thought he saw it begin to float away with the current.

Mazorca walked in the opposite direction. He needed to go into hiding, away from the eyes of people who had seen his photograph. He could not possibly check into a hotel— that would be the first place Rook and his men would have distributed pictures. Murder Bay was covered too. He could not even safely occupy a room in a whorehouse. There was always the safe house. Was it too risky? Or was it the best option among a set of worse alternatives?

* * *

There would be no escape this time. Rook would see to that. He was not interested in observing Mazorca from afar or trying to tail him anywhere. He wanted him killed or captured as quickly as possible. And if Mazorca was in the row house at 1745 N Street, one of those two things would happen in just a few minutes.

The house belonged to Robert Fowler. After Zack Hoadly had identified it, a lieutenant had looked up the address in the city's ownership records. Rook remembered Fowler as the man who had crossed the Long Bridge into Virginia with an overstuffed wagon on the day the news of Fort Sumter's fall had reached Washington. He knew that Fowler was a Southerner and a secessionist, but he was not sure that meant anything. To Mazorca, the Fowler residence might have represented nothing more than an abandoned building.

Everything rode on the accuracy of Zack's report. Could the account of a ten-year-old boy be trusted? Boys could have powerful imaginations. Yet Rook was convinced that Zack had bumped into somebody outside the front door of 1745 N Street—and the possibility that it was a chance encounter with Mazorca was his only genuine lead. Rook was determined to pursue it.

The brown-brick row house was three stories tall. It was not a mansion, but it was large—Fowler was clearly a man of some means. Several large windows lined its front. It did not appear as though anybody was inside. Mazorca, of course, would have wanted it that way.

The colonel had assembled two dozen men. They quickly took position around the building. A handful went around to the rear. Several others positioned themselves on N Street, where they would make sure Mazorca could not leave through one of the windows. The rest marched with Rook to the front door.

Rook gave the knob a cursory twist, but it held tight. He gestured to a burly private. The man raised an ax and slammed it into the lock. Two more hits and the door cracked open. Anybody inside the house would now be on alert. Rook rushed in with his troops. They fanned through the building, charging up the stairs and racing in and out of rooms. They swiftly reached the conclusion Rook had feared: the house was empty.

Had Zack led them to the wrong house? Rook did not think so. The boy had been certain about the location.

Starting on the ground floor, Rook walked through the entire house, searching for clues. He did not find anything of special interest until he entered a bedroom on the third floor. Clothes littered the bed. Several drawers rested near the headboard, turned upside down. They had been removed from a dresser along the wall.

A closet door was shut. Rook approached and pulled it open. On the floor he saw it: the dress and the ball of bloody clothes. The boy had in fact seen Mazorca and had led Rook to the right house. Once again, however, he was too late. Mazorca was gone.

XVII

Friday, April 26, 1861

When Mazorca opened his eyes, the dawn sky overhead was turning to a clear blue. The clouds from the previous night had disappeared almost completely, thanks to a cool breeze that must have pushed them away. It promised to be a very nice day—bright, brisk, and full of possibility.

Pain ripped through Mazorca's body as he sat up. He had known it would happen: sleeping on a hard granite surface, without a pillow or a blanket, had guaranteed the aching result. It diminished as he stretched and yawned. He stood and looked down at the city from his bird's-eye vantage point.

The night might have brought much worse than temporary discomfort. After leaving the crumpled body of the chaplain, Mazorca had walked swiftly along the canal, hiking up the collar of the coat and pulling down the brim of the hat—anything to hide his disfigured ear. There was no way he could remain in Murder Bay. It was probably dangerous to go anywhere in the city.

He briefly considered going back to the Fowler house but decided against it. They had found him at Tabard's, and they might find him there. Unsure of his destination and driven by an overwhelming desire simply to get away, Mazorca had set off to the east.

At Seventh Street, the canal came within half a block of Pennsylvania Avenue. The lights from Brown's Hotel and the National Hotel were exactly what Mazorca wanted to avoid. They were like those lighthouses Lincoln had described in their brief meeting—a warning for navigators to stay away. To his right, a small bridge crossed the canal. It led to the Mall and away from the buildings and people of downtown. Mazorca took it, and in a moment he found himself in a large open space of grass, shrubs, and pathways. In front of him loomed a structure that looked like a castle from the days of knights. This was the Smithsonian Institution, a red building that appeared out of its rightful place and time. One of its windows glowed. Someone was inside, poring over the museum's collections. Was there one person or several? Mazorca watched the window for several minutes. But he never received an answer. Given all that had happened, he was in no mood to take a chance.

The Mall itself was empty. As he passed the Smithsonian and continued to the west, Mazorca wondered about curling up beneath a row of bushes. But this would make little sense—if he was going to sleep outside, he would be better off leaving the city entirely. Although the Mall was deserted at night, it might very easily attract people in the morning.

Ahead, the moonlight fell upon the pale masonry of the Washington Monument—a big block of stone that was supposed to rise upward in tribute to America's first president. Mazorca knew from guidebooks that it was meant to reach a towering height of 555 feet, but work had halted several years earlier. The monument now stood at about 156 feet. To begin building such an edifice and not finish it struck Mazorca as worse than not having started it in the first place—its incompleteness seemed to dishonor the figure it hoped to glorify. Yet he began to wonder if it represented an opportunity.

The monument stood in the center of a spit of land that stretched into the Potomac River at the point where a small inlet channeled water into the city's canal. It was one of Washington's chief landmarks, but Mazorca had not given it much thought previously. He approached its base at the summit of a slight incline. When he arrived at the site, he walked around the four sides of its exterior, pulling his fingers along the cold stone. He confirmed that there was only one door, in the center of the eastern wall. He assumed it would be locked and was surprised to see it give way when he pulled on the handle.

The interior was dark. Mazorca's eyes were already well adjusted to the night, but he waited for a few minutes as they strained to give him a slightly better view. Right in front of him, a set of stairs began their ascent. When he had a good fix on their location, he closed the door. Pitch-blackness enveloped him. He took a few tentative steps in the direction of the stairs, tapping gently with his shoe as he got closer. He found the first step and felt for the wall on his right. Touching it, he began a cautious climb.

It was slow going. He hit a landing and turned. Then he hit another landing and turned again. He kept his right hand on the wall and his left hand in front of him to protect his head from low-hanging objects. In the passageway, it was impossible to see anything.

Eventually, however, Mazorca detected a faint radiance. He first saw it as he turned on a landing. It grew brighter as he continued upward, though it was never more than dim. After hiking a bit further, he saw its source: the staircase was open to the sky.

Mazorca clambered onto the top of the monument. He was on a square plateau, its edges perhaps fifty feet in length. Several blocks of stone were scattered about its surface. At a point near the center, a pole rose. A flag hung from it, showing signs of life from a wind whose blowing Mazorca had not noticed on the ground. He remembered having seen the banner fly during the daytime. It appeared as though nobody checked on it with any regularity.

From two sides of the monument, Mazorca saw almost nothing except moonlight glistening on the waters of the Potomac. On the other two sides, he saw the lights of the city. Somewhere down there, people were searching for him. He was exhausted and needed to shut his eyes. He gathered a couple of empty canvas bags and rolled them into something that resembled a pillow. Then he curled himself on the roof of the monument and fell asleep almost immediately.

Hours later, the sun woke him as it peeked above the half-finished dome of the Capitol, about a mile to the east. Above him, the flag flapped in the breeze. When he stood up, Mazorca surveyed Washington from his unique vantage point. Near the base of the monument, pigs and cattle roamed freely. To the south and the west, he saw the Long Bridge spanning the Potomac, the docks of Georgetown, and the Naval Observatory. To the north sat the city, or most of it.

He watched several groups of soldiers make their way to the Capitol. Mazorca figured that these were members of the New York regiment, reporting for duty at their new lodgings. More than a few would be drowsy or hungover, having spent their first night in Washington pursuing revelry rather than rest. Mazorca had seen more than a few of them in Murder Bay. No matter how sleepy or miserable they felt, however, they were now the toast of the city. He envisioned people from all over Washington heading to the Capitol to greet them.

The monument offered an excellent view of the White House. Mazorca counted second-floor windows until he found the one that he had seen from the other side, in the president's office, just a few days earlier. He wondered whether Lincoln was in there right now. He wished that he could just walk through the front door as he already had done and end his mission with a quick pull of the trigger. The impulse was powerful, but Mazorca resisted it. His mission called for patience and cunning, not haste and desperation. His general plan remained a sound one. He would just have to improvise the specifics.

Mazorca pulled the photograph from his coat pocket and examined it in the daylight. It remained what it had been the night before—good enough for purposes of recognition. He crushed it into a ball and tossed it off the side of the monument. When it disappeared from sight, he picked up his hat and coat and started down the steps. He carried his book in his left hand.

* * *

Every lead had gone cold, with a single exception. Standing in front of the house at 398 Sixteenth Street, Rook knew that he needed to confront Violet Grenier. The distribution of Mazorca's photograph had not produced anything useful. A handful of people claimed to have seen him at various times and places, but none could say where he was now or where he might go. The only report of significance was Zack Hoadly's, but it had merely permitted Rook to track Mazorca's movement up to a certain point. And then the trail had vanished once again.

Overnight, the body of Charles Calthrop, the bookbinder, had turned up—a soldier found it floating in the canal, where it apparently had been dumped a few days earlier. The corpse was swollen and starting to rot, and it had been difficult to identify, but a city policeman recalled hearing that Calthrop had failed to make an expected delivery. They went to the bookbinder's home and found the bloody scene.

There was no evidence that Mazorca had anything to do with it. Yet Rook had no doubt that he was the killer. It was the simplest explanation: the two men had been in recent contact, there had been some friction between them, and since then Mazorca had been revealed as an efficient and professional murderer. Rook was determined to stop him before he had a chance to strike at the president—and right now, his only hope lay with a woman who had quietly been his nemesis.

Grenier had been placed under an official, sanctioned watch ever since Rook presented Mazorca's photograph to Scott. It was the kind of observation Rook had wanted for days: a team of men holding various positions on Sixteenth

Street, in Lafayette Park, and in an alley behind the house. The only difference was that they now made no effort to conceal themselves. The operation was closer to a house arrest than surveillance.

"The lights were on until an hour or two before dawn," said Corporal Clark, who had kept watch through the night from a bench in Lafayette Park. "She was definitely up and about—I kept seeing movement near the windows. She's still inside right now."

"Is she awake?" asked Rook.

"Hard to say. The lights did go out before sunrise—maybe three or four hours ago."

"I'd like you to come to the door with me." Rook looked at Clark's belt, where the corporal had a pistol holstered. "Is that loaded?"

"Yes, sir."

"Good. I don't know what to expect."

Rook checked the chamber of his own pistol. It was loaded too.

At the front door, Rook grasped a metal knocker and banged it hard. He wondered what kind of reception he would receive. Would Grenier's servant answer and say her mistress was ill and could not see anybody? Or would Grenier receive him with a chilly formality? Rook even thought about the possibility of forcing his way through the door. It was thick and would not easily budge. Perhaps with Clark's assistance, however, he could get it open.

He reached to try the knocker a second time when he heard movement on the other side. A deadbolt unfastened and the door swung open.

Violet Grenier peered out. She wore a bright red robe and smiled warmly.

"Oh, Colonel," she said. "I'm so glad you're here."

* * *

Outside the president's office, John Hay scribbled furiously at his desk. He wanted to finish a short letter to one of his former professors at Brown before the next interruption, which was bound to arrive at any moment. Suddenly, he sensed that he was not alone. He stopped writing and turned his head. The tall figure of Abraham Lincoln loomed over him.

"Pardon my snooping, Mr. Hay."

"No worries, sir."

Lincoln was supposed to be reading his own mail—Hay had put a stack of letters on his desk earlier in the morning. Perhaps the president was just stretching his long legs.

"I'm restless in here—if I don't get out soon, the whole day will slip by, and I will have missed it."

"Sir?"

"I'm going to take a walk, Mr. Hay. You may join me if you like."

"Do you think that's wise?" Hay opened the top drawer of his desk and pulled out a picture of Mazorca. He held it up. "Aren't you forgetting something?"

"No, I haven't forgotten. I'm just not going to let anybody keep me caged in this house. It is good for the people to see their president."

"You're taking a risk. Aren't you concerned about what this man wants to do?"

"If I am killed, I can die but once—but to live in constant dread of death is to die over and over again."

Lincoln chuckled and then continued. "Besides, there probably isn't a safer place in Washington than where I would like to go."

* * *

"Please come in," said Grenier. She gestured for Rook to enter the house.

The colonel turned around and looked at Clark. "Stay here, on the porch," he said. Then he went through the door. Grenier closed it behind him.

"Take a seat, Charles," said Grenier as they entered the parlor. "May I call you that?"

Rook was struck by her beauty. He told himself to resist it. "I'll stand, thank you. And let's keep things formal, Mrs. Grenier."

"As you wish. I'm just glad you're here. You don't know how worried I've been."

"That's odd, because you've been the source of many worries, Mrs. Grenier."

"Then it will be such a relief for you to know the truth, because we are past the very worst," she said. "I must retrieve something. Please, make yourself comfortable."

Grenier left the room. Rook heard her climb the stairs. He considered stopping her, thinking that perhaps it was not wise to let her out of his sight. Yet she had not been in his sight until just now, and the house was surrounded by Clark and the other soldiers. She could not get away.

He took the opportunity to examine the room. He had seen Grenier's home from the outside many times, and he had always wondered what the interior looked like. He imagined Locke sitting here, telling Grenier about conversations with General Scott and meetings with the senior military staff. He thought of Davis and Stephens coming by to discuss plans for sabotaging the Capitol. He knew Mazorca had been here as well.

The bust of Stephen Douglas caught his eye. It sat on a table beside one of the parlor's red walls. Rook had not given Douglas much thought since seeing him at the inauguration. In a corner near the table, Rook noticed two boxes sitting on the floor. They were open on top, with wads of crumpled newspaper stuffed inside. A vase peeked through one of them. It appeared as though Grenier was packing. Rook reached into a box and pulled out a ball of newspaper. He smoothed it, revealing the front page of Wednesday's edition of the *National Intelligencer*.

"I'm leaving," said Grenier.

Rook had not heard her return. He crushed the newspaper again and dropped it into the box.

"So it would seem."

"I can't stay in Washington any longer. Not after what has happened."

"Before you go anywhere, you have quite a bit of explaining to do."

"It seems that there's been a terrible misunderstanding," she said. "This may begin to clear things up." She held out a piece of paper.

Rook accepted it and realized that he was looking at a letter for the second time: it was the note, dated April 19, that

Bennett had sent to Grenier. Springfield had intercepted it, shown it to Rook, and then let it go through to her. Only this time, it included a secret message between the lines of what had seemed an innocent missive:

> *I assume you have met Mazorca by now. Warn him to halt his mission immediately. His existence has been discovered. Future missions like his will be jeopardized if he fails. He must stop at once.*

"Do you know Langston Bennett?" asked Grenier.

"I've heard of him."

"He writes to me on occasion. He wrote this letter, including the words between the lines in a special ink that reveals itself only when it's heated."

"Why the secrecy?"

"Because it turns out that Langston has something awful to hide. He has consorted with the worst kind of person imaginable. Mazorca is a trained killer, and somehow I've gotten mixed up with him." Tears welled in her eyes. "You must help me," she said. She took a step toward the colonel.

Rook suddenly understood how a man could fall for her charms. Her imploring expression, the way she projected vulnerability—it summoned a masculine instinct to protect and defend. Rook had to remind himself that he was dealing with a manipulative seductress.

"First, you must help me," said Rook. "I want to know where Mazorca is right now."

"Have you been to the boardinghouse on H Street, where he goes by the name of Mr. Mays?"

"He's not there."

This did not seem to surprise her. She smiled confidently. "Then perhaps you can find him on N Street, at the former residence of Robert Fowler."

"He's not there either."

"You've been to 1745 N Street?"

"Yes."

"How did you know to look there?"

"It doesn't matter. How did you know he might be found there?"

"Because I told him the house was abandoned and that he might seek refuge in it. This was before I discovered his true intentions. I've been worried sick ever since I learned that he wants to kill the president."

"I wasn't led to believe that you were an admirer of Mr. Lincoln's."

"I'm not—horrors, no. But that doesn't mean I want him shot dead." A look of exasperation crossed her face. "No lady in my position would associate herself with the schemes of ruffians."

The tears came again, but Rook ignored them. "It sounds like you know about all of his hideaways," he said. "Where else could Mazorca be?"

"He must have left Washington."

"Why do you say that?"

"Because he knows that he's been exposed. You've been to his safe houses. You've been handing out pictures of him all over the city. And look at this letter I just gave you—Bennett is actually telling him to stop his mission."

"Actually, in the letter he tells you to stop Mazorca. You didn't try to do that, did you Mrs. Grenier?" Rook did not wait for a response. Instead, he reached into his pocket and removed the envelope he had found on the floor of Mazorca's room at the boardinghouse. He took out the note, unfolded it, and read: "I have reason to believe Rook is watching me. You may be in danger as well. Proceed with extreme caution." Rook returned the note to his pocket. "Here's what I think: you plotted with Bennett to hire Mazorca to murder the president, Bennett learned that Mazorca was compromised and asked you to call him off, and you told Mazorca to go ahead with the assassination anyway."

When she did not answer right away, Rook knew that she was having trouble making sense of her own plots. That was a difficulty for liars—the more lies they told, the harder it was to keep track of their deceptions.

"I'm frightened of him, Colonel," she pleaded.

"According to what I've heard, you weren't too frightened of him when he came to visit you. Nor were you too frightened to write him after receiving the secret message from Bennett."

"You must believe me. Only recently have I learned the terrible truth about him. I didn't know where to turn for protection."

Rook sensed her growing desperation. "How about your friend, Colonel Locke?" he asked. "Or didn't he drop by when you expected him?"

"Has something happened to Sam?"

"Nothing that he didn't do to himself."

"May I see him?"

"No."

"Then you must help me, Colonel." She stepped closer. "What must I do to make you believe me?" She touched him on the chest.

He pushed her arm away. "You must tell the truth. Unfortunately, you don't appear ready to do that. So I'm going to take you to a place that should make it much easier."

Grenier looked at him crossly. For the first time since laying eyes on her, Rook knew that she was not trying to charm him. "I suppose you mean the basement of the Treasury," she hissed.

Rook laughed. "No, Mrs. Grenier. You'll be staying at the Old Capitol Building—an actual prison."

* * *

Portia clutched the train ticket and studied the line of passenger cars that would take her north.

"Your next ride should be more comfortable than the last one," said Springfield. "Unless you want to hop inside of this." With the toe of his boot, he gently tapped a bag resting on the platform.

Portia smiled at him. "You've all been very good to me," she said. "Thank you for everything."

Since her midnight arrival at the White House and the meeting in the Winder Building a few hours later, Portia had stayed out of sight. She was still a fugitive slave—the private property of another person. Under the law, the government had an obligation to return her. It did not matter that she had fled from a regime of cruelty. It did not matter that her owner wanted to murder the president. It did not matter that her enormous personal sacrifice helped to turn the tables against a murderous conspiracy. She was still a fugitive.

The official policy of the Lincoln administration was to respect fugitive-slave laws. During the secession crisis, it wanted to do nothing to antagonize the slaveholding states, especially the handful that remained loyal to the Union. The act of letting Portia go, if it were to become public knowledge, would not sit well.

The solution was not to let it become public knowledge. "Make sure nothing bad happens to her," Lincoln had said to Rook. The colonel quietly issued orders to a few soldiers whom he knew to be abolitionists. Portia went to a private home where she ate, washed, and rested. Her caretakers prepared a bag of clothes and other necessities, obtained documents that would testify to her status as a free black, and purchased a train ticket to Buffalo. Once there, she would cross into Canada and join a community of escaped slaves who lived beyond the reach of fugitive laws and bounty hunters.

It fell upon Springfield to take Portia to the rail station in Washington. He was also the one to tell her that her grandfather probably was dead—information he had gleaned from the intercepted letter Bennett had sent to Grenier.

"When I went runnin' from the plantation, I knew that I might not see my family again," she said. "Then I watched Joe die. Now I'll have nightmares about what Bennett did to my grandfather. I'll get over the pain of gettin' to Washington 'cause that's just my body hurtin'. I'm not sure I'll ever get over the other parts."

"You're a hero, Portia."

"There are a lotta heroes, Sergeant, and some gave up more than me. Make sure it ain't in vain."

They stood in silence for a few minutes. When the conductor ordered passengers aboard, Springfield helped her with the bag and said good-bye. From the platform, he watched the train chug forward. Portia was on her way.

As the caboose left the station, Springfield turned and gazed at the Capitol. Plans called for a female figure— a statue of freedom—eventually to crown its dome. As he walked toward Massachusetts Avenue, Springfield said a quick prayer. He asked that by the time the statue was completed, all of Portia's people would have their liberty.

Just then, from near the Capitol, Springfield heard a loud commotion. Was it shouting? He took off in a sprint.

* * *

"And that's why we're going to leave the top off the dome of the Capitol," said Lincoln, with a big grin on his face. "You men must have proper ventilation!"

The federal soldiers erupted in laughter, cheers, and applause. Rook, Clark, and Grenier stood to the side. The colonel did not like seeing the president in the open, but he could not deny that Lincoln was in fine form. He talked to the troops with an easy camaraderie, demonstrating the political skills that had taken him to the White House.

When the men stationed in the Capitol had heard that Lincoln was coming for an impromptu visit, they streamed out of their temporary homes in the offices and committee rooms of senators and representatives. They assembled on the east side of the building, eager to greet their commander-in-chief. The new arrivals from New York were there, many of them bleary-eyed from a lack of sleep. The soldiers who had come to Washington before them joined in as well.

"Consider yourselves lucky," said Lincoln when the clamor died down. "Most people have to win an election to take a seat in the House!"

The men howled with delight again.

Grenier scowled. "Can we go now?" she asked. The question sounded like a demand.

Her destination, the new prison in the Old Capitol, was visible across the lawn and on the other side of First Street. Rook had thought about ordering transportation for her, but in the end he decided that they would walk. She did not seem to pose any kind of danger—not with Clark accompanying them on the march down Pennsylvania Avenue.

When they had rounded the Capitol and headed for the prison, they saw hundreds of blue-coated soldiers moving into formation on the eastern front of the building. At first, Rook assumed that they were going to drill. But then a carriage arrived. When it halted, John Hay stepped out, followed by Lincoln. The soldiers cheered him—the heavy majority appeared to be firm Lincoln men. A group of civilians began to gather nearby as well.

With any luck, thought Rook, the threat of Mazorca had passed, just as Grenier had claimed. Nobody had seen him since the day before. He was clearly on the run, with his boardinghouse and refuge raided, his picture distributed, and everyone seemingly on the lookout. Perhaps he had slipped away in the middle of the night. Mazorca could be far from Washington—either gone forever, or possibly biding his time in some local haunt until he believed the city had let down its guard again.

"I cannot listen to this obnoxious man any longer," snapped Grenier. She turned her back to Lincoln.

"Then don't listen," said Rook. "But we aren't going anywhere for a few minutes."

The colonel caught the attention of Hay, standing with the president about a hundred feet away. Lincoln's secretary knew what Rook was thinking. He shrugged his shoulders and threw up his hands, palms open wide, to indicate helplessness.

Just then, Springfield appeared. He was almost out of breath.

"I heard this hubbub from the train station—thought it was worth investigating," said the sergeant.

"Did you ship the package?" asked Rook.

"Yes. The train left a few minutes ago."

"Good. Stay here with our friend," he said, tipping his head toward Grenier. "I want to mingle a bit."

The crowd was growing larger. Rook estimated that a thousand people gathered in Lincoln's vicinity, and more kept arriving from the homes and stores nearby. A group of soldiers—a band carrying musical instruments—organized themselves near the steps. Rook walked toward them and climbed up for a better view.

Below, on the lawn, an officer from New York approached Lincoln. They exchanged a few words, and the president nodded.

"I've been asked to swear you in," said Lincoln, speaking as loudly as he could manage. "Would you like that?"

The soldiers burst out in approval. In New York, they had been sworn in for thirty days of service. But that was not long enough. Rook knew that one of their first orders of business in Washington was to swear in for ninety days.

"Before I do, allow me a few words," said Lincoln. Shushes and calls for quiet rippled through the crowd. Suddenly the racket in front of the Capitol dropped to almost total silence. "I have desired as sincerely as any man that our present difficulties might be settled without the shedding of blood," said Lincoln. "I will not say that all hope is yet gone, but if the alternative is presented whether the Union is to be broken into fragments and the liberties of the people lost or blood be shed, then I know you will stand for Union."

The throng roared its approval. The leaders of the Seventh Regiment broke their men into companies. Taking direction from Lincoln, they raised their right hands and swore in the name of God to be good soldiers. When it was done, they cheered again and congratulated each other. The band broke into "Hail Columbia," and many of the men sang the words. Their voices swelled when they hit the chorus:

> *Firm, united let us be,*
> *Rallying round our liberty,*
> *As a band of brothers joined,*
> *Peace and safety we shall find.*

As Rook hummed the tune, he watched the commander of the Seventh Regiment of New York lead Lincoln toward the Capitol. Apparently they were going to walk its halls. Their progress was slow, as soldiers and civilians approached Lincoln to shake his hand. The officer tried to fend them off, but Lincoln kept obliging. The president seemed utterly at ease. Rook noticed that rather than clenching hands, Lincoln kept grasping men at their fingers. The colonel realized that it was probably the only thing the president could do to prevent his hand from becoming sore from all of the squeezing.

Within a few minutes, Lincoln was near the steps, close to Rook as well as close to the spot from which he had delivered his inaugural address. A crowd continued to swirl around him. From the side, Rook noticed a man of the cloth advance toward the president. He was probably the pastor from one of the churches on Capitol Hill.

His presence reminded Rook of Lincoln's words on March 4. Toward the end of his speech, the president had commented that both Northerners and Southerners believed that they had justice on their side. If that was true, he said, then both should have the patience in "the Almighty Ruler of nations" to let justice prevail. Yet Lincoln was also resolute: "You have no oath registered in Heaven to destroy the government, while I shall have the most solemn one to 'preserve, protect, and defend' it."

Rook recalled the pledge he had made to himself on that day: he had vowed to protect and defend Lincoln, even with his own life.

When the pastor's head swiveled briefly in Rook's direction, a flicker of recognition gripped the colonel. He wore a hat, so Rook could not see the ear. Was it the shape of the chin? A look in the eyes? The pastor turned away before Rook could be sure of anything. Yet something told him to make good on his promise right now.

* * *

Mazorca adjusted the brim of his hat another time. It already flopped down well enough to hide his ear, but he wanted to be sure. Staring over his spectacles, which he had let slip to the end of his nose so that they would disguise his face but not distort his vision, Mazorca saw Lincoln standing just fifteen feet away. The president was pumping hands and listening to a soldier say how proud he was to have cast his first presidential vote for him.

When the band struck up "Yankee Doodle," Mazorca realized that he had found his moment. He might not get this close again. One shot. He knew he could get away. The noise and the crowd would create the confusion he needed. And nobody would suspect a preacher who clutched a Bible.

He had thought seriously about giving up. After descending the Washington Monument early in the morning, he walked to the edge of the Potomac River. Unsure about what to do, he headed east, toward the Capitol. He passed a few people who took no particular heed of him. With his hat pulled down tight, his collar up, his spectacles on, his cheeks covered in stubble, and his eyes cast to the ground, he avoided suspicion. The Bible—or a book that appeared on the outside to be a Bible—was a fortunate coincidence because it matched his outfit. Mazorca did not like to rely upon luck, but in this case he welcomed it.

Luck seemed to strike again as he went by the Capitol. Soldiers were gathering by the hundreds. He did not want to go anywhere near them, but he stopped to watch. A few minutes later, a carriage pulled up. A tall man in a black stovepipe hat got out. Mazorca did not believe in fate, but Lincoln's sudden appearance gave him pause. Rather than conceding defeat, he decided to claim victory.

He listened to Lincoln's jokes, his brief remarks, and his swearing-in of the soldiers. It was impossible to get close enough. He needed to arrive at almost point-blank range, and ideally when the crowd was starting to break up. If all eyes were locked on Lincoln, there was no way Mazorca could succeed.

Then it happened. The soldiers fell out of rank, the band struck up a tune, and a mass of people swarmed the president. Most were soldiers, but not all—and Mazorca plunged in behind a few civilians. He noticed that Lincoln was heading toward the Capitol. He worked through the crowd to get in position for the president to walk right past him.

When Lincoln was a dozen feet away, Mazorca fixed his hat a final time. He reached for his book's yellow ribbon and jerked it. The music muffled the click of the gun's cocking. When Lincoln was ten feet away, Mazorca grabbed the red ribbon and held it taut. With the book at waist level, he slanted it slightly upward so that its bullet would rip into Lincoln's chest. A soldier stood in front of him, blocking his shot. When Lincoln was five feet away, the soldier reached out to shake the president's hand.

"Sir," shouted the soldier, "I believe that God Almighty and Abraham Lincoln are going to save this country!"

Mazorca took half a step to his right. He remained behind the soldier, but the book had an angle. He pulled hard on the ribbon. The gun went off.

* * *

Rook did not hear the shot—nobody did, amid the noise of the crowd and the music of the band—but he felt the bullet dig into his left arm. What he heard, instead, was laughter: Lincoln had made another one of his wisecracks, telling the soldier who was shaking his hand, "Private, I believe you're half right!"

At first, Rook merely felt the bullet's impact. Uncertain about the pastor's actual identity, he had tried to force his body in front of the president. When he saw the man turn and move away swiftly, he knew it was Mazorca. He wanted to point and yell, but it was too late: the searing pain of his wound made him clench his teeth and double over. Lincoln kept walking and his pack of followers streamed by Rook. Nobody knew that a shot had been fired or that the colonel had been hit.

When Rook stood upright, he saw Mazorca darting toward a door beneath the Capitol steps. The assassin opened it, went in, and slammed it shut. Rook raced after him, stumbling at first and then gaining his stride. He finally yelled, "Get that man!"—but still nobody heard. He removed his pistol from his holster as he approached the door. Reaching to open it, he felt the pain tear through his left arm. Somehow, he pulled the door open. The sound of running footsteps echoed down a hallway.

Rook chased after them. He figured that he had at least one advantage over Mazorca: he knew his way around the Capitol, and Mazorca presumably did not. It was a large building, and Rook certainly did not know every twist and turn, but he had a general sense of its layout. He knew where its passageways led, where its staircases went, and where its exits were. From what he could tell, Mazorca had bolted through a foyer, turned right where it intersected with a long hall, and was running toward the Senate side of the building.

Rook hurried to the intersection and stopped. He could still hear Mazorca's footsteps, but he did not want to present himself as a target. On the ground, a book lay open—except that it was not really a book. Its pages were hollowed out. The gun was inside, with ribbons attached for cocking and firing. A hole on the bottom edge of its carved-up pages made Rook realize that this was the gun that had shot him moments before. Mazorca must have discarded it as he ran.

The sound of the footsteps grew fainter. Rook knew he needed to keep moving. He peered around the corner, down the long hallway. Mazorca was not in view. About forty feet in front of him, resting on the ground, he saw the black hat that Mazorca had worn.

The pain in his arm intensified. Rook tried to massage the wound, but the gun in his hand made it impossible. He knew he had to keep moving. If he stayed where he was, he would lose Mazorca. Again.

He sprinted down the hall past a series of closed doors that led to committee rooms. He still heard footsteps ahead, reverberating off the walls. It sounded like they fell on steps.

Rook knew exactly where Mazorca was headed: those stairs led up to a wide hallway just outside the Senate cloakrooms. When the colonel arrived at the staircase, he trained his pistol on the steps, but Mazorca was nowhere in sight.

Climbing the steps slowly, Rook kept looking upward. His arm throbbed, and he could feel blood begin to soak the sleeve of his uniform. It was not gushing out the way it would from hitting a major artery, but the warm dampness was becoming apparent. He did all he could to block the sensation from his mind.

At the top of the steps, Rook gained a view of the area just outside the Senate cloakrooms—it was technically a hallway, but it was wide enough to feel like an actual room. The bedding of soldiers covered the floor. The men who slept here were outside.

Rook wondered if Mazorca had gone to the right, through one of the cloakrooms and into the Senate chamber itself. Then he heard a door shut down a hallway to his left. If it was Mazorca, it meant that he was in the large room where the Supreme Court met. It was sometimes called the Old Senate Room because senators had used it before moving into their more spacious chamber at the north end of the building.

As he ran toward the room, Rook wondered why Mazorca would have chosen the door. If he meant to escape, there were better choices. Then he understood: ahead, in the rotunda, came the sounds of soldiers filing back into the Capitol. The assassin apparently wanted to avoid them. A new thought troubled him: if Lincoln had walked up the steps on the outside of the building's east front, however, he might very well be in the rotunda with them. Was it possible that Mazorca would have another chance to shoot the president?

The thick wooden doors outside the Old Senate Room were shut. Rook moved to open one of them. The door was heavy, and he might have leaned into it with his shoulder but for his injury. He turned the knob and forced it open with his foot.

Inside, he saw the majestic chamber—a semicircular room with a vaulted ceiling. Yet it was in a state of disarray, with desks and chairs shoved to one side to make room for soldiers who needed a place to sleep. Rook raised his pistol and stepped inside. The door swung shut behind him. He did not see Mazorca, but there was no shortage of places to hide.

Something glinted on the ground, catching his eye. Rook looked down. It was a pair of spectacles. His mind had registered nothing more than that when he sensed movement on his left. Mazorca emerged from behind a pillar and rushed toward him with a large knife in his hand. Instinctively, Rook tried to raise his left arm to block the attack, but the pain from his gunshot wound was so sharp that his knees buckled.

The move might have saved his life. Mazorca's dive was too high. The slash of his knife missed Rook entirely. Off balance, he fell to the floor. Meanwhile, Rook hopped to his feet and pointed his pistol directly at Mazorca, who rolled from his side to his back. The knife was still in his hand.

"Drop it," shouted Rook.

Mazorca closed his eyes and took a deep breath. When he opened them, he also appeared to loosen his grip on the handle of his knife. Instead of letting it fall, however, he flipped it up, grabbed the blade, and tried to throw it.

Rook pulled his trigger three times. Mazorca shuddered as each bullet hit its mark. The knife dropped harmlessly to the ground. The assassin's body jolted. Then it slumped. It did not move again.

* * *

"There you are!" yelled Springfield from across the rotunda. The large room beneath the Capitol's open dome was filling with soldiers. Lincoln had just passed through and was walking down a hallway toward the House chamber, away from Rook. The colonel gripped his left arm, as if by holding it he would lessen the pain.

Springfield ran over. Clark was with him.

"Where is he?" asked the sergeant.

"It's done," said Rook.

"You found Mazorca?"

"He's dead."

The sergeant explained that he had seen Rook chase a man into the Capitol and assumed the worst. He and Clark tried to catch up, but they started out too far away. By the time they entered the Capitol, they had no idea where Mazorca and Rook had gone.

"You've been shot," said Springfield, noticing Rook's wound for the first time.

For a moment, Rook said nothing. He just stared, first at Springfield, then at Clark, and then back at Springfield. "Where is Violet Grenier?" he asked.

The two soldiers looked at each other. They had forgotten. That was when Rook knew: she was gone.

EPILOGUE

Saturday, June 1, 1861

Langston Bennett was surprised to hear the sound of gravel crunching beneath the wheels of a carriage. He had not expected visitors. Hughes remained confined to his bed, though after three weeks at the Stark farm he finally had moved back to his own plantation. Bennett had paid him a couple of visits but still had not given the young man the excoriation that he thought he deserved for letting Portia slip away.

Perhaps it was a man seeking employment. Ever since Tate had quit—abruptly, and immediately following the burial of that runaway Big Joe—he had let it be known that he wished to hire an experienced overseer. So far, nobody had come to him for the job. Many of the men in the region were gripped with war fever. They were signing up to fight the North.

A minute ticked by as Bennett waited for Lucius to walk through the door and announce a guest. Then he remembered that the old slave would not appear again. Bennett was still unaccustomed to his absence. He had made no attempt to replace him.

Bennett rose from his desk and hobbled to the front door. He opened it and looked upon one of the people he least expected to see: Violet Grenier.

"Hello," he said, somehow making the greeting sound more like a question.

"Good afternoon, Langston," said Grenier. "It has been an exceedingly long journey. Are you going to invite me in?"

He did, and they settled into chairs in Bennett's office.

"This is certainly a surprise, Violet," said Bennett. "I anticipated a letter, not a visit. It has been quite some time since you wrote. I feared that something had happened."

"You wouldn't believe how much has happened—everything and nothing, all at once."

"What do you mean?"

"Mazorca is dead." She handed him a Brady's reproduction of the photograph. Bennett stared at it and sighed.

Grenier told her story: Mazorca's arrival, his pursuit, and his disappearance. She neglected to say that she had been arrested or that she had escaped during the tumult on April 26—she simply said that life in Washington had become too difficult for someone of her views. Bennett did not probe her on this point.

"How do you know Mazorca is dead?" he asked.

"I suspect strongly that Rook and his men killed him and then covered it up. The entire episode has been kept out of the papers. It's just rumors, really—about a lunatic who was shot in the Capitol and then given a pauper's burial. Nothing is confirmed, but it hardly matters. The bottom line is that Lincoln is still alive."

"How unfortunate," said Bennett. "It is such a shame to have failed."

Grenier narrowed her eyes and put her hand on Bennett's knee—the one above the false leg. "Mazorca failed," she said. "We have not."

Bennett looked puzzled. "What do you mean?"

She smiled wickedly. "The war is young."

AUTHOR'S NOTE

The First Assassin is a work of fiction, and specifically a work of historical fiction—meaning that much of it is based on real people, places, and events. My goal never has been to tell a tale about what really happened but to tell what might have happened by blending known facts with my imagination. Characters such as Abraham Lincoln, Winfield Scott, and John Hay were, of course, actual people. When they speak on these pages, their words are occasionally drawn from things they are reported to have said. At other times, I literally put words in their mouths. Historical events and circumstances such as Lincoln's inauguration, the fall of Fort Sumter, and the military crisis in Washington, D.C., provide both a factual backdrop and a narrative skeleton. Throughout, I have tried to maximize the authenticity and also to tell a good story.

Thomas Mallon, an experienced historical novelist, has described writing about the past: "The attempt to reconstruct the surface texture of that world was a homely pleasure, like quilting, done with items close to hand." For me, the items close to hand were books and articles. Naming all of my sources is impossible. I've drawn from a lifetime of reading about the Civil War, starting as a boy who gazed for hours at the battlefield pictures in *The Golden Book of the Civil War*, which is an adaptation for young readers of *The Ameri-*

can *Heritage Picture History of the Civil War* by Bruce Catton. Yet several works stand out as especially important references.

The first chapter owes much to an account that appeared in the *New York Tribune* on February 26, 1861 (and is cited in *A House Dividing*, by William E. Baringer). It is also informed by *Lincoln and the Baltimore Plot, 1861*, edited by Norma B. Cuthbert.

For details about Washington in 1861: *Reveille in Washington*, by Margaret Leech; *The Civil War Day by Day*, by E. B. Long with Barbara Long; *Freedom Rising*, by Ernest B. Ferguson; *The Regiment That Saved the Capitol*, by William J. Roehrenbeck; *The Story the Soldiers Wouldn't Tell*, by Thomas P. Lowry; and "Washington City," in *The Atlantic Monthly*, January 1861.

For information about certain characters: *With Malice Toward None*, by Stephen B. Oates; *Lincoln*, by David Herbert Donald; *Abe Lincoln Laughing*, edited by P. M. Zall; *Lincoln and the Civil War in the Diaries of John Hay*, edited by Tyler Dennett; *Lincoln Day by Day, Vol. III: 1861–1865*, by C. Percy Powell; *Agent of Destiny*, by John S. D. Eisenhower; *Rebel Rose*, by Isabel Ross; *Wild Rose*, by Ann Blackman; and several magazine articles by Charles Pomeroy Stone.

For life in the South: *Roll, Jordan, Roll*, by Eugene D. Genovese; *Runaway Slaves*, by John Hope Franklin and Loren Schweninger; *Bound for Canaan*, by Fergus M. Bordewich; *Narrative of the Life of Henry Box Brown*, written by himself; *The Fire-Eaters*, by Eric H. Walther; and *The Southern Dream of a Caribbean Empire*, by Robert E. May.

For background on Mazorca: *Argentine Dictator*, by John Lynch.

This is the second edition of *The First Assassin*. Except for a few minor edits, it is no different from the first edition.

ACKNOWLEDGMENTS

The AmazonEncore edition of *The First Assassin* would not exist but for readers of an earlier edition, which I published on my own through a print-on-demand service. They made *The First Assassin* a self-publishing success story. Their support was indispensible and is much appreciated.

At AmazonEncore, I'm indebted to Terry Goodman for having faith in this novel, Sarah Tomashek for helping promote it, Emily Avent and Jessica Smith for copyediting.

I'm also thankful for the advice and encouragement of friends, especially David Bernstein, Michael Carlisle, Ben Domenech, Robert Ferrigno, Vince Flynn, Andrew Klavan, Michael Long, Rich Lowry, Brian Meadors, Erika Meadors, Kristina Phillips, and Brad Thor.

Brendan Miller, Josie Miller, and Patrick Miller provided many distractions and delays, for which I am grateful.

My wife Amy has mattered most. This book is hers as much as mine. It would not exist without her encouragement and love.

ABOUT THE AUTHOR

John J. Miller is a journalist who writes for *National Review,* the *Wall Street Journal,* and other publications. He is the author of several books of nonfiction, including *The Unmaking of Americans: How Multiculturalism Has Undermined America's Assimilation Ethic; Our Oldest Enemy: A History of America's Disastrous Relationship with France;* and *A Gift of Freedom: How the John M. Olin Foundation Changed America. The First Assassin* is his debut novel. A native of Detroit, he lives with his family in Prince William County, Virginia. To learn more about John J. Miller and his work, visit his website at www.HeyMiller.com.